A PATH OF STORMS AND RECKONINGS
SILVERBLOOD RAVEN SERIES

NIKKI McCORMACK

ISBN: 978-1-7367938-7-9
Second Edition 2023

Published by
Elysium Books
Bellevue, WA

Written by Nikki McCormack (https://nikkimccormack.com/) Cover Design by Robert Crescenzio (https://robertcrescenzio.artstation.com/) Typesetting and Design by Brian C. Short Editing by M. Evan MacGregor

In loving memory of my grandmother, Ida.

Raven was never going to be able to fall asleep in a manor littered with dead bodies. Not even knowing the manor was Aldrich Darrenton's and the men his guards. Knowing how many of those lives she had taken only made it worse. She hadn't killed them for no reason. She did it to protect the ones she cared about in Amberwood from the attack Darrenton was planning and to avenge the murder of her adopted father and mentor, Jaecar. That second part was where the greatest conflict stemmed from. Revenge wouldn't erase the pain of his loss. She had understood that going in. But she hadn't expected to feel that loss more acutely when it was over.

Raven had been staring into the fire, sipping absently at her wine for about twenty minutes when the serving woman, Lily, returned to the sitting room to tell them their bedrooms for the night were ready.

"Go get some rest," Marek prompted when neither of them moved. "I'll keep watch and wake you in a few hours to trade off."

Raven looked over at him, her gaze going to a bit of dried blood in his jaw-length, dark-blond hair. "I don't think I can—"

"Try," he interrupted, his silver eyes narrowing slightly with a stubbornness that mirrored her own.

1

"You need the sleep."

So did he, but she could tell by his look that arguing would be an exercise in futility, one she didn't have the energy for right now. Lying alone in the dark, fretting over the lives she had ended, would probably only make her feel worse than she already did. But Lily had gone to the trouble of preparing them rooms. It would be rude to snub the offer now.

Raven shoved herself out of the chair, her muscles heavy with fatigue. Lily led her to a room down the north wing, away from most of the bodies. The young woman was quiet, perhaps sensing that Raven wasn't in the mood to talk. Or perhaps too afraid to speak after seeing how effectively she and Marek had finished off the manor guards.

She slipped off her leather armor in the room, trying not to think about how badly it needed cleaning and why. Then she lay down on top of the covers, prepared to stare at the ceiling for a few hours until Marek came around.

Sleep claimed her minutes after her head touched the pillow.

•

When she became aware within the dream, she was standing once more in the rear entry of the manor, slaughtered guards littering the floor around her feet. Every one of them looked at her. No. They *stared* at her, each of them blaming her for their deaths. Even those Marek had killed. And that was appropriate because she had brought him here. Some of these men could have played a part in Jaecar's murder. All of them worked for Aldrich Darrenton, who had ordered the death of her adopted father. His own brother. To make things worse, Aldrich had been gathering an army of mercenaries to attack Amberwood so he might lay claim to the town's natural resources. He lay there too, one of his eyes punched through with a crossbow bolt she had fired.

Why, even knowing all of that, did she feel so awful about ending their lives?

"Raven." Synderis's hands came to rest on her shoulders, drawing her back toward him. "You're alive."

She turned within the circle of his arms to face him, noting the distress that tightened his jaw and furrowed his brow when he looked around at the carnage.

He glanced down, his silver eyes reflecting the flickering light from a wall sconce. "Can I take us somewhere else?"

She nodded.

The dreamscape filled with Krivalen magic carrying the warm comfort of his presence. She willingly relinquished control, watching with a flood of relief as the bodies and the manor disappeared, replaced by lush forest. A shaded pond appeared next to them, teaming with life. Dragonflies and other insects danced around the water's surface. The intermittent deep croaking of frogs created an offset to the light twitter of songbirds. Two turtles rested on a log along the bank, basking in the sunshine. A family of ducks paddled through a spray of lily pads.

This was his counter to the death he had found her amidst.

She looked at him again, admiring the silvery-white hair that hung long around his face. Distinct cheekbones. A strong jaw, softened slightly by elegant elven lines. Lips she would never tire of kissing. "It's almost morning. How many times have you tried to dreamwalk me tonight?"

He brushed his thumb lightly across her lips, then

along her cheek. A faint tremble in his touch told her how worried he had been, waiting to see if she survived the assault on Darrenton's manor with no way to influence the outcome. Guilt twisted in her chest, not for the first time, at what she was putting him through. If only she could find a way to care for some of the people she loved without making others suffer.

A fond smile touched his lips, moving up to shine in his silver eyes. "More times than I can count."

The contrast between their dreamscapes pounded into the forefront of her mind. Her tableau of death against his beautiful forest bursting with life. She had killed. With minimal effort and almost as little thought, she had ended numerous lives that night. Somehow, she had even managed to fall asleep in that manor full of corpses.

Where was he sleeping? In his hut up in the trees? At the outer post where he had made love to her, unaware that she meant to leave him in the morning? Some other place surrounded by the beauty and vibrancy of that magnificent forest?

She lowered her gaze, a heaviness pressing upon her chest. "I don't know that I deserve Eyl'Thelandra after what I've done tonight. I don't know that I deserve you."

"You do. We've all done things we're ashamed of." His voice was soft. That sense of safety and comfort radiated off him, inviting her to lay her burdens aside.

"What have you done?" She made herself look up at him, demanding his answer with her eyes.

He leaned down and pressed his lips to hers. She accepted that for the evasion it was, but only because of how it eased her sorrow, bringing a glimmer of joy into her heart at a time when very little about her felt good. Still, the hollow in her chest persisted, refusing to set her free that easily.

When he drew back, his brows pinched together as though he sensed the depth of her lingering distress.

"You defeated Darrenton?"

She nodded.

"Are you safe?"

She nodded again, almost casting a look around before remembering that she was asleep, unable to see her waking world surroundings. "I think so. For now."

"Are you all right?"

She shrugged. "A few small cuts—"

He cut her off with a gentle finger over her lips and looked deep into her eyes. "I wasn't asking for a physical assessment. This night hurt you in a different way. How can I help with that?"

Raven stepped into him, leaning her head against his chest, and he folded his arms around her the way she had known he would. His heartbeat was steady and reassuring. Such an odd detail to capture in a dreamscape. Was it her expectation or his that created that effect? In that instant, this place seemed more real than the blood-soaked reality she had made for herself.

"Hold me a moment. Tell me the things I've done tonight haven't ruined me in your eyes."

His arms tightened around her. "Heleath le'athana, anweyn."

Tears sprang to her eyes, and sorrow tore through her as Phendaril's voice echoed in her mind, saying those exact Elven words. What had she done? Why did she still love him? Even now, after giving so much of her heart to Synderis, she longed to see Phendaril again. Why now, when she was closer to Phendaril in the waking world than to him, did Synderis have to offer precisely those words of love?

"Raven?" He spoke her name in soft inquiry.

She realized she had started to pull away from him. The urge to flee swelled in her, but she wasn't going to do that. Running from him again, with no explanation, would be cruel.

She looked up at him, opening her mouth to tell him the thoughts that tormented her.

Suddenly, she couldn't breathe.

•

Raven snapped awake to hands cinching tight on her throat. A cloaked figure crouched over her, leaning all of his strength into the vice-like grip he had around her neck. His hood shadowed his face, but her death lurked behind the pure loathing that burned in his eyes.

As she woke more to the desperateness of her situation, she grabbed one of his wrists. Her other hand reached for the dagger she had stashed under the pillow. The instant her fingers closed around the hilt, she bucked her body. Men often made the mistake of assuming she was weaker because she was female and slight of build. She was Krivalen, and those magic enhancements made her stronger than most men. The power of her movement flung him off to the side. She followed, throwing herself after him. They hit the floor with her straddling his body now, and she drove the dagger between his ribs.

His eyes widened with pain and the terror of realizing he had lost his last fight. He grabbed her hand on the weapon's hilt, holding it there. Perhaps he knew as well as she did that he would bleed out much faster when she pulled the blade free.

"I don't want to die." His voice shook, and tears spilled from the corners of his eyes.

Now that she got a better look at him with his hood knocked back by their struggling, she saw he was nothing more than a frightened youth. Her gut twisted. She yearned to take back the blade in his ribs and undo the damage, but it was much too late for that.

"Why?" She searched for anything familiar about his features. "Why did you attack me?"

He squeezed his eyes shut as he coughed up blood. It trickled from the corner of his mouth, spreading through the stubble of his beard. When he opened his eyes again, she was struck by how blue they were.

"You killed... my brother." He groaned, his breath coming in shallow gasps. His hand shook over hers, his grip weakening.

The room shrank around them. A dropping sensation in her gut left her lost and confused. "Your brother?"

"Captain... Karth." He coughed again, harder this time.

Raven turned her cheek to him, wincing when a light spatter of blood hit the side of her face. Revenge was never simple. Everyone had family somewhere. In her quest for vengeance and to protect Amberwood, she had inspired that same hatred that drove her in someone else. She had become this man's Darrenton.

Tears welled in her eyes, one spilling down her cheek.

His brow furrowed in response. "Why?"

She swallowed against the tightness in her throat. "He killed my father." She didn't know for certain that his brother, Captain Karth, was among the men who came for Jaecar that day, but it was as likely as not.

The youth squeezed his eyes shut. Fresh tears ran down the sides of the young man's face. A choking cough brought up more blood. "It hurts." His voice rose with fear.

"I know." The rest of her tears broke free. "I can stop the pain."

He met her eyes and nodded. Recalling how it felt when Wayland reached into her with his power, preparing to take her life from her, Raven guided the Krivalen magic

into him. She sought out that dwindling vitality that
made him more than an empty husk. While she did so,
she held his gaze and placed her free hand on his chest.
Fear still shone bright amidst the pain in his eyes, but his
face relaxed a little, and the hand over hers fell away.

Raven yanked the blade out as she drew on that faltering sense of warmth that was his life. He choked, his
body jerking under her. After several agonizing seconds
that seemed to linger on forever, the light left his eyes,
and he was still. A silvery mist swirled around her hand,
snaking up her arm and vanishing in to her chest. She
had expected pain, the way there had been when her
mother first turned her Krivalen. This was more like a
splash of warm water, except it sank inside her, spreading through her entire body before the sensation faded.

She shivered once, then shifted off him and sat back
against the side of the bed, bringing her knees into her
chest. Mere seconds had passed when she startled at the
sound of someone else entering the room. Closing her
hand around the knife hilt again, she looked up to see
Marek take a few steps toward her from the direction of
the open door.

"I heard a noise and came to check on you." His
gaze flickered to the dead youth. "If it makes you feel
any better, I do know for certain that Captain Karth
was among the men who killed Jaecar."

She heaved a shaky breath. "Not really. And, right
now, I'm not sure I want to know how you know that."
With a quick glance around the room, she spotted the
hidden door to the servant's passages standing open in
the back corner. That explained how the young man
had gotten in. Either he had been extremely quiet, or
she had been exhausted. Perhaps both.

"I met up with Darrenton's men on my way north
after killing that beast outside Andel. They had Jaecar's
body with them." He stopped a few feet from her. She

felt his gaze boring into her. "You took his life into you. How? In the Brotherhood, we're told that only the priests have that power."

Irritation prickled at her skin. She was tired, and the hurt that Synderis had so sweetly offered to help with was worse now. "Why would that be true? Priests are made using the same magic that made you and me."

"They teach us that the magic remakes some people differently every now and then, blessing them with the ability to make others of our kind."

"And it never struck you as odd that no one has been remade in that particular way since the first three men who started the Brotherhood?" She wiped her dagger on the frayed bottoms of the young man's trousers—he wasn't going to care—and stood up. "Control, Marek. That's called control. It's just another lie they fed you."

His hands clenched into fists for a few seconds, then he deliberately unclenched them and took a deep breath. "How did you learn how to do it?"

"Wayland tried to do it to me. I paid attention." She looked down at the youth lying at their feet. "He's not a guard."

"No. He was one of the stable hands. I met him when I brought the horses in. I got no sense of threat off of him then. He hid it well."

Raven nodded. "The dead, they're all human?" She looked directly at Marek now.

He met her eyes, his narrowing slightly. "Yes."

"Then we'll bury the bodies in individual graves as their families would."

"That will be a lot of work." There was caution in his voice and choice of words as if he feared upsetting her.

She walked to a basin on the vanity. The blood on her face was a spray of black specs in the darkness. She picked up a hand towel and dampened it, using it to start cleaning the blood away. Was it more amusing or

disturbing that neither of them thought to light a candle, relying instead on their enhanced vision to see? For
herself, she didn't want a better look at the dead man
lying behind her. It was terrible enough simply knowing
he was there.

"We've got fields full of mercenaries," she said. "I'm
sure we can find some willing to help for a bit of coin."

"If that's how you want to handle it."

"It is." She glanced at him in the reflection, noting
his wary regard. Part of her wanted to try to sleep again,
hoping that Synderis would dreamwalk her once more
and help ease her mind, but that would have to wait.
"Give me a few minutes to clean up, then I'll take watch
so you can get a little rest before morning. We have a lot
of work to do." A lot of bodies to bury.

He gave a nod and turned to leave.

"And Marek?" When he stopped, she said, "Maybe
put something in front of the servant's passage entrance
into your room."

He glanced down at the body of the stable hand
again. When he looked back up at her, some of the
wariness had gone, but she couldn't quite read what had
taken its place.

"I will. Thank you, Raven." He inclined his head to
her before leaving the room.

Once she was alone, she stared at her eyes and hair
in the reflection. Better light might reveal more silver in
them now, but she didn't want to see it. Not ever. She
walked over to the young man's body and bent down to
brush his eyelids closed.

"I'm sorry," she murmured, fighting hard against
the threat of fresh tears.

She had given him what she could. If the Krivalen in
Eyl'Thelandra were to be believed, Accepting his spirit
was an honorable act. She wasn't convinced, but it had
felt like the right thing to do at the time.

Karsima sat on her mount at the northeastern edge of town, watching a group working on the wall under the direction of one of the senior Stonebreaker builders. She didn't want to focus reconstruction efforts there right now, but with the threat from Lord Darrenton, they needed to build up their defenses. Walling in the entire town would take more time than they probably had. Still, it was coming along faster than expected with the expertise of the Stonebreakers. Whatever portion they completed would at least slow the army of mercenaries down, forcing them to circumvent it or pound their way through. What point was there in rebuilding the rest of Amberwood if that arrogant cur meant to destroy it again?

She nudged her mount with one heel, moving his hindquarters around until she faced south. Reconstruction continued on the town itself. They hadn't entirely abandoned other restoration efforts for the wall's sake. Everyone here was betting their future on this endeavor. Some show of confidence was necessary, or they might start giving up on their dream. At the top of the hill, a team had begun the process of clearing debris to rebuild the manor house. She and Alayne would call that home eventually if they managed to hold onto Amberwood.

She closed her eyes for several minutes, listening to

the clang of hammers hitting chisels and nails and saws cutting through wood. Snippets of conversation filtered in amidst those sounds. Some expressed concerns about Darrenton's army of mercenaries, but at least as many still spoke as if this would be their forever home. They discussed renovations and made plans for their lives here. The smells of stone dust, sawdust, and dirt reached her despite a light spattering of rain. Somewhere in there, she fancied she could even smell the forest outside of town.

The sound of fast-moving horses caught her attention. Opening her eyes, she spotted Jael and Ehric cantering up from the forest's edge. A flash of fear constricted her chest as it did whenever one of the scouts came hurrying it. She could not help dreading the day they would come racing in ahead of an attack. But they weren't sprinting in to warn of an impending threat this time. They had their mounts held to an easy canter rather than galloping in to sound an alarm. It was early enough that they must have news regarding the intruders at Darrenton's manor.

She urged her horse down toward the gate to meet them. They slowed when she rode through, easing back to a trot that set Ehric's magnificent mane of long black locs bouncing. They both had long black hair, but that was as far as the similarities went. Jael's hair hung smooth around his refined elven features, his skin as pale as Ehric's was dark. The two had become as close as brothers of late, working together to manage the scouts in Phendaril's absence, and now while he recovered from his injuries. They made an excellent team.

She met them a few hundred yards past the gate. The two looked troubled. Enough so that she knew their hasty return was a harbinger of something serious, if not an actual emergency.

"Good to see you both back." She offered a slight nod to each. "I take it you learned something more about Darrenton's nocturnal visitors."

Ehric looked to Jael. He commonly left the talking to the elf in these interactions, deferring to the longtime working relationship and friendship she and Jael had.

"Nothing else happened during the night, but there was something a bit odd going on near the third Away Post this morning," Jael said.

"Away Post" was the name they had given the three outposts where they had spies keeping tabs on events on Darrenton's property. The third was the one closest to the manor itself. Soon after learning of his purchase of the land, they started maintaining a daily watch for the arrivals of new mercenaries and any other comings and goings that might be of interest.

She tried to ignore the niggling worry in her gut. Sometimes it was hard to hide how much she dreaded the inevitable conflict with Darrenton. She was their constable. They looked to her for guidance and leadership. Any fears she had stayed locked behind doors where only those closest to her, primarily Alayne and Phendaril, ever heard of them.

"What's happened?"

"This morning, some of Darrenton's mercenaries and workers started digging graves on the south edge of the fields and carrying bodies out of the manor. Of the bodies I saw, it looked like most were wearing Darrenton's livery."

Karsima wasn't sure whether to be alarmed or excited. If last night's intruders had overpowered Darrenton and his men, that could be extremely lucky for them. But why would assassins take time to dig graves and bury the bodies? A mass grave or pyre might make sense, but multiple graves were a lot of trouble to go to for an enemy. Unless the attackers had managed to bring down several guards but had ultimately fallen. In that case, the survivors would surely tend to their dead in the aftermath.

"We should get to the bottom of this quickly? Gather a few more riders and meet me outside The Bear and Raven in half an hour."

They parted ways inside the gate, and she galloped up the road to the upper residential district. She left her mount tethered in front of The Bear and Raven where it could drink from the trough and jogged over to the house she and Alayne shared. When she departed that morning, Alayne and Phendaril had been in the study, discussing battle tactics. Since then, they had migrated into the sitting room and were drinking mead before a fire.

Karsima hesitated in the doorway. "Working hard, I see."

Phendaril glanced up at her from the chair he reclined in. "It is more comfortable here." He sat up straighter, his eyes narrowing as he took in her expression. "Something's happened?"

Alayne regarded her curiously. "Yes. Please tell me he's not on the march."

"No. But Jael kept watch over the manor the rest of the night. This morning, he saw them digging graves and carrying out the bodies of some of Darrenton's guards. I'm going to take a few riders up to investigate."

Phendaril's expression darkened. He didn't have to say anything. He still had healing to do before he would be fit to ride, and his frustration with that fact was written all over his face.

Sympathy softened Karsima's tone. "I want you both to know where we're going in case anything goes wrong."

Alayne got up and came to stand in front of Karsima, her green eyes bright with worry. "Why don't I ride with you?"

She shook her head. "If you don't already know all the reasons that's a bad idea, I'm sure Phendaril can explain them to you while I'm gone. The short answer is that you two are in charge if something happens to me. I need you safe."

Alayne's eyes sparkled with mischief. "I know that's not the only reason."

Karsima kissed her, loving how her lips tasted of wine. She let her hands rest on the familiar curve of the other woman's waist, yearning to show her exactly how much she wanted her. Now was definitely not the right time, however. She drew back, appreciating how Alayne licked her lips and smiled that sultry bedroom smile.

"I *want* you safe." Karsima took her hands away, needing to put a slight separation between them.

"Hmm. I want you too. Safe, that is. I want you safe too." Alayne winked, then the teasing look turned serious. "Please be careful. You can't trust that bastard."

"I second that," Phendaril offered, watching them with that hint of sorrowful longing in his eyes.

Karsima hurt for him. She wanted him to have what she had with Alayne. From the onset, she knew that falling in love with Raven would lead him to heartache. Still, the heart chose who it chose. Nothing could help that. If only Raven could have returned with him and Ehric without putting them all at risk.

"I'll be back soon," she assured them, though the words were as much to reassure herself as them.

After gathering her weapons and a few emergency supplies, she met Jael, Ehric, and two others in the square. They rode as fast as they could heading out of town, but when they reached the dense stretch of woods that created a challenging border between the two properties, they had to slow their pace. At the north edge of those woods, the lands were split by a run of steep craggy hills that were only traversable, at least without unreasonable effort, in a few spots. The route she chose had them winding back and forth down a precarious slope. It was ponderous going, and the trail up the other side was similar.

The landscape made social visits north difficult, but it would also make it harder for Darrenton to bring his mercenary army down to Amberwood. He could use the river to move some troops and equipment or trek inland to the east and around for a longer but less hostile route. It wasn't an insurmountable obstacle.

By midday, they rode along the end of the path into Darrenton's fields. A crude lean-to that served as a guard post stood empty. The light rain had let up. The mercenary camps still littered the north edge of the outer fields, though it looked as if a few were packing up to leave. As they got closer to the house, she spotted the mercenaries Jael mentioned on the south edge of the fields digging what were obviously graves, given the bodies lined up nearby. She stopped their mounts a fair distance away, wary of approaching too boldly after whatever had occurred here in the night.

A man at the near end spotted them. He jogged up the line of graves to tap on someone else's shoulder. When the second man turned to look their way, a swell of anger flooded in, only to be rolled over an instant later by confusion. She watched in disbelief as that man, Marek, leaned close to the more feminine figure digging next to him. When she cast a glance their way, Karsima barely managed not to fall off her horse in surprise.

"That's..." Jael began.

"Raven," Ehric finished for him.

Karsima kicked her horse to a trot, watching Raven wipe her sweaty brow with a cloth and hand her shovel to the man who had first spotted them. She walked toward them with a weary drag in her steps. Marek moved as if to follow her, but Raven stopped him with a gesture, saying something to stay him before she continued toward them alone.

They pulled their mounts up a few feet away from her. Karsima swung down and stepped out ahead of the horses. Jael did the same, coming to stand behind her. Ehric hopped off his horse as well, but he strode past Karsima and Jael and swept Raven into his arms, lifting her off the ground. A tired smile broke across the young half-elf's face, and she returned the embrace. The smile faltered when he set her down, her gaze moving briefly to the graves. It struck Karsima that Raven looked haggard, and not only in a physical way.

Trying to make sense of the situation, Karsima glanced around at the mercenaries and bodies. She watched with a deepening feeling of disorientation as a dark-haired serving woman trotted over to Raven, holding a water skin out to her.

"Lady Darrenton, you really ought to drink something. You've been working so hard all morning."

"Thank you, Lily." She accepted the skin and took a long drink before handing it back to the woman. "Take this to Marek."

Lily eyed them curiously, then offered Raven a slight curtsy and hurried back toward where Marek waited.

"Lady Darrenton?" Karsima raised an eyebrow.

Raven waved a dismissive hand after the woman. "Marek said I should let them call me that. He told them I was Jaecar's adopted daughter. He insisted they would be more likely to accept me if they thought of me as Lord Darrenton's niece." She grimaced as if she had swallowed something foul. "I'd rather not be considered any relation at all to that man, a sentiment I believe Jaecar shared, but it does seem to have the desired effect on his staff."

"And where is Lord Darrenton?"

Raven scanned down the line of graves, her gaze lingering on the ones at the far end that were already filled in. "We buried him first. The first grave on that end."

"He's dead?"

Raven nodded.

If Darrenton was dead, then Amberwood was safe again, wasn't it? "I don't understand how this happened, but you have our gratitude. Why didn't you tell Phendaril you were coming? We could have helped."

A darker shadow fell over her features. "I don't have the talisman anymore. Besides, Marek and I snuck into the manor last night to deal with Darrenton and his men. More people would have increased the chances of his mercenaries noticing something before we were through. This way, they didn't know anything was wrong until it was too late to intervene."

Along with her amazement and the excitement that was starting to bubble up, a wave of relief swept through Karsima. Phendaril would be so relieved to know there was a logical reason Raven hadn't reached out to him. "And you and Marek did all of this last night?"

Before Raven could answer, Jael spoke, an edge of awe in his tone. "You came all the way back here to help us?"

Raven glanced in his direction, not quite meeting his eyes. She didn't look that pleased with their accomplishment, but perhaps that was just exhaustion. "There's still Wayland to contend with."

"You've done an incredible thing here. Give yourself some credit," Ehric stated, giving Raven's arm a gentle squeeze.

A hint of moisture shimmered in her silver eyes before she turned away, looking back at the graves again. Karsima got the sudden sense that Raven was the reason they were burying the dead the way they were. It was guilt that visibly weighed her down. She was trying to atone for the lives she had taken in this small way.

Karsima glanced around at her companions. "Excuse us for a minute." Then she stepped up to Raven, gesturing away from the others. "Walk with me?"

Wordlessly, Raven turned and fell into step with her.

When they were out of earshot, Karsima said softly, "It's eating away at you, isn't it? Killing these men?"

Raven swallowed hard. Her nod was almost imperceptible.

Karsima stopped walking, and Raven did the same, staring into the distance for a few seconds before reluctantly facing her. For all that the half-elf had been through since Karsima met her, she was still the same Raven who feared social interaction more than any monster.

"You know you may have saved hundreds of lives by killing these men, right? Amberwood is in your debt. It's also still your home. There is no shame in protecting your home and the people you love."

Raven met her eyes, her gaze overflowing with more profound sorrow. She crossed her arms firmly over her chest, hugging them to her. "I know. But how many of these guards were loved by people who will never see them again?"

A break in the clouds let a ray of sunlight hit Raven's hair. Had there always been that much silver in it? Faint bruises were also visible around the other woman's neck that Karsima hadn't noticed until now. Life wouldn't ever be easy for her, especially as long as she cared the way she did. It wasn't in Karsima to suggest that caring was bad, so she left that alone.

"That will always be an unfortunate risk of this kind of conflict. I'd worry about you more if you didn't care about that. Some choices will never be easy. We just do the best we can. A whole town of men, women, and children won't die this year because of you. Hold that close to your heart, and it will heal." Karsima put a hand on her arms. "Come home tonight. Be with the people you saved. Everyone will be happy to see you. Especially Phendaril."

A tear slipped down Raven's cheek, and she lowered

her gaze to the ground. "He won't, Karsima. He really won't."

It was as if someone had tied bricks to her feet, dragging her down from the happiness that had come with learning the threat from Darrenton was over. Nausea made her stomach flip. "The Silverblood elf from the dream?"

Raven looked away.

Karsima stood silently, fuming for a few seconds. It was hard to stand there and support Raven, knowing the young half-elf was going to break Phendaril's heart. The first several things she came up with to say were cruel and scathing. But no matter what else happened, Raven had come back to help them. Somehow, she had to balance that knowledge against this new information.

"He deserves to know." Her voice was sterner than she meant it to be, but she couldn't help that.

Raven nodded, squeezing her arms in tighter. "I'll go to Amberwood after I take care of this." She glanced toward the mercenary camps. "Some of the mercenaries are heading out now. Others have expressed interest in staying on to help protect Amberwood for a while. I thought that might help in case Wayland tries to lash out. I've got the coin Darrenton set aside to pay them." She added the last quickly.

"That might be helpful," Karsima stated, still more curtly than she intended, though it was hard to be objective and kind at the moment.

Without a word, she stalked back to her companions, Raven following silently behind her. "I'm going to stay and help out with the bodies. Anyone else who wishes to do so can, though at least one of us needs to go back to check in with Alayne and Phendaril, so they don't get worried."

"I know the route best," Jael stated. "I'll go. What do you want me to tell them?"

"Tell them we'll be back by dark and that Darrenton and his men were killed last night by someone he had wronged. Don't mention Raven or Marek yet. I think it's best to leave that part quiet until the rest of us get there."

Jael inclined his head. "Milady." He swung up on his horse, not bothering with the stirrup, and trotted back the way they had come. None of the others followed.

Karsima turned to Raven. "Where can we help?"

aven heard Marek step in through the bedroom doorway behind her.

"You should come with us," she said without turning.

"I doubt they've forgiven me yet for what I did to you. We'll give them a few days to get used to the idea of me helping you save them before I show myself. Besides, whatever you're dreading isn't going to go away just because I'm there."

She didn't say anything. He wasn't wrong. To expect them to forget what he had done to her was asking a lot. It was probably stranger that she had forgiven him or at least set his betrayal aside to give him another chance. Forgiveness was a little too much for her to offer yet, considering that his actions had resulted in her death, temporary though it might have been. As to the other point, his presence wouldn't make talking to Phendaril any easier. It arguably had the potential to make that more difficult, given their history.

She stared at the armor sitting on her bed, trying to come up with a reason to put it on before riding to Amberwood. She didn't need it on this particular adventure, but she felt exposed without it, especially this time.

Marek stepped up beside her. "If you leave it here, you have an excuse to return sooner."

She glanced at him, watching as he strode over to the basin and used the damp cloth she had recently finished cleaning up with to wipe something off the back of his hand. The sound of construction reached them from the rear entry, where boards were being ripped up from the floor. Some of the bloodstains were on those boards to stay. It made more sense to replace them, though she wasn't sure why Marek bothered to keep the crew working on the manor. This place didn't belong to either of them.

"What makes you think I want to come back here?"

He glanced over at her, his eyes narrowing. "Because you're nervous as a bride about to meet her groom for the first time. I don't know why, but something has you uneasy about going back there. Aren't you eager to see Phendaril?"

Her stomach did a flip, and she brought her hands together in front of her face, using her fingers to rub at the slight ache between her brows.

He turned to fully face her. "You're *not* eager to see him?"

"I am. It's just..." She heaved a sigh and glanced away.

Not once on their travels together had she dared to tell Marek about Eyl'Thelandra or Synderis. He was a companion and had proven true so far, but she still didn't fully trust him. She had revealed more to Cyrleth in her rare moments alone with the animal than she had told him. Marek wasn't a confidant. She didn't have one of those.

She heard him walking over and caught the scent of a spice that recalled memories of Jaecar under the sweat and dirt of the day. Something about the way he smelled often reminded her of the quiet warrior who had raised her. Maybe that was part of why she had been foolish enough to trust him the first time. And here she was, doing it again.

He placed a hand on her shoulder. "If you want me there, I'll come."

"Please, don't be nice to me right now, Marek. The problems I'm dealing with are of my own making this time. I just need to figure them out."

His voice was gentle. "It is possible to fall in love with more than one person, Raven. The workings of the heart can be very inconvenient."

She jerked out from under his hand and stared at him. His assessment was too close to the mark. How much had he somehow figured out, and how much was simply a lucky guess? "I'll be fine."

"Take your sword and dagger, at least. It's a long ride, and there are beasts in the woods."

She grabbed the sword belt and buckled it on, sheathing her blade. "The others are waiting."

When she started walking from the room, he followed.

"I took the liberty of asking someone to bring Cyrleth around for you."

Raven stopped and turned to look at him, remembering the dead stable boy who had tried to kill her in her room. It was probably her imagination, but she felt as though she could still sense that distinct part of the Krivalen magic in her that had come from his life.

"Are you sure you'll be all right alone here tonight?"

"Lady Darrenton," he said, giving her a teasing smirk, "you do care."

Raven breathed a small laugh and shook her head at him. "You're insufferable, and I'm leaving."

He followed her to the door and out front. Karsima and others were there by their horses. Cyrleth was also there, being held by the remaining stable hand. The older gentleman wouldn't look at her, though he did watch Marek, who came out behind her and offered the adept a slight nod.

She paused a few strides past the door and turned to Marek again. "Thank you."

He raised an eyebrow. "For what?"

"For Cyrleth."

"Having him brought around or helping you steal him?"

She chuckled at that. "Both. Be careful. There may still be some here who aren't happy with the change of command."

"I took the liberty of hiring a few guards from the fields. I'll be fine." He inclined his head and lowered his voice. "You be careful as well. Love can be as cruel and sharp as any blade."

Her throat tightened at that. Seeing Phendaril again was going to be difficult no matter what she did to try to prepare herself. "I'll see you tomorrow."

She turned and hurried over to Cyrleth, forcing confidence into her strides. The stable hand released the reins to her abruptly and stalked away. Lowering his head, the black gelding shoved it closer to her, asking for her to scratch under his forelock. The simple act of doing so eased her nerves a little. Even the smell of dust and hay that clung to him was oddly comforting. She patted his neck once before moving alongside him, then swung up in the saddle.

"You've gotten more at home on horseback," Ehric commented.

Her cheeks warmed at that. "Yes. Cyrleth's been a good instructor." She stroked the gelding's shoulder, and Ehric nodded his approval.

"He suits you." As he spoke, they turned their mounts with the rest of the group and started away from the manor. "Where did you get him?"

"Marek helped me liberate him from one of the Lathwood guards who were hunting for me."

Karsima cast a sharp glance her way. "Speaking of

Marek, you two seem rather friendly, considering he's the one who handed you to Wayland."

Raven met her gaze. "Sometimes circumstances decide for us who our companions will be."

Karsima's expression tightened. "Does that also explain your situation with Phendaril?"

Raven winced inwardly, ignoring Ehric's questioning glance. It shouldn't surprise her that Karsima would get defensive about Phendaril. The two were as close as siblings. Still, it didn't help her feel any better about the situation. But maybe she didn't deserve to feel better about it. When she was with Synderis, it had been too easy to lose a piece of her heart to him. She had let herself believe it was all right because she couldn't have children, and she had not expected to ever find herself back in Amberwood. Maybe it had been naïve and foolish, but knowing that didn't make her love either of them less.

"I've been afraid to ask," Raven began, wondering as the words came out why she was torturing herself more, "if Veylin..."

As if responding to a planned cue, her companions looked away, most toward the ground. A palpable sorrow filled the cool, late afternoon air.

"Oh," she said softly. Tears pooled in her eyes, and she too stared down, unable to look at the others.

They upped the pace then, alternating between a swift trot and canter until they reached the craggy hills where they had to slow down and ride single-file, especially with dark falling. About halfway through, a light drizzle began to rain down on them. Raven didn't mind. It helped mask her occasional tears as she fought to keep her thoughts away from Veylin and how her friend must have suffered.

In his dream, Wayland told her they had tortured Veylin by inflicting on her the same injuries Raven endured the night she fought him. It was hard not to imagine the vivacious elven female bleeding from cuts over her entire body. Wounds like those Raven suffered, mostly when the glass ceiling burst, though a few of the deeper ones came from Wayland's blade, such as the one that left a long scar down her breastbone. Had they struck Veylin across the head the way he had Raven? A blow that broke her cheekbone.

She shuddered in the saddle, feeling nauseated.

Cyrleth needed little guidance from her. Reliable and steady, he was content to follow the other horses as they made their way through the steep crags into the denser forest. They picked up the pace again when the path opened some. When they cantered out of the trees below the lower edge of town, the number of windows with lights in them struck her. So many more homes were occupied. The wall had progressed considerably as well.

Jael and Sameth waited by an open gate. Sameth's eyes popped wide when he saw her ride in with the others.

"Raven!" He gave Jael a mock chastising look. "They didn't tell me you were the wronged party who took care of our northern threat."

She managed a smile and a nod of greeting. "I had a little help," she answered.

Strange how, now that she was here, she couldn't wait to see Phendaril, even though she knew the encounter would be difficult and might end badly. Seeing him and knowing he was all right would be worth the pain. At least, she hoped it would.

The streets were cleaner, cleared of weeds and debris. As they approached the square, she noticed the beginnings of new cobble being placed. When they finished it, this town would be a wonderful home to so many. Maybe she could find solace in that. For every life she and Marek had ended last night, dozens of humans and elves would get their chance at a happy existence here.

Karsima stopped them alongside The Bear and Raven, turning her attention to the others. "Why don't you three get some rest or enjoy a drink. I imagine Phen and Alayne are waiting at the house."

The three broke off then, though Ehric paused beside Raven to tell her how happy he was to see her before heading to the public house. A block of icy dread weighed her down as she followed Karsima toward the home she and Alayne shared. Outside the door, they dismounted, and Karsima tied her mount to a post.

Raven hesitated, holding Cyrleth's reins. "Should I put him somewhere?"

"They'll be fine here for a few minutes."

The other woman's cold tone expanded that block of dread in her gut. Forcing a calming breath, she tied Cyrleth and followed Karsima in. They had barely stepped inside when Alayne burst through the doorway of the sitting room as if she meant to run to Karsima. She stopped dead when she saw Raven and stood there for a few seconds with her mouth partly open. Raven's legs were gradually turning to mush under her.

Her gaze stern, Karsima gestured to the sitting room. Raven gave a slight nod and made herself walk toward it. The shine of joy in Alayne's eyes only made it worse. The other woman didn't know what Karsima knew. Not yet.

"Is everything all right?"

Phendaril's voice coming from the room froze Raven in her tracks. It would be a dreadful time to throw up, but she was beginning to feel like it was a real possibility. Alayne glanced from her to Karsima, her joyful look starting to fade. Raven ground her teeth and moved forward again. When she reached the doorway, Alayne walked to intercept Karsima, who followed a few steps behind.

Taking one last deep breath, Raven entered the room.

Phendaril sat before the fire, the light of the flames enhancing the red in his long, nearly black hair. His dark eyes widened when he saw her, his mouth opening with a gasp of surprise. He struggled to his feet, one leg encased in a complicated-looking jointed brace.

Karsima stopped in the doorway next to Raven. "Alayne and I are going to take the horses to the stable around the corner, then go get a drink. Feel free to use the house as long as you like."

With that, the other two women left Raven standing there, drinking him in with her eyes. Tears shone in his eyes as he stared at her that she knew were reflected in her own. With tentative steps, she walked over and stopped in front of him, taking in the scar that ran down the right side of his nose, so close to that eye. She appreciated the slightly more pronounced nose and stronger brow that made his features quite different from Synderis's but no less handsome.

He reached out and touched her face, his fingers light upon her cheek as if he feared she might disappear from under his fingertips. A tear slipped from one eye, running along the scar. Then he took a limping step forward and pulled her into his arms, squeezing her tight against him.

Raven returned the embrace, pain lancing through her chest like someone had driven a blade into her heart.

"I didn't know if I would ever see you again." His voice was strained by the strength of his emotions.

Raven didn't know what to say. It was so wonderful to be in his arms again. It was as if she had never left for just a moment, but it wasn't fair to him or Synderis to let it continue. She started to pull away, and he released her only enough to capture her lips in a kiss. For a second, she kissed him in return, needing to feel his love in case she never got another chance to do so. Then a sob broke through her. He let go of her immediately, pushing her back to meet her eyes.

Raven avoided his gaze. "I can't, Phen. I..." She had no idea what to say. She wanted him. She loved him. And yet, she loved Synderis too.

Worry furrowed his brow. "Raven? What is it?" He stared at her then, and something slowly changed in his regard, something she had feared. "You pulled away because I kissed you." His voice was soft, almost as if he were talking to himself.

"Phen, I'm sorry. I didn't think I would ever see you again." Why did that sound like such a weak excuse now, especially standing there watching the sorrow crash across his face?

"Do you love him?"

She noticed the tremble in his chest as he struggled to calm his breathing and control his emotions. The hurt was bright in his eyes.

"I love *you* too." Her voice cracked as she said it.

He closed his eyes, the muscles in his jaw jumping as he clenched his teeth. He turned away from her before opening his eyes again, staring into the fire instead. "You need to leave now."

"Phen—"

"Leave!"

She flinched at his shout. A powerful pain burst through her chest as though her heart had physically broken. The agony made her feel trapped, like an injured animal. Raven spun and bolted from the house.

She didn't slow until she reached the stable, where Alayne and Karsima were talking. They had the horses in ties but hadn't unsaddled them yet. Raven wiped brusquely at the tears streaming down her cheeks, not that it helped much. Then she strode past them and hastily untied Cyrleth.

Karsima took a few steps toward her. "What happened? I thought you two had things to talk about."

"He told me to leave. I'm leaving." She hauled Cyrleth out into the street and swung into the saddle. It was raining harder now. That seemed appropriate somehow.

Alayne caught her hand as she adjusted her hold on the reins. "You can't leave tonight. It's raining and dark. It's not safe."

"This is still your home," Karsima added, stepping up beside Alayne.

Raven squeezed her eyes shut for a second, fighting the threatening sobs. "Not anymore."

She jerked her hand away from Alayne and kicked Cyrleth hard. The startled gelding lunged forward, almost leaving her behind. Then she bent over his neck and turned him toward the gate.

Karsima watched as Raven disappeared down the road, a sense of helplessness flowing through her.

Alayne reached over and took her hand. "Should we send someone after her?"

She considered it for a minute, but what would be the point? This was Raven. "No. She's better suited to navigate this place in the dark than any of the rest of us. Besides, if she doesn't want us to find her, we won't."

"She has gotten a lot more comfortable around horses."

Karsima breathed a soft laugh, though it didn't ease the ache of sorrow in her chest. "She must have discovered that they're much easier to get along with than people. It's a shame Jaecar taught her everything about fighting and nothing about love."

"A good reason not to judge her too harshly. Most of us start learning how to interact with people *before* we turn twenty-two." Alayne released her hand. "Why don't you go check on Phen. I'll unsaddle your horse."

Karsima gave her a teasing smirk. "Always taking the easy jobs." She leaned in to give her a quick kiss. "Don't be long. I'll probably need some comforting after this."

Alayne grinned and shooed her away.

Back in the house, she found Phen sitting before the fire again, though this time he leaned to one side, resting his head in his hand. The raven-headed cloak pin sat on the table next to him. It made her chest hurt to think that he carried that link to Raven everywhere with him.

Karsima stopped in the doorway. "Phen?"

He didn't lift his head when he spoke. "Is she all right?"

It encouraged her that he asked after Raven first. That meant he had already begun to calm down and consider the complexity of the circumstances.

Karsima made her way around to sit in one of the other chairs. They had placed three before the fire specifically so Phendaril could join them. Having him there so much of the time reminded her of when they had all lived together while she was still attending the university in Chadhurst. He was family in every way except blood, and always would be.

"She left."

He lifted his head. His eyes were rimmed in red, the hurt in them tearing through her so that she had to blink back her own tears.

"Left? As in, she's returning to Darrenton's land in the dark? Alone?"

She shook her head at the worry in his voice. "This is Raven. The semi-feral Silverblood you brought back from Manderly. She can see herself back to the manor in one piece."

"I'm not worried about her physical wellbeing."

That wasn't Karsima's concern either if she were being honest, but she didn't want to exacerbate his fears. "She won't be alone there. Marek's with her. He helped her bring down Aldrich."

"Comforting." His sarcastic tone was probably appropriate, given how little they all trusted Marek.

"I hoped you two would talk. You couldn't have said

more than ten words to each other in the time between when Alayne and I left, and she showed up to take her horse. What happened?"

"You expected us to talk?" His eyes narrowed sharply. "You knew?"

"I only found out earlier today." She shrugged, a little uncomfortable before his gaze now. But it wasn't as if there had been an opportunity to warn him, and she doubted it would have helped the situation if she had.

He looked down at the cloak pin before turning to stare into the fire. "What do I do now?"

Karsima considered her words for several seconds, taking a sip of wine from the cup that had been Alayne's. The front door opened and closed. She heard Alayne's soft footsteps going up the stairs.

"What do you want to do? As I see it, you can either focus on healing and rebuilding life here, without her, or, if you still love her, you could try talking to her. She's young and extremely inexperienced in matters of the heart. More importantly, she's here. The Silverblood elf isn't. I don't know if this can be saved, but you won't know if you don't try. What I do know is that she still loves you, and you still love her. That seems like it should be worth a conversation, at least."

He leaned back in the chair. "It isn't as if I can go running after her," he growled, gesturing curtly to his injured leg.

"That might be for the best. I suspect you could both use a couple of days to calm down and think things through." She swallowed the last of the wine.

"What if she leaves?"

"I think she'll be around for a few days at least. She's concerned that Wayland might lash out after this. Apparently, they found the funds Lord Darrenton was using to pay his mercenaries, so she was planning to bring some of them here to help protect Amberwood."

He nodded, the firelight reflecting in his dark eyes as he stared into it. "It's a reasonable concern."

Karsima considered him a moment. He was walking a little on the leg with the help of the brace, but he'd need assistance to get to his place. His home, where he had lived a few blissful months with Raven before Wayland ruined everything again. Perhaps he would rather not go there tonight.

"You can use one of the extra rooms if you like, unless you want me to wheel you home."

"No. I don't want to be there alone right now."

Karsima nodded at the expected answer. "Is there anything I *can* do for you, Phen?"

He dredged up a weak smile for her. "No. Thank you. Get some rest."

"Goodnight." She stopped in the doorway and watched him for a moment. Maybe it was wrong to encourage him to try. It might draw out the heartache. Raven loved him, though. She didn't doubt that. It was apparent in the suffering this situation caused her. Whatever happened next, Karsima could only hope they would be kind to each other through it because of the love they shared.

•

Finding the trail in the dark with the rain coming down harder now was more than enough to keep Raven from having an opportunity to think about things. The route wasn't heavily used and followed animal paths in places, making it especially difficult to spot, even with her enhanced vision. The rain had developed into a full downpour by the time she reached the craggy hills. It soaked her through, and her shivering began to sap her energy. At least with the inhospitable weather, she was far less

apt to encounter hostile creatures. They were typically smart enough not to be out in such conditions. She
didn't like what that said about her wisdom for coming
out here, but she couldn't stay in Amberwood.

The long day was also wearing away at her. She'd
had little sleep the night before and spent much of the
day digging graves. Now, with midnight looming near,
she was running significantly short on stamina.

Cyrleth was still strong and steady beneath her,
though he slipped a few times on the wet ground. When
they reached the fields outside the manor, the gelding
broke into an extended trot without her urging. He
took them past the remaining mercenary camps, where
they had erected numerous tents to shelter from the autumn weather, and around to the stable. The horse was
smart enough to know where comfort and food could
be found.

She wasn't sure how long she sat on his back in the
barn aisle before someone pried the reins from her wet,
cold fingers. It could have been seconds or hours. The
stable hand took her arm and helped her dismount. It
was the same man who had brought Cyrleth out to her
that morning. He looked like he had just woken up,
probably roused by the unexpected visitor trotting into
the barn at this hour.

He looked her over once and waved toward the
house. "Get inside, milady. I'll take care of him."

Raven nodded and stumbled away. She made it over
the threshold of the back door before she sank to her
knees and curled in on herself, shivering as sobs tore
through her. A few minutes later, someone closed the
door behind her and wrapped their arms around her,
lifting her to her feet.

"Come," Marek said softly, "you're soaked and must
be exhausted. Let's get you dry and warm."

He took her to her room and dug around for a minute

or two while she stood shivering. If he was looking for a change of clothes, he wouldn't find anything clean. She hadn't brought that much with her. It occurred to her that she should probably tell him that, but by the time her cold lips were willing to form the words, he had given up.

He held up a finger to her. "Give me one minute. Please don't wander off."

When Lily came in a few minutes later, Raven was staring at her bedraggled reflection in an ornate mirror. The woman shut the door and strode over, tossing clothes on the bed.

"Here, milady. I brought you something clean and dry to wear. They aren't appropriate clothes for a lady, but Marek insisted you wouldn't wear a dress, so I had to get creative. I'll get your things washed first thing in the morning." When Raven didn't move, Lily came over and took her shoulders, turning her away from the mirror. She smiled at her. "Help me get you out of these soaked clothes. Brek and a few others were down with a nasty flu not long ago. You're like to catch it if we don't get you warmed up."

Raven tried to help her peel off the wet garments. Her fingers were still too numb from holding the reins in the cold rain, so she gave up after a time and allowed Lily to do most of the work. Once her wet clothes were off, Lily hesitated, looking at her with tears welling up in her eyes. Then she shook herself and quickly dried Raven off with a towel she had brought.

"Milady hasn't had an easy life for one so young, judging by your scars, if you don't mind my noticing."

Raven held her silence, staring at the wall. Neither Phendaril nor Synderis had ever been turned off by those scars. The only reason they really bothered her was because they reminded her that she would never be accepted by society at large and would always be a danger to the people around her. Maybe, if she ended Wayland, she could at least stop the current chain of madness before she fled to Eyl'Thelandra. Assuming she survived the encounter. Figuring out how to get to him was the first problem.

Lily wrapped the towel around Raven's shoulders and turned to grab the clothes from the bed. "The trousers belonged to one of the younger men, but he's slender enough. We should be able to make them work."

When they finished, Lily led her to another room down the hall. She could hear someone moving furniture before they stepped into the doorway. Brek and Marek were inside, shifting a four-poster bed closer to the fire that crackled in the fireplace. Raven watched them, still unable to stop her shivering. Finally, Marek stepped back, eyeing the space between the fireplace and the side of the bed where two comfortable chairs sat, and nodded.

"Brek will fetch more wood," Lily said, shooing the man off with a wave of her hands. "Anything else I can get you?"

"Bring warm food and drink if you could, Lily," Marek requested.

Raven took distant note of his polite tone. She appreciated that he was treating the serving staff respectfully. As soon as they had gone, he pulled a blanket from the foot of the bed and came to wrap it around her. He then guided her to one of two chairs and pushed her into it with gentle pressure on her shoulders.

"Let's get you warm inside and out before we put you to bed." Once she was seated, he knelt next to the chair. "Things obviously didn't go well in Amberwood. Is there anything I can do to ease the hurt I see in your eyes?"

A tear slipped down her cheek, hot against her chilled skin. She shook her head.

"All right. If you change your mind, I'm not as bad a listener as you might expect." He smiled and brushed a lock of her damp hair back over one pointed ear.

"Thank you, Marek," she said softly. "Don't take this badly, but you're the last person I expected to ever find taking care of me in a moment like this."

He grinned. "I would have said the same."

When the shivering eased, Raven dozed off for a time before the food arrived. Marek woke her with a gentle squeeze on her arm and mothered over her until he was satisfied she had eaten enough. She dozed off again for a time after that. When next she woke, she was lying in bed, shivering again despite the blankets and the still blazing fire. Marek and Lily were talking nearby. Their voices seemed strangely loud and rushed. Enough so that she might have covered her ears if not for the effort required in doing so.

"Brek was down for two weeks with it. He had a fever for five days straight," Lily was saying.

Marek looked at Raven. "She's Silverblood. It won't take half that long."

"Krivalen," Raven mumbled.

Marek walked over to her. "What was that?"

No. She wasn't supposed to talk about that. "I'm tired."

He placed a hand on her forehead as she closed her eyes. His voice sounded distant when he spoke again as if it were echoing across a vast chamber.

"Sleep, then."

Synderis fired one arrow after another into the furthest target. His grouping was decent, though his precision wasn't as good as usual. He was distracted. For the last four nights, he hadn't been able to dreamwalk Raven. The first night, there had been no dreams to enter, as if she never went to sleep. The next three nights, his efforts were met with confusing flashes of images and emotion, like fever dreams. Once again, he could do nothing from this far away. It was eating at him the way Koshika would eat a rabbit, shredding him into ribbons of frustration.

He reached for the last arrow in the quiver and grabbed air. When he turned to see where it had gone, he found Telandora standing there, grinning at him. Her long brunette hair was worked through with an elegant weaving of braids. Something her sister, Ilanya, had probably done for her, which suggested the two were still talking, despite Telandora recommending to the Delegate that she not be made Krivalen. Or perhaps Ilanya didn't know her sister was the one behind that. Telandora looked a little less like a creature of the forest now, cleaned up and dressed in casual clothes.

He glanced over at Koshika, who hadn't even paused from grooming her feathered coat. "Some guardian you are."

Telandora laughed. "She knows I'm no threat." She held up the last arrow between them and arched one brow. "Arrow for your thoughts?"

A couple of days ago, the Delegate summoned him, Telandora, and Lindyl back to the inner post, replacing them with other Krivalen scouts. The scout master insisted it was because they had spent so much time away from the village lately, and the Delegate believed they deserved a break. Given that no one ever got called back from the outer posts when they were willing to stay, Synderis doubted that was the reason. At least in his case, he suspected the Delegate wanted him where she could more easily monitor him after their last conversation.

He snatched the arrow from Telandora and fired it, striking dead in the center of his grouping. "I haven't been able to dreamwalk Raven for four nights now. I'm worried, and I'm sick of feeling helpless."

Telandora glanced around surreptitiously as though looking for anyone close enough to hear them. Then she hopped up to sit on a tree that had grown at such an angle it was almost parallel to the ground. The trunk bounced several times under her weight, far more dramatically than it did when his brother's daughters sat there to watch him shoot.

"If you decide to go, Lindyl and I have already agreed that we'll go with you."

Synderis gave her a wary look. "Go?"

"I spent some time catching up with Dell yesterday. I told her I've been concerned about you since Raven left. She told me what you said to the Delegate about it being our fault Raven is in this situation. Then she asked me to keep an eye on you to ensure you don't do anything reckless.

"You're right, though." She picked at a bit of moss on the tree. "Our ancestors are the reason Raven isn't safe outside of our borders. None of the Krivalen are.

They're the reason a small brotherhood of human men has control of the Silverblood magic. Maybe it's time we changed that."

He shook his head at her, breathing a soft laugh. "I'm relatively certain this isn't what Dell had in mind when she asked you to watch me so I don't do anything reckless."

She offered a wry smirk, then leaned forward on the branch, intensity burning bright in her silver eyes. "Think about it, Syn. Raven is half-elven, half-human. She's Krivalen to us, Silverblood to them. Maybe her mother was following more than her heart when she made Raven. Maybe Raven is meant to be a bridge between our worlds. She's out there alone, trying to protect those she cares about from a danger our people have allowed to exist. Even though she has literally paid with her life once already, she went back out there. That takes a special kind of courage."

She sat up then, swinging her legs enough to make the tree bounce. Her calculating gaze made him feel as if she were trying to manipulate him and, truth be told, doing a reasonable job of it. "Maybe the world should know Raven isn't just some anomaly of the Silverblood magic that should be erased. Maybe they need to know that not only can elves be Krivalen, but we're more likely to survive the transformation than humans. And the idea that women can't be Krivalen is just ludicrous."

How reasonable it sounded if one didn't consider the risk to everyone else hidden away in Eyl'Thelandra. As Krivalen, they were tasked with protecting this place. That was part of the oath they took before becoming Krivalen. This was not the way to fulfill that oath.

He drew in a deep breath, hoping it would help keep his mind rational, and started walking out to retrieve his arrows. Telandora hopped off the tree, letting it spring back up behind her, and followed him. Koshika joined them as well, probably sensing his rising tension.

"I don't know, Tel. I'm willing to bet the Brotherhood would love to get their hands on someone who could translate the Acridan book. Given what they did to Raven, I don't expect they would hesitate to use any means necessary to get information out of us before they executed us." His long strides got them to the target quickly, and he started yanking the arrows out with a little more aggression than he needed. "What would happen if the Silverbloods learned more ways to use the Krivalen magic, or worse, if they found out about Eyl'Thelandra." He met her eyes, hoping to drive the point home.

She put her hands on her hips. "Really. You sound more like a council member than a man worried about the female he loves."

He yanked on the next arrow roughly enough to snap the shaft in two. His hand tightened around the half that came away. "Am I supposed to ignore what's best for our people because my heart is breaking for one half-elf?"

Her expression softened. Reaching out, she pulled the other half of the arrow from the target. Then she wrapped her free hand around the back of his hand and turned it palm up. He opened his fingers, and she placed her half of the arrow next to the half in his hand. "Maybe you're supposed to put the pieces back together. Our world and theirs. Your heart and hers."

He stared down at his hand. Was there actually sense to what she was saying? He wanted to say that she was right, but he couldn't tell if that was his head speaking or his heart.

She closed his fingers around the two halves and released his hand. "I'll be around if you need me."

He said nothing as she walked away. One by one, more carefully now, he pulled the rest of the arrows from the target.

Maybe there was something to what she said. Raven's mother had gone out into the world to seek out other elves who might wish to join their hidden sanctuary in Eyl'Thelandra. Instead, she fell in love with a human. When they were savagely attacked by a group of men, she used the last of her strength to make her daughter Krivalen. Had changing Raven merely been the ingrained response of someone who grew up viewing becoming Krivalen as good and natural. Or could there have been something more to it? Even if it was that simple, didn't Raven's mere existence force them to question the way things were arranged? Obviously, the half-elf had already changed the heart of at least one Silverblood.

Raven told him in one of their dreamwalks about her past with Marek. How he had earned her trust working together in Amberwood, only to turn on her by dragging her off to the Silverblood Brotherhood. And yet, he had helped her escape the temple in the end. Even knowing that, Synderis wasn't sure he would have given the man the second chance she was offering him. But to have an ally who was a sanctioned Silverblood could be helpful if she wanted to change more hearts and minds.

And how many more could she change if she had Krivalen elves at her side in addition to that Silverblood human?

Late that evening, he sat on the elevated platform, leaning back against his hut in the trees. Koshika's head rested on his lap. Her contented purring vibrated the muscles in his leg. He trailed his fingers through the soft emerald feathers, scratching gently between her ears and along her cheek.

The two pieces of the arrow lay on the platform on his other side, the broken ends lined up.

He missed Raven. He would consider doing almost anything to see her again, which made him wary of any choices he might make regarding the situation.

Above them, he could see the stars sparkling to life in the dark sky between some of the branches. One particular star, the one that made the point of the Scout's arrow, was the one he used to determine if it was late enough to try dreamwalking Raven. It was visible now, shining bright with a faint red halo.

He patted Koshika's shoulder, and she sat up, recognizing it as a symbol that cuddle time had ended.

He stood. "Let's see if I have better luck tonight."

Koshika rubbed her head into his palm, then she turned and loped off down the elevated walkway. She often wandered out to hunt at night. Like most cats, the lalyx were naturally more active at dusk and dawn. The hours she kept at his side weren't natural to her. It amazed him that she chose to keep them for the sake of staying near him.

"Good hunting, my friend," he murmured before heading in for the night.

Once he settled in the hammock hanging in one corner of the hut, he closed his eyes and focused on that vibrant connection that linked him to Raven.

•

He entered the dream next to the pool at the base of the waterfall where he had found Raven once before, the night he brought Dellaura into the dreamwalk with him. Raven was there, and the burst of relief was dizzying. He might have run to her, but she wasn't alone. She knelt next to a fallen male with two arrows buried deep in his chest. He was elven, with hair the red color of leaves in autumn. As Synderis watched, the elf stopped breathing. She leaned over and placed a kiss on his forehead. When she sat up from the kiss, the male had changed to someone he recognized. The elf Phendaril now lay dead before her.

Raven buried her face in her hands, her shoulders shaking with sobs. The ferns that surrounded the pool began to wither as he watched. The trees in the woods around them started to warp, twisting into angry shadows. Water coming over the falls turned a rust brown, the color pouring into and spreading across the pool. The stone around the falls and under his feet began to turn black, cracks radiating through it.

He rushed over and sank to his knees beside her. "Raven!"

She turned into his embrace, wrapping her arms tightly around him. She started telling him things then, so quickly it was difficult to follow, her voice broken by her sobs. "I was attacked… the last time we dreamwalked, but I killed him. Then I… I took his life. We buried the bodies, all of them. And I saw Phendaril. I still… love him, Syn, but I let him… know I love you too. I broke… his heart. I got sick… with a fever. Now I… I don't know what to do." She was trembling. The anguish of the waking world brought fully into the dream with her.

"First," he said, pushing her back far enough to meet her eyes, "you need to give yourself a chance to breathe."

He met her eyes and took several slow breaths in and out. After the first one, she started to follow his example, her tears gradually abating as she did so. While her attention was on him, he took control of the dreamscape, altering it around them.

He brushed some moisture from her cheeks with his fingers and smiled. "You love me?"

A fleeting smile broke across her lips. "Of course, I do." She scowled at him then. "Did you hear anything else I said?"

"Everything."

Her dubious look was adorable. It made him want to kiss her, but he had heard her, and some things did need to be addressed. "You were attacked but survived, which is the first positive thing. Then you Accepted the life of this person who tried to kill you, which was an honorable and generous thing to do." As he said it, he noticed a hint of more silver in her hair. "You got sick, which explains why I couldn't dreamwalk you, but the fact that I could do so tonight tells me you're starting to feel better."

"And Phendaril?"

The tremble in her voice told him she feared his reaction. It also suggested that Phendaril hadn't reacted well to the revelation. He couldn't hold that against the other elf. Unlike humans and many of the elves that had grown up among them, Synderis's people understood that love was not such a finite thing. If he remembered correctly, that was another aspect of the Acridan culture they had absorbed. It was acceptable if life bonds were not always exclusively between two individuals.

Synderis had never intended to seek out such a relationship for himself. He hadn't really considered seeking out a more substantial relationship at all yet. But when he chose to act on his attraction to Raven, he had known Phendaril was already in her heart. Phendaril, however, had fallen in love with her before Synderis came into the picture, and he was raised in a different culture. Their two experiences were not the same, though it hadn't been painless for either of them, given the way she had unexpectedly left Synderis in Eyl'Thelandra after their night together.

"I always knew that you loved him." He sat down, crossing his legs, and leaned back against the wall of his hut.

Raven glanced around, taking in the elevated platform

and the structure behind him, built against the massive tree trunk. She sank back to sit on her heels. "How did you..."

"You were upset and, I suspect, are still recovering from your illness. Your dreamscape was fracturing, so I took over. I hope you don't mind."

"You are good at this."

He smirked. "One of the best dreamwalkers in Eyl'Thelandra."

A hint of a smile touched her lips, then she shook her head, turning her attention back to the previous subject. "Doesn't it bother you that I love him?"

He drew a deep breath and glanced down at his hands as though he might find answers there. He couldn't honestly deny that it concerned him, knowing Phendaril was unlikely to accept the situation, and he wasn't going to lie to her. He made himself meet her eyes before he spoke. "Of course it does, but I knew it would before you came to me that night. I never expected my love to erase him from your heart, Raven, any more than your love for him stopped me from falling for you."

"Or me from falling for you." She lowered her gaze. "What now?"

"We figure it out as we go." He drew another deep breath and exhaled slowly to give himself the courage to say the next words. "I'm not there for you, Raven. Reach out to him. Be with him if you need to."

Her eyes narrowed. "You're not serious."

He stood then and offered her his hand. "I am."

She gazed up at him, ignoring the offered hand. "I don't want to hurt you."

A flicker of lingering anger kindled in response to that. "Unless you stop loving me, nothing you do will hurt as much as your leaving did."

Raven flinched slightly at his words. "I deserve that."

He reined back the anger and offered a gentle smile. "You do."

She took his hand, letting him guide her to her feet. "I think it might be too late to reach out to Phen."

"Then that's his loss."

He drew her near and slid his arm around her waist, leaning in until their lips were only a few inches apart. He didn't close the last bit of distance, allowing her to choose. She looked into his eyes for a few eternal seconds, their breath mingling. Then she closed that space, her lips pressing against his in a soft, sweet kiss that took his breath away.

"Heleath le'athana," she said softly when they parted.

It was strange how his heart felt like it was breaking and taking flight simultaneously. He kissed her again, and she opened her mouth to him this time, sharing a more passionate connection with him. When they parted a long moment later, they were standing in the bedroom she used when she had stayed at Dellaura's house.

She looked up at him. "Was that me or you?"

He grinned. "Were you thinking of this room too?"

She pressed her lips together as if trying to fight the smile that threatened and nodded.

He chuckled. "Perhaps it was a combined effort then."

Mischief sparkled in her eyes. Her hands moved under his shirt as he guided her back toward the bed.

M arek left after breakfast the following day. He had watched her like a mother tending her young while they ate, his eyes narrowing a fraction every time she put a hand on something to steady herself. If she sighed too deeply or closed her eyes for a few seconds, she would find him staring intently at her. She refused to give him an excuse to postpone leading their selected group of mercenaries down to Amberwood for another day. He eventually relented and struck out with the sizeable party.

For three days, she hadn't left her bed. Yesterday, the fever broke, much sooner than Lily expected it to, though Marek hadn't appeared surprised. Fortunately, the weakness from her sickness had not followed her into her dream, giving her a chance to spend time with Synderis. She still felt uncertain about some things, but after last night, she had no doubts about loving him.

As the day wore on, the sky, which had seemed welcoming enough that morning, darkened, and rain began to fall. She fell asleep around midday, only to be startled awake sometime later by a crack of thunder overhead. Lily, who knelt by a pile of blankets near the fireplace, looked at the ceiling and then over at her.

"How are you feeling, milady?"

Raven sat up. The nap helped restore a little of the

energy she burned walking around that morning. She took a deep breath, then held it for a few seconds, turning one ear in Lily's direction. "Did those blankets just squeak?"

Lily flushed and reached into the pile. She lifted out a wriggling black-and-grey striped kitten. It latched onto one of her fingers, chewing enthusiastically, its tiny tail whipping back and forth.

Raven got up and walked over, taking the little bundle of teeth and claws from her. She held the feisty creature up and looked into its eyes. The nubs of small horns poked up from two black spots on its brow above those bright yellow eyes. She glanced down to see a couple more kittens stumbling around in the blankets like drunk mercenaries.

"Where did you come from?" She asked, bringing the black-and-grey closer to her face. It swiped at her nose, the tiny claws just missing their mark.

She laughed softly and handed it back to Lily.

"They've been living in the barn, milady. Something got their mother. I was afraid they might die out there alone." A hint of unease tightened her tone as though she expected her actions to be met with disapproval.

With Aldrich, they undoubtedly would have been.

Raven offered a warm smile. "They are more than welcome in the manor."

Another startling crack of thunder punctuated her words, this one louder than the last, and a bright blue light flashed outside. Lily gasped and got to her feet, leaving the kittens in their pile. Raven followed her to the window to look out at the ravaged fields. Marek and the others should be in Amberwood by now, but he wouldn't be returning in this.

Another flash of blue lightning lit the storm-darkened sky. The wind whipped up outside. The rain was oddly lighter now, but a strange mist was rolling in to take its place as if the clouds had sunk to the ground. Thunder cracked, and she felt the electric charge as lightning flashed bright blue again, illuminating the thickening mist.

"That's no normal storm," Lily breathed.

Raven glanced at her, but the answer occurred to her before she could ask. "A storm drake."

Lily nodded. "For certain."

Excitement burst through Raven. Storm drakes were one of the rarest forms of drake. They were typically quite elusive, only creating this chaotic weather when something upset them. "Stay with the kittens. I'll be right back."

She left Lily there. After getting her boots and cloak, she walked to the front entrance and opened the door. The cracks of thunder and flashes of lightning were becoming more frequent. The mist was thick, despite the wind and a light rain still falling through it. That meant the drake must be close.

"Milady, you shouldn't be going out there." It was a man's voice, though she didn't look to see whether it was one of their recently hired guards or a servant.

"I'll be fine," she answered dismissively before heading out.

When she started to close the door behind her, he blocked it with one foot. Refusing to let him distract her, she left it open and stepped out into the storm. The wind grabbed at her cloak, pulling her hood back. Tiny raindrops, whipped about by the gale, stung her cheeks as she continued away from the house. Thunder cracked, painfully loud without the insulation of the manor walls. Lighting struck down not far from her, making her flinch, but she kept going.

The storm drake must be extremely agitated to bring on a storm this violent.

Glancing back, she could barely see the outline of

the house in the mist. She stopped and drew upon the Krivalen magic, using it to seek out the drake through the energy in the storm it had created, searching for the source. Thunder cracked repeatedly. Lighting flashed on all sides, sometimes striking the ground. Her magic ran up against the beast almost directly above her. Closing her eyes, she reached into the drake, making her presence calm and welcoming.

A shriek rang out from above. Cracks of thunder were coming seconds apart now, the flashes of lighting snapping out all around her, many hitting the ground close enough to make the hair on her neck and arms stand up. The wind swirled violently, tugging at her cloak and hair. She looked up, squinting against the tempest, and made out the outline of the drake's form descending through the mist in front of her.

Then the mist opened around her, and the massive slate-blue beast sank down, vast wings creating a buffeting wind of their own. The other wind disappeared, moving outside the area they occupied with the mist, no longer touching them. She resisted the urge to cover her ears when the drake shrieked again, crying out in challenge as it landed on its hind legs in front of her. It was easily twice the size of the wyvern she and Phendaril had fought in the Amberwood forest the day they drove the harpies from their original nesting grounds.

Lightning crackled in horizontal arcs across its wings. Its eyes were a metallic version of the slate-blue color of its scales when it inclined its head to look at her. Raven's breath caught when she gazed back into those eyes. She struggled to remember her magic and continue radiating that sense of calm.

It shrieked once more before settling forward on its front legs and lowering its head down level with her. Its wings remained partially spread, electricity still crackling over them, ready to take off in an instant. Her heart

pounded violently as she approached. One careful, calculated step at a time, she brought herself close enough
to touch her fingertips to the creature's nose. It jerked
back a fraction, a low growl rumbling deep in its chest.

She paused there for a moment. When it didn't try
to eat her, she took another few steps, moving close
enough to run a hand gently over the smooth scales on
the side of its face. She was trembling now, but not from
fear. Excitement and an overwhelming sense of wonder
made it hard to breathe.

The drake lowered its head a little more, wings
gradually folding in closer to its body. The cracks of
thunder and flashes of lightning became infrequent and
less severe. Even the wind started to die, and the mist
began dissipating.

Then she noticed it. An arrow. A lucky shot had
managed to wedge precisely up under a scale in the drake's
shoulder. Raven smiled, remembering how Synderis told
her he used his magic to tame Koshika so he could help
her with her injury.

"It's all right, my friend," she murmured, keeping
her tone low and soothing as she worked her way to the
offending projectile.

The beast's claws and incisors were the size of her
forearm. She stroked along the scales of its neck, feeling
a shiver of electricity buzzing through her with the contact. When her hands moved to the arrow, the creature
growled a warning. Was her magic sufficient to keep it
from lashing out at her if she caused it pain? Was it intelligent enough to recognize that she was helping it?

For a second, she hesitated there. Then the beast
brought its head around, nudging her hip with its nose.
She met its eyes. It closed and opened them in a slow
blink, a sound that was more like a purr rumbling in its
chest now.

Acutely aware of how big those lethal jaws were,

Raven swallowed and took hold of the arrow. It had wedged in tight. She wrapped both hands around it, got a firm grip, and took a few deep breaths, recalling how Synderis used breathing to calm her in her dream. Jaecar had implemented a similar method to help her maintain her focus when they were training. Raven yanked as hard as she could. For a second, she didn't think it would work, but then it gave and pulled free, releasing a trickle of bright blood over the slate-blue scales.

The beast roared in pain, but it didn't strike at her. Raven backed warily up until she was standing in front of it again. She placed the arrow on the ground before it like an offering and retreated several more steps. The drake sniffed at the bloodied projectile, a menacing growl rising in its throat. Lighting crackled wildly over its hide now.

Raven let out a small cry, jumping back when two strikes of lightning hit the arrow. All that remained when her vision cleared was a charred spot on the ground. She gazed at the spot considering the implications.

"So it's not all chaos," she commented softly. "You can be precise."

The beast brought its head out toward her, and she stepped forward, placing a hand on the side of its muzzle once more. The thunder and lightning stopped. The wind faded, and the mist rolled away. The drake stayed there a few seconds longer, then it drew back and reared up on its hind legs, its wings spreading wide. It inclined its head to her one last time before lunging skyward.

Raven tracked its course for several seconds as it flew up and away. Then she glanced around her. The remaining mercenaries were standing to her right, staring at her with slack-jawed wonder. Many workers and servants had gathered in front of the house or observed from the front windows. Turning to her left, she saw a lone horseman watching her.

A jolt of surprise coursed through her, and she started walking toward him. Phendaril urged his mount forward. He rode with his braced leg hanging outside the stirrup, grimacing with every step the horse took. She stopped alongside the animal, placing an absent hand on its strong shoulder.

"What did I just see?" Phendaril's there was wonder in his voice, but pain caused tightening around his eyes and mouth.

She shook her head at him. He was a stubborn elf. "You shouldn't be riding."

He smirked. "True. And if what Marek said about you being sick is true, you shouldn't be out here in the foul weather working miracles on one of the most dangerous creatures in these wilds."

A valid point.

Raven glanced up in the direction the drake had gone. The beast had vanished in the clouds, leaving nothing more than light rain and a lingering breeze in its wake. She took his reins and led his mount to the front of the house. There she had one of the stunned-looking guards help him down and directed the man to assist him to the sitting room. She tasked another with taking the horse to the stable.

With the excitement gone, fatigue swept back in. She leaned against the door frame for a long moment and gazed out into the fields where the drake had been. She could barely see the charred spot where she had lain the arrow.

When she went to join Phendaril a few minutes later, Lily was in the sitting room with him. She had thrown a blanket over the chair to help protect it from his damp and dirty clothes. Raven heard Lily's whispering voice and stopped around the corner to listen.

"You know Lady Darrenton?"

"Raven," Phendaril corrected. "Yes, I do."

"Does she do things like that often?" It wasn't necessary to say what Lily was referring to, though Phendaril apparently felt the need to clarify.

"Like administering wound care to storm drakes?" A brief pause. "No, I've never seen her do anything like that."

"Oh."

Raven stepped around the corner and walked in.

The young woman hurried out, nodding to her on the way past. "I've sent for some food, milady."

"Thank you, Lily."

In the sitting room, she noticed that Lily had already burdened Phendaril with a glass of wine and a lap full of frolicking kittens that he was entertaining with a string from the blanket.

Raven breathed a laugh. "Making friends, I see."

A faint smile curved his lips. "They are rather charismatic, in a somewhat painful way," he added, digging a tiny claw out of the bandage on his healing hand.

"What are you doing here, Phen? You're not supposed to be riding?"

"Trust me, I felt the truth of that in every stride, but I don't think I did any lasting damage." He glanced at her only to quickly turn his attention to the kittens. The little black-and-grey leapt down from his lap, spotting a new victim, and toddled over to climb up her leg. "I was... concerned about you. We didn't exactly part on the best of terms. Then there was no word at all for several days. When I ran into Marek, he told me you had been ill."

She nodded, feeling the weight of her weariness sinking back into her very bones. She snatched the kitten that was now halfway up her leg and went curled up in the other chair with the fluffy beast. "I came down with a fever after riding back that night, but it broke yesterday." So Synderis could finally dreamwalk her.

She took a sip of the wine Lily had left sitting out for her, hoping he wouldn't notice the sudden flush in her cheeks.

"The two of you got rid of Darrenton together, and now Marek is what? Your loyal guard?" He gave her a curious look, an edge of something, jealousy perhaps, in his tone.

"He's just a companion. We've found ourselves common ground in Wayland's bad graces. It seemed as good a place as any to build an alliance from."

Phendaril raised an eyebrow at her. "When we spoke earlier, he acted like your safety was his chief concern."

She focused on petting the kitten, who had worn himself out trying to kill a wrinkle in her shirt and lay curled into a purring ball of fluff on her lap.

Marek was more solicitous of her needs since the night they took over the manor. He had not pressed her further on her Acceptance of the young stable hand, but there hadn't been much opportunity for him to do so with her being sick. Now that she was feeling better, that would undoubtedly change.

The rain picked up audibly outside, and she glanced out the window. A charge of remembered excitement from her encounter with the drake shivered through her.

Phendaril followed her gaze. "I'm a little mystified by what I saw outside. If I'm not mistaken, you were petting a storm drake."

She glanced over at him, noting that the two kittens in his lap appeared to be nodding off. "Do you want something to put your leg up on?"

He gave her a long-suffering look, but he allowed the evasion. "If it wouldn't be too much trouble."

"I can get that, milady," Lily said, striding back into the room with a tray full of a selection of edible items she set on the table between them.

While Lily hurried off to get something to put his

leg on, the kittens came to life again, roused by the smell of food. They began a single-minded effort to make their way to the tray, which was more of a problem for Phendaril, who had two kittens and only one good hand.

Raven picked up the black-and-grey kitten and got up to help Phendaril with his predicament. He turned his right shoulder into the path of one kitten. Raven leaned over to grab the kitten as it accepted the challenge, trying to climb onto his shoulder. For a second, she was tempted to lean in and give Phendaril a quick kiss as she might have done before. That disconcerting resurfacing of easy affection left her confused. When she moved away again, he closed his eyes, jaw clenching, apparently party to similar thoughts.

"Oh. Milady!" Lily rushed in, setting down a small bench she'd brought. "I'm so sorry. I'll take these little monsters to another room and feed them something."

Raven handed her the two kittens she was carrying. "It's all right, Lily. They're just kittens. I'll move the footrest into place."

Lily took the third kitten, managing to hold all three in one arm as she bent over to grab their blankets. "Sorry, milady." She offered an awkward curtsy and hurried from the room.

Raven took a minute to situate the bench and put a folded blanket on it to make it more comfortable. While Phendaril lifted his leg up on the bench with a groan, she shut the doors to the sitting room, then curled back into her chair, tucking her feet under her. She listened for a few seconds to determine if anyone was eavesdropping. Satisfied that they had some privacy, she turned to look at him, raising her wine glass for the odd comfort holding something gave her.

"Remember the incident with the horses outside of Andel?"

Phendaril nodded.

"This was a little like that, though not as dramatic. In the sense of how much control I had," she added at his raised eyebrow. "I didn't take away the drake's will like I did with the horses. I merely offered it a compelling invitation. The drake had an arrow wedged under one of its scales. I was able to calm the creature and remove it. Better for all of us that way, I suppose."

"Better indeed." He cleared his throat. "Did you learn how to do that from your mother's people?"

She knew what he was really asking. He wanted to know if Synderis taught her. She decided it best to answer vaguely for the moment. "The concept, yes."

They picked at the food in silence for a time. Raven sank deeper into the chair and rested her head back. Exhaustion clawed at her. For a second, she closed her eyes, relenting to the weight that pulled her down.

aven opened her eyes. For a few seconds, she pondered the possibility that the storm drake and Phendaril's arrival might have been a dream. Maybe Marek was just now preparing to lead the mercenaries to Amberwood.

"Under normal circumstances, I would have carried you to bed myself, but I'm afraid I had to get someone else to do it."

She rolled on her side and looked at Phendaril where he sat before the bedroom fireplace. Someone had carried in the small bench so he could put his leg up, and a black-and-grey ball of fluff slept curled up on his shoulder.

She breathed a laugh, and a hint of a smile tugged at his lips.

"Lily was worried I might get lonely while you were asleep."

Raven sat up and propped a pillow behind her to lean on. "That was thoughtful of her."

"I don't know. I think she might be trying to get me to keep it, so she has one less little monster on her hands."

Raven smiled drowsily. "I'm sorry I fell asleep. I guess I'm still recovering."

His brows lifted. "Perhaps you should refrain from charming storm drakes until you're healthier."

She mirrored the expression back at him. "The man who ventured out on a long, difficult ride while recovering from several broken bones doesn't get to lecture me."

He cracked a smile, then it faded, stolen away by sorrow.

The sound of heavy rainfall drew her attention to the darkness outside the windows. "What time is it?"

"Early evening."

"Is Marek back?"

He started to shake his head, then caught himself, glancing at the sleeping kitten from the corner of his eye. "I doubt he'll be back tonight. The storm picked up again after you dozed off. Though it appears to be a natural storm this time."

"Won't Karsima and the others be worried about you?"

He shrugged, and the kitten lifted its head, its eyes opening a tiny crack as it mewled in protest. Its complaint heard, it shifted and curled up again. The soft smile he offered the little creature made her heart ache.

"They'll be worried, but they know where I am. I left a note."

"Thoughtful of you."

Silence stretched between them. Phendaril brought his leg down from the bench and lifted the kitten from his shoulder. He set the animal in his lap and dug into a pouch drawing out a small vial of something. He took a sip from it, grimacing as he swallowed, then followed it with a sip of wine, swishing it around his mouth before swallowing that as well.

He met her eyes. "One of Synal's healing tinctures. It also helps me sleep with this uncomfortable contraption." He tapped the side of the brace.

She grinned. "I think she's picking on you. The ones she gave me when I was healing didn't taste that bad."

He laughed softly. "She probably is. I haven't been a great patient."

Raven couldn't stop a fond smile. "I'm not surprised."

After putting the tincture away again, he lifted the kitten and stood. Holding the little ball of fluff in one hand, he limped over to the side of the bed and held it out to her.

"I should see if there's a room I can use for the night. I don't think I could manage the ride back tonight even if the weather was good."

Raven braced another pillow against the headboard beside her and shifted over. "Sit with me. Just for a little while." She gestured to the bed next to her in invitation, then accepted the kitten from him.

While she set the soft creature on her lap, he regarded the spot as though she had offered him a choice between two equally ponderous books to read. Breathing a sigh, he sat on the bed, swung his good leg up, and then pulled the injured one up after. She could only imagine how exhausted his muscles were from holding up the heavy brace while riding without being able to let his foot rest in the stirrup. It took him a few minutes to get comfortable with the leg. When he finally settled, he stared in uneasy silence at his injured hand where it rested in his lap.

"I didn't mean for this to happen." She knew it wasn't going to help, but she had to say it. "When I learned that I could never have children because I'm Krivalen—"

"Krivalen?"

She hesitated, but this wasn't Marek. Phendaril had no reason to want to expose the elves or their knowledge of the magic to the Brotherhood. Of course, the less he knew, the less he could be forced to tell or risk saying accidentally, but she had already spoken the word.

"That's the proper name for the Silverblood magic

and those that can use it."

He gave a thoughtful nod. "I didn't know Silver-bloods couldn't have children." His tone and expression offered no insight into how that made him feel.

"When the magic changes you, it takes that away."

"I'm sorry."

She shrugged, trying not to care. Ilanya was probably right. It was better that she couldn't have children. Mixed blood wasn't a blessing. "When I learned that, I told myself it was better if I never came back. You would be safer without me, and you would still have the opportunity for children of your own if you wanted them. We never talked about that." She drew a shaky breath. "I never expected to love Synderis. Then, when I did find myself falling for him, I expected that I would somehow fall out of love with you. It hasn't happened that way."

He nodded to himself. Then he inhaled deeply and exhaled slowly before speaking. "Does he know?"

"He does." She blinked against the sting of tears. The selfless way Synderis had responded to that made her wonder if she deserved him.

The silence dragged out. She stroked the fuzzy coat of the black-and-grey kitten, focusing on how that contact felt rather than on the desperate ache inside or the powerful urge to run from it. It hurt to be close to Phendaril but being apart had been just as painful. At the same time, she yearned for the comfort of Synderis. He had told her he wasn't here with her, but he was. He was everywhere she went, connected to her by Krivalen magic and love.

Phendaril reached over and slid his hand into hers, twining their fingers together. "I'm not sure I know how to stop loving you."

She leaned back against the headboard and gave his hand a soft squeeze. "You know, Jaecar used to tell me that once I pick my target, I should never let myself become distracted by another, or I would come away with neither. I always thought he was just talking about hunting."

Phendaril chuckled. "The way you shoot, Raven, I suspect you would come away with both."

She glanced at him, searching for the intent behind that comment. The urge to lean over and kiss him struck her hard enough that she looked quickly away. Synderis told her to reach out to him and be with him, but she couldn't reconcile that within herself. It would hurt him, wouldn't it? And yet, wasn't she hurting Phendaril now? How was she supposed to safeguard one of them and cause the other pain when her heart loved them both?

"Tell me more about Jaecar."

Raven smiled at him, hoping he could see her gratitude in the expression. "What would you like to know?"

"He trained you, didn't he?"

She nodded. "He told me once, when I was grown, that he hadn't known how to raise children, only soldiers, so he raised me that way. Most of my childhood was spent learning to hunt and fight. Not that he didn't try to make it fun. As he got used to working with a child instead of adults, he started making obstacle courses, sometimes with silly objectives, like saving an imaginary puppy from a rampaging, rabid cow."

Phendaril laughed at that. "He sounds like a good man."

"He was. He never quite got used to being a father, but he tried. When I got older, he put me in charge of most of the hunting and keeping dangerous animals away from the keep. That didn't get me off the hook from training with him most days. He never did tell me much about himself, though. I didn't even know he was from a noble family until after he died."

"And you didn't know he had adopted you?"

Raven gazed down at the sleeping kitten in her lap, swallowing against the lump in her throat. "No. I assume he meant to tell me when the time was right, but he wasn't one for talking about emotional things. I'm not sure the time would have ever been right."

Phendaril extracted his hand from hers and put his arm around her shoulders.

Raven let herself lean against him. "Tell me about your time in Chadhurst with Alayne and Karsima."

Phendaril relaxed into the bed a little more, and she sank down with him, resting back on his shoulder. He began to tell her some of his adventures from living in Chadhurst with the two women. He talked for a time about playing chaperone to Karsima once she realized she had a romantic interest in women. Imagining the strong woman blushing and giggling when she and Alayne first got together made Raven smile. She closed her eyes and listened until she drifted off to the sound of his voice.

●

"Well played, my little Raven."

Raven's pulse quickened. She spun from the fire to see Wayland standing by the window at the other side of the room, his liquid silver hair reflecting the firelight. Phendaril lay asleep in the bed. When she looked at him, his features started to transform, his hair turning to a silvery white.

With a flash of panic, she changed the setting, taking them into the field outside the manor. Her gaze drifted to the charred spot at Wayland's feet. The placement wasn't an accident. The thought of him being blasted with lightning from a storm drake might have made her smile if the implications of his presence here didn't carry such overwhelming dread.

"It took a little while, but I seem to have figured out how to tap into our connection." He grinned. "You're wishing you hadn't taken that power from me now, aren't you?"

Raven narrowed her eyes at him. "Keep this up, and I'll take a lot more."

A hint of worry tightened the corners of his eyes for an instant, then he donned his false smile, taking a step toward her. "And who will help you? Silverblood Marek?" He offered a lock of mock concern. "I'm not sure I would trust him if I were you. But it doesn't have to be this way. Come to Pellanth, and we can work everything out."

"Of course. You'll leave my friends alone if I come to Pellanth and let you kill me. I don't think you need me to tell you that isn't the most compelling offer." She dropped her hand to the sword now sheathed at her waist.

A sword appeared in his hand in response. He was getting too comfortable in the dreamscape for her liking. It dawned on her then that he was in her dream. What would happen if she woke with him there? Had he somehow figured out anchoring, or would he end up trapped here?

She smiled and drew her sword.

"I don't want to kill you, Raven. I only want to know what you learned from your mother's people. I want to know where they are." He moved slowly forward as he spoke. "We could come to an arrangement."

"No." Raven backed away, maintaining a constant distance. Whether he understood the risks he took by entering her dream or not, the confidence in his gaze was unnerving.

"I've already made my move. I reached out to the Brotherhood temples in Chadhurst and Alm. Soon, every Silverblood on the continent will be hunting for you with orders to bring you in alive and kill anyone with you, including Marek." He smirked. "No. *Especially* Marek."

His advance was so sudden she almost didn't have time to move out of the way. His blade nicked the leather armor at her ribs as she twisted to the side. Their last dream encounter proved how painful injury could be, even in the dreamscape, so she preferred not to test it again. She expected his failed lunge to leave her an opening, but he turned fast enough to block her blade, moving with uncanny speed.

They traded attacks, Raven narrowly avoiding his sword until he managed to catch behind her hilt, cutting into the side of her hand and ripping her sword free. She sucked back a scream of pain and leapt away from him, grabbing the bleeding hand. It didn't matter here. This pain and injury wouldn't follow her to the waking world, but it was hard to ignore how real it felt.

She made a lunge for her sword. Wayland cut her off, and she checked herself, twisting clear of another strike.

Wayland stepped back then, moving away from her weapon. He gestured with his sword for her to pick it up. His elated smile chilled her. "It's so rare that someone can hold their own against me. I've forgotten how refreshing it is to have a challenge."

Raven let go of her bleeding hand, fighting to convince herself the pain and gash weren't real. She snatched up the blade, gritting her teeth as the hilt pressed against the open wound.

"I'm sure we could keep this up all night, but I know you're at Darrenton's manor. There's no point in playing games now."

"Not an impressive feat of investigation, given I announced my presence rather boldly." She sneered at him, hoping to draw him into making a mistake. "What I want to know is, if you know where I am, why bother starting a hunt for me?"

"I want you to come to me, Raven. I want you to acknowledge your defeat and come to me of your own free will. To that end, I decided to send you a little gift. It should be there when you wake."

His hand came up fast, the sword becoming a crossbow. She leapt to the side, the bolt tearing through the outside of her shoulder. Agony ripped a scream from her this time, but Wayland was no longer there to hear it. He had disappeared. She grabbed the shoulder with her wounded hand, gasping as she sank to her knees.

She squeezed her eyes shut and shouted at the sky. "This isn't real!"

The rain started to fall, fat drops pounding down faster by the second. Her cry echoed through the dreamscape. Where was Synderis? Why hadn't he come into her dream?

She screamed again, an incoherent roar of pain, rage, and fear. No one was there to hear.

R aven!"

Phendaril was shaking her gently. She opened her eyes and sat up, trembling. The kitten, who lay curled up between them, squeaked a tiny meow of irritation at being disturbed.

Phendaril placed a hand along her jaw, running his thumb over her cheek in a light caress. "You were crying out in your sleep. Loud enough to drag me up from under the influence of Synal's tincture. Are you all right?"

She stared at him for a few seconds, trying to disconnect him from the image of Synderis in her head. Wayland's voice echoed through her mind.

"I decided to send you a little gift. It should be there when you wake."

She lifted the kitten and threw off the covers, sliding quickly out and setting the kitten back on the bed behind her. It trotted to the edge and stopped there, unsure about the drop to the floor.

"Raven?"

"I need to check something."

Phendaril started to climb out of bed. She grabbed her sword and dagger from where they sat near the door, then stopped and listened. She could detect no unusual sounds from the hall or nearby rooms, though the rain pounding outside wasn't helping. After a few seconds, she heard the creak and click of Phendaril's brace as he went to collect his sword from his things near the chair.

She glanced over her shoulder at him. He was still in no condition to fight, but she knew better than to try to talk him out of following. Instead, she eased the door open and peeked down the dark hallway. A few sconces were lit, though most had been snuffed for the night. She looked both ways before stepping out and starting a slow creep toward the central part of the house. Nothing was obviously amiss. Phendaril didn't emerge until she was well ahead of him, perhaps cognizant of his brace's potentially distracting noises.

Everything appeared normal until she reached the back entry. The two guards on duty lay on the floor, throats slit and drained out on the recently replaced floorboards. The door stood open a few inches, spray from the hard rain mixing with the blood that darkened the floor near the threshold. The quantity of water inside and the fact that the guards had finished bleeding out was enough to tell her their killers had been here a while. A chill swept through her.

Raven nudged the door shut. She turned and started across the entry, catching Phendaril's eyes as he stepped around the corner and gesturing with her head toward the men by the door. His jaw tightened, and the tension in his posture amplified. Injured or not, he looked ready to kill.

Raven made her way to the much grander front entry. The two guards standing inside the door caught sight of her instantly and hurried to meet her halfway across the foyer.

"What's happened, milady?" one asked in a low voice, glancing at her bared blade.

"The guards at the back door are dead. Gather some more men and do a sweep of the house. My companion and I will start searching the lower north wing."

To her surprise, the young man answered with a firm shake of his head. "Milady, you've been sick, and your companion is injured. I'll come with you. Gerrod can gather more men to help search the rest of the house."

She considered arguing with him, but he was right. Neither she nor Phendaril were in the best condition to face someone who had managed to slip in and dispatch two guards as effectively as she and Marek had not that many nights ago. If this was Wayland's doing, they were likely dealing with one or more Silverbloods.

"Your name?"

"Davon, milady."

His voice was familiar. This was the guard who had attempted to stop her when she went out to the help storm drake. She liked that he hadn't been too aggressive in his attempts to hold her back. It showed a willingness to recognize her autonomy, even if he didn't always agree with her actions.

She nodded and turned to the other man. "Gerrod, we may be dealing with Silverbloods. Group your men accordingly."

The man paled a little at that, but his nod was resolute. "Yes, milady."

Gerrod slipped off in the other direction. She started back toward the north wing with Davon beside her now. Phendaril had already gone that way. When they rounded the corner into the hallway, he was pushing the door to the servants sleeping quarters open with the tip of his blade. The mere fact that it hadn't been shut when he got there sent a chill of dread through her. Raven broke into a jog when the color drained from his face. He took a limping step forward and caught her by the shoulders, trying to block her path.

"No. Raven, you don't need to see this."

The cloying metallic stench of blood reached her. She twisted violently, managing to escape him with relative ease given his injuries, and stepped into the room.

Bodies lay on or alongside every bed. Those she could see clearly had their throats slit before being left to die in bed or dumped on the floor. She spotted Brek next to one of the closer beds, his eyes and mouth opened wide with horror. At the back of the room, Lily lay prone across the mantle, a dagger still buried in her chest. Drying blood ran down one arm that hung outstretched toward the bundle of blankets she was keeping the kittens in.

Raven dropped her sword and stepped back against the wall, sliding down it to the floor. Phendaril limped past her into the room, checking among the bodies for anyone who might still be alive.

"Milady?" Davon's voice was tight. It appeared that even mercenaries weren't hardened enough for this kind of senseless slaughter.

"The killers are likely gone," she said, struggling to speak past the hurt inside. This was because of her. Wayland was leaving a message. He hadn't done this to kill or capture her this time, but to show her that she wasn't safe and to feed her fear of endangering those she cared about. He had accomplished his goal. "Take some men and search the rest of the house. Be careful, just in case they're still here somewhere."

"Yes, milady."

Phendaril reached Lily. He brushed her eyes shut and glanced into the blanket next to the hearth. Then he closed his eyes and shook his head. He stood that way for a moment before limping back to her. He avoided looking at anything but her this time. The stench of blood was suffocating.

He offered her a hand when he reached her. "Wayland?"

She didn't want to stand. She didn't want to do anything. These people died because they were associated with her. They died because Wayland wanted to make her feel trapped and vulnerable.

"I'm not sure I can do this anymore, Phen."

His hand remained extended before her. "Don't let him win."

She looked up at him. "Hasn't he already?"

"Only if you believe he has."

She glanced toward the end of the room at the pile of blankets Lily's hand dripped blood into. "The kittens too?"

He bent over awkwardly with the brace and took hold of her hand. Raven grabbed her sword and made herself stand, sparing him the pain of trying to drag her to her feet in his condition.

He gestured toward the hallway. "You knew something had happened when you woke. Is Wayland in your dreams again?"

She nodded. It appeared it was possible to reach a point where she couldn't cry anymore. The pain was a savage beast ripping its way out from the inside, but the tears wouldn't come.

"Is there a way to stop him?"

She let him lead her into the hallway. "I don't know. It's still night. I could try to ask Synderis."

"Do you need the cloak pin?"

"No. We have..." She glanced at him, a twinge of guilt piling on top of the monumental ache of sorrow.

"You don't need to explain. How can I help?"

She led him back toward the bedroom. "Can I anchor to you? It will make it easier for you to wake me if something goes wrong."

"Is that likely?"

"With Wayland coming around, I'd rather not take chances."

The kitten was still on the bed crying when they reached the room. She lifted it and hugged it to her chest, the soft little creature whose siblings were now gone. A shattering sensation inside her made the tears run down her cheeks.

Phendaril put an arm around her shoulders and drew her into his embrace, careful of the purring kitten in her arms. She didn't allow herself the indulgence of his support for long. She had things to do before dawn.

Extracting herself, she handed him the kitten and stepped toward the bed, pausing at a knock on the door.

She turned. "Come in."

Davon entered, offering a slight bow. "Lady Darrenton, the house is clear. I've got men searching the grounds as well. How would you like us to handle the bodies?"

"We'll bury them in the morning. Thank you, Davon."

A hint of a weary smile touched his lips when she said his name, then he bowed again and left the room. Raven straightened the covers before lying on top of them. Phendaril sat on the bed next to her, stroking the purring black-and-grey fluff in his lap. Raven couldn't look at the kitten. Somehow, at that moment, he became the physical embodiment of all the lives lost that night.

She closed her eyes and anchored her magic to Phendaril. Even though he wasn't Krivalen, it was almost as easy as anchoring to Synderis. That didn't serve to ease her heart any. Searching for the connection to Synderis, she took hold of it and used her magic to take herself into sleep and dreaming.

•

Synderis was working through sword forms along the elevated walkway near his little hut in the trees. The slight bounce and sway of the walkway didn't appear to detract any from the grace and precision of his movements. His forms differed from those she had learned growing up under Jaecar's tutelage. Synderis also wasn't wearing a shirt, so his muscles gleamed with a sheen of sweat. It was a picture she might have appreciated more under other circumstances.

He stopped and turned suddenly. Then he was in front of her, his sword gone and a loosely laced shirt over his torso. "What's happened?"

"Sometimes I wish you weren't so perceptive, my love." She offered a shaky smile.

"Your very presence feels as haunted as you look." He spoke softly, cupping her cheek in his hand. "I couldn't reach you when I tried to dreamwalk you earlier."

Raven told him what had happened in the dream with Wayland and what she had found when she had woken. When she finished, he pulled her into his arms. She sagged against him, willing, for a few seconds, to let him support her.

"You're not safe there." He let go of her, stepping back to meet her eyes. "Marek and Phendaril are with you?"

"Marek's in Amberwood. Phendaril..." She hesitated, not wanting to hurt him.

Synderis raised his brows at her in question. "I told you to reach out to him, did I not? Besides, I can feel your anchor to him. I recognize his presence."

"You remember what his presence feels like from one dreamwalk encounter?"

He cleared his throat, glancing away for a second. "It was a poignant experience for me. I hadn't realized, until that moment, that you already loved someone else."

Raven took his hand. "I'm sorry, Syn."

"I'm fine," he answered dismissively. "What can I do? You sought me out for more than just comfort."

"I need to know if there is some way to block Wayland

out of my dreams. There's too much he can learn from them."

Sorrow stole across his features. "There is, and I think we should do it, given the situation."

"But?"

"As you figured out before, we can't eliminate the magic connection you have to him. We could break the emotional one, but the other is part of you now. The only way to block him now that he knows how to use that would be by using a talisman to shield your dreams. Unfortunately, that will block everyone else out as well."

Her hand tightened convulsively on his. To be cut off from him completely? That was the last thing she wanted, yet what choice did she have? If she let Wayland torment her dreams and learn from them, gleaning information about her locations and the people she cared for, the situation could get much worse for all of them.

"If you need me, you can still dreamwalk me, but you'll have to take off the talisman to do it, leaving you vulnerable to him."

"No. I can't risk you or Eyl'Thelandra."

Dark anger sparked to life in his eyes. "To the wolves with Eyl'Thelandra. You are my anweyn. I am here for you if you need me."

Raven held his gaze for a few seconds, acknowledging how deeply he meant those words. Something more lurked behind the anger in his voice when he spoke of his home. Now wasn't the time to dig into that, however.

She nodded. "Show me how to make the talisman. Will I need to remember a chant?" She asked, recalling the strange words her mother had spoken the day she made Raven Krivalen.

"No. You only need words the first time to bind the magic to yourself or someone else. Once it's part of you, intent is enough to make it work."

She startled when they snapped from their place on

the walkway to the front room inside Dellaura's house.

"Sorry. I'm usually gentler with my transitions when someone else is in the dreamscape. I'm worried about you, Raven. I'm sick of not being able to help you." He brushed his fingers along her cheek.

Frustration was apparent in his tight voice and the abruptness of his actions in the dreamscape. She was doing this to him.

"You're helping me now." Raven bounced up on the balls of her feet and kissed him.

For a second, he resisted, then she slid her hands around his waist, feeling the lean muscle as she shifted closer to him. He responded, moving his arms around her to pull her against him, and deepened the kiss. When the urge to take it farther was almost too much to resist, she made herself pull away.

"Do you know that I love you?" she asked, holding his gaze.

He gave her one more light kiss. "I do." He retreated another step then. "I'd best show you how to do this before someone wakes one of us."

Raven nodded and reluctantly let go of him.

*

When she eventually woke, Phendaril was still sitting next to her, alert for any sign that she was in trouble. A hint of distress tightened his expression, but he didn't put words to it. She suspected it had something to do with watching over her while knowing she was with Synderis.

"Did you get what you needed?"

Raven nodded and sat up. "I need something I can wear to use as a talisman to block Wayland from my dreams."

Phendaril reached out, slipping his fingers under the edge of her collar. He drew them back, letting the string around her neck slide through his fingers until the arrowhead pendant he had made her from the remains of her father's bow rested in his hand.

"Would this do? I've never seen you take it off."

She met his eyes. "I don't." She took the arrowhead from him.

How ironic to use the pendant Phendaril had given her to block not only Wayland but also Synderis from her dreams.

"That will do quite well."

The storm broke sometime before dawn. By mid-morning, a band of mercenaries was engaged in the messy work of burying the dead. Raven put another smaller group in charge of hauling siege equipment out of the barn and setting fire to it so that a large bonfire now blazed in one of the empty fields. Neither she nor Phendaril was in good enough shape to help with the work. Instead, they spent the morning in the kitchen preparing a meal for those who toiled outside, burying the serving staff who typically would have done the cooking.

A few guards protested the idea of Raven engaging in such menial labor. Davon, in particular, made something of a fuss about it. Her attempts to deny noble standing or any need for privileged treatment were met with disappointment. She eventually diverted him by assigning him the task of selecting new guards to replace the two who had died in the night. Once he departed on that mission, she busied herself with the process of cooking. It wasn't her strongest skill, but she had learned enough over the years she spent sharing the burden of keeping herself and Jaecar fed.

The kitten helped as well, if it could be called helping. He climbed everything he could get his claws into, including their legs, to try to reach the food above.

After numerous failed attempts to keep him on the floor, he wound up perched on Phendaril's shoulder, making a vocal fuss between the nibbles Phendaril gave him. Observing their interactions lifted her spirits some.

She was watching Phendaril pass the little beast a morsel of cheese when Davon entered the kitchen and offered her a bow.

"I've found a couple of new guards, milady, if you wish to approve them."

His gaze took in the room, a hint of confusion in his slight frown making it apparent that he had grown up around a specific type of nobility. One that wouldn't dirty its hands on menial tasks. The fact that he didn't make another attempt to discourage her behavior this time, however, told her he could adapt.

Raven considered him for a few seconds, wiping her hands on the apron she had donned. "I trust your judgment. I would like to make you captain of my guards, Davon, if you would accept that post."

Her words caught Phendaril's attention. He stopped cutting a slab of meat and turned to watch them, one hand rising absently up to scratch his fuzzy passenger. The kitten pushed his back into Phendaril's fingers, tiny claws snagging the shirt as he kneaded happily.

Davon bowed more deeply this time, a lock of dark brown hair falling in front of his hazel eyes. "I would be honored, milady," he said, brushing the hair back as he straightened.

"I'm pleased to hear it, Captain Davon. Would you be so kind as to find a few men to carry a some tables out front so those digging the graves can sit to eat?"

Davon inclined his head. "Of course, milady."

After Davon had departed, she turned to find Phendaril watching her with acute interest. It was hard to take his thoughtful gaze seriously with the puff of black-and-grey fuzz still enthusiastically kneading his shoulder.

She found a tired smile tugging at the corners of her mouth. "You have something to say?"

He took a few limping steps toward her. "Well, mi-lady," he said with a hint of teasing in his tone, "we—the bottomless pit of hunger—and I," he clarified, gesturing to the kitten, "were thinking you should come back to Amberwood with us for a time while you finish recovering. With all the scouts, fighters, and your mercenaries hanging about, it would be considerably safer there."

Raven breathed a soft laugh. "The two of you were thinking that, were you?" She reached up to fiddle with the arrowhead pendant. Synderis would probably agree with Phendaril on this, though she couldn't ask him as long as she wore the pendant.

"It was mostly his idea." He held a nibble of meat up to the kitten, who grabbed his hand with both front paws and dug in his claws as he devoured the morsel.

"Honestly, Phen, the poor little smudge will explode if you feed him much more."

The door to the kitchen opened. Whatever Phendaril started to say in response to her comment died on his lips, along with his smile. Even before she turned, she knew who she would find there, primarily because of the hatred that cast a shadow over Phendaril's features. Raven watched Marek as he crossed the room to her, not acknowledging Phendaril with so much as a glance.

He stopped a few feet back and looked her over. "Your new captain told me what happened. Are you all right?"

"I'm not injured." That was all she wanted to say on the subject. She couldn't let herself think too much about the events of that night because she didn't feel anything close to all right about it.

"I knew I shouldn't have left."

Raven considered arguing with him—he might be

dead now, had he stayed—but it would serve no purpose. Those choices were in the past, which wasn't their concern now. "Marek, Wayland came into my dream last night. He's reached out to the other Brotherhood temples to set the Silverbloods hunting us."

Marek shrugged. "I'm a little surprised it took him this long."

She drew a breath and let it out. "It's worse than you think. He wants them to take me alive, but you..."

Marek met her eyes. After a moment, he nodded, his expression unreadable. "I suppose that shouldn't surprise me." He clenched his jaw and glanced briefly in Phendaril's direction. "I think we should go to Amberwood. We can take the remaining mercenaries and guards with us and send the construction crew back to their homes. You can take a little time to recover the rest of your strength while we figure out our next move."

At least part of that plan sounded somewhat familiar. She glanced at Phendaril.

He was scratching the kitten's head. He met her eyes for a second, avoiding looking at Marek. "As much as I hate to admit it, Marek and I agree on this rare occasion."

Raven gave him a wry smile. "I'll note it in my journal."

She wandered to one of the windows to gaze at the bonfire where the siege weapons were burning. There was little reason to want to remain here now. The manor practically floated on a foundation of blood. Wayland made it apparent that it wasn't a safe place to stay, though she supposed she and Marek had taken the first step toward that end. Amberwood, as both of them pointed out, with all the scouts, warriors, and mercenaries there, would provide a great deal more protection while they figured out how to proceed. She didn't feel up to the ride, but Marek and Phendaril were right. It was time to leave Darrenton's manor.

She turned to Marek. "When the bodies are buried, and the fire burned down, we can head out."

Marek shook his head. "No. I think you and Phendaril should take the guards and head down now. I can follow with the rest of the mercenaries when the work is done."

Raven was ready to argue, but she caught Phendaril's supporting nod out of the corner of her eye. Fighting with them both sounded like too much effort in her current state. "Fine. Let Captain Davon know we'll head out in an hour. That will allow him and the other guards time to eat before we ride." It would also provide her and Phendaril a chance to rest and eat. Neither of them were in prime condition for being on their feet this long, especially given the poor night's sleep.

Marek nodded and started to turn away, then he paused, his gaze boring into her as though he meant to dig out some secret. "The men also told me you tamed a storm drake."

Oh, that. "I didn't tame it. You can't tame such a creature. I only aided it. It was nothing."

Phendaril cleared his throat, and she gave him a warning glance. Far too many people witnessed that encounter for her to try hiding it. Still, she didn't want anyone, Marek especially, digging too deeply into it.

"The men are in awe of you now. Be careful how you wield that influence." He turned and strode from the room.

Raven stared after him, extremely uncomfortable with the idea that she might have sway over the mercenaries beyond the mere coin offered for services. How did one avoid abusing such a thing? Would she know if she did?

Phendaril lifted the kitten up in front of him, the motion breaking her out of her thoughts. "Hear that, Smudge? You're moving to Amberwood."

"You can't call him Smudge."

Phendaril grinned at her. "You called him Smudge."

"I called him a poor little smudge."

"Exactly."

Raven shook her head, though the sight of the moody elven scout smiling at the squiggling kitten before him did ease her heart a little.

They relaxed in one of the sitting rooms to eat. It was all Raven could do not to fall asleep after, but the day was far from done. They had a hard ride ahead of them. Smudge slept soundly in Phendaril's lap. She envied him both the sleep and the warm body he got to curl up against. When the hour was nearly up, Raven went to her borrowed bedroom to put on her armor and gather the few items she had into her pack. She returned to the sitting room and sat back down moments before Davon and Marek came in.

Raven stood, noticing that it took Phendaril a little longer to get to his feet now than it had that morning. Their exertions were taking a toll on him too. He needed a peaceful night's rest as much as she did. Perhaps more. Returning to Amberwood would help him get that.

Davon offered her a bow. At some point, she hoped to discourage that behavior. It wasn't worth the effort now, especially given the impression her encounter with the drake must have made on the young guard. Marek started to lean forward as if also intending to bow, then caught himself. She would have to put a stop to that before it became a habit.

"Captain Davon said there is a small craft Darrenton kept down at the dock. He and some other guards could escort you two downriver to Amberwood and spare you the strain of riding."

"What about Cyrleth?"

Marek smiled. It was a shockingly open and affectionate

expression. "Your horse will be there by nightfall. I'll see to it myself. I promise. For now, I'll leave you in Captain Davon's capable hands." He chuckled as he walked away.

Phendaril was staring at her. "Did I just see you get anxious about being parted from a horse?"

Her cheeks grew warm. "He's a good horse."

"A horse you named Regret in Elven?"

She shifted her feet and glanced at Davon, who watched them curiously, before turning to Phendaril. "Perhaps we should go?"

"Where did you get this horse?"

Her brief hope that Davon would support her comment vanished when he gazed on in curious silence. She wasn't going to avoid answering Phendaril that easily it appeared. She let out a huff. "I stole him off a Lathwood guard with a little help from Marek."

A sound came from Davon that fell somewhere between a laugh and a choke, though his expression turned carefully neutral when she arched a brow at him.

Phendaril inclined his head to her. "Well done. As I recall, they owed us at least one horse."

She met his eyes, the pain of that incident sweeping back through her. The moment Dusk went down, forcing them apart. So much changed for both of them after that poor gelding was shot out from under them. How might things have been different if that hadn't happened? She supposed there wasn't anything to be gained from dwelling on it now.

She looked to Davon. "We're ready when you are?"

The young guard offered her his arm. "Milady."

Phendaril breathed a soft laugh.

Raven sighed and slipped her arm through his. She would clarify with Davon what she expected of him, which wasn't that much, really. Right now, however, she was weary enough that she was quietly grateful for the support he offered.

It was a long way across the fields to the river. Davon and another guard helped them both up into the back of a cart they had brought out for the purpose. The mercenary-turned-guardsman rode attentively along-side, taking his duties to heart. She was beginning to appreciate him. He had been an excellent, if purely cir-cumstantial, choice for captain.

"What happened with you and Marek?"

She glanced at Phendaril where he sat next to her, close enough that their arms touched. "What do you mean?"

"You say he's merely a companion, but there is more to it than that, at least for him. I see respect and affec-tion in his regard. How did he go from the man who betrayed you to Wayland to this?"

Raven caught a narrowing of eyes from Davon at the mention of Marek's betrayal. Maybe that wasn't a bad thing. Having Davon attentive to Marek's behav-ior meant he could act as an extra level of protection should the Silverblood decide to switch loyalties again to save his own hide. Given their history, she couldn't completely dismiss the possibility.

"Marek's only a companion," she asserted again.

"I think he would argue that."

Raven shifted her position, trying to ignore how uncomfortable that observation made her. Her relationship with Marek was complicated. More so all the time. "I told you, we found ourselves on the same side of Wayland's hatred. And... it was nice not to be alone after leaving my mother's family."

She kept the reference to her time in Eyl'Thelandra intentionally vague. Synderis might be willing to throw the hidden village to the wolves in a moment of passion, but she didn't expect that sentiment to last. She refused to be the one to expose them after generations of peace and safety there.

Phendaril said nothing. Instead, he reached out and took her hand, cradling a sleeping Smudge, worn out after a long morning of cooking, in the crook of his other arm.

ynderis stood staring at Koshika in the dark. The big cat sat and glared back at him, her flattened ears making it clear that she had run out of patience with his games. They weren't games from his perspective but admittedly feeble efforts to drive her off. His heart wasn't in it. Earlier, he attempted to remove their magic link. The one he had initially created between them so she would seek him out when the claw that grew into her foot needed trimming again. The link had changed without his noticing it. The big cat's increasing trust and devotion had mutated the magically forced connection into an authentic bond, one he couldn't eliminate without first destroying her trust.

He sank to a crouch, and her ears swiveled forward. She trotted over to him, pressing her head into his offered hand. He scratched behind her ears, the emerald feathers soft under his fingertips.

"You can't come where I'm going, my friend."

The cat shoved her head into his chest, knocking him back hard enough that he had to catch himself with one hand behind him. He wasn't going to admit it out loud but leaving Koshika had become connected to the idea of losing Raven in his mind. He had given Raven permission to be with Phendaril, knowing it would help her. Now the fear that she would decide that the other elf was the one she really wanted plagued him. If she and Phendaril had grown up in Eyl'Thelandra, where having more than one committed love wasn't such a strange concept, he might not worry. He longed to have more faith in her, but the way she left without warning had fractured the fledgling trust between them.

Telandora, a little too perceptive to his moods, placed a hand on his shoulder. "Maybe she'll turn back after we get out of the forest."

"Regardless, we should get moving," Lindyl commented, gazing over his shoulder the way they had come.

Like Synderis and Telandora, the other male had two braids worked into his long blond hair along each side of his head. The lower braids hung behind their ears while the two upper ones were pulled and bound together in the back, helping to hold the rest away from their faces. It was a traditional warrior style among the scouts, one they rarely adopted in earnest since they stayed hidden away from danger in Eyl'Thelandra.

He scratched Koshika behind the ears once more and stood, adjusting his pack on his shoulders. When he had arrived at the rendezvous point earlier, a mix of dread and relief filled him at finding the other two already there. They had agreed to meet shortly after nightfall, making their way separately past the inner scout posts. Being Krivalen scouts themselves, they knew the posts and the elves on duty well enough to avoid notice.

He loved Raven. Asking anyone else to do this for her felt wrong. But that wasn't the only reason Telandora and Lindyl were coming. They were done with hiding and letting the Silverbloods hold power. In that way, he couldn't help a sense of dread that he was providing the catalyst for something that could quickly get out of control. Still, even he had started humoring thoughts that it might be time for things to change. He just wasn't sure if those inclinations came from a place or reason or emotion.

They had kept up an easy jog through much of the night, making quick time on the trek to the outer posts. Once again, their knowledge of how the post patrols worked and who was on duty helped them sneak past unnoticed. Now, they were technically outside the boundaries of their forest, standing in the cover of trees near the old monument.

He was glad he would not be making this journey alone, but he didn't like knowing they were heading into danger with him, no matter their reasons for coming. It was a confusing spot to be in. They had made their choices, even before he had, so he would respect their right to do so. Now, if only he could explain the situation to Koshika.

"I've never been much farther than this." Lindyl was gazing out into the dark, his silver eyes gleaming in the occasional spears of moonlight that broke through the clouds.

"None of us have," Telandora answered.

Lindyl met her gaze. "Are we doing the right thing?"

Synderis watched Lindyl and Telandora, waiting until they looked his way. "I can only answer that for myself. I will not blame either of you if you wish to turn back."

Lindyl grinned. "See that, Tel. He's trying to get rid of us already."

Telandora smirked and clapped Synderis on the shoulder. "You had better reconcile yourself to our company quickly, yilesk," she said, using the Acridan term for brother. "We're with you at least until you find your wayward Raven."

Synderis smiled at them and nodded, finding it a little easier to breathe. The relief was definitely stronger than the dread. "We had best get moving, then. We'll want to put as much distance as possible between us and the forest before sunrise."

He absently touched Koshika's shoulder before moving. It was a habit now and not one that would help discourage her from coming with them. For now, they meant to avoid populated areas and travel as much as possible at night. They would head north the way Raven and Marek had gone. It was the fastest way to get to where Raven was. There would also be less risk of being seen that way. It made sense not to let anyone know a trio of elven Krivalen was roaming the countryside. Raven's experiences were enough to make that obvious.

They crossed the road that headed east to Branwill and dove back into the woods beyond. From there, they made their way north, angling east toward where a branch of the road also trended northward. They hadn't gone much past that point when a shimmering figure appeared in the trees ahead of them. All three had their bows in hand with arrows knocked before the image had fully formed.

The figure wore silvery elven robes, and her liquid silver hair made his breath catch in his throat. He lowered his bow and held a hand out, gesturing for the others to do the same. They put their weapons away as they approached the Delegate. Her form was flickering and inconstant, like that of an uninvited dreamwalker. Still, it wasn't so unclear that they couldn't easily see the displeasure in her narrowed eyes and the thin line of her lips.

"How?" Synderis asked when they stopped before her.

Her icy gaze homed in on him. "You will never know the answer to that if you continue down this path."

"A waking dreamwalk," Telandora breathed. "I came across mention of it in an Acridan text once. One of the more difficult uses of Krivalen magic."

The look the Delegate turned on her was not kind. "You are at the heart of this, Telandora. You've always been restless and impulsive."

Koshika growled, reflecting Synderis's flash of irritation. "Tel is not the reason I chose this path. She merely shares my views. We have done more harm than good by living in hiding, and, this time, it isn't just some stranger the Brotherhood is hunting as an illegal Silverblood. It's someone we know and care for. The Brotherhood will make an example of Raven and then go back to murdering people to make more of their Silverblood mercenaries. How many lives is enough?"

Would he have had the courage to speak to her that way without Telandora and Lindyl standing next to him, nodding their agreement? Or was it the fact that she wasn't here in the flesh that made him bold? Of course, he had stood up to her that day outside his hut. Maybe his experiences with Raven really had changed him.

The Delegate stepped closer to him and placed a hand on his cheek. It was unnerving that he could feel the cold of her touch despite her not being there in the flesh. A silvery tear tracked down her cheek.

"Synderis. My best dreamwalker." She smiled fondly. Another shimmering tear broke free. "Your loyalty to our people was unquestioning not so long ago. Think about what you are doing? Raven broke your heart and continues to do so again at the end of every dreamwalk. With such raw pain always fresh within you, how can you be expected to make reasonable choices? You must ask yourself if this female who left you without any warning is truly worth risking the safety of all of Eyl'Thelandra. Hundreds of elven lives hang upon your choices now. Do not let the pain in your heart and the hot blood of your companions decide your path. You are better than that."

Her words chipped at his resolve. She was right. Raven

had hurt him, and that hurt cut through him anew every time he saw her. He wouldn't be seeing her again now unless she chose to remove the talisman he assumed she would have made after their last dreamwalk. Perhaps he was being hasty. Should he take more time away from her to consider his path with a clearer head?

Koshika pressed against his leg. He let his fingertips sink into the feathery coat over her shoulders. Telandora and Lindyl were silent. They respected him too much to try to influence him one way or another at this moment. The choice was his to make. That didn't necessarily mean they would turn back with him if he chose to do so, but they would not force their decision upon him.

And he would choose the same way again and again. Not because he loved Raven, at least not only because of that, but because no one should have to suffer the persecution of the Brotherhood. Their power was built on lies, and the people in the best position to prove that were doing nothing.

He stepped back from the Delegate's phantom touch. "We have a responsibility to every soul that has died at the hands of the Brotherhood. We let the Silverbloods become what they are now. If we let it continue, we might as well kill their victims with our own hands. I think I can safely say that all three of us will do everything in our power to keep Eyl'Thelandra from being discovered, but it's time someone tried to fix this."

The Delegate took a step back from him. "You are resolved in your path. And perhaps you are right. I hope you don't come to regret your choice, Synderis. For your sake as well as ours."

The Delegate disappeared.

He turned to the other two. When he opened his mouth to speak, Telandora glowered at him.

"Don't, Syn." An edge of warning sharpened her tone. "You already presented us the option to turn back.

Do not question our resolve again. We heard her words. Nothing has changed. All we ask from you now is your trust."

Synderis met Lindyl's eyes, and the other elf's sober regard was enough of an answer.

He faced forward. "Let's see how far we can get before dawn."

They resumed their fast, easy jog. Rest could wait until they were further from Eyl'Thelandra.

A few hours after dawn, they stopped for a break. Telandora took the first watch, declaring that she was far too on edge yet to sleep. Even Koshika seized the opportunity to rest, stretching out with her back against Synderis to take advantage of his warmth. The arrangement worked well for both of them. Later, while Telandora slept and Lindyl kept watch, Synderis and Koshika went hunting; he for edible plants and berries to supplement their supplies, while Koshika sought out more lively game.

The forest was dryer here than around Eyl'Thelandra. The green of the foliage was not as vibrant, but there was still great beauty to the woods. The late season had turned the color of many leaves and stolen them from the trees, leaving those branches bare among the more constant evergreens. The dry fallen leaves crackled under foot, making it hard to move with as much caution as he would like, not knowing what life they might encounter in this region.

Koshika had split off to hunt on her own, finding that his scrounging for roots and berries did little to quell her appetite. She hadn't been gone long when a child's shout cut through the gentle birdsong.

"No!"

It came from close by, and whoever made it sounded panicked. Synderis sprinted in that direction.

"Please! Don't eat him!"

This was another voice, this one also young but

more girlish than the first. He broke through the trees next to a low cliff and immediately spotted Koshika. The lalyx had cornered a goat in an alcove at the base of the cliff. Two human children, around the same age as his brother's girls, stood shouting at the big cat from the other side. Koshika wasn't paying them much attention beyond the brief swivel of one ear. The emerald feathering of her coat appeared to have dimmed down to a shade closer to the duller green of the bushes here. She moved in a low stalk, almost ready to pounce on her prey.

When Synderis came out into the open, the children stopped shouting and stared at him. The girl threw an arm out in front of the boy as if she meant to protect him from the well-armed elf.

"Koshika." Knowing it would take more than his voice to break through her bloodlust, he reached along their bond to discourage the cat. "Let it go."

She resisted for a few seconds, then shook herself and glanced around at him, growling softly to tell him how she felt about his interruption. With a single huff in the direction of the terrified goat, she turned away, coming to stand beside him.

Synderis placed a hand on her shoulders. "Thank you."

The children were still staring, though the young girl, who appeared to be the older of the two, took a few steps toward the trembling goat. She eyed Koshika nervously.

"Thank you, sir. We can't afford to lose our last goat."

"You're welcome." He watched quietly as she hurried over to tie a rope around the animal's neck.

Emboldened by her approach, the boy walked closer, his wide-eyed gaze jumping from Koshika up to Synderis. "Never seen a cat like that one before. Nor an elf with eyes like yours."

Synderis grinned. "And I've never seen a child with such round ears."

They laughed as if they thought he was teasing, which he was, though he truly had never seen a human child in the flesh before.

"What're you doing out here?" the girl asked, leading the goat in a wide arc to where the boy was standing, staying as far from the lalyx as possible.

"I'm merely passing through. I was searching for some edible plants." He crouched beside Koshika, bringing himself more to eye level with the children. "You don't know where I could find any good roots or berries in the area, do you?"

"'Course we do," the boy answered, standing a bit taller now that he had knowledge to offer. "There's an abandoned farm a little farther on. The plants there have grown wild, but you can still find all sorts of food there."

The girl eyed Koshika, a faint smirk touching her lips. "Sometimes it's hard to find stuff the rabbits haven't chewed on, though."

Synderis raised his eyebrows. "There are rabbits there?"

The girl grinned. "Lots of yummy rabbits," she said, speaking more to the cat than him now.

Synderis chuckled.

The boy gave him an unexpectedly shrewd look then. "If we show you where, that's a fair trade for saving our goat, right? We wouldn't owe you a debt anymore. 'Cuz Pa says it's better to pay your debt to fey things right away, afore they can come up with some price you can't afford to pay."

The girl elbowed him. "You're not supposed to tell them what you're doing," she hissed.

Synderis stood, doing his best not to laugh. He gave

the boy a sober nod. "I would consider the debt paid."

"Come on, then." The girl gestured for him to follow.

They started walking away, dragging the reluctant goat after them. Synderis followed at a distance with Koshika, keeping the "fey things" where the children would not feel threatened by them.

As they had claimed, the remains of an old farmhouse stood a little further in. The forest was in the process of reclaiming the gardens and fields. Within seconds of emerging, Koshika was off, sprinting after a rabbit they startled with their arrival. In an instant, the hunt was over, and she trotted back to him with her kill dangling from her jaws.

"Well done." He scratched between her ears before following the children to the overgrown remains of a vegetable garden.

Koshika settled to eating her kill a short distance away, keeping an eye on them as she did so. The girl tied their goat to a tree, and the two joined him in digging up edible roots and gathering nuts from the nearby orchard. The two laughed and played as they worked, seeming to forget the scary fey. When they finished, he had a fat bundle of foodstuffs to take back to camp. The girl had her own bunch wrapped up in part of her skirt.

"We're good now?" the boy asked.

Sensing the adventure was over, Koshika came to stand by Synderis, still licking at the blood around her mouth.

"We are," he answered, inclining his head to the children.

The two sprinted away like they were narrowly escaping death, dragging the bleating goat behind them. Knowing their parents might not find the story of their interactions with strange elves amusing, Synderis turned back toward the camp and broke into an easy jog, Koshika loping along beside him.

"Fey things." He chuckled under his breath, glancing over at the big cat.

Koshika's coat, still muted to blend with the less vibrant forest, rippled with each stride. A lalyx cat and a Krivalen elf. Perhaps, to the people out here, they were fey things. As strange to them as children with round ears were to him.

CHAPTER ELEVEN

Karsima stood in the shadow of one of the buildings, watching Raven select a bow with a light draw weight for Phendaril to try out. His hand wasn't healed enough for the heavy draw on his usual bow. Still, Synal reluctantly approved his request to start practicing archery again as long as he used a lighter bow with a lesser draw weight.

Occasional patches of clear sky brightened the practice field alongside the armory. Their shadows danced as the clouds marched overhead before a stiff breeze.

Raven handed him the bow she had chosen. "This should be light enough. Smudge could probably pull this one if he had thumbs."

Phendaril accepted the weapon, his lip lifting in a slightly disgusted sneer. Raven grinned in response, picking up her bow to step into shooting position beside him. There might still be hope for the two of them, though a hint of distance and reservation marked their interactions now that hadn't been there before. Given time, they could work past that, assuming they wanted to.

The kitten they brought back from the manor with them, Smudge, was clumsily attacking a twig that had gotten caught up in his tail.

"Are you just going to stand here and spy on them?" Alayne slid her arms around Karsima's waist, letting her chin rest on Karsima's shoulder.

"Yes," she answered without shame.

When the two let their arrows fly, releasing at the exact same moment, the kitten startled, leaping straight up with his fuzzy coat puffed out around him. Both Raven and Phendaril laughed. Karsima and Alayne did as well, though more quietly, Alayne respecting that Karsima was not yet ready to have their presence noted. Phendaril bent over and held a hand out to Smudge, who came sprinting up to him, the moment of panic instantly forgotten. He picked the creature up and set it on his shoulder.

"How did that feel?" Raven asked. When she turned to face him, her gaze flickered past to where Alayne and Karsima stood, taking quick note of them before returning her attention to him.

"Painful." He scowled at the injured appendage. "I'm afraid it isn't going to be pleasant getting my strength back in this hand."

Raven's smile was warm and sympathetic, her tone unyielding but kind. "Nor in that leg, but it will happen. Just be patient with yourself."

Karsima shifted to glance at Alayne. "Does she seem more... mature to you?"

Alayne let go and moved over to stand beside her. "She's had to learn a lot in a short time. That was bound to have an effect."

A chill swept through Karsima. The two had come down in a boat yesterday afternoon along with four guards. Synal checked Phendaril's injuries and looked Raven over as a precaution after her illness. While she did so, they shared the story of Wayland's reappearance in Raven's dream and how he had his Silverbloods murder all the servants at the manor. The haunted look in Raven's eyes when she mentioned the servants told Karsima how effective Wayland's strategy had been. Wayland also informed Raven that he had all the

Silverbloods hunting her and Marek. A tactic almost certainly intended to keep her from disappearing again.

They had talked for a while, mostly learning about the events that led to Raven and Marek arriving at the manor. Raven was incredibly vague about her time before joining up with Marek. Eventually, Synal badgered her two patients into taking healing tinctures. The two wandered off to different rooms in the house. They slept through until morning while Karsima and Alayne happily took charge of the kitten.

Marek had arrived an hour or so after dark with another contingent of mercenary soldiers. It took nearly an hour to get them settled outside town, where temporary structures had been constructed to give the first group of mercenaries someplace to get out of the weather. They would figure out longer-term arrangements for those who wanted to stick around over the next few days. Several from the first set had already started working on houses in the lower district, expressing an interest in possibly making a home in Amberwood.

"Come on." Alayne nudged her in the ribs before striding toward the two archers. "I'm hungry. Let's move this along."

Karsima followed, watching as Raven and Phendaril released another set of arrows, again at almost exactly the same time. The synchronicity continued as they nocked the next two arrows. It was that natural rapport they'd had since before their relationship began to develop into something more intimate that made Karsima believe they were right for one another. What about Raven's entanglement with the other elf had eclipsed this?

The two let a third set of arrows fly, then turned together, attentive to the sounds of the women's approach. Raven reached for Phendaril's bow the exact moment he lifted it to pass it to her. Neither of them appeared aware of that effortless synergy. Phendaril rubbed at the palm of his injured hand, grimacing as he did so.

Raven nodded to each of them, a hint of reservation in her regard. She still saw them as Phendaril's friends, which wasn't an inaccurate assessment, though she continued to miss the fact that they cared about her too now.

"I see you're getting him back in shape," Alayne remarked, giving Raven a wink.

The barest of smiles curved her lips in response, although the sorrow that had found a home deep in her eyes remained. Karsima could only imagine what effect those servants being murdered while she slept in another room must have had on her. She still looked weary too, though the sound night's sleep under the influence of Synal's tincture had helped.

"We were hoping the two of you would join us for some refreshment." Karsima cracked a grin when Smudge nipped at Phendaril's ear.

He snatched the little creature off his shoulder and set it at his feet. His attention flickered over to Raven, soliciting her thoughts with a glance.

She met his eyes for an instant before narrowing hers at them. "There's something you wish to discuss."

Alayne shifted her weight, an uncommon show of impatience or unease, and nodded. "We had a few ideas for addressing your current predicament."

Raven opened her mouth to speak, hesitating when something behind them caught her attention. The tension that had appeared in her jaw and around her eyes when they approached relaxed a fraction. Karsima didn't have to turn to know who she was looking at. Marek and two of the guards who had accompanied her and Phendaril down the river stood talking across the street from the armory.

"In that case"—Raven met Karsima's eyes as she spoke—"I would ask that we include Marek in the conversation."

She caught Phendaril's deep scowl before he looked away. Karsima wanted to argue against the idea, but Raven was right. No matter how little love they had for the Silverblood, he had helped Raven stop Darrenton and protect Amberwood. His life was in danger now too, partially because of that. She still didn't trust him, but she could see the counter-resistance building in Raven's eyes. Sometimes it was easier to acquiesce.

She breathed in the smell of the freshly watered earth before nodding. "There's plenty of room for one more." She would apologize to Phendaril for that later.

Raven glanced back toward where Marek stood and waved him over. Karsima and Alayne moved to the side, making space for the Silverblood and the two guards to join them. It was a little disconcerting to watch the guards bow to Raven. More disturbing than that, however, was the adoring way they gazed at her as if they held her in complete awe. What else had happened at Darrenton's manor to inspire such a reaction in these men?

"Marek, I was hoping you would join us for some refreshments."

The adept inclined his head. "I would be pleased to do so."

Raven's gaze moved to the young guard with striking hazel eyes. "Captain Davon, if it isn't too much to ask, would you and Gerrod check in with the mercenaries and see that they're getting settled?"

Davon inclined his head. "Of course, milady."

As Raven watched the two men depart, Karsima glanced at Alayne, who merely shrugged.

The group moved to the larger of the two sitting rooms in the house she and Alayne shared. Alayne and Karsima sat together on the couch. Raven, Phendaril, and Marek sat in three chairs, one of which they had to bring in from another room, making it a little crowded.

A fire crackled in the hearth, its light and warmth burning through some of the chill caused by Marek's presence. A warm spicy mead also helped with that.

"What's on your mind?" Phendaril asked, his tone more interrogative than usual, perhaps because of the adept. However, she suspected his conflict with Raven played a part too.

Alayne pulled her legs up onto the couch to sit cross-legged there. Her gaze lingered on Phendaril for a second before settling on Raven. "I know you're being hunted by the Silverbloods, which means guards in the cities will also be watching for you. That will make it especially hard to get close to Wayland unless you think you can draw him out."

Marek shook his head. "Wayland hasn't left the temple in my lifetime. I couldn't tell you why, but I'd say the odds are against him venturing out now. He'll find other ways to convince Raven to come to him or have someone else bring her there."

Alayne nodded to him, recognizing his contribution, though neither Karsima nor Phendaril bothered to acknowledge him with as much as a glance. "That's what I figured. And the Brotherhood has King Saldin's ear. You would need an extremely compelling argument to gain his sympathy. That makes Pellanth the worst place you could go right now."

Raven's silver eyes flashed, the muscles in her jaw jumping. "What am I to do? Run again? I might be able to disappear, but I will always have a connection to Wayland. It could be disastrous if he ever figured out how to follow me using that connection. And he has already made it clear that he won't leave Amberwood alone so long as I continue to defy him." She looked at the Silverblood adept. "Besides, Marek can't follow where I would go."

"Who gives a shit about Marek," Karsima blurted.

She cast a quick look at Marek. "No offense."

"Of course not." Marek's chair creaked as he sat back. He glowered at her, his hand sinking to the hilt of his dagger.

Smudge sprinted across the floor and pounced on a shadow created by the fire, before bolting over to climb Phendaril's leg. The kitten came to a stop, crouched in his lap. After a second, it let out a tiny huff and curled up there. Phendaril glanced at Raven, who met his eyes, a brief fond smile passing between them.

Maybe...

Raven faced Karsima then, her expression sobering. "I care what happens to Marek," she stated, though she pointedly didn't look at the Silverblood as she spoke.

"There may be another option," Alayne said in the awkward silence that followed. "Once you've had time to recover your strength, we could go to Chadhurst and meet with my uncle."

Raven tilted her head slightly to one side, her brows lifting with a hint of skepticism. "King Navaran? Is he not also swayed by the Brotherhood? He never responded to your request for aid against Darrenton, did he?"

A slight tightening of Alayne's hand on the arm of the couch hinted at uncertainty, but she forged ahead. "I'm sure there are good reasons for that. Regardless, he's never had much love for the Brotherhood, and he's a good man. If we could sway him to your cause, I think we could get him to take a stand to protect you."

"And how would we do that?" Marek asked, his tone sharp with cynicism.

Alayne smiled patiently. "The mere fact that Raven gives lie to some of their doctrines will endear her to him. At the very least, we might be able to improve her situation south of the border. It would be a step in the right direction. If we tell him about how Wayland was funding Darrenton's efforts to take Amberwood, we might be able to get him to reach out to King Saldin as well."

Marek sneered at Karsima. "I think your... lover, is it? I think she's underestimating the influence the Brotherhood has in Chadhurst."

Phendaril leaned forward in his chair before Karsima could react to Marek's attempted jab. His gaze drilled into Alayne. "You think we should try to change her status. Convince King Saldin that she is not an anomaly to be turned over to the Silverbloods for judgment. That's a significant undertaking, though I can see how taking that power away from the Brotherhood might appeal to him." He looked at Raven, a slow smile touching his lips. "But, if it worked, you could live free wherever you pleased and be recognized as Jaecar's legal heir, at least in one kingdom."

The smile Karsima expected from Raven didn't come. The shine of unshed tears rose in her eyes, and she stood abruptly. She looked down at Alayne. "I appreciate your willingness to try on my behalf, but I can't..." She trailed off, avoiding their eyes as she strode from the room.

The front door opened and closed firmly behind her. Marek and Phendaril both stood.

Alayne reached out a hand toward Marek to get his attention. "Marek, if we tried this, would you support her?"

Marek's eyes narrowed as he watched Phendaril set Smudge on his shoulder and limp from the room. He glanced down at Alayne. "With everything I am." The front door opened and closed again. "If you'll excuse me." He offered a curt nod before following Phendaril. A few seconds later, the door opened and closed for a third time.

Raven wasn't sure where to go. Her feet took her across the square and partway along the street leading out of town toward the river. At a different time, she would have gone to the house she and Phendaril shared. That seemed to be where her memories were taking her, given that she was only one building away from it now, but that wasn't appropriate anymore. Things had changed since she was last here.

Plenty of townsfolk were still working in this area, though the center of reconstruction had shifted down toward the lower part of town. None of those passing now were familiar to her. Several offered polite nods, but a few stared too long at her eyes and hair. Perhaps they had heard of her from others, perhaps not.

She drew the arrowhead pendant out of her shirt, comforted by the feel of its smooth surface in her hand. Her ears caught the sound of Phendaril's brace clicking behind her. Another set of familiar footsteps were coming her way, quickly overtaking Phendaril.

Raven turned to face Marek. Though his pace was undoubtedly fueled by a desire to reach her before the elf did, genuine concern showed in the lines that furrowed his brow and the tightness around his eyes.

"Are you all right?"

She met his eyes. Silver, like her own, only not as

bright. Not even close. "Yes. I just need to think."

He cast an irritable glance at Phendaril, who was closing in on them, keeping a good pace despite his current limitations. "Alayne's idea might be worth thinking about. If we went before King Saldin, I would stand with you."

It was a generous offer, considering how profound a betrayal that would be in the eyes of the Brotherhood. Raven gave him a look she hoped conveyed the depth of her gratitude. "Thank you, Marek."

He stepped up close to her. "I can provide you an excuse not to talk to him right now if you want it," he offered under his breath.

She touched his arm, giving it a light squeeze. How odd that she would have once shied from such contact. Was that a sign that she had grown, or was she merely too numb to feel that anxiety now? What made her anxious was that Marek had figured out the problem between them without her telling him about Synderis. She didn't understand relationships well enough to guess what could have tipped him off, but she didn't want him any more involved than he already was.

"No. I appreciate the offer, but Phendaril and I need to talk things through at some point. It might as well be now."

Marek nodded once and strode away, casting a warning scowl at Phendaril on his way past. Phendaril stopped next to her and turned, following Marek's departure with his gaze for a moment before speaking.

"He is very protective of you now. Ironic, given that he abducted you and nearly got you killed not so long ago."

"Did get me killed," she corrected. "It's his choice."

Phendaril nodded. "I suppose it is. Come inside?" He gestured to the house with one hand.

Was it really a good idea to be alone with him?

The temptation to ease back into the way things were when they lived here together was almost irresistible. A powerful part of her didn't want to keep turning away when the inclination to be more intimate him grew more intense. She longed for things to be easy between them the way it was before they left Amberwood. That couldn't be, though, because part of her heart belonged to Synderis now, and every time she looked at Phendaril, she saw the other elven man in her mind.

Raven reached up to scratch Smudge's chin, her chest aching with memories the kitten dredged up. For a few seconds, she struggled to chase away images of the room full of dead servants, of Lily lying prone on the mantle next to a silent bundle of blankets.

Phendaril touched her arm, offering tacit comfort. He, more than anyone, understood what haunted her.

She took a deep breath, then nodded and walked to the house with him, matching her pace to his. Once inside that familiar space, a different surge of memories struck her. These were of the times they had spent here together, sharing this home, their lives, and each other. Did all of that mean nothing now?

Of course, it didn't, and yet... why did love have to be so complicated? Wasn't being actively hunted by the Silverblood Brotherhood enough of a challenge to deal with?

She considered turning and leaving for a few seconds while he focused on building a fire in the hearth. She wouldn't do that to him, though. Treating Synderis that way was a mistake that continued to torment her thoughts. One she refused to make again with either of them. The pain she had caused them to this point was more than enough.

Raven wandered into the kitchen and pulled out a bottle of elven wine and two goblets. She knew where to find it. This had been her house too, after all. If Wayland could have had the decency to forget her, she might have lived the rest of her life without ever knowing Synderis existed. She and Phendaril could have continued building their home here in Amberwood. Would that have been so bad?

"Raven?" His voice was soft and inquisitive.

"Sorry, Phen. I got lost in thought."

His smile was gentle and edged with sorrow when she turned to face him. "You have plenty to think about. Too much, I'd venture. Come sit by the fire with me."

She did as he asked, though the act of doing so was so achingly familiar and natural that it left her ill at ease. Synderis told her to be with Phendaril if she needed that. Still, she couldn't take comfort from him without being able to fully offer herself in return. It felt selfish to do so.

He filled her goblet, and she took a long drink of the wine, grimacing as the sweetness of it in quantity overpowered her sense of taste and smell. It was not meant to be drunk that way.

Phendaril arched an eyebrow at her but said nothing. He took a chip of wood from beside the woodpile and flicked it across the floor to Smudge, who was investigating a frayed carpet edge. The kitten sprang into the air, startled, then pounced on the offending wood chip. He attacked it, biting and clawing at it until a kick of his hind legs sent it flying toward the door. He gave chase.

Raven breathed a small laugh, her gaze following the energetic little creature. Then she turned and faced the fire again, catching a glimpse of Phendaril's thoughtful gaze as she did so.

"What is it about Alayne's proposal that bothers you so much?" he asked, though he didn't leave space for her to answer. "If we went to Chadhurst, you wouldn't be here, so there would be no need for the Silverbloods to bother Amberwood. A few of us, including Alayne, given that King Navaran is her uncle, would have to travel with you, but we all know the risks. Your odds of getting to Chadhurst and King Navaran are at least as good as those for getting close enough to Wayland in Pellanth to try to kill him. Maybe better. Especially given that, even if you succeeded, it would not solve the issue of the Brotherhood hunting you."

Raven stared into the fire. He was right about her odds and the problem of being hunted by the Brotherhood, even if she eliminated Wayland. In their eyes, she was an illegal Silverblood, an abomination, and killing one of their priests wasn't going to earn her their clemency. If anything, it would make them all the more determined to find and execute her. If she fled to Eyl'Thelandra after committing such a public crime, the ensuing hunt would put them at greater risk of discovery.

He took a sip of wine, giving her a chance to speak now. When she didn't, he continued. "If Alayne's plan worked, you would have the backing of a king. You might even get a chance at a more normal life. It's a long shot, but why not try? What do you have to lose that you aren't at least as likely to lose going after Wayland?"

She set her goblet down and gave him a pleading look. Didn't any of them understand? Could they? Veylin and all of Darrenton's servants were dead because of her. She wasn't sure she could carry the weight of more lost lives. "I would be putting people in danger again. Wayland's orders were to take me alive and kill anyone with me. That means Alayne and anyone else who accompanied me to Chadhurst would be executed if they caught us. I can't have that on my conscience. There are too many lives there already."

He set his goblet down and leaned forward in his chair. "We know who's hunting you, Raven. No one would be forced to go. Alayne made the offer. Don't imagine for a second that she hasn't already thought through the risks."

Raven stood and paced to the window that looked out toward the forest. "I can't, Phen. I don't have it in me to hope for a good outcome anymore. Not after..." The painful tightening in her throat cut off her words.

The soft clicking and creaking of his brace warned of his approach. She imagined she could feel him there, the warmth of his body close behind her. She touched the arrowhead pendant. He had returned to the woods after the wyvern destroyed her father's bow and retrieved a piece to craft it from. A genuine act of love. Now it also protected her dreams from Wayland and blocked her from Synderis.

He placed a hand on her shoulder. "You've been ill, and what happened at Darrenton's manor would be hard for anyone to deal with. Give it a few days. Let your body finish recovering before you make any decisions. You might find that hope you think is gone."

"I'm almost more afraid to find that you're right. If I dare hope, and something happens to someone else because of me..." She turned and saw the stubborn resistance rising in his eyes. Frustration answered it. Didn't he realize what it would do to her if he died? She had thought him dead once already. She couldn't lose him that way again, no matter what the future held for them. "Can you imagine what Alayne's death would do to Karsima?"

His expression hardened, and her attention flickered to the scar that ran down along the side of his nose. The scar he had gotten taking vengeance on the men who raped the elven female he loved. She had killed herself rather than bear the child conceived by that awful act. He knew exactly what it felt like to lose someone he loved. She was wrong to imply that he didn't. Very wrong.

"I'm sorry. I didn't mean to suggest..."

He clenched his jaw, wrestling down the hurt and anger in his eyes.

"Phen, I remember what it felt like when I thought you might be dead. I can't go through that again, and I can't put anyone else through it. You must understand that, given the people you've lost."

He looked into her eyes, his expression softening a little. "I lost you once too if you recall."

He reached out, brushing a lock of hair behind her ear. Though the easy intimacy of the gesture made it obvious he'd merely slipped into the comfort of their former situation, it sparked a gnawing longing in her chest. His gaze moved to her lips, and he pulled away, going back to stand next to the fire. She followed, sensing he had more to say.

"You know, after Lysanna's death, I swore I would never give my heart to anyone else. I was doing a decent job of that. Then I met you." He turned to her again, the profound affection in his gaze warming her more effectively than the fire had. "Even before I saw your face, I was drawn to something about you. Then, when I saw what you were, I knew loving you was guaranteed to break my heart again. I tried so hard not to."

A fond smile tugged at the corners of her mouth. "Is that why you were so angry and cold to me at first? You were trying to protect your heart?"

There was pain in his answering smile. "I didn't trust my heart not to betray me. I was trying to make you want to keep me at a distance because I already didn't want to stay away from you. I couldn't stick with it, though."

"Do you regret it?" She swallowed hard, finding that she dreaded his answer more than she would have expected to.

His expression turned serious, a few light lines of distress showing across his brow as he considered her. "No. Not even now."

More than anything, she yearned to step into his

arms and find the comfort and reassurance she knew he would offer. Not only because of the love swelling within her but because she longed for distraction in ways he could provide. He could help her forget and feel something good, if only for a short time. She wanted to take that sweet, intimate comfort and let it chase away her sorrow as it had in the past. It would be different now, though. Not because she didn't love or desire him. She very much did. But with Synderis always in her thoughts, any comfort she found with Phendaril would add to her sorrow as much as it took away.

She met his dark eyes. Eyes she had let herself sink into many times in the past. She wished he would kiss her the way the longing in his gaze said he wanted to and make a choice for her. Maybe then the resulting guilt would be less consuming.

He didn't, however. Past pain made him wary now. He took a step back from her and lowered his gaze. "The main bedroom upstairs is useable now. You're welcome to it for as long as you're here. The collection of books you found is up there waiting for you. I can't really manage the stairs yet, anyhow."

Raven nodded. "Thank you. I think I'll go up for a bit now. I could use some time to rest and think."

Without waiting for a response, she stepped around him and hurried up the stairs. The bed in the room upstairs was larger and more comfortable than the one they had shared for so many months in the downstairs bedroom. Sitting on it, leaning back against the headboard, she felt more alone and lost than she had in a long time. By diverting her plan and coming after Darrenton instead, she inadvertently left herself open to new options. The way forward was uncertain.

She glanced at the sword and dagger resting next to the door. They were gifts from Jaecar. Expensive ones, if what Phendaril had said when he first saw them was true, and she had no reason now to believe otherwise. Given that Jaecar was nobility, she supposed he might have had a fair bit of coin stored away with little to use it on. They had lived a relatively meager life, using the forest and the land to provide for their needs. He had taken trips to town on occasion. Usually for things like clothing, given that his skills as a seamstress were sorely lacking.

She smiled wistfully at the weapons. "Before you died, you were the only person I had spoken to for most of my life. Can you believe that now they want to put me in front of a king? What would you think of that?"

When her plan was simply to confront Wayland, the odds of surviving the experience were abysmal enough that she didn't consider what would come after that. If she went along with Alayne's idea, the odds were still poor, but there remained a slight chance of a future in it. If it did work, she would have to figure out what her future would look like. It also meant that what she chose to do now could have consequences beyond the next few days or weeks.

Raven leaned back against the wall and rubbed the arrowhead pendant between her thumb and fingers. The temptation to remove it and reach out to Synderis was fierce, but she wasn't ready to face Wayland again. Not yet. Not after what he had done.

CHAPTER THIRTEEN

Once the shock of their defiance wore off, Synderis and the others settled into a pattern. They maintained a steady jog throughout the days, resting in shifts at night. Synderis and Koshika typically rested first, the big cat stretching out against him to share his warmth, which was welcome with the increased chill of the season. Telandora and Lindyl did the same through the second part of the night, though the added layer of intimacy in their sharing of warmth brought Raven to mind with an acute pang of longing.

In the mornings, they foraged together, gathering local plants to keep their stores from running low. The threat of snow in the air meant it might get harder to find the foods they ate. Koshika offered to share her meals more than once. They appreciated the gesture, but none of them were eager to start eating meat.

They were able to keep up a swift pace even without horses. The scouts of Eyl'Thelandra maintained a rigorous fitness level, always prepared for fights that never arrived because they used magic to turn threats away at the borders of their forest. With all three of them having the extra Krivalen enhancements as well, they had no trouble consuming the miles. They stuck to the woods between the main road and the shallow river that paralleled it until they reached the crossroads. There, they turned west, heading in the direction that would take them toward the lands north of Amberwood that Lord Darrenton owned before Raven and Marek summarily ended him.

After confirming their route at the crossroad signpost, they disappeared into the trees again, staying hidden from any travelers on the road. The closer they got, the more anticipation set his nerves on edge. Raven wasn't expecting them. He had hoped she would dreamwalk him before they entered the town so he could give her some warning. That she hadn't didn't come as much of a surprise. After what Wayland had done, she wasn't going to risk opening her dreams to him if she didn't have to. But if she had reached out to Phendaril as he suggested, his sudden arrival might put her in an awkward position.

It was late morning when he noticed the unnatural quiet of the forest. The lively birdsong and chitter of small animals that serenaded them since they entered the woods on this side of the river had ceased. Telandora and Lindyl slowed on almost the same stride as though they too had just become aware of the change. Koshika dropped to a walk, moving closer to him. A low growl rose in her throat. Synderis touched her shoulders, and she pressed up against his leg for a single step before turning and bolting into the trees to their left.

He glanced at Telandora and Lindyl. They both gave almost imperceptible nods in response. Something in this part of the forest didn't belong as far as the wildlife was concerned. Not that they belonged here, but animals responded differently to them. They were, in a sense, also woodland creatures, and they moved and acted as part of that natural world.

They proceeded with more caution now, stepping lightly to avoid making noise. All three had drawn their bows and nocked arrows. Whatever or whoever waited ahead, the fact that they hadn't spotted anything yet told him their trio of elves had been seen and were unlikely to get a warm reception.

He heard the soft chink of chain mail to his right about the same time he caught a hint of motion behind one of the trees on that side. He turned his head enough to see Telandora hold two fingers down next to her thigh. How she had figured out they were facing two opponents when he had only now caught a sound from one was beyond him, but he didn't doubt her. The breeze shifted slightly, and the scent of a recently doused campfire reached him. A twig cracked nearby as someone adjusted in their hiding place. Then he heard the nearly inaudible creak of a bowstring being very slowly drawn. One of them was being targeted.

Following the sound, he spotted the tip of someone's arrow edging out from behind a tree several yards ahead an instant before they stepped out to shoot. The bow released, but Telandora had also seen it coming. At a hand signal from her, Lindyl leapt aside, his Krivalen reflexes moving him out of the path fast enough that the arrow flew harmlessly past. Another arrow came flying from a different direction, exposing a second opponent.

Synderis released an arrow before leaping behind a tree for cover. The enemy's arrow cut a deep gouge into the armor over his right shoulder. The man he had fired on dodged his shot as quickly. Synderis's arrow missed its mark, flying through where his opponent's eye had been a second before. Behind the cover of the tree, Synderis felt along his connection to Koshika. The big cat was circling around behind his opponent, still hidden in the undergrowth. He grinned and stepped out the other side of the tree. Taking a quick, somewhat reckless shot, his arrow cut a deep gouge in the tree the archer was hiding behind and sliced into the armor over the man's thigh. The man startled, swiveling his attention toward where the shot came from. Koshika leapt from the brush on his opposite flank and closed her teeth around the back of his neck. The power of her jaws, meant for severing the spine of large prey, was enough to take him down.

The other attacker, seeing his companion go down, lunged out with his sword, ready to go after the lalyx cat. Two arrows sank deep into his right thigh from Telandora and Lindyl. As he collapsed to one knee, a third arrow appeared in his left side that didn't come from any of them. Synderis peered past their assailants and spotted a cloaked figure stepping from behind a tree farther out. The stranger was lowering their bow, though they still had an arrow nocked.

Satisfied that her prey was dead, Koshika turned on the injured man, snarling. Synderis jogged toward her, sending calm along their bond.

"No, my friend, I'll handle this one." He glanced over to catch Telandora's gaze. "See that our unexpected ally doesn't drop an arrow into any of us if you would."

She smirked and gave a nod, gesturing for Lindyl to join her as she strode confidently past Synderis.

The injured man was struggling to breathe. The third arrow had gone deep into his left lung. Synderis caught his breath when a set of hate-filled silver eyes looked up at him. A distinct edge of fear joined that hate when he noticed Synderis's silver eyes.

Synderis welcomed it. A pair of Silverbloods wandering the woods this close to where Raven was staying couldn't be a coincidence. These men were guilty of terrible things.

"What are you doing out here?" Synderis demanded, crouching in front of the man.

"My job." The Silverblood grabbed ineffectually at the arrow in his side, unable to get a strong enough grip to pull it out.

"Your job wouldn't involve killing a Kri—Silverblood

half-elf, would it?"

"What's it to you? Freak bastard. All you magic-stealing abominations need to die." The man spat blood at him.

Hatred swelled in Synderis. It was a strange feeling and not one he was fond of. He reached down and jerked one of the arrows out of the man's leg, eliciting a grunt of pain from him. "Ambushing a trio of Silverblood elves isn't as easy as killing sleeping servants, is it?"

The man grabbed at his leg, his breath rasping. "How... do you know about that?"

Synderis hesitated. The urge to stab the arrow he was now holding through the man's throat was powerful. A quick motion and this world would have one less Brotherhood mercenary to worry about. And yet, he had never killed anyone like this. The man was injured and at his mercy. For all that he trained his entire life to fight and kill if necessary, it felt wrong to do so now that the choice lay before him, even when it was someone who deserved it this richly.

Synderis started when another arrow struck the Silverblood in the back with enough power that the point jutted out through the front of his chest. He looked up to see the cloaked stranger lowering his bow.

"Because Raven is a friend of ours," the stranger snarled.

The Silverblood fell sideways. For a few seconds, Synderis debated whether he should Accept his spirit, but this man had killed innocents to terrorize and hurt Raven. He didn't deserve that honor.

Synderis stood to face the approaching stranger. Telandora and Lindyl held their bows ready, though they weren't aiming at him. They didn't need to. He drew his hood back, revealing elven ears and features. Unsurprisingly, he was not Krivalen. He wore his long black hair bound back, and there seemed a curious lack of concern in his violet eyes as he sized Synderis up. Given his words, he was their ally in at least one way.

"I'm Jael." He started to put his bow away, then his gaze came to rest on Koshika, and he hesitated.

Synderis lowered his hand, and the big cat stepped in beside him, pushing her head against his fingertips. He scratched behind her ears. "You needn't worry about Koshika. She's with us."

Jael arched a curious brow and resumed putting his bow away. "Phendaril said a Silverblood elf followed Raven into his dream the first time he met her there. Given the scarcity of Silverblood elves, I'm going to guess that the three of you are somehow connected to that one?"

Telandora and Lindyl were putting their bows away now. Synderis did the same.

"I am that one."

Jael nodded as though he had expected as much. "I know Raven and some others were planning to leave Amberwood soon, but I don't know if they've done so yet. I've been out here three days keeping an eye on those two and waiting for an opportunity to do something about them."

Telandora glanced at the two dead Silverbloods. She smiled at Jael. "You're welcome."

Synderis gave her a chastising look, then regarded Jael thoughtfully. If this elf was out here spying on two Silverbloods alone, he was either reckless or highly skilled. Perhaps a bit of both. "Since we've helped you solve this problem, would you consider showing us the way to Amberwood?"

"I would."

Synderis offered his hand. "I'm Synderis. Those two," he introduced, gesturing to each in turn, "are Telandora and Lindyl."

Jael accepted his hand in a firm grip. "A pleasure."

"Do we need to do anything with the bodies?" Lindyl asked as he stepped in to shake the other elf's hand in turn.

Jael shook his head. "There are wolves and harpies aplenty in this area. They'll be gone by tomorrow morning."

Telandora grinned as she accepted his hand last. "I like you. Are all Raven's friends this skilled and sensible?"

Jael smirked. "I think you'll find that many of us are." He released her hand, his gaze drifting once more to Koshika. He offered a respectful nod of greeting to the cat. "Follow me. If we keep up a good pace, we should be able to reach Amberwood before full dark."

CHAPTER FOURTEEN

Karsima stared into her mug of mead. She couldn't shake away the nervous roiling in her gut. Alayne and the others had been gone for the better part of two days. Alayne had traveled without her dozens of times. The other woman could take care of herself, and she had several skilled fighters with her. But this was different. Two of her traveling companions, Raven and Marek, were actively being hunted by the Brotherhood. Aside from Raven and Marek—and Phendaril, who was still healing—none of them had faced a Silverblood in combat before.

Besides those four, they had taken along Ehric and two of Raven's guardsmen, Davon and Gerrod. They had tried to find a balance between the safety of numbers and the need to not draw attention to themselves. Word had come up from several vessels heading toward Pellanth that a mandatory checkpoint had been established at the narrowest part of the river west of Lathwood. Because of that, they took seven horses with them, preparing to disembark north of Andel a little past where the river veered east. They could unload the horses and riders at the poor elven village of Finyel on the north side of the river and take the less-traveled overland route through the forest the rest of the way to Chadhurst.

Jenner sat across the table from her. "Milady," he

greeted her with a nod. "Are you planning to drink from it or strangle the poor thing?"

She loosened her death grip on the mug. "I'm worried about them."

"Believe in them. Put your love and your confidence out into the world. Your worry won't do anything for them." Jenner watched her finish off the rest of her drink. He signaled one of the servers to bring her more. While they were filling her mug, he gazed into the drink he'd brought with him and smiled wistfully.

Curiosity and the need for distraction got the better of her. "What are you thinking about?"

"You recall when we first met."

Karsima grinned. "It was outside of Lathwood. Sameth was getting ready to set fire to some slaver's tents to create a diversion. You were ready to free the slaves they were taking to the port in Alm."

He chuckled. "Then you, Alayne, and Phendaril come along, driving a dragon's hoard of sheep into the camp. As soon as the slavers started beating on those sheep, trying to drive them back out, that dragon came swooping in like death on wings. We barely had time to get the slaves out of there before she showed them the error of their ways. As I recall, when it was over, Phendaril went and apologized to the dragon while the rest of us helped the folks we freed make their way to town."

"Then we all sat down for a drink at the Lazy Dragon public house."

"You and Alayne thought the place's name would help Phendaril find us."

She took a swig of her mead. "And he did, eventually."

"After he found the dragon three new sheep to add to her hoard. I always wondered where he got those extra sheep from." He took a long swallow from his mug.

She remembered the sly grin on Phendaril's face when

he refused to disclose his source for the sheep. A wistful smile tugged at the corners of her mouth. "He never told. The dragon apparently wasn't as amused by our efforts as we were. But she was appeased by his offering."

She spotted Talis standing in the doorway of the public house, peering around as though looking for someone. When he saw her, he gestured for her to come.

She smiled her appreciation at Jenner. "Thank you for the company and the memory. It looks like I'm needed."

He started to stand. "Shall I accompany you?"

Karsima shook her head. "Stay and finish your drink. I doubt it's anything serious."

"Yes, milady." He sank back down.

As she neared the door, Talis stepped out, waiting for her in front of the building. His expression vacillated strangely between bemused and troubled.

"What is it?"

"Jael just arrived with some unusual guests. I hurried them to your house. They were drawing a bit of attention."

Her eyebrows crept up as she glanced toward home. As constable, she often had visitors from the town waiting on her return to address some issue or other, but there appeared to be a few more people than usual milling about in front of the house. Rather than waste time questioning Talis, she took off at a brisk walk that way. He fell into place alongside her in silence, content to let her discover these *guests* for herself. At the house, he jumped ahead to open the door for her. Karsima strode in and turned toward the sound of voices in the larger sitting room.

She first noticed a cat bigger than any she'd seen before, with a strange coat of leaf-shaped emerald feathers sitting next to the fireplace. Standing beside the hearth with one hand resting on the cat's shoulders was an elven man with silvery-white hair and bright silver eyes. He inclined his head respectfully when he saw her enter. Two braids were woven along the sides of his head. Some hair from on top had escaped to hang loose in the front, framing features that were both elegant and masculine.

Two other strange elves, a female and another male, stood up from the couch. They were as attractive as the man by the fire, though something in their regard struck her as a hint more feral. When they rose, there was a closeness to how they leaned ever-so-slightly in toward each other. They wore their hair the same way the first male did. Most notably, all three elves were Silverbloods.

Jael, who had been sitting in one of the chairs, got to his feet with the rest of them.

The cat glanced around at the lot of them and, apparently deciding she didn't want to make waves, also stood, leaning against the elven male's leg until he moved to approach Karsima. The cat came with him.

"You're Karsima," he stated, stopping in front of her. "Raven spoke highly of you."

That caught her a bit by surprise. Her relationship with Raven had always struck her as awkward and uneasy. Primarily because of her desire to protect Phendaril from having his heart broken again. That hadn't worked out well, and part of the cause of his pain was standing before her now. As much as she hated to admit it, even she could see why Raven might have gone astray.

"I am. I'm afraid you have me at a disadvantage."

He smiled. It was a most disarming expression, though she noted that it didn't fully reach his eyes. Something worried him enough to push back against that warmth.

"I'm Synderis." He gestured to the other two, who nodded in turn as he introduced them. "They are Telandora and Lindyl." Then he glanced down at the cat next to him, and the smile crept a fraction more into his eyes. "And this is my guardian, Koshika."

It was hard not to back away from the cat. She was nearly as large as the couch. Karsima forced herself to stand her ground. "You are welcome here. Can I offer you some refreshments?"

"Thank you. I believe Jael already sent for something."

Karsima glanced at Jael, offering a look of gratitude. He inclined his head slightly without taking his intent gaze entirely away from the others. Typically, she would have ascribed his attentiveness to caution, but in this case, something more like fascination shone in his eyes as he considered the strangers.

She gestured to the chairs. "Please, make yourselves comfortable."

After the other two sat and Synderis went to reclaim his spot before the fire with his impressive companion, Karsima joined them, taking the remaining seat. Once they all settled, she met Synderis's eyes. He didn't wait for her to speak.

"Am I to understand Raven has already left Amberwood?"

Karsima crossed her legs and set her hands on the arms of the chair, doing her best to convey calm and confidence. She gave him an appraising look. Like his companions, he appeared fit to fight, and the collection of weapons she had noticed resting next to the door on the way in said they were prepared to do so. "Yes. They struck out the day before yesterday. You came to help her?"

"We did."

"She's on her way to Chadhurst with some of our companions. They are hoping to speak with King Navaran. He has no love for the Silverbloods and might be persuaded to stand up against their efforts to take her. My life-bonded, Alayne, is with them. She is the king's niece, so they at least have that working in their favor."

He glanced down at the cat, who looked up at him, their eyes meeting. There was something unnerving about the moment of silence that passed between the two. Then he scratched behind the cat's ears. The big predator pressed her head into the affection, purring loudly, a response so ordinary that it reminded Karsima a kitten was running around the house somewhere, assuming this beast hadn't already eaten poor Smudge.

"Phendaril is with her?" Synderis asked.

Karsima hesitated, searching his expression for any indication of how he would feel about the answer to that question. Not that it would change anything if the truth upset him. Phendaril was with Raven, and while she had nothing against Synderis, she still hoped their interactions over the days before they left were a sign the two were reconciling. What would Raven do if Synderis showed up now?

"He is," she replied tentatively.

On the couch, Lindyl took Telandora's hand. The gesture was absent-minded and comfortable, suggesting a fairly established relationship between the two.

"Good," Synderis answered, his gaze also drawn briefly to the other two Silverblood elves. "She needs someone she can rely upon with her."

Karsima shifted in her seat and glanced at Jael, who shrugged unhelpfully. "You do know—"

"That he loves her?" Synderis interrupted, his eyes narrowing with a flash of irritation that surprised her. "That she still loves him? I do. What I don't know is why you seem to feel that should be of concern to me right now. Her life is in danger. My greatest concern is that those who are with her have her safety and happiness as their priority. Even if Phendaril and I were to agree on nothing else, I am confident we feel the same about that."

Karsima hated him for how much his words made her want to like him. He was right. The Silverblood Brotherhood was hunting Raven. Jealousy was a luxury they had no time for here. Either he cared for her, in which case her safety should matter most to him, or he didn't.

At a knock on the door, Jael hopped up, hurrying to answer it. He reappeared a moment later with two of the elves that helped out at The Bear and Raven. They had a couple of platters of food and drink in hand. Curiously, there was no meat in sight. She suspected that meant their new acquaintances refrained from eating animals, which didn't surprise her somehow.

Koshika lifted her nose to sniff the air and huffed her disappointment.

Jael glanced down at the big cat. "Sorry, I didn't think to request anything for her."

Synderis chuckled. "No need. She'll go hunt once she's satisfied I'm safe here." He looked up at Jael then. "Though that assumes she can do so safely. If she's likely to get shot, perhaps it would be better to get something for her."

"Perhaps we should be cautious. We've had enough trouble with wild beasts in this area that some people might be too quick to draw their bows," Karsima suggested.

They sent the two elves back with a request for meat for the cat. Karsima set her thoughtful gaze on Synderis again, observing as he exchanged a few words in the elven tongue with his companions. She paid less attention to the words than the unfamiliar accents they spoke with. Jael was staring at the cat with one ear turned toward the others as if also listening.

When they finished talking, Synderis rested his silver-eyed gaze on her again. "Would it be possible to catch up with them?"

Part of her didn't want them to catch up with the

others. That part of her wished for Raven and Phendaril to have as much time together as possible before this captivating elf had a chance to ruin what they were re-building. That part of her had no place here. Three more Silverbloods fighting on their side was an advantage she couldn't begin to scoff at.

"With our boat gone, we don't have a fast enough way to get you downriver. You'd never get past the checkpoint outside of Lathwood anyhow. However, it is possible, given that they're going to have to cut across land through some difficult terrain, that you might be able to meet up with them about the time they reach Chadhurst or shortly after if you went down the eastern road." She turned to Jael. "We have horses we could loan them, don't we?"

Jael nodded. "And a guide."

Karsima's expression hardened. "No. You're needed here. We can send someone else if a guide is necessary."

"Three Silverblood elves can't march into Chadhurst and start asking around about the king's niece. I know the city and the inland routes to get there. Sameth and Talis can manage the scouts for a few weeks."

Karsima frowned at him, shaking her head. "You remind me of Phendaril sometimes."

Jael answered with a crooked smile. "I drive you mad and make you want to kick rocks?"

She exhaled a slight laugh, but weariness lingered beneath it. She didn't want to add one more, not after what happened to Veylin. Too many of the people she loved were at risk.

"If Jael has duties here, perhaps there is someone else who might be able to assist. We would be grateful for the help. These lands are new to us."

She glanced over fast enough to catch the softness of sympathy in Synderis's regard. Why did he have to be considerate and handsome? He probably didn't have a scar on his entire body, either. Of course, that also suggested he hadn't ever known real hardship the way so many of them here had. If what little she derived from Raven and Phendaril was true, which wasn't much, she got the impression Raven's mother came from elves who lived hidden away from the world. They were protected from all the horrible realities the rest dealt with daily. Sheltered.

Then again, wasn't that an even more compelling argument for sending someone with them who knew the route and the city?

She met Jael's eyes, and his slight smirk told her he recognized where her thoughts had taken her.

"Perhaps Jael would be the best suited," she admitted. "We can select horses and get supplies together this evening. There should be time as long as you head out early tomorrow. We can offer you all food, drink, and a warm place to sleep tonight."

Smudge came bounding into the room at that moment. Koshika leaped to her feet, and the kitten skidded to a halt in the middle of the floor, back arched and fur puffed out so he looked like a ball of fuzz with legs. Before anyone else could react, Telandora snatched him up and sat down again, holding him protectively in her lap. Koshika stalked over, her ears pricked so far forward that Karsima noticed the red tips for the first time.

Smudge hissed and spit at the big cat, and she flinched, earning several low chuckles from around the room. Then Koshika rested her head on Telandora's knee, gazing curiously at the little black-and-grey kitten. Smudge sank back into Telandora's arms and stared at the big cat warily.

Synderis drew his gaze away from the cats. "The public house is called The Bear and Raven? Is there something to that name?"

Karsima smiled. "She didn't tell you about the dire bear?"

He shook his head.

Grinning, Jael pulled his chair in closer and settled into it as if preparing for a good bit of entertainment. The smells of mead and firewood filled the room. The fire crackled as it bathed them in its warmth.

Karsima arched one eyebrow at her friend. "You were there, Jael. Perhaps you should tell the tale."

Jael inclined his head to her, a wistful smile tugging at the corners of his mouth. "It would be my pleasure."

As he eased them into the story, expertly setting the scene, Karsima found herself feeling oddly like a parent listening to someone tell tales about her child.

CHAPTER FIFTEEN

Raven placed a hand against Cyrleth's neck, feeling how his pulse ran strong, but calm beneath the surface. The big gelding munched at hay they had provided for the horses where they stood, divided by rails and supported by slings on the deck of the river galley. All the animals were the same. They rested quietly in their spots, chewing at the hay as if they ate in a stall on dry land.

She looked up to find Davon watching her. He glanced at the horses, then smiled and inclined his head before sauntering off along the port side railing. Since the incident with the drake, he seemed more than willing to believe her capable of almost anything. Not that he was wrong about the horses. And perhaps that was good, given that it also appeared to have instilled in him a powerful determination to see her protected. Wasn't that the kind of attitude one wanted in a guard captain?

Phendaril strolled up behind her, reaching around her to stroke Cyrleth's neck, his hand stopping beside hers. "Your Cyrleth is a handsome animal, though I never thought I would see you fussing over the wellbeing of a horse."

He was near enough that his breath warmed her ear when he spoke. Whether intentional or not, she caught herself leaning slightly into his warmth. He smelled fantastic, too. That didn't help.

She breathed a soft sigh and shifted her stance a fraction so he was no longer so close, though she remained within the circle of the arm he had reached around her. She couldn't pretend that wasn't on purpose.

"He has you to thank for helping me learn that horses aren't all teeth, hooves, and chaos."

"Not always." Phendaril smiled. His gaze moved down the line of animals. "They've been unusually calm all this way. Is that your doing?"

She glanced around, catching sight of Marek up near the bow of the boat talking to Narene. She listened for a moment, unable to make out what they were saying. That was good. His hearing didn't have the range hers did, which meant he wouldn't be able to eavesdrop at this distance. Still, she kept her voice low when she responded.

"I'd prefer not to talk about it. I don't want Marek learning more about the other ways to use Kriva... Silverblood magic."

There was approval in his brief regard. "Good to know you aren't placing too much trust in him."

She didn't respond to that. In truth, she had come to trust Marek a great deal. Still, she wasn't going to trust anyone enough to expose the secrets the elves of Eyl'Thelandra were keeping. Phendaril and Ehric were privy to the fact that the magic had other uses, but only because they had been there when she inadvertently stole the will from the horses before.

Phendaril moved around her to stand closer to Cyrleth's head and scratched the horse under his forelock. Cyrleth responded, nodding his head up and down vigorously to encourage the attention. "You've figured out how to manage it without harming them," he murmured, a hint of appreciation in his tone.

"Yes. I don't want to incapacitate them. Just keep them from injuring themselves."

Ehric joined them then. "We're almost to the Finyel dock. Get your things together and be ready to unload the horses. We can't stop long, or we risk a river patrol spotting us. It's an unusual place to be stopping with a galley this size."

Raven and Phendaril both nodded. Marek, Gerrod, Alayne, and Ehric were already heading down into the hold to gather their belongings. Davon was striding toward them. He stopped and bowed slightly to her.

"Shall I bring your things up, milady?"

"That's not necessar—"

"Actually," Phendaril interrupted, "it isn't a bad idea. There are already enough bodies below deck. Why don't you start making sure Cyrleth is ready to be moved. We'll be back in a moment."

Raven glanced at him, trying not to take insult at his interruption, then at Davon. They were right, she supposed. She'd spent enough time in the hold to know the quarters were cramped. More so with the cargo they were carrying that the crew picked up in Pellanth before the trip to give them a legitimate reason for their journey this way. The boat could keep going past the checkpoint and into Chadhurst without them aboard. There it could pick up supplies for Amberwood and possibly paying passengers or other cargo.

She nodded and turned her attention to removing hay bags from the horses. A few of Narene's crew were cautiously working their way among the animals to saddle them. They would be able to unload faster if the horses carried their own gear, and since they were uncommonly calm, it was safe enough to do so.

Raven smiled as Cyrleth lowered his head to let her put on the bridle. She hadn't done that much to influence the animals. A little soothing here and there, delivered in measured doses throughout their time on the boat, was adequate to keep them from panicking.

They weren't such awful creatures. Her former fear of them felt misplaced now. As mammals went, humans were proving far more dangerous than horses.

The others came back up from below and began helping, each taking over preparations for their own mount. All except Alayne, who went to speak with Narene for a few minutes. Raven could hear her thanking the captain for risking her ship and crew to bring them this far. Narene shrugged it off as if it were nothing, though her gaze shifted to Raven as she spoke, and her eyes softened. Helping save the captain and crew all those months ago in Manderly still carried weight with her.

Raven smiled back, her cheeks warming. Then Davon stepped into her line of sight, offering over her pack, weapons, and an escape from awkward social interactions.

"Would you like me to hold onto any of this for you, milady?"

"Thank you, Davon, but I can manage." She donned her sword belt and attached her pack to the back of Cyrleth's saddle before taking her bow and quiver.

He bowed. His gaze lingered on her, a glimmer of fondness and admiration lighting his eyes. Then he turned his attention to his own mount.

According to Phendaril, the route they would pick up outside Finyel meandered along the north side of the river, weaving through swampy forest land. The path tended to be mucky and slick. Still, it would keep them away from the heavily traveled roads where they were more apt to encounter Silverbloods or those who might report them to such men.

Finyel was an entirely elven village. Though it appeared poor, with its ramshackle houses and muddy streets, the elves that watched them lead their mounts down the gangplank didn't look less happy than those she'd met in places like Lathwood and Manderly. Laugh lines around their eyes and mouths suggested they might be quite happy if there weren't a band of primarily human strangers disembarking into their town.

Would the Silverbloods even look in such a place, or was it beneath their notice?

Raven considered trying to offer smiles to some of them. Would they reciprocate if she did? But she couldn't quite bring herself to do so. Inviting interactions with complete strangers was still too far outside her comfort zone. Proof that she was destined to botch the process of meeting a king. Did Alayne have a clue how the mere thought of attempting to present herself to such an individual made her gut shrivel into a ball of quivering fear? How ridiculous was it that she could approach a storm drake more easily than a man?

She cast a sidelong glance at Davon. He caught her doing so and answered with a dashing smile and friendly nod. He and Gerrod were the only ones here who had never seen her shudder in terror at the sight of a crowd. At least they might leave off calling her milady when they saw how brave she was not.

Narene waved them on as she exchanged a few words with one of the village elders. They had barely unloaded the last horse when she hurried back on board, and the crew pulled in the gangplank to cast off. Phendaril, who seemed familiar with the village, mounted up and rode off in the lead. It took all of three minutes to pass through the little village in which every building had a lean to it and was painted with enough dirt to make them all roughly the same color as the muddy streets.

Raven felt the horses relaxing into familiar habits as they followed the path leading east from Finyel. She eased her influence away from them, careful not to do so too abruptly. When she had fully withdrawn the magic with no one the wiser, she smirked to herself and patted Cyrleth's neck.

"Milady looks pleased." Ehric offered a teasing grin

as he moved his mount up next to her.

"You do not get to call me that. We've been through far too much together." She couldn't hold back a warm smile, though regret still shadowed some of the memories they shared, tempering the expression. "I only hope this goes better than our last journey in these parts."

"You must believe it will," Ehric answered, his bold tone exuding confidence. He shifted his mount a little closer and lowered his voice, glancing at Phendaril, who still held the lead with Alayne. "The two of you are not as easy together as you were before."

Raven looked at Phendaril, his dark auburn hair bound into a long tail that hung down his back. They had fashioned a wider stirrup for him to accommodate the brace more comfortably. She had considered trying to discourage him from coming, but he was an adult. It was his choice. Besides, after what had occurred the last time they were separated, she didn't imagine she could say much to convince him that staying behind was the better decision. Part of her was glad he had come. Nothing she thought or did to persuade her heart that she did not still love him had any effect.

As Synderis said, he wasn't here, and she had no way of knowing if she would ever see him again. Was it inappropriate of her to enjoy being around Phendaril? Was it wrong to want a little happiness in whatever life she had left to her? Not that she doubted Alayne, but she didn't have a great deal of optimism regarding the Silverbloods. Besides, what human king would support a half-elven anomaly over the powerful Brotherhood? It was sweet of Alayne to want to try, even if it only delayed the inevitable confrontation between her and Wayland.

So why had she let them talk her into this?

Next to her, Ehric was speaking of his travels through this area with his sister when he was younger.

Behind them, Gerrod, Davon, and Marek were conversing about something they all seemed to find amusing,
given their measured laughter. Ahead, Phendaril had
turned toward Alayne, a faint smile curving his lips as
he nodded to her. They were all here for her, risking
their lives to win her freedom. Her future mattered to
them. Even to Marek, who was now an exile to his order
and hunted alongside her because he chose to let her
escape the night she nearly killed Father Wayland.

This was why she was doing it? Even when Jaecar
decided to take her north, hoping to make a home for
her where she would be welcome, she had not dared to
dream of this. Of having people who cared about her
and accepted her for who and what she was. This was
precisely what Jaecar wanted for her. She wanted it too.
Now that she was here with them all, she couldn't bring
herself to let go quite yet.

"You didn't hear any of that, did you?" An amused
smirk pulled at Ehric's lips.

Her cheeks burned. "I'm so sorry. I truly do want
to hear the story. Would you forgive my distraction and
tell me again?"

Ehric grinned. "Whatever thoughts took you away
made your eyes glow. I can handle being ignored for
that, and I'm happy to start again."

Ehric entertained her with his stories until the muddy path narrowed and began winding through trees
and shallow pools that hid deep, sucking mud. The terrain forced them to follow single file after that. When
evening fell, they found a dryer area to make camp. It
looked as if it had seen such use before, judging from
the chunks of wood conveniently positioned like seats
around a depressed spot perfect for setting up a fire.

They ate and settled in for the night with little chatter.
They were weary from long hours of riding and sobered
by the knowledge that dangerous men were hunting

some of their number. Raven spread her sleeping roll next to Phendaril's, watching with veiled amusement as Marek and Davon rushed for the spot on her other side. Not surprisingly, the Silverblood adept was faster, so Davon laid out his roll not far from the top of hers.

Phendaril met her eyes, shaking his head and barely suppressing a grin.

Raven shrugged and sat cross-legged next to him. "How are your injuries after a day in the saddle?"

"I won't lie and say they don't hurt, but it's tolerable." He flexed the wrapped hand and grimaced.

"Did Synal send anything with you for the pain?"

"Some tincture and a salve. I'd rather not take the tincture while we're in unfamiliar territory." He drew a small container out of one pack.

Raven took it from him and set it between them. Then she took his hand and began to gently remove the bandage. He followed her every movement with his gaze, the intensity of his attention making her question her own behavior.

She set the wrap aside, still holding his hand in one of hers, and reached for the salve. "Is it all right if I help you?"

He nodded, his gaze suffused with warm affection. "More than."

Raven's face grew warm. How she loved it when he looked at her like that. Trying to ignore the insistent flutter in her chest, she took a dab of the salve and started to massage it into his hand around and over the healing scars. It was nice to touch him. To have a hint of that physical contact she longed for.

"I miss you, Raven," he said softly.

There had to be many ways she could answer that without encouraging anything. She could think of nothing, however, because she missed him too. Even though they had spent considerable time together over the last several days, she missed being close to him. Perhaps more so because of that.

"I know," she murmured.

CHAPTER SIXTEEN

Raven woke abruptly, her heart racing. Something had ripped her from her slumber, though she couldn't place what. The chatter of the unfamiliar insects and amphibians that lived in the swamp filled the night. An owl hooted nearby. Tiny flying bugs with white bodies that glowed in the spears of moonlight flitted about, creating an effect like snow or ash falling through the bare trees.

She could hear the breathing of the three closest to her. Marek, Phendaril, and Davon were all still deeply asleep. Whatever woke her hadn't disturbed them.

She sat up slowly, wary of waking her companions yet, and peered through the darkness. Alayne slept on the other side of Phendaril. The horses shifted at their line. Not restless enough to suggest approaching danger, but not entirely calm. Gerrod and Ehric should be on watch, though she couldn't see either of them anywhere near the camp.

Raven climbed carefully to her feet. She didn't want to raise the alarm yet, but she did strap on her sword belt before investigating further. With delicate steps, she moved between the sleepers and retrieved her bow and quiver from where they leaned against a stump next to Davon.

Still stepping lightly on the moist ground, she made

her way to the edge of the path they followed during the day and peered around, searching for Gerrod or Ehric in the darkness. The trees and bushes in this dank, musty wilderness were devoid of foliage. With her elven Silverblood vision, it shouldn't be hard to spot the two men if they were somewhere close, which they should be.

The sucking sound of footsteps in the mud drew her attention back the other way, toward where the mist rising off the swamp waters limited even her eyesight. Drawing her sword, she struck out in that direction, the hair on her arms standing up. As she approached the edge of the water, a figure began to take shape, standing with their back to her. From the build and hair, it appeared to be Gerrod.

She crept closer, her feet starting to sink into the mucky soil. He didn't move. Didn't turn to find out who was coming up behind him. She could see now that he stood knee deep in the water.

She stopped and called out to him in a low voice. "Gerrod."

Something was wrong with the stiff way he moved as he turned to face her. Raven shifted back a step, putting a little more distance between them. When his face came into view, she sucked in a sharp breath. His eye sockets were empty, part of the flesh of his cheeks torn away to the bone. Some of his teeth were visible through the side of his mouth. He reached one hand out toward her.

Raven's stomach turned. She caught a scream in her throat. Whatever had done this might still be around. She couldn't afford to draw its attention. Instead, she stepped back enough to stay out of his range.

"Gerrod," she choked out.

He continued toward her with his arm outstretched, his movement strange. He didn't act as if he was in pain. He didn't act as if he felt anything at all. Swallowing terror, she grabbed his wrist tightly enough to feel his pulse. Only he had no pulse.

She shoved his arm away and began retreating again, unsure whether she should call for help and risk alerting whatever had attacked Gerrod. Then she caught the sound of low, raspy breathing behind her. She stopped backing up and had started to turn around when something touched her arm.

●

Raven's legs were wet. She held her sword in a loose grip by her side, the end of the blade submerged in the swamp pool she was standing in. Terror gripped her, squeezing her gut and forcing her to fight a sudden urge to vomit. She turned a circle, searching for anything that might help her orient herself in the dark mist. Gerrod and whatever had touched her arm were gone, or at least far enough away as to be hidden from sight.

Clenching her teeth against the spike of fear, she started slogging in a direction that appeared to have more trees, which she hoped meant the edge of the pool she was standing in. As she waded through the water, her feet sinking almost a foot in the mucky soil beneath, she reached out with her magic, searching for someone familiar. Phendaril. Marek. Anyone. Even Cyrleth would do.

What she found first was something else entirely. It was the purest darkness. A tempest of hatred, anger, and pain. Trying to reach into it was like trying to hold onto water in her hands. Her magic slipped through the mire of black emotion and fell away.

"Raven!"

Marek.

A large shadow in the mist separated from a cluster

of trees. Its shape was so unfamiliar that she couldn't associate it with any creature she had ever seen.

Marek called again, and she turned in that direction, wading through the mucky depths as rapidly as she could without stumbling. At the same time, she kept an eye on the shadowy form. Then the large figure sank down and disappeared amidst the shadows of the underbrush.

Raven tried to move faster, but the sucking mud and water made it next to impossible.

"Marek," she called.

When he didn't answer, her chest grew tight, making it harder to breathe. Then, as she finally emerged from the pool, a familiar figure appeared out of the darkness. After her encounter with Gerrod, her terror gained potency until she was close enough to see his face and the relief in his eyes.

"There's something else out here," she hissed.

He nodded, his gaze darting around, jumping from shadow to shadow. His voice held an edge of panic. "Someone woke it."

"Woke what?"

"The eliket. We need to get back to the camp. Fast."

He took her hand, his palm damp with nervous sweat, and headed off at a swift jog. Relieved that he seemed to know which way camp was, she made no effort to pull away or slow him. When she matched her pace to his, he released her hand.

"Gerrod's dead."

"Dead, or dead and still moving around?"

Raven glanced over at him. He obviously knew a fair bit about what they were dealing with. "What is this thing?"

"A curse given flesh was always the popular theory. The Brotherhood was hired to get rid of it several years ago. Seven Silverblood warriors went into these woods. Only two of them ever came back. They claimed that the thing killed the other Silverbloods and took control of their bodies, giving them no choice but to fight their own dead comrades. They couldn't remember what had happened after that. One said he came to alone the next morning, standing chest deep in swamp water. His weapons were gone. The armor he still had was tattered and bloodied, though only a little of that blood was his. The other survivor showed up wandering outside of Chadhurst a day later. He said almost exactly the same thing. However, the beast hasn't been seen since, so they assumed the Silverbloods managed to kill it or drive it off."

Raven shuddered and focused on keeping pace with him. When they reached the camp, Davon, Phendaril, and Alayne were standing near the horses. Gerrod's body, now headless, lay several feet away, Davon's brows pinched tightly as he stared at it. All three appeared immensely relieved when they saw her with Marek. Raven scanned over them. An elf and two humans. None of them Krivalen. She glanced down at the dead man's head, his face torn apart, the eyes missing. This wasn't a beast looking for a meal. This was something else.

"I don't think we need to worry about the horses," Raven stated. "I don't think food is what it's after."

"Then what does it want?" Alayne demanded, her voice tight with fear. She pointed at Gerrod. "He was already dead when he attacked us. What does that?"

Raven considered the hatred, anger, and pain she had felt in the creature. The eliket, if Marek was right, which evidence suggested he was. "It's after something more personal. Emotional."

Phendaril and Marek were eyeing her with disturbingly similar looks of curiosity. Davon's expression bordered on reverence, which wasn't all that comforting. She turned her attention to Alayne, whose demanding gaze was somehow easier to face.

"What is this thing?"

Raven glanced at Marek. "He can explain. I'm going to look for Ehric."

Marek stepped forward, silver eyes flashing in a manner that reminded her of the day he knocked her out and carried her off to Pellanth. "No. He's almost certainly dead."

"I'm afraid I agree with Marek," Alayne stated, her jaw clenching to fight back the moisture rising in her eyes.

Raven stepped away from Marek. Wary of him attempting to force his opinion on her with Silverblood magic the way he had that day. She was surprised that neither Davon nor Phendaril argued with her stated intention.

Davon's hand sank to his sword hilt. "I'll go with you."

Raven shook her head, keeping a close eye on Marek. "No. None of you are Silverblood. This thing gets inside your head somehow. You have no defenses against that." She regarded Marek. "The magic will come to your defense. I think that's how I survived it. Stay with them and keep an eye out for it. Don't let it get close to you. If I can't find Ehric quickly, I'll come back, and we'll get out of here."

She turned to the others. Phendaril held a hand out to her, and she automatically took it. Alayne and the rest conveniently chose that moment to return to the fire.

"Be careful." He moved close to her. "I've seen you do amazing things, but I feel like this is something different. Something darker."

She met his eyes. "I expected you to argue with my going." He took her other hand then, and she wondered, feeling the bandages against her skin, if it hurt him to do so.

"I want to argue. I really do. But you have proven

yourself time and again. It's time I trusted you to make your own decisions." He let go of one hand and reached up to cup her cheek, his palm warm on her face. "Don't you dare prove me wrong."

A little of Raven's fear melted before his adoring, worried gaze. He didn't hesitate to meet her halfway when she leaned in to kiss him. He slid his hand into her hair, the other moving around her waist to encourage her closer. He kissed her ardently then, like he expected it might be his last chance to do so. Perhaps it was.

When she pulled away, she felt a little stronger and more confident. Why a kiss should affect her so, she couldn't say, but she even managed a smile for him. Then, deliberately not saying anything, she turned and strode to the edge of the camp to search out Ehric's footprints.

"His tracks leave from there," Marek stated, coming over to join her. "I found them when I was going to search for you." He frowned when she sidestepped out of his easy reach but said nothing about it.

"Thank you." She inclined her head to him, hoping to convey her respect and gratitude for his rescue to ease the current mistrust. If he tried to knock her out now, she was confident he would be doing it to try to save her, but that wouldn't make it any less of a betrayal.

"Are you sure about this?" He kept his voice low as he asked. "You seemed rather turned around when I found you out there."

"I am... and I was. I have a better idea of what we're facing now than I did before. It got close enough to touch me earlier. I suspect it needs that physical contact to get around the protection of the Silverblood magic. I need to make sure that doesn't happen again. If I lose the trail or find Ehric dead, I'll come directly back here. I don't plan to go looking for trouble."

He gave a nod. "Then I will do my best to keep

anyone else here from dying if you promise to do the same for yourself."

"I will."

She shifted the weight of the bow and quiver, then trotted off to follow Ehric's footsteps into the darkness. It didn't take long for the tracking to become difficult as the trail wandered closer to some of the swamp pools. The glowing bugs were also more densely packed near the water, making it hard to breathe without the risk of inhaling them. She constantly had to wave them away from her face.

His trail led her around and through several pools before it turned her back toward the main path. She finally found him standing in the middle of the path, staring at nothing. Blood ran unchecked from a ragged cut down one arm, but he appeared otherwise unharmed. She reached out and took his wrist, dread forming a cold lump in her gut as she felt for a pulse.

"Ehric," she breathed, relief sweeping through her when she found the sign of life she'd hoped for.

He didn't do so much as blink in response. She started to reach into him with her magic when the sound of something larger moving down the path caught her attention. She was almost relieved to see a Silverblood warrior emerging from the shadows, a manageable enemy, at least until his companion joined him. With Ehric apparently comatose on his feet, she would have to deal with both of them alone.

The first one's eyes widened when she turned to face them. Then he smiled smugly as he strode forward, his long legs eating up the ground between them. "My idea to travel at night was the right one, I see."

"What's wrong with your friend?" The other, a stockier man with dark hair pulled into a high knot, was staring uneasily at Ehric as they approached.

Raven drew her sword. "He likes to sleep standing up."

The first held his hand up. "No need for that. We aren't here to kill you."

Raven forced a grin, hoping to unsettle them. "Maybe I'm here to kill you."

He shrugged, and they both drew their weapons. He carried a long sword that would add to his already greater reach. His companion carried a comparatively light battle axe, one that might be small enough to use as a throwing weapon, though it was plenty large enough for hand-to-hand combat as well.

She focused on her breathing, moving away from Ehric. Wayland's orders said to kill anyone with her, and he wasn't in a state to defend himself. No matter what came of this, she had to at least try to keep them from going after him.

With a quick, unexpected lunge, she drove the taller man back. He jumped away in surprise, raising his blade just in time to block her strike. Raven leapt to the side to keep herself out of range of the other man and swung again. The taller one took her bait, following as she moved away from Ehric toward the mist that crept in at the edge of the path. He matched her aggression, coming in fast with a fierce volley of attacks she managed to dodge or block and counter with equal ferocity.

Behind him, the other Silverblood hurried in, moving around to flank her. She kept him away with calculated direction changes, her circuitous route leading them to the edge of one of the pools. The game was exhausting, though. Trying to fight the first while avoiding the other left her zero room for error.

The taller man leapt in with a jab that turned into a twist to the side, blocking her planned move to get away from the one with the axe who was attempting another flanking maneuver. Raven changed her direction, darting forward instead. She felt a blade bite into her thigh as she narrowly avoided worse injury. The swordsman shifted to block her, and, this time, she altered course again in a different way, lunging toward him rather than trying to bolt away.

Her blade, aimed low, slipped in above his leg armor to one side of his groin, driving in deep. As she darted back out, he fell to one knee, crying out in agony. The other man's axe caught her with a glancing blow to the back of the arm. Her armor took the brunt of the strike, though she felt the steel edge open a cut where the armor didn't fully cover.

She hissed with the pain and bolted out into the mist, away from the injured Silverblood. The man with the axe gave chase.

Raven led him into heavier mist, losing herself amidst the strange, crooked trees. She quickly lost track of him, frequently stopping to listen for his breathing and footsteps. She could hear him pausing to do the same. The tall man's moans of pain were the loudest sound in the darkness. Her blade had gone deep, which meant the wound could easily be fatal.

Raven moved, stopped, listened, and moved again. She was making her way around back toward the injured man, intending to finish him off. Then his groans ceased. She hesitated, straining her hearing, but all she got was the breathing and footsteps of the other man navigating in the muck as he followed her trail. She waved the bugs away from her face and peered through the heavy mist. Something moved near where she had left the wounded Silverblood. She took a few steps that way, getting close enough to see his shape, standing now. Then the other Silverblood changed direction. She stopped next to a tree, listening as he cut around to where his companion was.

Raven crept closer still, getting near enough to make out more details of the swordsman as his companion crept cautiously toward him. The tall man would have been staring over her left shoulder had he eyes to stare with, but his sockets were empty, like Gerrod. Whatever haunted these woods had gotten to him.

The other Silverblood reached out, placing a hand on the tall man's arm. He didn't have time to react when his companion turned to face him because something else stepped out of the mist behind him.

CHAPTER SEVENTEEN

The creature emerged crouched on all fours, though the front limbs looked more like arms. External bone created a natural armor that extended along its arms, legs, back, and shoulders. That bone appeared chipped, cracked, and caked with dirt. The limbs were long. When it rose upright on its legs, it reached an easy seven feet tall, hovering over the stocky man. She could see every rib along its torso pressing against the grime-coated skin.

Long claws extended beyond the tips of its overlong fingers, and it closed these together, making a spearhead of the nails. Then it stabbed them through the Silverblood's back, piercing leather armor, flesh, and bone with such ease that its hand and part of its arm burst out the front. The man's mouth opened as if to scream, but his eyes emptied of life too quickly for him to do more than make a few gurgling noises.

The eliket, if that's what it was, lifted him in the air and flung him aside. Its long face, rotten vines tangled in the back-swept horns that crowned its forehead, swiveled toward her. It took two steps in her direction, making a strange chattering sound deep in its throat. Its eyes looked sunken, its cheeks hollow, but something about it struck her as eerily familiar.

Her moment of curious uncertainty was all the time

it needed. It flashed forward and swung into her with one long arm, sending her flying. Raven landed hard, losing her bow and quiver as she rolled. She came to a stop on her back, her whole body aching from the impact. She reached for her sword, but it was gone too. All she had left was her dagger, so she grabbed for that.

The beast dropped down over her, crouching so its face was only a few inches above hers. Then she saw it. The nostrils were little more than slits in its face. The eyes angled sharply up. Wash away the grime and put some flesh on its bones, and it was familiar. Something she had seen only in another's dream.

She gasped. "Acridan."

The creature drew back a few inches, its eyes, a solid metallic black from edge to edge, narrowed.

She spoke in elven, hoping it might recognize the words. "You're Acridan, aren't you? An Acridan Krivalen. But how?"

One of the clawed hands grabbed her wrist, and she was plunged into something like a dreamwalk, only this was a memory. Memories of its kind dying of disease, an illness introduced by humankind. Death was everywhere. Too many dead to Accept them all. It was dying too. Weak and sick, without hope. But somehow, it lived on. It and a few of its kin survived the illness, struggling back from the edge of death after the humans left.

They had barely regained the strength to start tending to their dead by the time some of the men returned. The three brothers who had taken the Krivalen magic and used it to remake themselves and several others. They began killing off the few weary survivors, so it fled with another, and the men gave chase. Long and far, they ran, fighting lingering weakness from the devastating illness. Raven felt the terror, the desperation, and the evolving hatred. Emotions it had never experienced like that before.

The men caught its companion collecting water from a stream and cut them down without mercy. A sense of overwhelming sorrow poured into her at being unable to Accept their spirit. It escaped again and came to the swamps. A dark place as unwelcoming to the humans as it was to the Acridan. It hid there, using Krivalen magic to avoid discovery, magic that woke the dormant fey magic that ran through the dank forest. Over time, the two magics mixed within it, changing it, making it something else, a beastly creature full of nothing but hatred and fear.

With a sensation like falling, Raven collapsed into herself again, back in the swamp forest. Tears streamed from her eyes as she stared at the beast still holding her pinned there.

"I'm so sorry," she murmured.

It met her eyes for several tense seconds more, then her vision changed again. Suddenly she was standing apart, looking at herself with the Acridan crouched over her. The creature moved back, sinking onto its heels as Raven stood up. As she watched, her other self drew her dagger and drove it into the Acridan's chest. It collapsed, and she placed a hand on its chest, drawing out its life. Accepting it.

When she returned to her body this time, the Acridan moved away from her and sank back on its heels the way it had in the vision.

Raven got to her feet and shook her head. "No. It doesn't have to be this way. I can help you heal."

The creature placed one muck-coated hand over its chest, the sharp claws as long as its fingers.

She reached into it with her magic. The anger and hatred were less powerful now, but the pain was greater. It suffered enormous physical agony. Every part of it hurt. Every joint and muscle ached. Its stomach cramped with the pain of hunger. Overshadowing it all was the misery of crushing loneliness. A longing to be among its own kind that could never be fulfilled. And yet it never let itself die. She understood that too. Synderis told her the Acridan believed that dying without being Accepted would leave their spirit trapped between worlds.

Raven felt tears running down her cheeks again. "You want me to Accept you?"

It made a soft noise in its throat, much like a purr. Its strange gaze sank to the dagger at her belt. Raven drew the weapon, and it moved its hand out of the way. It met her eyes, watching her as she came closer. As unfamiliar as its features were to her, she was certain hope and relief were in its expression. Even sitting back on its heels, it was nearly as tall as her.

She wiped at her eyes, her throat tightening. "You're sure?"

The Acridan stared up at her in silence, waiting.

Raven placed the tip of the blade between two ribs. It was easy to see where to put it with how gaunt the creature was. It continued to hold her gaze. She could think of nothing she wanted to do less at that moment than kill this being, the last of its kind. But how cruel would she have to be to deny it? Centuries of loneliness and pain could finally end.

She drew a deep breath, letting it out as she drove the blade in with all her strength, determined not to let it suffer more than necessary. Its expression softened, the tightness of pain and hatred leaving its features. Raven eased it to the ground, surprised at how little it weighed.

It was impossible not to recall the young stable hand when she placed her palm against its chest and prepared to pull out the dagger. The Acridan gave a slight nod, its eyelids sinking with the call of endless sleep. Raven drew the blade out as she moved her magic into the creature.

Rather than defend the Acridan, the Krivalen magic in it embraced hers, welcoming it and merging with it. If that wasn't proof enough that this was what it wanted, the rage and torment she had felt before were fading. The power that flowed into her when she opened herself to the creature rocked her back so hard she had to fight to keep the physical contact. It burned through her as though someone had set fire to her blood. The unexpected pain ripped a cry from her throat, and the forest went black.

She became aware that she was lying on her back with someone gently shaking her.

"Raven." Ehric's voice was thick with concern.

"Ehric." She blinked her eyes open, and he jerked away from her. "What is it?"

"Your eyes... just like your hair."

Raven sat up, panic spreading swiftly from her core. "What about them?"

He stood, offering her his hand as he did so. His gaze moved to her hair and back to her eyes. "The silver seems more intense but also much darker. Though it could just be the moonlight."

The panic intensified. Had any human or elf ever Accepted an Acridan? Synderis might know, though, in this case, that Acridan also carried fey magic in them. She was confident no one had Accepted an Acridan like this individual, possibly not even another Acridan. Would the fey magic affect her too? Not that she could do anything to change it now. There hadn't been much chance to think the situation through before she granted the tortured being its wish.

She took a deep breath and looked at the husk of the Acridan lying next to her, all muck-covered skin and bone. How could she have refused it? That kind of suffering was too much for any creature. Perhaps reminding it of what it was helped it to remember itself. It had certainly stopped it from killing her, but she hoped that had also allowed it to find some peace in the end.

Raven grabbed her dagger with one hand and took Ehric's hand with the other. As he helped her up, she realized the moonlight had broken through the overcast, enough so that she could clearly see his arm was still bleeding.

"We need to see to that wound." She winced as putting weight on her leg reminded her of the cut she had received fighting the Silverbloods. Her whole body ached, though she wasn't sure if that was more from the blow the Acridan dealt her or from the Acceptance process. A faint tingle still moved in her limbs that she was confident was from the Acceptance.

"How did you kill two Silverbloods and that thing?"

She exhaled a rough laugh. "You give me too much credit. It killed the Silverbloods, though I did help, I suppose. Then it asked me to kill it."

His brows pinched together. "Asked you?"

She placed a hand on his arm and looked around, spotting her bow and quiver, the arrows scattered across the ground. "Come. Help me gather my weapons so we can get back to camp."

The taller Silverblood had fallen and was still now. She assumed that happened when the Acridan died, probably the same instant Ehric woke from his strange trance. She avoided questions by telling him she needed all her senses to lead them back to the others. That was a lie, given that they were near the main path, but it allowed her a reprieve.

When they reached camp, the rest of their companions rushed over. Phendaril gave Ehric a quick embrace before Alayne wrapped her arms around the Stonebreaker in a mighty hug. Davon smiled at Raven, the confidence in the expression telling her he never doubted her return. He also didn't look bothered by the change in

her hair and eyes, though Marek and Phendaril regarded her with concern.

"You took its life?" The tone of Marek's question
said he wasn't asking if she merely killed it.

"It wanted me to. We can talk about it more later."

The unease didn't leave his regard, but Phendaril
was willing to accept her answer for the time being. He
limped past Marek and pulled her into a tight embrace.

"I won't lie. I was terrified you wouldn't come back."

Raven shifted to ease the pain from her bruised chest
where the Acridan had struck her, then she let herself lean
against him, stealing a moment of comfort. She glanced
over to see Alayne leading Ehric to the fire, where she sat
him down to look at his wound. Marek and Davon joined
them, Marek asking Ehric to explain what had happened.
Not surprisingly, Ehric had little to offer. He didn't
remember much until he woke to Raven's cry. He told
them about the two Silverbloods that were already dead
when he got to her, then started describing the body of
the Acridan, though he still called it the eliket.

Phendaril pushed her away, his gaze moving over
her to take in the cuts on her leg and arm. "You fought
Silverbloods?"

"Mm." She was exhausted. Now that she was safe, fatigue washed through her, making her unsteady on her feet.

"Are you all right?"

She nodded. Darkness swept up to meet her.

•

When Raven woke again, it was early morning. She felt
strong and refreshed, though she had only slept a few
hours. Her wounds from the nighttime encounters had
been bandaged. None of them hurt anymore. When she
sat up, she saw that everyone except Ehric was awake.
Raven pulled the wrap off her arm to find that the cut

had already healed. When she removed the one from her leg, the deeper gash there had nearly closed up.

"Milady." Davon sank to one knee next to her, the first to notice she was awake. "There's food and a warm fire. I can bring something to you if you like."

Raven allowed him to help her up, though she felt more than capable. Phendaril glanced over from where he stood, talking to Alayne at the edge of the camp. His eyes widened a fraction when he saw that she was up. She offered him a nod and a faint smile she hoped was reassuring before sitting next to Marek by the fire.

The adept looked her over once, his expression troubled. "You took the life of the eliket into you? Was that wise?"

Phendaril limped to them. His curious gaze told her he also wanted to know the answer to that question.

Raven sighed and stared into the fire. "The eliket, as you call it, wasn't some beast. It was an Acridan, altered by the native magic of this place."

"One of the beings that gave us the Silverblood magic?" Marek's brow furrowed with disbelief. "They died out hundreds of years ago."

Raven answered him with a sour look that she hoped conveyed both her disgust with the Brotherhood and her disinterest in explaining it at the moment. "It *was* Acridan. It wanted to die, and it wanted me to Accept its spirit. Whether or not it was a good idea remains to be seen, but it's already done." She pulled her hair forward. It was black as night, so black it almost had a hint of blue to it, but now the metallic silver shine was more intense than before. Her fingernails were the same silver-black. "Are my eyes this color now too?"

She looked up at Phendaril, who met her gaze and nodded.

She sighed. It was done.

"We should wake Ehric and get on the road."

The day was immaculate, with bright sunshine contrasting the bitter chill in the air. The group had dismounted, walking to give the horses a break from long hours at speed. Of the four of them, only Jael held the reins to his mount. Synderis and the other two Krivalen used a minuscule amount of magic to encourage their horses to stay close to them. They also influenced all four of them to keep them calm around Koshika. Although the animals were almost accustomed enough to her presence after a few days of travel together that it was no longer necessary.

Synderis listened to Jael tell of how he first met Raven in Manderly. Numerous revelations came out in the story. He now knew how she had come to know the Silverblood, Marek, and who the dead elf he had seen in her dream was. He had not quite realized how little contact she had with the rest of the world before that. In less than a year, it seemed, she had gone from a life of complete seclusion with her guardian, Jaecar, to this. In many ways, he did not know her that well.

Yet here he was, risking a great deal to help her. Was he right to do so? Telandora and Lindyl knew her even less, and they had come, but they wanted to change Eyl'Thelandra. He wasn't sure he did? For the elven people to have such a sanctuary was a precious thing in a world that could be extremely cruel. He had seen a hint of that cruelty, but only secondhand through dream-walks with Raven.

Like the other two, he wanted to expose the Broth-erhood's lies, and not just to make the world safer for Raven. Their power had gone unchecked for too long. Was there a way to do that without risking the safety of Eyl'Thelandra? Could they separate the two?

"Raven and Phendaril, it seems as if they quickly developed a significant rapport working together once she arrived in Manderly," Synderis observed when Jael finished.

Jael gave him a wary look but didn't attempt to avoid the subject. "Phendaril tried not to like her at first. He lost his former love in an awful way. It made him quite reluc-tant to risk his heart again. Given that their relationship essentially started with her saving him from two guards in Manderly, I don't think he ever had much of a chance."

They continued a little farther in silence, then Jael asked, "What is it that you hoped to hear?"

"He's just trying to reassure himself that Raven is in good hands," Telandora offered before Synderis could speak. "Even if they aren't his." She gave him a good-humored grin and wink.

Synderis answered her with an indulgent half-smile. To Jael, he said, "Tel isn't wrong."

Jael reached over to scratch his mount's neck, a faint smile curving his lips. "I can respect that."

"Do you..." Synderis trailed off, catching the sound of someone crying out in the distance.

Telandora and Lindyl had already stopped and were mounting up. Jael, who didn't share their enhanced hearing, gave Synderis a questioning glance, though he also halted to swing up on his horse.

"Sounds like someone's in trouble," Lindyl answered for him.

They urged the horses to a canter, Koshika loping along beside them with relative ease. The big cat
was built for speed and agility. When they neared the
source of the cry, they slowed their mounts. The meaty
thwacks of fists against flesh and accompanying grunts
of pain came from behind an old shack.

"Go see who's here," a man's voice ordered, hearing
the horses approach.

"I'm sure it's just riders passing on the road. Nothing to worry about," another man answered.

Telandora gestured with two fingers, indicating
Synderis and Jael should head around the building to
one side while she and Lindyl went the other way. They
raised the hoods of their cloaks before splitting up.

"Not feeling so pretty now, are we, ye pointy-eared
bastard," someone shouted.

Another thwack, followed by a grunt. Synderis
eased his sword from the sheath. Jael drew his bow, letting his horse fall back behind Synderis's. They circled
the building to where a group of seven human men
gathered around an elven male. The latter had taken a
substantial beating, given the blood and bruising to his
face. He hung in the arms of two of the men. Another
man with greying red beard and a bald pate had a fistful
of the elf's long hair in one hand and was about to slice
it off it with a dagger. He hesitated when they rode into
sight. Telandora and Lindyl rounded the other side of
the building in a similar configuration, her leading with
her blade out and Lindyl following with his bow ready.

"Bother off," a man shouted. He had a thin black
mustache that emphasized his sneer. "This doesn't concern you."

"Unless you want to help," another man offered,
gesturing to the elf.

An arrow flew from behind Synderis and knocked
the dagger from the hand of the balding man about to

cut off the elf's hair.

"What's your problem?" the man shouted, taking a menacing step toward Synderis. "This pointy bastard had the gall to smile at my sister. He needs to learn a lesson."

"I think you'll find us unsympathetic to your cause," Synderis answered, drawing back his hood.

Telandora did the same, though Jael and Lindyl didn't, choosing to keep their bows drawn and aimed. The balding man let go of the elf's hair and backed away from him. Two other men drew daggers, and Synderis offered them a cold smile.

"You're welcome to try."

Koshika arrived at the edge of the building's roof and snarled down at them. The men holding the elf dropped him. They dashed away from the big cat, whose coat had dimmed to a dirty green about the color of the moss on the roof. A few men turned to the man with the mustache who had spoken first as if waiting for guidance.

The man glared around at them, then looked up at Koshika. He retreated a few steps. "You can have the bastard, but if he ever looks at my sister again, he's dead."

With that, he turned and jogged away, his companions following. A few cast furtive glances back as if they feared pursuit. The way Synderis's blood boiled, he longed to give it to them, but others needed tending to. He and Telandora dismounted while Jael and Lindyl kept their bows trained on the retreating men. On the roof, Koshika lay down and proceeded to groom one paw as though nothing of note had occurred. He could feel heightened irritation from her, probably brought on by the tension and the scent of the man's blood, but she was going to play it cool and keep an eye on things.

The young elven man remained knelt where they had dropped him as though he lacked the strength to stand alone. He glanced up at them. One eye was swollen mostly shut.

"Thanks. I appreciate the help, though I suspect it will only be worse next time." He turned to spit blood in the direction the men had gone.

Synderis took one arm and Telandora the other. They lifted him up and back a few steps so he could lean against the side of the run-down building.

"This was all for smiling at some man's sister?" Dark anger swirled in Telandora's eyes as she asked.

"Wasn't even her I was smiling at," he answered, pulling a corner of his shirt up and bending his head down to wipe away blood running from a cut over one eyebrow.

Now that the men were out of sight, Jael and Lindyl dismounted and joined them, drawing back their hoods. Lindyl dug a cloth out of his pack and handed it to the young elf. He accepted it with a muttered thanks, pressing it to the wound, and looked around at them more closely now.

"They must have beat me worse than I thought because I would swear three of you is Silverblood elves."

Synderis managed a ghost of a smile, trying to ignore the sick feeling in his gut. "We are. You're in no shape to be left alone. Is there someone we can take you to?"

He spit more blood before answering. "I'm Jeys. My family has a house on the edge of the elven slums around the bend."

Synderis glanced at Jael for guidance.

"Wretched little town called Dince," Jael offered. "We were going to skirt around it, but I can take him home if you three want to wait."

Synderis nodded. "We'll accompany you far enough to see the edge of town. Make sure there aren't any surprises waiting."

Jael gave a quick nod of agreement. They helped Jeys clean up before getting him mounted behind Jael on his horse. They kept to the trees going around the bend, so the three Krivalen could stay out of sight. Jael rode alone from there toward the edge of a run-down town. The streets in the elven slums were thick with mud, and Synderis could smell the stink from where they waited. The houses he could see were in ill repair, most poorly prepared for the coming winter, and many listed heavily to one side or another.

When Jael returned alone about an hour later, the light was starting to dim with the arrival of evening. His jaw clenched with the same unassuaged anger that had set Synderis pacing the whole time he was gone.

"Do many elves live like this?" Telandora demanded as soon as he reached them.

Jael's eyes narrowed. "Yes, many elves do," he snapped. "We can't all be hidden away in some secret paradise, free to use forbidden magic and frolic with our forest pets."

Telandora's hand dropped to her sword. Synderis stepped between them, and Lindyl moved up behind her, placing a hand on one shoulder.

Confident the message was clear, Synderis faced Jael. "Is Jeys home safe?"

Jael didn't answer immediately. The anger coming off him was almost palpable, so Synderis used the Krivalen magic to project a hint of calm into him, diverting a little of it back to Telandora as well.

Jael heaved a deep breath and blew it out. "He's home. As to safe, I doubt any of them will ever be safe there."

Synderis lowered his gaze and swallowed back against the guilt that rose in him. Jael was right. They had led an easy life by most any measure. Sure, they weren't allowed to leave Eyl'Thelandra, but that was a minuscule sacrifice for an otherwise pleasant existence. Of course, they had broken that rule now, so they didn't get to expect things to be easy anymore. In some ways, they were as naïve as Raven had been when she left her hidden home in the woods.

He placed a hand on Jael's arm. "One battle at a time."

Jael stared at nothing for a moment, then lowered his gaze to look at the hand on his arm and nodded. "Yes. We need to find someplace to camp away from here before it gets dark."

Telandora appeared calmer now, though she cast him a shrewd look as she mounted up, telling him she suspected he had a hand in that. He shrugged and gave her a wry smile in return.

Jael led them into the trees, moving away from the main road. It was difficult for Synderis to turn his back on the situation they were leaving behind. He had a feeling it was hard for all of them. The young elf expected this kind of treatment or worse to come again. That was no way to live. It was foolish to believe they could do anything about it now, however. As he had told Jael, they had to focus on one battle at a time.

They kept a swift pace, weaving through the trees to keep out of sight of the village. Helping Jeys was risk enough for one day. They didn't need to draw any more attention to themselves.

A meadow opened ahead of them, the dry golden grasses blanketed with fallen leaves from the surrounding trees. In the lead, Jael's mare was stepping out past the last trees bordering the clearing when Koshika snarled and bolted off to one side, startling Synderis's mount even with the calming influence of his magic. He gripped with his legs as the horse leapt in the opposite direction and pulled around on one rein, circling the animal quickly to regain control.

The other three reined in their mounts, their attention shifting to him. Across the meadow, a group of mounted men emerged from the trees.

"Trouble," Synderis hissed, pulling his hood up.

The others did the same as they turned forward again.

Five men in matching green-and-black livery trotted their horses across the clearing. They rode in a wedge formation around a man with several insignia of rank or reward embroidered upon his surcoat. When he halted his mount about ten feet from Jael, the other four fell into line to either side of him, stopping their mounts a few strides back to maintain their order.

The leader's blond mustache lifted with his sneer. "We got word of four pointies stirring up trouble in the town. Not much chance you aren't them." He spat on the ground, then glanced over them with open disdain. "Don't suppose you'll come along peacefully."

"We've done nothing wrong," Jael countered.

His voice was calm, but he rested his right hand on his thigh, close to the hilt of his sword. Synderis followed his example, subtly adjusting his position to make drawing his blade easier. They were human, so they wouldn't be as fast as Jael was, let alone be any match for three Krivalen, but there was no point in taking risks.

"That's my job to decide." He looked around at the rest of them, licking his lips when his gaze settled briefly on Telandora. "Pull your hoods back."

Synderis exhaled softly. He saw no way this could end peacefully.

CHAPTER NINETEEN

Synderis could hear Koshika's low growling coming from the tree she had chosen. Had her coat changed again to match the woods around them? He didn't dare look and risk giving her away.

"We're merely passing through," Jael tried again. "We want no trouble."

The leader tilted his head, his eyes narrowing. "And you can go on your way once you all comply with orders."

Jael's voice hardened as he too seemed to accept that this wouldn't end peacefully. "We're not asking for your permission."

Synderis heard something in the trees off to the left, a twig cracking underfoot, followed by the sound of a crossbow firing. He ducked low over his mount's neck. The bolt skimmed through the air above his back at what would have been chest level mere seconds ago. Lucky for him, he didn't sit up again right away. An answering arrow flew past from the other direction. The attacker in the trees twisted out of the path of the return fire a little too fast for someone with ordinary human reflexes.

Synderis cast Telandora a questioning look for her risky return shot as he slid from his mount and drew his sword. She merely shrugged.

Jael was already out in the clearing, engaged in

mounted combat with the leader of the five men. Lindyl had dismounted and joined him, drawing off two of the others. One of the others kicked his horse hard, charging at Synderis. Telandora nocked a second arrow, preparing to fire, but Koshika leapt onto him from above before she could release it, tearing him off the back of his mount.

With that threat handled, Telandora turned her attention to the others ahead of them. Synderis sprinted in the direction of the attacker in the trees. It didn't come as a surprise when the man who stepped out to meet his charge was a Silverblood. Given the speed with which he dodged Telandora's shot, he had to be that or elven. The latter was unlikely in this situation.

Synderis lunged at him without hesitation, hoping to throw him off balance. The Silverblood managed to parry his first strike. He was unprepared for the speed of the following attacks, however, and fell back, eyes widening with surprise as Synderis forced him onto the defensive. The sound of another crossbow firing caught Synderis's attention, and he twisted to one side. He wasn't fast enough this time. The bolt sliced along his cheek and ear, ripping back his hood.

The pain heightened his focus. He spotted the second Silverblood a little farther out, leaning against a tree as he hurried to reload his crossbow. The man he had already engaged with looked more surprised now that he could see what he was fighting. Then his eyes narrowed, his lip curling in disgust, and he charged in.

Synderis had to put most of his effort into his opponent, blocking the man's lightning-fast attacks while searching for an opening. The Silverblood was well-trained in utilizing the speed and strength of his magic enhancements. The added complication of keeping his opponent between himself and the man with the crossbow now required him to split his attention. The sting of the cut and the warm blood trickling down the side of his face and neck were enough to keep him cognizant of that danger, but the odds weren't in his favor.

Unfortunately, the man he fought was also keenly aware of the problem. With each strike, he tried to maneuver Synderis into a vulnerable position, directing his attacks in such a way as to provide a clear target for his companion. The effort led the Silverblood to take risks, however, and Synderis caught him with a deep cut to the side, near the same place Raven's wound had been when she first arrived in Eyl'Thelandra. They exchanged several more blows, the Silverblood struggling to hold up his half of the battle between the injury and his human disadvantage. The same magic changed them both, but only one of them had the extra advantage of elven agility and speed.

An animal roar proceeded Koshika's charge. The sound startled Synderis's opponent, dragging his attention away for a split second of opportunity. Synderis brought his elven blade up at an angle. The edge cut into the Silverblood's chest near the armpit and continued through the front of his neck, shearing off the lower right side of his jaw.

When the man fell, Synderis had a clear view of the other Silverblood turning his crossbow on Koshika. Fear stole his breath away at seeing the big cat sprinting straight into the line of fire. He grabbed a dagger from his belt and threw it, catching the crossbowman in one shoulder. An arrow came from behind him and sank deep into the other side of the man's chest. His finger jerked on the trigger of the crossbow. Koshika leapt out of the way, snarling at the bolt when it hit the ground beside her.

The man staggered and fell. The instant he hit the dirt, Koshika lost interest and changed direction. She trotted over to Synderis, who sank a trembling hand into her feathers with a surge of relief. He turned to take stock of the situation. Jael, who had apparently fired the last shot, lowered his bow. Synderis nodded his gratitude to the other elf, not quite ready to speak. Seeing the big cat threatened frightened him more than he would have expected. She was his companion, but he was only now realizing how deep that bond went.

Farther back, Lindyl was walking among the fallen guards. He stopped next to one and knelt, placing a hand on the man's chest. Telandora, who stood a few feet behind him, met Synderis's eyes, a question in her look. After a moment's hesitation, he gave a nod. It was fitting to honor one's enemies. They had not done so before, and the choice nagged at him. This time, they would handle it differently.

He turned back to the Silverbloods. It was too late for the man at his feet, so he walked to the other. The man had his fingers around the arrow, trying to pull it free, but he was already too weak from his injuries. His grip on the shaft slackened, and his hand sank to the ground at his side. As his eyes started to lose focus, Synderis knelt next to him, murmuring a few words of passing in Elvish as he placed his palm against the Silverbloods chest and Accepted the departing spirit. It was easy enough to avoid triggering the magic in the other man to react in his defense. This wasn't a hostile act. It was a generous and honorable one. The Acridan had believed that, and the elves of Eyl'Thelandra believed it too.

"We should get out of here," Jael stated, a hint of unease apparent in the way he avoided looking at Synderis after he Accepted the Silverblood.

Synderis appreciated that the other elf had at least waited for him to finish before saying anything. He was developing a great deal of respect for Jael. "Yes, we should."

They rejoined the other two.

Telandora was standing up from Accepting another of the guards. She glanced at Synderis and smiled wryly. "You've got a bit of a scratch there, Syn. Looks like you came close to losing an ear."

He answered with a weary smirk that made the cut hurt more. "It can wait. Anyone else hurt?"

"Also a scratch," Lindyl commented, taking hold of his horse's reins. Blood trickled down his left forearm from a cut near the elbow. "We can deal with it when we're away from here."

"A sound plan," Jael agreed as he mounted up.

They were galloping away from the scene within minutes, Jael leading the way. They cut across the river in the early evening, finding a shallow spot to ride through rather than risking the bridge on the main road. It was dark when they finally stopped to make camp, staying away from more established camping sites along the route. They made a small fire, more for the purpose of caring for wounds than cooking. They had foraged enough in their earlier travels that cooking wasn't necessary.

Telandora unsurprisingly put her attention to Lindyl's injury first, which left Jael tending the slice along Synderis's cheek and ear. The other elf wore an amused smirk as he wiped away the blood with a clean rag from his pack. Synderis could only sit still for so long before he had to question it.

He cocked an eyebrow at Jael. "You find this humorous somehow?"

"Don't talk. You'll make it bleed again." The other elf breathed a small laugh then. "I couldn't help wondering if perhaps you did this to yourself. Trying to compete with Phendaril for the role of ruggedly handsome elven warrior in Raven's heart."

Synderis cracked an unintentional smile.

"No smiling, either."

Telandora glanced over at them and grinned. "I like it, Syn. It's a good look for you."

He rolled his eyes at her, trying hard to keep still while Jael finished cleaning the wound. If he were to be honest, he had no desire to compete for any position in Raven's heart. It wasn't realistic to think that he should have to anyhow. Her heart had more than enough love in it for both of them. It was her life, and what she wanted it to be would decide who she had room for in it. For the moment, whether she had room for them both or not, he suspected she needed them both. Though it was going to be extraordinarily awkward if she disagreed.

"That's the best I can do now, other than putting some of Synal's salve on it. Her treatments are miraculous. Between that and you being a Silverblood elf, this should be well on its way to healing by morning." Jael bent over to dig into his pack.

"Krivalen," Synderis corrected. He could no longer stomach being called a Silverblood. "Silverblood is the name humans gave to the magic they took from the Acridans."

Jael sat up again, opening a small container. He scooped up some of the translucent green substance with one finger, then closed it and tossed it to Telandora. She caught it and offered a nod of gratitude. He began to wipe the salve over Synderis's wound.

"I know that," Jael said, catching Synderis by surprise. "I also know your people prefer to keep those things secret, hence my avoidance of the term."

Lindyl looked over at him, curiosity lining his brow. "What else do you know?"

The amused smirk returned. "Not a great deal. I did travel with an elf from Eyl'Thelandra for a time. He tried to convince me to go there and start a better life for myself."

"And you turned him down?" Synderis couldn't keep the incredulity from his tone. Why would anyone trade that for this?

Jael met his eyes and pressed his lips together before answering, a hint of regret in his expression. "I wanted to go. I truly did. It sounded like a paradise. But there were people out here who needed me. People like Karsima, Alayne, and Phendaril, were all counting on me. People with whom I shared a common dream." He wiped the excess salve from his finger on the rag, then went to set a small piece of wood on the fire. "Not all decisions are easily made."

"Feylarin?" Synderis posited.

Jael's warm smile was answer enough. "I suppose you would know him."

"Not well, but I have met him. One of a small number who have gone out into the world to bring back like-minded others."

A hint of sorrow stole across Jael's features. "Believe me, I was of a like mind, but my heart felt otherwise."

"I can't imagine anyone would fault you for that," Telandora said softly in the ensuing silence, her expression hidden from him in the shadows beyond the firelight.

"No," Synderis agreed, sinking his hand into Koshika's fur as she curled up next to him now that Jael had moved away.

Jael met Synderis's eyes. "I get the feeling Raven will be happy to see you." He paused to draw a breath, his brows pinching together. "And it eases my heart to know that the elf she broke Phendaril's heart for is at least someone of worth."

Synderis bowed his head, turning his gaze into the fire. "Thank you."

Jael stood. "We should all get some rest. I'll take first watch." He turned towards the dark woods but didn't move. "You know, I thought you were looting the corpses earlier before I realized what you were actually doing. Feylarin explained the act of Accepting to me, though it still unnerves me, just to see the brighter silver in your eyes and hair and know how it came to be." He glanced at all three of them as if noticing that subtle change again. "I know, to you, it is a way of honoring those who die, though I have some trouble seeing how those men deserved to be honored."

"There is something good in everyone, no matter how deeply it is buried," Telandora stated, her tone gentle but confident.

Synderis was silent as he suppressed a shudder, the memory of his blade shearing off part of the Silverblood's jaw etched horrifically in his mind.

Jael only nodded, and Synderis watched him walk into the trees. If Phendaril had such friends as this, he was also someone of worth. That thought was both comforting and a little unsettling.

They waited until after nightfall to make their way into Chadhurst. More people were passing in and out of the city than Raven could bring herself to count. Even in full dark, when they finally dared to emerge from the edge of the woods, the number of travelers was above her comfort level. Though, if she were being honest about it, anyone she didn't know was above her comfort level.

They had discussed, over the course of the last few days, how they would get Marek and her into the city unchallenged. Given Wayland's active manhunt, a couple of hooded figures would almost certainly be questioned before being allowed to pass through the gate. She couldn't enter without some concealment because, given the rarity of *Silverblood* half-elven females, she was obviously the individual the Brotherhood was hunting for.

Raven watched from the shadows as Alayne rode confidently to the gate along with Phendaril, Davon, and Ehric, all with their hoods up. They led along with them three riderless horses. Another trio of travelers on foot was being questioned by the guards when Alayne tried to ride past them. The nearer of the two guards glanced up at her, mouth gaping open in disbelief at her audacity. When she didn't look at him or slow her mount, he closed his mouth and strode over to take hold of her reins.

"I don't know who you are, but you and your companions can't march in like you own the city."

"Can't we?" she demanded. "Do you know who I am?"

His eyes narrowed as he peered up into her hood. "Not a clue."

She pulled the hood back with a fierce jerk, looking convincingly incensed. "I'm Alayne Valassian, King Navaran's niece."

The man stared up at her a moment, then he glanced at his companion, who had just finished giving the other group permission to enter.

He looked up at her and shrugged. "Could be."

She held up her hand, displaying the signet ring that represented her family line. The king's family line.

The guard holding her reins heaved a sigh. "It doesn't matter who you are. Your companions, who are not related to the king, must go through the same process as everyone else. Pull back your hoods, give us your names and your business in the city."

"That's ridiculous," Alayne snapped, raising her voice more sharply than Raven had ever heard, drawing backward glances from the trio heading into town. "Where's the guard captain? My companions and I will be allowed our privacy."

Another two guards emerged from the gatehouse. One of them, wearing a fair number of ranking emblems on his surcoat, leaned against the door frame, folding his arms over his chest. When Alayne tried to yank the reins away from the guard holding her back, he pushed off from the frame and strolled over.

"Lady Valassian," he greeted her, a certain weariness in his deep voice. "While I do recognize you, I'm afraid I can only allow you through on the merit of your name. Your companions must go through the same process as everyone else."

She pressed her lips together, scowling down at him. "This is absurd."

While all eyes were on Alayne, and with the darkness for cover, Raven and Marek started climbing the city wall, finding purchase between the stones. Raven didn't just feel stronger than normal. She felt strangely powerful. The sensation was unnerving. There wasn't time now to fret over it, but the temptation to reach out to Synderis in the night and talk to him about the Acridan was becoming harder to resist. If not for Wayland...

With little effort, she overtook Marek and, after a quick glance to make sure no one was around, pulled herself over the battlement and onto the flat walk behind it. Marek joined her moments later while she plotted the best way down the other side.

"You did that with remarkable ease," he whispered.

"As did you." Though she tried to be dismissive, his dubious look left her feeling unsettled. She turned her attention to the task at hand.

After briefly scanning the street below, Raven pointed to a low storage building alongside the wall. Directly across from it was the entrance to a narrow alleyway that could keep them out of sight long enough to get away from the gate. From there, they could find a place to merge with the others farther up along the main street. Marek nodded agreement. He started to move, pausing when she didn't follow.

She tilted her ear back toward the gate, where she could still clearly hear Alayne and the guards talking.

"You've got three extra horses. What happened to the rest of your party?" the guard captain was asking.

"We were attacked by some beast on the swamp road," Alayne answered, her tone defensive and a little haughty. Just enough to be sure the guards kept their attention on her party and not elsewhere.

"No one with any sense takes that route. Why didn't you and your... peculiar collection of companions take the south road?"

They must have pulled their hoods down if he had seen enough to deem them an unusual group. Though she couldn't help wondering if it was the presence of an elf and a Stonebreaker in the party or the fact that they were reasonably well-armed that he found unusual.

"My friend had business in Finyel."

Raven could imagine her gesturing to Phendaril. Finyel hadn't struck her as the kind of village humans typically had dealings in.

"Raven," Marek hissed softly.

The guard captain sounded civil enough. She doubted that he would detain the others much longer. They had no Silverbloods among them, and with Alayne's familial relationship to the king, little good was likely to come of harassing them needlessly. Satisfied that the others would soon join them, she turned to Marek and nodded.

They dropped to the roof of the low storage building and down to the street from there, darting quickly into the alley when they were sure no one was watching. Other than a few beggars huddled for warmth and a fair assembly of rats, the alley was quiet. Quiet and a bit rancid. Raven exhaled through her nose, trying to chase away the stink of the city. Mostly, it smelled like horse manure and urine, though the alley had a stench of rot to add to the mix, making it even less tolerable.

At the first opportunity, they turned toward the main street, finding a dark corner to wait in where they would be able to see the others coming. Raven sat on a barrel pushed up against the wall of the building. She drew her knees in to her chest and wrapping her arms around them as she watched for their companions. Marek leaned on the wall next to the barrels she had made a seat of. He stared at her with a strange intensity.

"What?" she whispered.

"You know, in the moonlight there are reflective flecks in your irises now, like stars in a silver-black night sky." He tilted his head to one side, his expression softening.

"Don't say that like you find it beautiful," she grumbled, pulling her knees in tighter.

"I do."

She gave him a stern look. "Don't."

"What happened when you took the spirit of the eliket into you? What did it feel like?"

Raven squirmed a little in her seat. This line of conversation was going to creep dangerously close to things she didn't want him to know. If he desired her confidence, he should never have given her to Wayland. That wasn't something she was likely to forget.

"Later," she said, evading the question.

For a few seconds, he was quiet, and she thought he might stay that way, then he started watching her again. "Are you and Phendaril reconciled? You seem to have gotten past whatever or whoever came between you."

Raven turned a little away from him, not wanting him to see how uncomfortable the topic made her. "You could have found a more appropriate time over the last several days to ask me these things."

"When has Phendaril not been by your side since the eliket attacked? You seem inseparable."

He was right. They had been together nearly every waking moment since that encounter. They had not kissed again—not for lack of wanting on her part or his, she was reasonably sure. A sense of uncertainty created a rift between them that she was afraid to cross again. Where would it stop if she dared to let that intimacy return? She longed for him to kiss and hold her. Synderis wasn't here. He had encouraged her to be with Phendaril, but where did it end? Where was the line drawn? Was there a line?

"Who is it that haunts your thoughts?"

"Marek," she hissed, irritation providing a brief release from her tumultuous thoughts. She spotted their companions then, riding along slowly with the extra horses in tow, and met Marek's eyes, gesturing toward the street with a jerk of her head. "Time to go."

Marek glanced out, spotting them quickly. "Later, then."

He pulled his hood further forward before moving casually into the evening street. He walked at a measured pace, allowing the group of riders to start catching up with him. When they were past her hiding spot, Raven did the same, though she set her pace a little faster so that she would eventually overtake them if they stayed on this route for long.

About the time they overtook Marek, they turned down another street. Raven did the same, closing the last distance to wander up alongside Cyrleth. Phendaril let go of the black's reins when she reached up, letting her take them. When she dared to glance up at him, he smiled at her, genuine warmth in the expression that caused a flutter in her chest. Was love always this difficult, or was she doing something wrong?

She touched the arrowhead pendant. Odd that it had turned into a symbol for both of them. One male had carved it for her. The other had shown her how to make it into a tool to protect her dreams from Wayland. She'd become used to seeing Synderis every night in her dreams. It made his absence much more bearable. But now...

The group continued along a maze of streets for a time. Alayne knew all the routes to keep them away from guards and the majority of prying eyes. Raven stayed on the ground, walking between Cyrleth and Phendaril's horse where she wouldn't be easily seen. Her hood was up, but that was more likely to draw the attention of the guards. Marek was also walking alongside his horse, letting the group of animals obscure him from view. Alayne's careful navigation would hopefully be enough to get them to their destination without trouble.

Eventually, they angled the horses across the street to stop behind a large building with ornate carved wood ornamentation generously distributed over the entirety of the exterior. The fancy woodwork and bright colors—red, blue, orange, and even splashes of gold—made it stand out amidst the tame décor of its neighbors. It struck Raven as a rather flamboyant destination for a group attempting to remain unnoticed, but this was Alayne's former home. They would trust her to manage this.

Alayne disappeared through double doors at the back of the building. It was all Raven could do not to chew at her lip or wring her hands while they waited. She might feel more powerful than she ever had before, but that didn't mean she could protect herself and everyone with her if things went badly. They were all here for her, and they had already lost Gerrod. If something happened to any of the rest of them, even Marek, it would weigh heavily on her. Enough lives had ended because of her.

A hand settled on her shoulder. She turned to see Phendaril standing there.

"Are you all right?"

She glanced around them, catching Marek and Davon as they hastily looked away. Ehric was watching them openly, concern in his eyes.

"I don't feel like we should be here. This extremely remote chance at some freedom is just putting you all at risk."

His indulgent smile made her face grow warm.

"We're putting ourselves at risk. Stop taking credit

for our choices." His tone was gentle, taking the edge off his words.

She glanced away, only to catch Ehric's nod of agreement. She made a point of not looking at the other two men, reasonably sure they would have the gall to agree.

"But why?" She met his eyes, realizing it was a foolish question as soon as she asked it. The open affection in his gaze was all the answer she needed.

"They're ready," Alayne declared, striding up to them. "You have two adjacent rooms on the second floor." She handed two keys to Phendaril. "I expect you can manage room assignments." Her gaze flickered briefly from Phendaril to Raven and back as she said the last. "All I ask is that you not leave Raven alone tonight."

"What about you?" Marek asked, a hard edge to his tone that Raven suspected had to do with her putting Phendaril in charge of divvying up who would stay in the two rooms.

"I am going to the castle to stay in my rooms there. I want to catch my uncle first thing in the morning. The longer we linger here, the greater our chances of running into trouble." She swung up on her mount and then met Raven's eyes.

Raven dug into her pack and pulled out the leather case that held Jaecar's papers. It was almost painful to hand them up to her. She let go reluctantly.

Alayne took the case and tucked it in one of her saddlebags. "I'll take good care of them. Stay out of sight until I'm back."

With that, Alayne trotted off. Two youths, a boy and a girl of about thirteen or fourteen came from the rear of the stable alongside the inn. Phendaril gave them his horse and Gerrod's before turning to the others.

"Ehric and Davon, can I trust the two of you to get the rest of the horses to the stable while I accompany these two inside."

Meaning her and Marek, though she suspected he was avoiding names in case any eavesdroppers lurked about. Davon and Ehric took the remaining animals. Raven lingered a moment, scratching Cyrleth behind the ears before she turned to follow Phendaril inside, Marek hovering close beside her.

The inn's interior was no less garish than the exterior, awash with lavish decor accented in red and gold. Raven didn't see much of it, however, as they were greeted inside the door by a burly man who stepped in front of them, making a wall of himself. He put a hand on Phendaril's chest to stop him. The man glanced down at Phendaril's braced leg and grunted.

"The other two taking care of your horses?"

Phendaril gave a nod. Raven kept her head down, and her hood pulled forward, aware that Marek was doing the same beside her.

"Good. Go up these stairs." He pointed to a dark staircase on their left. "First two doors on the left. Alayne said there was a regular human among you. Send him down if you need food. The owner is fond of Alayne, so you won't be harassed. But this is an upscale establishment, meaning no elves, no Stonebreakers, and no whatever you two in the rear are in the common areas. Get my meaning?"

Raven got his meaning well enough that she wanted to shove it back down his throat. She made herself stay silent. The fact that they wouldn't be bothered here was undoubtedly the reason Alayne had chosen the place. That was worth a little insult.

"Understood," Phendaril answered, his sharp tone telling her he appreciated the message no more than she did.

The man gestured up the stairs. "I'll direct the other two up when they come in."

They followed Phendaril up to the second floor. When he unlocked the first room and opened the door, Raven was surprised by both the size of the room and its fine appointments. A big four-poster bed stood against one wall, and a couple of chairs for sitting were positioned beside a large fireplace in which a fire already burned. The linens and furnishings appeared almost as expensive as those in Darrenton's manor. The next room had two slightly smaller, though still as luxurious looking, beds and a similar sitting area near the fireplace.

Phendaril handed one key to Raven. "The first room is yours, but it isn't safe for you to be alone. You can decide who else will sleep there. There's more than enough room near the fire for someone to set up a bed on the floor."

Raven disliked Marek's knowing look. She accepted the key, closing her hand around it tightly enough that its edges bit into her palm. "Might I have a few minutes to myself first?"

"If you wish it."

She nodded. "I do."

Raven retreated to the first room and shut the door behind her. She set the key absently on a side table and then curled into one of the chairs by the fire. The blaze crackled softly as if talking to itself. She took off the arrowhead pendant and folded her hands around it, staring deep into those flickering flames.

For someone who had spent most of her life wandering the woods near that remote keep all by herself, it surprised her how much she had come to dislike being alone.

A knock on the room door broke Raven from her thoughts. She wasn't sure how long she had been staring into the fire, but she didn't feel inclined to move. After a few seconds, the door cracked open. She glanced over her shoulder to see Davon leaning in.

"Milady, I have food if you're hungry."

"Thank you, Davon. Could you set it on the table?" She turned back to the fire.

He was silent as he brought the meal in and set it down as directed. The aromas woke her taste buds, but she didn't have the desire to go investigate yet.

"Would you like me to stay?"

"No, thank you, Davon."

"Should I send someone else over?"

She exhaled a soft breath. "No, thank you."

"Milady—"

"No," she repeated more firmly this time.

"Of course, milady."

After a moment of silent hesitation, in which the pressure of his desire to say more filled the room, he turned and left her alone with her thoughts. The mouth-watering aromas of fine-cooked food wafted from the plate.

The quiet only lasted for a few minutes before someone else knocked. When she didn't say anything, the door opened. She continued looking into the fire. She recognized the new pattern of Phendaril's footsteps, changed by the brace, as he entered and closed them in together. He brought the plate of food over and set it on the table next to her.

"I'm not that hungry."

He limped around in front of her chair, where she had no choice but to look at him. "Are you certain? I've already had some, and it was as delicious as this place is gaudy."

She couldn't stop a smile.

"I can send someone else if it's the company you object to. Ehric or Davon, perhaps."

Not Marek. He would never suggest Marek. "No. You're welcome to sit if you want." She gestured to the other chair in a manner that was more dismissive than intended.

His gaze caught upon the pendant in her hand, but he didn't remark upon it. Did he wonder if she thought of Synderis?

"The main dish is exquisite. Some sublime preparation of duck." He sat in the chair and leaned over to cut away a piece of the meat, which he offered her on the end of a finely made fork.

Raven laughed softly. "Will you feed me all of my supper?"

He grinned. "Only if you'll let me."

She smiled and shook her head at him, taking the fork so she might feed the morsel to herself. The alternative was too intimate, and she was too confused. As he had said, it was sublime. Possibly the best bite of anything she had ever tasted. A small sound of delight escaped her lips, and Phendaril smirked.

"I told you so."

"Don't be smug." She left the pendant in her lap and leaned over the platter to cut away a second bite.

"Who's paying for this?"

"Alayne assured me all our needs and expenses were covered. I didn't press her for more."

Raven swallowed another bite of something she wasn't even sure what was, though she didn't much care. It was delicious. "Did you get enough to eat?"

"I did, thank you. Though, if you feel like you can't eat it all, I'd be happy to assist."

She raised one eyebrow at him, giving him a look of mock gratitude. "So generous of you."

Yet another knock on the door came then. Phendaril got up and answered it. Ehric stood outside holding a decanter of wine and two goblets.

"They brought three decanters and five goblets to the other room. I thought you two might appreciate one." In a lower voice, perhaps forgetting her Krivalen-enhanced hearing, he asked, "Is she all right?"

"I think she just needed some time alone," Phendaril answered.

"Good thing you're here, then," Ehric replied, a hint of good-natured sarcasm in his tone.

Raven smiled to herself. Ehric was a good man and an excellent warrior. It was nice to have him there.

"Thank you, Ehric. You may go." The smile in Phendaril's voice as he dismissed the Stonebreaker made her wonder what *unspoken* exchange may have passed between them.

Phendaril shut the door and brought the decanter and goblets back. He set them down on the table and filled the one closest to her.

"Do you want me to go?"

A simple question that caused a tightening of the painful knot in her chest. She did, and she didn't. Knowing how it would sadden and worry him if she sent him away, Raven took the decanter from him and gestured to the other chair. When he went to sit again, she filled his goblet. She finished the meal, sharing a few choice morsels with him to little objection on his part. When she was done, she carried the plate to the table by the door. He refilled her wine when she curled back into the chair, and it surprised her to see that the decanter was over half empty. Though that did explain the warmth and calm that suffused her now.

"You lived in this city with Karsima?"

He took a drink and then nodded. "Yes, for a few years."

"Before Alayne, was there ever a time the two of you..." She wasn't sure how to phrase it, so she trailed off, hoping he would fill in the blanks.

He gave a laugh. "Karsima and I? No. She has always been one to appreciate appearances, regardless of gender, but she never had any interest in the opposite sex beyond friendship."

"What about you? Did you have interest in her?"

Phendaril smirked. "No. She's pretty enough, but her ears are much too round for my taste." He gave Raven a wink. "Besides, I'm more attracted to darker hair. Nothing is more beautiful than glossy silver-black locks and eyes that reflect light like fine blades in the darkness."

Her pulse quickened at the heated appreciation in his regard. She took a quick drink of the wine, searching for that calm again, and changed the subject. "What does one do when they meet a king?"

"Curtsy. Although, in your case, I suppose a bow might be more appropriate."

"Why?"

He looked her over. "I'm guessing you mean to appear before him in your armor."

"I do." The mere thought of wearing a dress after her experience with Wayland still made her shudder. "How does one bow properly?"

Phendaril set down his wine glass and stood, then

he gently took hers from her, his fingers lingering a moment where they touched hers. Her pulse was racing again even before he took her hand. She let him guide her up.

"Like this." He bowed deeply to her, the execution formal and elegant despite the hindrance of the brace. "Now you."

She did her best to mimic his movements, feeling awkward and inept as she straightened. "I'm afraid I need to practice. I was quite clumsy."

She met his eyes, and the deep adoration in them caught her by surprise. When had they gotten so close?

He took her hand, his grip gentle. "Stars, no. You have the effortless grace of an elven warrior. I've never seen anything so magnificent. If he isn't taken with you the moment he meets you, then he's blind." The ache of sorrow stole across his features. "I'm sure Synderis would agree," he murmured, starting to pull his hand away.

Raven stared into his eyes. She felt her whole being sinking in them. The first time they kissed swept in on her, like a memory, but more somehow. She could smell the wood dust and the salt of his sweat from working on rebuilding the town. The house's walls, the staircase still needing repairs, and the rough-made furniture all closed in around her. Her heart raced as it had then, at that moment when she told herself that if she could face a wyvern, she could kiss him. That intoxicating fear of rejection, blended with a longing to feel his touch, burned through her like wildfire as if this were that moment. It stole her breath away.

Raven tightened her grip on his hand, pulling him closer. That little encouragement was all he needed. Suddenly, she was wrapped in the warmth of his arms, her lips pressed to his. Those memories blended into the present, confusing her sense of what was real. Of what was important. It felt as if something gave within her, and she let herself become lost in that moment, kissing him with all the passion she held locked inside for him and for Synderis.

•

When morning came, Raven woke to a soft kiss on her forehead. She opened her eyes to see Phendaril sitting on the bed beside her, fully dressed and holding the arrowhead pendant.

"I take it Wayland didn't haunt your dreams."

Raven sat up, a shot of alarm piercing through her. She took the pendant and put it on again. "No. He must not have tried after being unable to for so long." Neither had Synderis, not that it surprised her. He knew she wouldn't be available to him as long as she had the pendant. Even so, it hurt to think she might have reached out to him last night but had been too focused on Phendaril to consider doing so.

Phendaril cupped her cheek in his hand and placed another kiss on her forehead. "He'll understand," he said softly as he pulled away, that sorrow from last night returning to cast a shadow over his features.

She wasn't sure what to say to that. Instead, she watched him stand and walk toward the door.

He turned partially back to her. "I'm going to make sure the other three didn't kill one another in the night. Alayne's likely to come early, so you might want to get ready."

Raven watched him go. Their night played back in her mind. Has she used him? She didn't like feeling as if she had. It wasn't as though she didn't love him, nor as if he didn't love her, and yet... the power of her strangely lucid memories overwhelmed a moment she perhaps should have handled differently.

She leaned back against the headboard and stared at the canopy over the bed. "Oh, Jaecar, I think I'm starting to understand why you hid away in that keep. Life in the world of others is much too complicated."

There wasn't time or place to linger on these troubles. She needed to be ready for Alayne to arrive at any time with news of when they could go before the king, assuming he agreed to meet with them. There was always the chance he would refuse outright or, worse yet, send his guards to arrest her and give her to the Brotherhood.

Unease spurred her out of bed. They were making a significant gamble that King Navaran held his niece in high enough esteem that he would consider defying the Brotherhood to hear them out. Alayne said he had no love for Silverbloods, but how much risk was he willing to take upon himself and his kingdom for the fate of a mere half-elf? The more she thought about it, the more she suspected fleeing the city might be the wiser choice. The prospect of facing Wayland was less terrifying than that of being declared irrelevant in the eyes of the court and cast aside.

Raven hastened, pulling her clothing and armor on. If she hurried, she might be able to slip away before anyone noticed.

She put on her sword belt and grabbed her bow and quiver, slinging them over her shoulder. She headed for the door with quick strides, freezing when someone knocked on it. She glanced at the window, trying to recall the lay of the roof and how far the drop would be.

"Raven. Can I come in?"

It was Alayne.

She stared at the window for a few more seconds, a sinking sensation in her chest.

"Raven?"

"Come in."

Alayne opened the door and stepped in. Just as she started to close it, Marek appeared, blocking it with one hand. Alayne scowled back at him, then moved out of the way so that he, and the other three following close on his heels, could enter. Marek and Davon, both of whom easily outpaced Phendaril in his brace, came to stand to either side of her. Ehric settled for leaning against the wall near the window she had considered escaping through mere seconds ago. Opportunity lost.

Phendaril closed the door and stopped next to Alayne. He didn't quite meet Raven's eyes, and his words when he kissed her forehead played back in her mind. Perhaps he did feel used. She yearned to tell him that it hadn't been that way, but far too many people were in the room for that now.

"My uncle has agreed to meet with us, but for discretion, he has requested that I bring only Raven and Marek with me."

"No." Phendaril's tone was final.

Alayne gave him a withering look. "He's my uncle, Phen. You've met him."

"Under far different circumstances," Phendaril countered, his stern gaze offering no concessions. He still wouldn't look at Raven, however.

"These are his terms. He sent two guards with me to ensure we don't run into problems along the way. The rest of you will have to wait here. To be safe, I've already secured these rooms for another two nights."

Raven shifted her weight, settling her hand on the hilt of her sword. She understood Phendaril's concerns all too well, and they reflected in the eyes of Davon and Marek as well.

"Alayne and I will go," Raven stated. "The rest of you can wait here."

"No." This time it was Marek who objected. "I will

not let you face this alone. The support of a Silverblood will carry weight."

Raven faced him. "A headsman's axe also carries weight; you're headed straight for one if the Brotherhood gets their hands on you."

Surprise widened his eyes then, surprise and something else that made her want to look away, but she wasn't going to this time.

"He's right, Raven," Davon said, breaking into their silent exchange. "One of us should go, and the king has asked that it be Marek. It might be prudent to play by his rules if we wish to gain his favor."

Raven blew out a breath and nodded. "All right. I guess we do it his way."

She moved around Marek to grab a hairband she had left on the vanity. Alayne stepped forward and placed a hand on her arm.

"No. Leave your hair down. Let my uncle see you for the unusual and beautiful individual that you are."

Raven met her emerald eyes, a little startled by her words. After a second, she set the hairband down, then put her bow and quiver on the bed. Pulling up the hood of her cloak, she nodded to Alayne, who returned the gesture and turned to leave. Marek also pulled up his hood, and they followed Alayne from the room. At the foot of the stairs, he placed a hand on Raven's arm. When she looked down at it, he held a folded parchment out to her in his other hand.

"In case I don't get a chance to give this to you later. You needn't read it now."

Raven glanced up at his face, but he turned away, the hood hiding his expression from her. She took the letter. Her fingers itched to open it, but this was not the time for such things, so she slipped it into a pouch on her sword belt.

aven immediately regretted not running away. Two of the king's personal guards fell in behind her and Marek as they followed Alayne from the building. The two guards, one male and one female, made her uncomfortable. Their presence drew attention, enticing many people out on the streets to gawk curiously at them. There were a lot of those people on the streets too. Every five feet at most, it seemed another person walked or rode by, or a carriage passed.

There were voices and colors and smells and movement everywhere she looked. People laughed. People shouted. People stopped and stared at the two hooded figures striding along behind Alayne with their escort of the king's guards.

Raven found it hard to remember to breathe. She closed her eyes for a second, and a hand came to rest on her shoulder. She looked at Marek, and he moved closer to her, offering an encouraging nod.

"I'm not leaving your side," he said in a low voice.

For once, Raven found that prospect immensely comforting.

"Focus on Alayne or me if you need to."

"Thank you," she answered softly.

She took his advice and stared at Alayne's back while attempting to maintain some peripheral awareness of their surroundings in case something went wrong. Marek left his hand on her shoulder, and she made no effort to remove it.

After a walk she doubted was half as long as it seemed, they passed through the inner wall. With Alayne and the two guards in the entourage, they were waved through at the gate. Once inside, far fewer people milled about. A small group of soldiers marched past, but Raven found them less alarming than the flurry of uncontrolled civilians outside the wall.

Of course, now they were approaching the massive stone structure of the castle itself, which presented new problems. Setting aside the fact that the architecture reminded her somewhat of the Brotherhood temple in Pellanth, anxiety about meeting the king flared up with fresh vigor. How did they honestly expect her to win over a king when she couldn't handle passing through a crowd?

The guards at the entrance pulled the doors open for them, and they were greeted by a tall woman with close-cropped blond hair. She was armed and armored like the other guards, though the king's crest on her armor was edged in gold, and ornate gold vinework was inlaid into her silver pauldrons. Symbols of rank or achievement, Raven assumed. The woman's grey eyes fell upon them with suspicion before she inclined her head to Alayne.

"Lady Valassian. The king is in a brief meeting. He will send for your group as soon as he is done. For now, you will leave your weapons here." She used a key to open a cabinet set into the wall. "Then, I'll escort you to the east waiting room."

Alayne, already in the process of removing her sword belt, inclined her head in turn. "Thank you, Captain Reysa."

Raven wondered, as she reluctantly handed over her

sword and several daggers if Marek hated leaving his weapons here as much as she did. Being unarmed made her feel naked, not a comfortable sensation in most settings.

Reysa gave a curt nod of approval when they finished and locked the cabinet. "Your companions are asked to keep their identities hidden until they are in the meeting chambers."

Raven took note of the pouch where she tucked the key away. Just in case.

"Understood," Alayne answered.

With that said, Captain Reysa led them down several hallways that reminded Raven uncomfortably of the halls in the Brotherhood temple. All stonework with ornate carpets and occasional fancy side tables set in alcoves along the way. They eventually turned in to a large chamber with a blazing fireplace on one wall and an array of cushioned white-and-gold chairs set around a carved marble table.

A few tapestries hung from the other walls. One, an image of a mounted warrior hefting a spear as his mount reared up over a sea of fallen soldiers, caught Raven's eye. The splashes of red throughout, like spatters of blood, made her shiver. She pointedly chose a chair that put her back to the piece. Marek sat on one side of her, and Alayne took the other.

The two guards flanking them stayed at attention inside the door they entered through. Captain Reysa went to stand beside another door, staring dead ahead as if there were nothing in the room to look at.

Raven leaned to the side, bringing herself closer to Alayne to keep her voice low. "Are you certain this is a good idea?"

Alayne shrugged. "Is it any worse an idea than going after Wayland in Pellanth?"

That remained to be seen, so Raven said nothing.

They were offered tea and cakes, which Raven

thought she might be too anxious to eat. However, the scent of them as Alayne and Marek brought them to their lips quickly had her stomach grumbling. She relented and took one of the sweet morsels, washing it down with the light, fragrant tea. The flavors and smells were soothing enough that her nerves settled a little. Perhaps there was some hope for this. They were at least being treated quite civilly for the moment.

Then the door next to Captain Reysa opened, and a young man leaned in. He glanced quickly around the room before settling his eyes on Alayne.

"The king will see your company now, Lady Valassian."

Raven's stomach turned, and she had a moment of near panic when she thought she might throw up the cakes and tea. Then Marek set a reassuring hand on her shoulder again.

Less than a second later, Alayne placed a hand on her other arm and smiled. "Remember, he may be a king, but he's also a father, an uncle, and many other things that are far less intimidating."

Raven nodded, standing when Alayne stood. If there was ever a time to follow the other woman's lead, it was now.

The original two guards fell in behind them again, and their small party entered the adjoining room. The young man who had called them in announced their names as they passed through the doors.

"Your majesty, may I present Lady Alayne Valassian, Lady Aneiris Raven Darrenton, and Silverblood Adept Marek."

Raven glanced at Marek in question and he leaned close for a moment, whispering, "We give up our family names when we become Silverbloods."

"Oh." It seemed a strange practice, but she supposed it didn't matter if they couldn't have children. It wasn't as if they would pass the name along to anyone. For herself, the claim to the Darrenton name hadn't been legally recognized, given her illegal status. Still, she was willing to go with it if that was the name Alayne saw fit to give them for her.

The room they entered was long, with a row of tall arched windows along the right wall letting in daylight. Between each window hung a long orange banner bearing the king's crest. The opposite wall was the same, only there were arched alcoves mirroring the windows on the other side, each with an ornate sconce within. Before each sconce or window stood a guard bearing a halberd.

The only seats were a pair of large and a pair of smaller thrones at the head of the room. For the moment, only one throne was occupied, with two more guards behind it. A finely dressed gentleman stood quietly to one side. An advisor of some kind, perhaps. A few elegantly painted room dividers hid the rest of the room beyond the thrones.

King Navaran had the build of a warrior, and his attire strongly resembled the armor his guards wore. Though his short, dusty blond hair and close-cropped beard were woven through with hints of grey and lines showed at the corners of his eyes, he wore his age well. His bearing was that of a man who was confident in his power and ready to defend it. He had grey eyes, like Captain Reysa. In fact, there was enough resemblance between the king and his guard captain that Raven wondered if there might be some relation.

Reysa looked at her then, her eyes narrowing. "Remove your hoods in the king's presence."

Raven did so, and Marek followed suit. She mimicked the other two as they bowed deeply.

"You may rise." The king leaned forward, eyes narrowing in an expression that made the resemblance between him and his captain even more apparent. She was sure now that there was some blood relationship. An illegitimate child, perhaps? "Come forward, Lady Aneiris."

Raven drew a calming breath, trying to bring Jaecar's training to the forefront of her mind. This wasn't a hunt, or rather, she wasn't the one hunting, but remembering to focus and breathe as if she were helped. The leather case containing Jaecar's papers sat on the floor next to the throne, making it marginally easier to bring the old warrior to the fore of her mind. Marek touched her arm discreetly, offering his support before she took a few steps forward.

The king cocked his head to one side a little. "Closer, if you will."

Raven drew a deep breath and took a few more steps forward, increasing the distance between herself and the companions she felt safer around.

"You really are a half-elven Silverblood. Remarkable. No wonder the Brotherhood is so determined to get their hands on you. Can't have such a one wandering around unchecked, can they? Their whole doctrine could unravel."

He chuckled and stood, catching her by surprise when he started to come toward her. It also apparently caught the four guards and their captain by surprise, all of whom put their hands to their swords.

Captain Reysa stepped forward. "Your majesty."

He waved a dismissive hand. "Don't concern yourselves. This young half-elf is not here to hurt me. She is here to ask me to support her in defiance of the Brotherhood. She's here to ask me to deny their laws. I must admit, these things do instantly endear me to her." He stopped a few feet from her and looked her up and down. Despite his words, she noticed that his right hand remained close to his sword. He glanced at Marek, then met her eyes. "Your eyes are not the same as his. The silver is darker, with flecks of starlight in it. Fascinating. Is that because you're female? An elf?"

"I'm not certain, your highness," she answered cautiously, fighting the urge to turn away. She wasn't yet comfortable with those new differences. Certainly not comfortable enough to explain them to this unfamiliar man.

"Do I frighten you?"

How was she supposed to answer that? "You do not, your majesty. The power you have over my life does."

"Clever," he said in a low voice, almost as if speaking to himself.

He made a slow circuit around her, looking the rest of her over as if she were a prospective mount. It went against her nature not to track his movement, but she made herself stand still. He was the king. That apparently afforded him the right to be rude. When he had finished his pass, he went back to sit on his throne, his penetrating gaze offering no insight.

"And is it your desire that I should defy the Brotherhood? And that I should recognize you and your adoption by Lord Jaecar Darrenton as legal in my kingdom?"

Raven was caught off guard. She hadn't realized Alayne meant to go that far with it this fast. Merely getting his support against the Brotherhood was a big enough ask.

"That was Lady Valassian's plan, your majesty."

His gaze flickered briefly to his niece behind her, his expression guarded, then back to Raven. "And what was your plan?"

She met his eyes, a flare of old hatred bringing her courage. "It was my intent to confront Father Wayland directly."

His eyebrows rose slightly at that. "To what end."

Raven opted for silence.

The king chuckled. "You're wise for your years to

answer that with silence." He reached down beside the throne, his fingers resting on the leather case. "One of these legal documents is a deed of ownership for Amberwood."

"Uncle—"

He held up a hand to silence Alayne and left his words hanging between them. Not a question, an invitation for comment.

She started to shift her feet and stopped herself. No need to make her discomfort any more evident than it most certainly already was. "I have no interest in that, your majesty. I am content to see Amberwood in Alayne's capable hands."

He gave a slight nod. "Clever, wise, and generous. Not quite what I expected." He drew a deep breath, exhaling it slowly. "I appreciate your courage in coming here. You seem honest, and Alayne speaks well of you. As such, I must apologize in advance for this."

At some unseen cue, the four guards struck the ends of their halberds on the marble floor. The door at the back of the room flew open, admitting seven more royal guards and five Silverbloods. Raven glanced around at them, panic igniting her blood. Then she faced forward, her attention drawn by the sound of a new set of footsteps toward the front of the room. Another man stepped out from behind one of the dividers that blocked off the back of the room.

Raven forgot the danger behind her. The man who walked out from behind the throne had short, liquid-silver hair and matching eyes. His features were youthful and robust, and a hint of amusement showed in his smile as he strode out past the throne. Like the king, his attire looked more suited for combat than court, but it had the Brotherhood's distinctive black-and-silver coloring.

"Father Markon Mallebron, Lady Darrenton. I believe you are acquainted with my brother." He stopped in front of her and bowed slightly, offering his hand.

Raven stepped back from him, swallowing hard against the bile that rushed to the back of her throat.

"Uncle! What have you done?"

Raven dared a glance over her shoulder at Alayne. The woman's panicked gaze was locked on the king. Two of his guards had lowered their halberds, creating a block between her and Raven. Behind Alayne, two Silverbloods had already taken hold of Marek while a third started to bind his hands behind him. A look of deep despair darkened his eyes. The look of a man who knew he would die soon.

"My dear Alayne, you'll soon see this is for the best. This woman may seem a friend, but the Brotherhood has assured me that the Silverblood magic will poison her mind and eventually drive her mad. She cannot be trusted." The gaze he cast upon Alayne, and then Raven looked genuinely sorrowful. "I am sorry for deceiving you both."

"Raven." Alayne's voice cracked with emotion when she called out to her.

In front of Raven, Markon had retracted his offered hand. He turned to King Navaran, giving a bow no deeper than the one he had given her. "Your majesty, your assistance is much appreciated in this matter. I shall take these two off your hands now."

The king stared at Raven, his brow furrowing deeply. "No. Not the girl. You may do as you wish with the Silverblood warrior. Lady Darrenton will stay in my holding cells for the time being."

Raven could see enough of Markon's face to tell that he was caught off guard by the king's words. "This wasn't our agreement."

A hardness to the king's regard when he met Markon's eyes told her Alayne had not been wrong about his dislike for the Brotherhood. That was small comfort as several of his own guards moved between her and the three Silverblood warriors who had started toward her. It was a brave move, considering they weren't likely to win if it came to a fight. The Silverbloods stopped, however, and looked to Markon for guidance.

"Our agreement," King Navaran began, standing up now, "was contingent upon my meeting with the young female in question. It is my determination that our meeting has not yet reached its conclusion, but as I have other business to attend to, I will keep her here until such time that we may resume said meeting." He met Raven's eyes then, and she wished she had the insight to read what thoughts lurked behind them. "Leave my castle, Father Markon. I'll send word when I'm ready for your men to come collect her."

"She's dangerous," Markon argued.

"Indeed. I'll keep her under guard."

"In Lathwood—"

"I'm aware."

Markon didn't move right away. He stared at the king, who met his gaze unflinchingly. Tension crackled in the air, then Markon turned and glared at her.

"I look forward to our next meeting, Lady Darrenton." He gave another slight bow to her before turning sharply away. At an abrupt gesture from Markon, the Silverbloods holding Marek's arms started to move him.

"Marek!"

It would be easy enough to wrest a weapon from one of the guards, but Marek met her eyes and gave a sharp shake of his head. Then he turned and went with them out the doors they had entered through. Raven stared after them, a painful twisting in her chest.

"Take her away," King Navaran ordered as the doors shut behind the Silverbloods.

Alayne ducked around a guard and grabbed Raven's

arm, her eyes wide with desperation. "I'll make this right."

Raven looked into her emerald eyes as one of the guards moved his halberd between them, the blade coming close to Alayne's arm. Another took hold of Raven's other arm.

"Tell Phendaril that I love him," Raven said before letting the guards lead her away.

Alayne turned to the king. "Uncle! You can't do this."

"I can, Alayne. Captain Reysa, please escort my niece out."

Raven stopped trying to listen as they led her out, and someone shut the doors behind them. For now, she would allow them to lock her up. She could get away if she wanted to. Of that, she was confident. Still, Navaran had reservations about handing her over to the Silver-bloods, and Marek had discouraged her from helping him. She would wait and give the king a chance to make his next move.

For a little while, she would wait.

ynderis and the others waited for dark to head for the Chadhurst gate. They had made their way around the city to a less frequented entrance, but even then, too many people moved through for them to attempt entry during the day. Once night fell, they mounted up, ready to make their approach.

Jael hesitated, glancing at each of them, his brows pinched together. "I still don't quite understand how you expect to get them to let us through."

Telandora smiled at him. "Have faith. By the time we reach the gate, they'll be opening it for us."

"It's a Krivalen thing," Lindyl added.

Synderis glanced back at Koshika, who stood in the deeper shadows. For now, the lalyx cat seemed willing to stay behind in the cover of the tree line. He urged his mount toward the gate. He had finished waiting. Raven was somewhere inside those walls. Already, he reached out with his magic to one of the guards. "Tel, it's time."

She trotted up alongside him, the distance in her gaze telling him she was going to work on the second guard. Lindyl rode up on her other side, his focus shifting as he reached into the gatehouse for the third guard they had spotted earlier. When evening moved in, the five daytime guards they had been watching cycled out. Only three had taken their place, making this notably easier.

The two guards outside the gatehouse had also started passing a wineskin back and forth some time ago that, based on how simple it was to manipulate them, held something much more potent than wine. As Telandora had boasted, when they reached the gates, the guards opened them as if a royal entourage approached, bowing to them as they rode through a swift trot.

Jael glanced back over his shoulder as the gate closed behind them. "I never..."

"Don't forget, you're in charge now, love," Telandora said, giving Jael a wink when he looked at her.

He answered with a faint grin and urged his mount into the lead. His winding route took them down a series of narrow side streets, carefully avoiding patrols. Before long, they stopped across from the rear entrance of a large, gaudy building.

"Alayne and Karsima used to come here for private escapes after Phendaril moved in with them. We also often used one of their rooms as a meeting place to plan our return to Amberwood. It isn't the most elf-friendly inn, but they're known for their discretion, and I'm familiar with most of the hired muscle that works the place. Unless she took them all directly to the castle, which seems a bit brash for Alayne, then she'll have brought them here." Jael watched the street for a few minutes, then nodded and led them across.

They dismounted behind the building. He left his horse with Synderis, jogged up the steps, and disappeared through the door. Synderis didn't have time to get restless before the other elf came out again and hurried over to them. A burly man followed him, waving over two youths standing by the back entrance to the stable.

"Alayne's here," Jael stated.

The two youths snapped to attention and hurried over to them. It took a few minutes to grab their packs off the horses. Even at an upstanding establishment, theft was a risk. They might not be here long, but they weren't going to take any chances. They left the mounts with the two and followed Jael back inside. The burly man gestured up a set of dark stairs on their left.

"First two doors on the left," he growled. "I'd prefer you all didn't stay much longer, Jael."

Jael nodded absently and turned to the stairs.

Synderis fought the urge to sprint up the steps, allowing Jael to take the lead since he was familiar with Raven's companions. At the top, Jael knocked on the first door.

"Yes," a woman's voice called from within.

Whoever it was, it wasn't Raven, and she sounded unhappy. Jael, apparently recognizing the voice, yanked the door open and strode in. The rest of them followed, pulling back their hoods once they were inside.

Synderis noticed a couple of things as the red-headed woman sitting nearest the door stood up and embraced Jael. Foremost was the fact that Raven wasn't in the room, although her weapons were lying on the bed along with some others. The second was that having enhanced senses wasn't always a good thing. He could smell Raven here, and he could smell that Phendaril, who stood up from the other chair when they entered, had been with her in an intimate sense.

It took considerable effort to stamp down the surge of jealousy that threatened to overwhelm reason at that instant. The similar battle he saw play out across Phendaril's features made the struggle a little easier. Whatever had passed between the two in the night, Phendaril clearly didn't feel like it had changed things regarding Raven's feelings for him. Besides, for the moment, none of those things mattered. He could worry about her relationship with each of them when he knew she was safe, which her absence suggested she might not be.

Their eyes met, and Phendaril stepped forward with a noticeable limp, offering his arm. Synderis took it, gripping below the elbow in a firm greeting.

"As much as I never expected to find myself saying this, I'm actually glad to see you," Phendaril stated, looking almost as confused speaking the words as Synderis was hearing them.

Unfortunately, the meaning behind those words was readily apparent. Raven was in trouble.

He released Phendaril's arm and turned to the woman. "You're Alayne?"

Jael stepped in, hastily running through introductions before asking, "Is Ehric—"

"Next door with Davon," Alayne interrupted.

Jael glanced around at them, a hint of apology under the relief in his eyes. "If you would excuse me a moment."

Phendaril gestured toward the door with his chin. "Go. We promise to behave ourselves."

Jael smiled gratitude at the other elf and disappeared back into the hall.

"Ehric's fine," Alayne said, watching him go. "Raven, however." She kicked at the chair in front of the vanity, knocking it to the side. "King Navaran decided to welcome us in and betray us. He arrested Raven and handed Marek over to the Silverbloods."

"Isn't he your uncle?" Telandora questioned.

Alayne gave her a sour look. "He is, though that seems to matter far less than I expected it to."

"He didn't give Raven to the Silverbloods?" Synderis asked, feeling that was the more important fact to be clear on.

"Not so far," Phendaril offered, his concerns aligning more with Synderis's. "He's decided to spite the Brotherhood for the moment by keeping her in his dungeon. In Raven's typical way, she seems to have unintentionally captivated him."

Alayne glanced at Phendaril, a smile tinged with sorrow curving her lips. "She faced him with such courage, Phen. You would have been proud of her." Then she turned to Synderis, her look telling him she was aware of the more complicated relationship going on, and cleared her throat uncomfortably.

He opted to let the moment go without comment. "If she's there, then why are you all here instead of trying to get her free?"

"King Navaran told Alayne to come back here for tonight, and he would meet with her to discuss Raven again in the morning," Phendaril explained. "We were trying to come up with a plan. We need something to bargain with. Some way to convince him she isn't the danger the Brotherhood wants him to believe she is."

Alayne's face lit up then. She smiled at Synderis with such delight that he almost backed away. "I could kiss all three of you," she declared. "If you three are willing to go before my uncle with us, we can prove beyond a doubt that elves and females can be Silverbloods. One exception can be dismissed easily enough, but four?" She held his gaze, hope brimming up in her striking emerald eyes. "That's assuming you're willing to reveal your existence to the king to save Raven."

Her choice of wording didn't leave him much of an option. He met Phendaril's eyes, seeing the expectation and underlying resentment. "I would do anything to help her."

Phendaril gave a slight nod of approval, or perhaps it was only agreement.

Alayne looked to Telandora and Lindyl.

Telandora took Lindyl's hand, their fingers twining. "That's why we're here," she stated.

Synderis briefly wondered if she meant they were here to help Raven or to expose their existence to the outside world. Ultimately, it didn't matter. The result was going to be the same.

"Excellent. First thing in the morning—"

"Why wait?" Synderis interrupted.

Phendaril nodded. "I agree. Let's not leave her in the dungeons overnight if we don't have to. King Navaran played his hand without any concern for you or Raven. I see no reason we should wait to play our hand at his convenience."

Alayne's expression hardened. He hoped that meant she was angry with her uncle for what he had done. She turned and strode over to lean against the mantle, gazing thoughtfully into the fire. As she did so, Synderis walked to the bed and reached out to touch the hilt of Raven's sword. Was she angry? Afraid? There had to be a way to protect her. If this failed, then he would find another way to break her free and get her out of there. If she didn't want to hide away in Eyl'Thelandra, he would go wherever she wanted to go. It didn't matter as long as he didn't have to be without her again.

The creak of Phendaril's leg brace caught his attention then.

What if she didn't want him with her? It was a possibility and not one he cared to consider, but it would be foolish to ignore it.

He glanced at the other elf, who had gone to stand beside Alayne, the familiarity of long-time friends in their ease with one another. Phendaril knew more of hardship than he did. That much was evident in more than just his scars. The dark edge to his gaze said that he had seen terrible things and perhaps done some as well. He loved Raven, though. That much had been obvious the night Synderis followed Raven into his dream. For now, that meant they at least had the same purpose.

Telandora set a hand on his shoulder, and he met her eyes. "All that matters right now is helping her," she said softly, echoing the direction of his thoughts. "We can figure out the rest later."

"Alayne," Phendaril said in a voice that might have been soft enough to be private in different company. "You can't expect us to leave her there any more than we would expect you to leave Karsima in such a position."

"Not fair, Phen," she answered under her breath.

"Isn't it?"

A few minutes passed in silence, during which Synderis met Telandora's eyes. She glanced surreptitiously at Alayne, and he shook his head. If they needed to, they could use their magic to push her the way they wanted her to go. Still, he would prefer not to accomplish their goals by unfairly manipulating one of Raven's companions. If Alayne continued to hedge, he suspected Phendaril would go on arguing the point or take matters into his own hands.

Alayne exhaled heavily, blowing a lock of wavy red hair out of her face. "All right. I'm not sure it's a great idea to push him, but I'm not convinced waiting is the best option, either. Get the others. I don't intend to leave anyone behind this time."

They gathered everything, including the weapons on the bed that were Raven's and Marek's. From there, they went to the stables and pulled out their horses and three others, two of which Synderis assumed belonged to Raven, Marek. Now, when Alayne appeared to have set herself single-mindedly onto the task of going back for Raven, seemed like the wrong time to question the extra horse.

They followed her at a brisk pace along several backstreets, making their way indirectly to the castle gates. As they made their final approach, Alayne pushed ahead, no doubt expecting the party to be challenged. With their hoods pulled up, he and the other two Krivalen elves hung back behind Alayne, Phendaril, and the Stonebreaker, Ehric. Jael rode on their left, and the other man, Davon, paralleled him on their right behind Phendaril.

Unsurprisingly, the two of the castle guards moved out in front of the gate. Two more stood on the rampart above, aiming crossbows down at them.

"Have some manners. You know who I am," Alayne snapped at them.

One of the guards acknowledged her with a slight nod. "Sorry, Lady Valassian, but it is a little late to bring a group of strangers to the castle."

This time, when Telandora glanced at him, he gave a subtle nod, holding out two fingers without lifting his hand from his horse's neck. Her eyes flashed a brighter silver for a second, as did Lindyl's, who had watched their silent exchange. Synderis left all four guards to the two of them, ensuring he could remain free to react if trouble arose.

"I meant to be here earlier, but things don't always go according to plan," Alayne was saying. "Couldn't you just..." She trailed off as the two men's expressions slackened, and they moved abruptly to the sides while the guards above lowered their bows.

"Of course, lady," one guard stated, his voice now monotone. The two men walked stiffly in to pull open the gates.

What Synderis hadn't accounted for was the need to calm the horses when Koshika came loping out of the darkness. Ehric and Phendaril were the fastest to react, but Jael grabbed Ehric's arm when he reached for his sword. Synderis kicked his mount, driving it into Phendaril's line of fire before the elf could knock an arrow. At the same time, he spread his influence among the horses to keep them calm.

"Koshika!"

The big cat stopped in her tracks, sinking into a wary stance, and looked up at him, her ears slightly back.

Karsima, who also had a hand on her sword hilt, glanced from the big cat to him. "Is this a friend of yours?"

"Yes. There's not much we can do about her now. We need to move before the influence wears off." He gestured toward the guards.

Alayne glanced around at the men, seeing how they didn't respond to the unusual cat, and blanched. "How?"

Davon was also staring at the guards with a look of near panic. Ehric and Phendaril appeared far more composed, which told him they must have experienced something with Raven that made this use of Krivalen magic less alarming.

"We don't have time for explanations now," Phendaril said, putting his bow away.

Alayne gave a sharp nod and urged her mount ahead.

Synderis glanced down at Koshika. At this point, however, the lalyx had managed to get into the city and find them, it was safer to bring her along than to send her back out through the streets alone. "Come along."

When they got to the castle's front doors, two more guards were waiting outside. Koshika disappeared into the shadows. This time, Alayne held a hand back to them in a stopping gesture. Since she hadn't done so at the gate, he suspected she was telling them not to use their magic. A request they would respect for the moment.

She dismounted and strode confidently up to the guards.

"Send for Captain Reysa, please, and someone to tend our horses."

The guard glanced around at them uneasily, his gaze lingering longer on the three with their hoods up. Then he gave a nod and his companion, probably the more junior in rank, disappeared into the structure. The rest of them got off their mounts to wait. A short time later, a gentleman in the king's livery, followed by two young girls, came and began collecting horses. They each led two at a time, taking six on the first trip and returning for the remaining five a few minutes later.

When the second group of animals was being led away, the castle door opened, and a tall woman stepped out, dressed in fine armor with the king's colors on it. She swept over them with her gaze, taking inventory of the party and their weapons.

"What is this about, Alayne?" she snapped.

"Captain Reysa," Alayne greeted her stiffly. "We want to talk to my uncle."

The woman scowled, fingering the hilt of her sword. "And it can't wait until morning?"

Alayne turned, giving Synderis a meaningful nod. He drew back his hood. Telandora and Lindyl followed suit.

The captain's eyes widened. "More elven Silverbloods," she breathed. She stared at them a moment, then looked at Alayne. "I can't take all of you to see the king. The Silverbloods and you, perhaps, but the rest will have to stay in one of the sitting rooms. And no weapons. You'll disarm inside the door, just like before."

"You're referring to this morning when my uncle betrayed me," Alayne spat.

Captain Reysa gave her a stern look. "You follow the rules, or you leave now."

"We'll abide by the king's rules," Synderis stated. All he wanted now was to see Raven and know that she was safe. Getting her to that point was all that mattered.

Koshika chose that moment to sprint from the shadows to his side as if she feared being left behind. The two guards and Captain Reysa startled, but Reysa gestured for them to stand down when the cat pressed against his leg, and he set a hand on her shoulders. After a minute, she shook her head at Alayne.

"This is highly irregular, Alayne. You know that. You and your unusual company will have to remain here while I summon more guards. Several more if you expect to bring that thing in with you."

Without waiting for a response, the captain disappeared inside again. The two guards eyed them warily, especially Koshika, keeping their distance with their hands on their swords until Reysa returned. The captain shook her head at the big cat, then led them through the door in pairs, watching every movement as they stored their weapons in a cabinet inside the entrance. Two more sets of guards waited further down the hall.

When they finished, she led them to a sitting room where the rest would have to stay while Alayne and the Krivalen went before the king. He could see the burn of frustration in Phendaril's eyes as he watched them follow Captain Reysa from the room. The captain took them down several richly decorated hallways to a set of ornate double doors. Two guards stood outside the doors, one of whom had his armor buckled on a little crooked, making it clear he had rushed to answer the call to duty. The two opened the doors and proceeded them inside what turned out to be a formal dining room. Twelve more guards had been stationed around the room's perimeter, far more than Synderis suspected the king usually dined with.

"Your majesty." Captain Reysa bowed deeply to the man sitting at the head of the table.

Alayne bowed as well. Synderis inclined his head, Telandora and Lindyl following his lead. The man stood, his fine clothes fitted nicely to a strong frame, though age was starting to show through the hints of grey in his hair and fine lines around his eyes. He came around the side of the table and looked over them thoughtfully, the faintest glimmer of unease tightening his eyes when he spotted Koshika standing against Synderis's leg.

"I was only expecting one guest to dine with me tonight." A door at the near end of the room opened, and two guards stepped through with Raven escorted between them. "And here she is now."

Synderis's breath caught in his throat as she looked at him and her eyes widened with surprise. When a genuine smile of joy and disbelief brightened her features, he found that he could breathe again.

CHAPTER TWENTY FOUR

Raven had spent the day in a cell in the dungeon, an experience she was becoming uncomfortably familiar with for someone who had only been out in the world less than a year. This cell, at least, was surprisingly pleasant compared to the ones below the Brotherhood temple in Pellanth and that in the Lathwood jail. Soft cushions lay over the hard bench against the wall, and a few fresh blankets were set out for warmth. The cell was large as well, with a washbasin on a table in one corner that she used to clean her face and hands. A fireplace blazed across the hall, keeping it from getting too cold.

She had seen less pleasant cells along the way as they escorted her to this one. Cells that brought back the stink and the dampness of the other two cells she had stayed in before. She could feel the remembered cold of damp stone beneath her feet, even as she walked upon the worn carpet covering the floor in this one. It was as if she stood in three places at once, her memories as vivid as the ones that led her back into Phendaril's arms. These weren't like ordinary memories. They were more like relived experiences. Similar to the memories the Acridan had shared with her.

The fact that the king placed her in this more comfortable cell gave her a cautious hope that he might be someone they could still reason with. Unfortunately, unless he provided her a chance to appeal to him, it wouldn't matter. Every hour that passed made Marek's demise more likely. Perhaps it was foolish to think she could do something about that, even if the king did experience a change of heart. It was probably foolish to even care, but for all the reasons she had to despise the Silverblood, he had aided her many times and proven a faithful companion since they joined up outside Eyl'Thelandra. She couldn't help wanting to save him.

The most frustrating thing she lacked down here was any indication of the time of day. This part of the dungeons had no windows. The only light came from the fire and sconces outside the cell. If they didn't let her out by nightfall, she had every intention of setting herself free the way she had in Lathwood, hopefully without any fatalities this time. Since she was aware when they brought her down here, she knew the way out already. She needed an indicator of time, such as an evening meal, to tell her when the waiting had gone on long enough.

It seemed an eternity before a group of guards came to her cell. One of them opened the door and gestured for her to step out.

"King Navaran has requested that you dine with him, Lady Darrenton."

"Requested?" She got up from the bench and strolled out into the midst of the guards as if they scared her not a whit. "I get a choice?"

The guard shifted his feet, his brows pinching together. "Not really, my lady. He just indicated that I should phrase it politely."

That was encouraging. If the king wanted to be polite, maybe he was also interested in hearing her out. Unfortunately, she had no idea how to win over a king, and she only had a few more minutes to figure it out.

They led her back up the same way they had come down. Once they reached the castle's first floor, they finally deviated from the route they had taken earlier, leading her away from the throne room. One of the two guards in front of her opened a door, and they stepped into a long formal dining room. Before she entered, she spotted the king, dressed in less militaristic attire, standing next to a long table, talking to someone. The last person she expected to see when she stepped inside the room, however, was Synderis, standing there along with Telandora, Lindyl, and Koshika.

For a few seconds, she froze, torn between the rising joy and intense fear that she had lost her mind and was hallucinating. Was this a living memory invading her reality now? How could he possibly be here, in the king's dining room? He would never leave Eyl'Thelandra, would he?

His silvery-white hair was braided back on the sides, a few shorter strands slipping free around his face. It reflected the candlelight and the fire that burned in a hearth on the opposite side of the room, giving a surreal quality to his ageless allure. A relatively fresh cut stood out red against his pale skin.

The injury made him real. It was not a detail she would have made up for him. Especially now that her memories had taken on such a vivid life of their own.

His silver eyes met hers, and she smiled. He reacted instantly, long strides devouring the space between them, and swept her up in a fervent embrace.

Raven wrapped her arms around him, closing her eyes and burying her face against his neck while he held her. It didn't matter that they had an audience or who that audience was. Only now, with his arms holding her tight, did she realize how intensely she had missed him. So much it hurt. So much she had buried it as deep as she could to keep from letting it consume her. Now she clung to him. If how tight he held her wasn't enough to tell her he had missed her as much, then the surge of happiness and relief through their link when he touched her made it clear.

"I get the impression they haven't seen each other in a while," the king commented.

"Uncle, I—"

"Let them have their moment. Alistair, please send to the kitchen for three more place settings here. And have the table in the Autumn Dining Room set for Alayne and her companions."

Synderis eased Raven back from him, though only far enough that he could look at her, his hands coming to rest at her waist. She left her hands on his shoulders, meeting his searching gaze.

"Your eyes." He raised one hand to cup her jaw, his thumb brushing lightly along her cheek.

That would be too hard to explain just then, so she placed her hand over his and tried what the Acridan had done. It came easily, moving across the bond they already shared. She showed him her memories of the encounter in the swamp forest, along with a few select memories the tormented Acridan had passed to her. When she finished, he met her gaze, his brow furrowed, and his features shadowed with concern.

He leaned closer, his breath upon her lips. "We need to talk more about this when we're alone," he whispered.

She gave a slight nod, then closed the remaining distance, pressing her lips to his in a soft kiss. He responded with gentle passion, the hand still on her waist pulling her closer. The one on her jaw slid back into her hair.

Someone cleared their throat. A fierce flush burned Raven's cheeks as they parted. A hint of red in Synderis's face told her he had forgotten the others for a moment too. They both turned to face the king. Raven slid her hand into Synderis's, and he took it in a gentle grip.

A hint of displeasure narrowed Alayne's eyes when she looked at them, but she quickly glanced away. Guilt pierced through Raven in response to that brief look. The problem she thought she might not even live long enough to have to deal with had suddenly become a much more immediate issue. Synderis and Phendaril were in the same city. Possibly in the same building if Phendaril was one of the companions the king had mentioned.

"Alayne, you and your other companions may feast in the Autumn Dining Room. I would like to speak with this startling quartet of Silverblood elves alone."

Alayne curtsied. "Yes, uncle." She walked swiftly from the room.

Koshika chose that moment to remind Raven that she had not received any greeting. The big cat moved in front of her and reared up, settling her front paws on Raven's shoulders. Then she pushed her head into Raven's cheek, purring loudly enough that the sound filled the room. Raven let go of Synderis's hand and buried her fingers in the soft feathers over the cat's shoulders. She pushed her cheek back against the powerful press of the cat's head.

"I missed you too. Though why they brought you to the city, I'll never guess." She arched one brow at Synderis.

Telandora laughed. "Do you really think she gave him a choice?"

"No. I don't imagine you did," Raven said, placing a kiss on the big cat's head before the animal dropped back to the ground.

Synderis arched a brow at her. "I don't believe I've ever gotten such a fond greeting from her. I'm almost jealous."

Raven smiled faintly, aware that the time for reunions was at an end.

Captain Reysa shook her head at them, but the king appeared amused. "I'm sure my kitchens can provide something for your companion," he said, looking to Synderis. "They keep some fine cuts of raw meat for my hounds."

Synderis inclined his head. "That would be much appreciated, your majesty."

A group of servants hurried into the room, adding three more place settings to the two already there. Now there were two settings on either side of the table and one at the head. When they departed, King Navaran gestured to the table. "Please. Join me. The meal will be served shortly."

The guards around the room watched with an almost tangible unease as they walked to the table. Synderis pulled out the chair closest to the king on his left for Raven before seating himself next to her. Lindyl did the same for Telandora across from them. The elves from Eyl'Thelandra appeared to have more formal experience than Raven did. She hoped she wouldn't be the one to make them all look like savages as she settled into her seat. Her chair shifted a fraction when Koshika laid down against the back of it and Synderis's next to her.

King Navaran looked around at them. "There are more like you? More elven Silverbloods?"

Telandora didn't hesitate. "Many."

"Then it stands to reason that there are also those among you who can make more Silverbloods, correct?"

Raven pushed past the fear in her throat. "There are, your majesty," she answered vaguely, not sure it was wise to let on that all four of them could do so. "I feel it's important to point out that the elven Silverbloods don't kill people to make more like themselves. They only do so when someone is already dying as a way to protect and honor their spirits."

The king regarded the three Krivalen elves, all of

whom offered nods of confirmation. Then his scrutiny fell upon Raven again, and she fought the urge to look away. "You explicitly referred to your fellows as *they.* You do not include yourself among them?"

Raven glanced down at the fine place setting in front of her. An actual glass plate with ornate rose vines around the edges painted using what was probably real gold. She didn't belong in this place. She didn't belong anywhere. Not really. "I'm half-elven," she admitted with a flush of shame. "I did not grow up among them, though my mother did."

Synderis took her hand under the table. "Raven is one of us, your majesty."

"More than that," Telandora added, "she is the bridge that connects us all."

Raven flushed brighter, unsure how to respond to their words.

King Navaran regarded her with a thoughtful smile. "Your friends think highly of you, Lady Darrenton. And my niece was willing to risk asking me to defy the Brotherhood to protect you. In addition to those things, I see no evidence among the group of you that race or gender makes you any less capable of adapting to the Silverblood magic, which makes it clear the Brotherhood has been lying to us all. I will have to think hard on the information you have brought before me. While I do so..." A door to one side of the room opened, and a line of servants filed in, bringing an array of dishes and extraordinary aromas. "Let us dine," the king finished once the platters were laid out and wine poured.

They mainly spoke of food while they ate. The initial presentation was meat-heavy, with pork belly, two different preparations of quail, and a fine cut of lamb. Two of the three choices of starting soups had meat-based broth. The king's kitchen faced an immediate challenge to come up with a selection of more appropriate dishes for the Eyl'Thelandran elves who did not consume animals. King Navaran appeared initially disturbed by the idea. What pleasure could they possibly get from their meals without savory, fatty meats? The three elves began to regale him with descriptions of dishes popular among their people, a few of which Raven had tried in her time there. Lindyl especially seemed to enjoy the subject, describing in detail the proper preparation of each ingredient and the exact measures of which spices. Exactly how much or little heat to apply and how.

The king warmed to the conversation. He began offering insight into many foods on the table, explaining what regions the recipes were adopted from and which were his favorites. Raven quietly enjoyed the flavors as the four spoke, sticking primarily to the non-meat dishes for the sake of her companions. Jaecar's idea of a gourmet dining experience had been a slab of venison spiced with one or more of the same three spices he used for every meal. This was not her area of expertise. Despite how delicious everything was, she ate lightly, her stomach knotted with nerves.

Eventually, the feasting ended, and servants came to clear the table, leaving the goblets and bringing a fresh decanter of wine.

The king reclined in his chair and sipped from his wine, his gaze falling upon Raven again. "My niece took you to stay at that fancy inn she's so fond of, the Ambris, did she not?"

Raven nodded, suppressing a shiver of unease at becoming the object of his attention once more.

"It's owned by one of the wealthiest noblemen in Chadhurst. A powerful man. He's generous with his funds as long as the city is managed to his liking. He's one of many who are happy to help keep the palace coffers well-lined in exchange for a modicum of influence over the city's politics. Unfortunately, many of these powerful nobles like feeling powerful. They find it easier to do so by keeping others down. Specifically, through keeping elves and those they deem unsavory out of their businesses. If I'm to be honest, while I have nothing personal against your kind, I haven't bothered myself with trying to change your plight because it has worked out to my benefit."

Raven could feel the tension in the room rise at his words, but no one interrupted. Perhaps they were as curious as she was to see where he was going with this inflammatory confession.

He took another sip of his wine before continuing. "There is another group that has had considerable influence in how this city, and others like it, function. The Silverblood Brotherhood's narrative that joining their ranks is an elite privilege restricted—by the magic itself, no less—to young, strong human men has contributed to the racial strife. It also lures young men away from the royal military, nearly half of whom end up pointlessly dead when the magic kills them."

Telandora jumped into his brief pause. "Perhaps it would interest you to know, majesty, that it makes no difference if you are male or female. What does make a difference is race, but not in the way you might think? Elves are far *less* likely to die from the transformation. We are, in some way, better suited to it."

He arched a brow at her. "If I declare that, per royal decree, elves and women can legally be Silverbloods, I am undermining a delicate balance, albeit one that comes with many issues of its own. To suggest that elves are *better* suited than humans for something most people have come to view as an elite status would upend society completely. However, if we leave that part out, for the time being, the revelation that elves and women can be Silverbloods would be enough to undermine the foundation of the Brotherhood."

Raven shifted in her seat, sudden irritation with the conversation putting her ill at ease.

"You have something you wish to add, Lady Darrenton?" The king now arched a brow at her.

"If I understand correctly, you want to support us because it would undermine the Brotherhood, but you're concerned about the effect it will have on the social order much of your nobility is so fond of if the elves start feeling less inferior?"

"There would be anger and unrest," Captain Reysa stated, stepping out from the wall where she had stood between two guards throughout the meal. "Tell a man he is better than his neighbor, and he will build himself up with that knowledge. Take it away, and you tear him down. You leave him feeling uncertain and betrayed. Such feelings, shared by many, can lead to violence."

"Isn't there already violence?" Raven asked, arching one brow. "Or is the current violence more acceptable because the elves are its victims?"

The king cleared his throat. "Thank you, Reysa."

A stern look pushed her back to her post, but Raven noted the lack of title when he addressed her.

"It is a delicate issue," the king acknowledged.

"What happens if you choose to deny us legal status?"

"Well, that is a complicated issue, made more so by the fact that I suspect the four of you and that..." He glanced at the floor behind their chairs.

"Lalyx," Synderis offered.

"Lalyx could probably overpower my guards and me, so it is in my immediate self-interest not to deny you."

Raven glanced around the room. The guards there wore their weapons comfortably, their eyes alert and their postures ready. She glanced at the king and caught the hint of a smile when he met her eyes. They both knew the four Silverbloods and the cat might do some damage. Might even harm or kill him, but they weren't going to escape this room with their lives. Not with that many trained guards standing ready.

Telandora cocked her head to the side, and Raven was struck by the bold way the other woman stared at the king. "It's unlikely that's true, though not impossible." She grinned, pausing just long enough to make a few guards shift uneasily. "But we mean you no harm, your majesty, so long as you mean us none."

"Tel," Synderis growled in warning.

King Navaran held up a hand. "No. It is a perfectly reasonable statement, given the impact my decision could have on your future. However, it could also significantly impact the peace in my kingdom, at least for a time. These are things I must think about."

He stood, and they rose with him, a move made difficult on Raven's side of the table by Koshika's weight against the back of their chairs. The big cat, who had been grooming after devouring the slab of meat the kitchen brought out for her, got up with a growl of protest.

"Rooms have been arranged for you all here tonight. Alistair will show you to them and to where the rest of your companions are waiting. I shall call upon you in the morning to discuss my decision. Until then, you have my gratitude for joining me this evening. I have not had such an interesting meal in some time. Rest well."

He inclined his head politely before turning away.

Alistair came forward and gestured for them to follow him from the room.

CHAPTER TWENTY FIVE

Telandora and Lindyl claimed the first room they were shown to, making it evident that they intended to stay together and had no interest in anyone's opinion on the matter. Synderis and Raven continued after Alistair to the next rooms when the group from Amberwood entered the hall from another direction. They fell upon Raven, Jael slipping in for a fleeting embrace before Ehric did the same. The guardsman, Davon, bowed deeply to her, his eyes gleaming with a powerful devotion that caught Synderis by surprise. It seemed he had missed a few things in the time since they stopped walking each other's dreams.

Phendaril came forward and took her into his arms, pointedly not looking at Synderis, who stepped closer to Alistair to give the two space, even though part of him objected to the action.

"Is there somewhere I could take Koshika out to stretch her legs?" Synderis asked in a low voice.

Alistair gave Koshika an anxious glance before nodding to him. "The others know where the remaining rooms are. I can show you to the yard. Follow me, my lord."

It was impossible not to notice the intensity of Phendaril's embrace or that Raven returned it in kind. That made it easier to walk away in a sense, knowing he left her among those who cared for her. It also made it more difficult because he knew how much the elf holding her at the moment loved her and that he would undoubtedly prefer to keep her to himself.

Alistair led him out a side door of the castle to a large grassy yard closed off from the rest of the garden by a wrought iron fence. Koshika growled low in her throat, sniffing the air. Alistair gave her an uneasy glance and moved a few steps farther away.

"Apologies, but this is where the king's dogs are let out. Perhaps she smells them."

Synderis placed a hand on Koshika's shoulders, sending a sense of calm to her. "It's just for tonight, my friend."

The cat leaned into his leg for a second before bolting across the yard like the wild creature she was. With minimal effort, she leapt the fence and began to explore the garden beyond.

"Oh, dear." Alistair's brow furrowed.

Synderis chuckled. "She's no dog. I don't think she'll hurt anything, but I'll keep an eye on her."

He started to walk out into the yard in the direction Koshika had gone. After a few minutes of staring worriedly after the cat, Alistair left Synderis to handle the problem and went back inside. That put him alone with his thoughts, which weren't thoughts he was particularly excited to be alone with. He focused on the garden beyond the fence that Koshika was loping around. A bright moon and clear, star-filled sky let him appreciate the array of plant life, even if it was too organized for his taste. The flowers were arranged in orderly rows. The bushes were precisely trimmed to shape.

Koshika batted at some kind of late-blooming flower with a fat, round blossom. A burst of petals flew into the air and began floating down around her like snowflakes. The cat attacked several petals, looking every bit like an oversized kitten frolicking before she moved on. Behind him, he heard the door of the castle open. Familiar footsteps started to cross the yard toward him, and he smiled to himself as the scent of her reached him. The anticipated pleasure of being near her made it almost impossible to wait for her to come to him, but he needed to let her take the lead.

A light laugh as she came to stand beside him told him she had noticed Koshika's antics in the garden.

"I don't know how the gardeners will feel about her redecorating." She laughed again, a hand coming to her mouth when the cat bounded through a bunch of plants. Then she turned to look up at him, her gaze penetrating. "Does it hurt?"

He faced her now, the healing cut on his cheek stinging more since she brought his attention to it. Her eyes narrowed slightly as she considered the injury. "Not much. Does it bother you?"

"Only in that you got it because of me." Her hand came up then, her fingers lightly tracing his jawline beneath the wound, setting his blood on fire with a single touch. She smiled, an expression full of warmth and affection. "When I saw you standing in the king's dining room, I thought perhaps I had lost my senses and imagined you. No one has ever looked so wonderful as you did at that moment."

He started to lean in, intending to kiss her, and her look changed, her brows knitting in distress. She began to move her hand away, but he caught hold of it, keeping it there. "What is it?"

"Last night... Phendaril and I—"

"I know."

His knowledge didn't appear to surprise her any. She looked into his eyes, searching for something. "I still love him, Syn. And I love you. So very much. I don't know what to do."

Perhaps he had lived with that understanding long enough that he had come to accept it, but it didn't hurt that much to hear her say it. He leaned down, answering her worry with a kiss that she responded to immediately, sliding her hand around the back of his neck, into his hair, fingers pulling him closer. He deepened the kiss, tasting the wine upon her lips and longing to ask for more, but they needed to discuss some things before he pushed that line.

Reluctantly, he drew away. Flecks of bright silver sparkled in her darker silver eyes, gleaming in the moonlight. He brushed the backs of his fingers lightly against her cheek, and she closed her eyes, smiling softly.

"What you did earlier, showing me your memories—I didn't know that was possible."

Her eyes snapped open. "Oh. I assumed you would be familiar with that kind of sharing. The Delegate was there when the Acridans lived."

He shook his head, finding it hard not to get lost in those unexpected eyes. "If she knows about this, it's knowledge she kept to herself."

"There's more I should show you. The Acridan shared more of its memories with me. Not just its desire to die, but how it came to be there in the first place."

He nodded. "Perhaps we should go inside. Somewhere more private."

She gave him a coy smile. "Are you asking me to come to your room?"

As hard as he tried to be serious, it was impossible before her smile. He wrapped his arms around her waist and pulled her close. "Whenever I get the chance, Lady Darrenton."

He kissed her again, barely able to think past the glorious feeling of having her in his arms. No matter what came of this undertaking, he would do it all over just to hold her like this for a moment.

Koshika, who had returned sometime while they were distracted, rubbed against their legs hard enough to make them stumble apart. Raven grabbed his upper arm, and he caught her elbow in his palm, finding balance in the contact as much as giving it.

Raven placed a hand on the lalyx cat's head. "I think Koshika's ready to go in."

They strolled back into the palace halls with the cat between them, playing chaperone. When they turned the corner to the hall their rooms were in, Phendaril was walking away from one of the doors.

"Your room," Synderis asked softly.

Raven only nodded.

Phendaril looked them over as he approached and held her weapons out to her. "I was just bringing these to you."

Raven accepted the items. "Thank you."

When Phendaril moved to step around them, she passed the weapons to Synderis and caught Phendaril with a hand on his arm.

"Phen—"

The other elf shook his head. "We can talk tomorrow." He inclined his head slightly to Synderis. "I believe Alayne put your weapons in your room," he said, gesturing to another door.

Synderis returned the slight nod, recognizing the pain in the other elf's eyes with a twist of remorse. He didn't wish Phendaril ill. It would be petty to do so over circumstances neither of them had planned. "Thank you."

Raven removed her hand from Phendaril's arm. "Goodnight," she said softly.

"Goodnight," he answered, his voice tight as he strode away from them.

Synderis drew a deep breath, noting the fresh gleam of distress in Raven's eyes when she turned back to him.

"If you don't want to talk tonight..."

"No. I want to show you what the Acridan shared with me. And..." She took her weapons from him, not meeting his gaze for a moment. When she finally looked up at him, the shine of unshed tears lurked in her star-touched eyes. "I missed you, Syn. More than I even realized. I want you close to me a little longer."

He nodded and continued down the hall, opening the door to her room for her. It was the nearer of the two and felt like the better choice. If she wanted time alone, she could ask him to leave rather than having to do the leaving herself.

A fire already warmed the room when they entered. Raven set her weapons on the floor next to the vanity. Then she moved the chairs out from in front of the fire and sat cross-legged on the floor. She gestured for him to sit in front of her. He did so, shifting in close so their knees touched. The moment they were both settled, Koshika curled up between them and the fire, her back in contact with their knees on that side.

Raven took his hands. "Are you ready?"

A chill of unease swept through him, but he nodded.

She shared the Acridan's memories. The room around them vanished, and he was somewhere else, re-living the horror of the death of the Acridans from the eyes of one. Then he learned things he had never heard in the histories the elders told of them. Probably because they left before these events occurred. How the men had come back to eliminate the few who survived the illness. About how this one had escaped with another who was later killed. After that, it hid away in the swamps that ultimately changed it into the creature Raven had faced. She also shared the images it had given her, asking her to kill and Accept it. The memories were so vivid it was as though he could smell the musty dampness of the swamp and feel the anguish the moment that Acridan became the last of its kind.

When the images stopped, he saw Raven in front of him again, tears on her cheeks, her changed eyes soft with affection. She let go of one hand and reached across to brush away a tear that ran down his cheek.

"I'm sorry you faced that alone," he said gently, "but I think you handled it as well as anyone could have." He took her hand and placed a kiss on her palm.

Raven's smile was tremulous. "I'm a little scared, to be honest. These memories. Could you feel how real they are?"

He eyed her a moment, seeing the fear in her changed eyes and feeling the faint tremble in her hand. "Yes. It was like I was living them rather than merely witnessing them."

"All my memories are like that now, and they come upon me suddenly. It's as if I have no control over them anymore." She drew a shaky breath. "Has any elf or human ever Accepted an Acridan before?"

"Not that I know of. Not many have been around long enough to ever have seen one alive. We might ask the Delegate if she'll speak to me after what I've done."

"You left without permission?"

He nodded, clenching his teeth against the dread that admission brought.

Raven squeezed his hand. "You shouldn't have done this for me."

He offered a warm smile. "I would do anything for you, but you aren't the only reason we left. Telandora said this had gone on for too long, and she was right. The Brotherhood needs to be challenged. Perhaps we can create some changes that will help many people."

Her smile warmed, only to falter an instant later. "What about the fey magic in the swamp? I know that's why my eyes changed this way. This isn't because of the Acridan."

Synderis nodded in agreement. "It isn't. The Acridans had bright silver eyes, like us, though the Delegate
tells us the entire eye was that way. I don't know what it
means. I wish I could reassure you, but what I can do is
say that, as long as you will allow it, I will stand beside
you. You don't have to face this alone."

Raven leaned in, and he moved to meet her, their
lips touching in a soft kiss. He could taste the salt of
new tears upon her lips. He pressed his forehead to hers,
sliding one hand along the side of her neck and into
her hair, fingers trailing along her silky-smooth skin. He
closed his eyes, feeling her breath on his lips.

"I love you, anweyn."

"Heleath le'athana," she murmured in return.

He moved up on one knee and stood, taking her
hands to lift her with him. When they were both standing, he brushed her hair back over one pointed ear, trying not to dwell on how the silver-black was somehow
both more silver and more black than it had been before.

"We should get some sleep."

Raven nodded. She stepped in closer, sliding her
arms around him and resting her head against his shoulder. "I didn't think I would ever see you again. It's hard
to want to let you out of my sight."

Synderis chuckled. "If only you could know how
much I don't want to let you out of mine. But it would
be unkind to risk letting Phendaril see us leave the same
room in the morning. We must figure things out between the three of us, and it should not be handled
carelessly."

Raven stepped back, lowering her gaze. "I know."

He could feel her worry, her fear, through their connection. For a second, he considered using his magic
to calm and comfort her the way he had when he first
started dreamwalking her. It was a little jarring to realize that he was afraid to do so. She had magic in her now

that he didn't understand. He had no way of knowing how it would react to such an intrusion.

He slid his fingers under her chin, and she looked up at him, giving to the slightest pressure. "If you need me to stay, just say so. You are my priority."

She frowned up at him. "No. You're right. Though sometimes I hate how thoughtful and reasonable you are."

More than anything, he wanted to undress her and show her how rash and spontaneous he could be. The longing was almost too much to bear. "So do I," he whispered, trembling with the need to touch her.

Raven kissed him, her mouth opening when he brushed his tongue across her lips. He kissed her needfully as if she was the source of life itself, pulling her tight against him. His head swam with the surge of desire and emotion. The way she matched his passion told him she understood his longing. That didn't make it easier when he finally made himself move away. He was breathing hard, and he wasn't sure how much of her his hands had explored over her clothes, experiencing each remembered curve while they kissed. She was at least as flushed and out of breath as he was. They had shared so many nights together in dreamwalks, but he had only been with her once in the waking world. It felt unfair to have to walk away from her now to spare the feelings of another.

"You'd better go."

"Yes." He pulled back from her and started toward the door. "Koshika." The big cat barely lifted her head enough to glance at him. "Right. Perhaps you should stay with Raven."

Raven breathed a laugh. "Goodnight, my love."

He smiled back at her, hoping she hadn't noticed the relief that came with the cat volunteering to stay. For all that they were guests here, he didn't trust these people. Knowing Koshika was there to warn her if anyone tried anything made him a little more comfortable leaving her.

"Goodnight, my beloved Raven," he answered, slipping out the door.

•

Synderis wouldn't have expected to fall asleep so soon after leaving Raven, but he now stood in the enclosed glade of the evergreen temple in Eyl'Thelandra, clearly able to drift into the dreaming despite his distraction. The Delegate stood at the edge of the small crystalline creek that meandered through the center. She glanced over at him. Her eyes widened with a hint of surprise and curiosity. To his relief, she didn't appear angry, though he undoubtedly deserved her anger.

"I was angry," she answered his thoughts, catching him off guard. "But the three of you are not wrong. I used to tell myself that I would find a way to fix things when the moment was right. I could have gone on telling myself that forever, perhaps. Maybe we needed something as strong as the bond between you and Aneiris to force a change."

It wasn't what he expected to hear, but he was not about to waste this time questioning her words when he had more important concerns. "You dreamwalked me to tell me this?"

A smile tugged at the corners of her mouth. "I did not dreamwalk you, Syn. You must have had some great need to bring you to me like this."

His thoughts veered off course. "Is that possible?"

"We have a connection, you and I. Perhaps because I have long looked upon you as family. A sentiment you must share to some degree. I blocked that connection after it formed to hide the fact that you are favored by me, Syn. I am not supposed to have favorites, but you remind me of my brother's son. He was kind, smart, and devoted to those he loved, like you." She smiled, wandered over toward the pillar with the white stone basin on top, and brushed her fingertips across the water's surface. "When you left, I removed the block upon our connection so that I could know you were alive and so you could reach out to me if you had need. That time apparently has come."

A jolt of alarm shot through him. "I'm not anchored."

The Delegate waved a hand dismissively. "That's not really necessary when you share a connection with the dreamer. However, it is still a good habit, which is why we don't tell you that. Now, what is it you need?"

"Something happened with Raven. Something perhaps only you might understand." A possibility struck him then, and he walked up to her, reaching one hand out. "Perhaps, it would be faster if you simply looked at the memories."

The Delegate started to reach for his hand in turn, but then she stopped, her eyes narrowing. "How do you know of that?"

He pushed his hand toward her again, his suspicion proven true. "It will be easier if you see what she showed me."

The Delegate warily took his hand. A few minutes later, silvery tears sparkled on her cheeks, and delicate lines of worry were etched across her brow. "I didn't know any survived." She let go of him and turned to gaze at the creek. "The Acridan didn't want us to Accept them. They weren't sure how it might change us. A few tried anyhow, unable to take the pain of watching them die and become lost, but the Krivalen magic always blocked them out. It wasn't possible to trick it in them."

"Then how could Raven..." He trailed off when she held up one delicate hand.

"In this case, the Acridan invited her to Accept it. I think that must be what made the difference. After the book they had written for us was taken by the Brotherhood's founders, the one who wrote it came to me in confidence. They were dying and did not want the knowledge of the magic to die with them. They and I were bonded by our love of history and lore. They asked me to Accept them when they died to preserve their knowledge for our people. I did so."

A glimmer of hope rose in him. "Then you know what Raven can expect."

The sorrow in her regard made his hope flicker out. "Some, yes. The intensely real memories and the ability to share them in that way are part of the Acridan nature. Its memories are hers now, as is the ability to recall memory in that way. The Acridan she Accepted was altered, however, by magic we know little about. We know it has had some effect based on the changes in her appearance. Beyond that, all she can do is wait and see if there are other consequences. If she would consider coming here, I would do my best to help her, Syn. If not, then you should both be very careful." She waved a hand dismissively at him. "Now go. I must think about this news."

Synderis woke abruptly in the castle bedroom he'd been given. A strange place that he found oddly uncomfortable despite how soft and warm the furnishings were. Or perhaps because of that. He considered slipping back to Raven's room for a few minutes, but he had already made that choice. There was no value in changing his mind now. Instead, he stared into the darkness and wondered what, exactly, they should be careful of.

aven woke abruptly to the clack of wooden blades striking together. It took her back for a confusing moment to the mornings she had spent sparring with Jaecar. As she became aware of her surroundings, she noticed that she lay curled up on a tiny portion of the right corner of the bed. Koshika had unapologetically commandeered the rest of it. The clacking of practice swords outside caught her attention again, and she slipped out of the covers, a little surprised that she hadn't lost them in the night with the cat nudging her around. She crept to the window, nearly bursting into laughter when it dawned on her that she was being quiet to avoid disturbing Koshika, and peeked through the heavy drapes.

It was still early, judging by the light, and cold, given how visible Telandora and Lindyl's breath was as they danced back and forth in the fenced yard. Their beautiful faces twisted into masks of fierce determination, looking for all the world like they meant to kill one another. At the far side of the fence, Synderis, Davon, and Captain Reysa stood observing the mock battle while they conversed. Raven watched Synderis for a few seconds, delighting in the shape of him and the way his silver eyes followed the fighters moving around the yard in their violent dance. After a minute or two, she turned and went about sponging the night sweat away with water from the basin and dressing in the marginally cleaner set of clothes she had in her pack. Once she finished with that, she pulled open the curtains to let in the light.

Koshika made a displeased noise and wrapped one paw over her eyes.

"One night in a castle, and you've gone soft as an old hound."

Looking away from the cat, who appeared utterly unconcerned with her accusation, Raven spotted her weapons lying on the floor. A memory slipped through her mind of Marek handing her a letter as they left the inn yesterday morning. She could feel the parchment between her fingers again for a second. That seemed so long ago now. Surely the Brotherhood wouldn't have put him to death yet. They would give him an opportunity to defend himself, wouldn't they? Perhaps they would hold him as leverage against her or torture him to force him to tell them more about her. At least, under the relatively peaceful circumstances of his capture, there was a chance he would remain alive for now.

She dug the letter out of the pouch and hopped back on the bed to sit cross-legged next to the cat, who made a slightly louder protest at her disturbance. A soft knock came at the door before she could unfold the parchment.

"It's unlocked."

Alayne leaned in and scanned the room. When she spotted Koshika, a grin cracked her features. She strode in, Phendaril on her heels, his limp already less pronounced than it had been when Raven first saw him at Darrenton's manor. He cast a surreptitious glance toward the bed, a hint of relief smoothing the tightness of dread from his expression. His dark amber hair hung elegantly free, contrasting the fierceness of his sharp features. He hadn't put his armor on, and his shirt was loosely laced, hanging open enough to show the edge of a scar on his muscular chest. A scar she knew well enough that, for a thankfully brief moment, she could feel the texture of it the first time she had traced it with her fingertips. A different time and place, but as vivid as Koshika's feathers under her hand for an instant.

"I see you didn't sleep alone after all," Alayne commented, chuckling at the cat, who reluctantly rolled up on her stomach to glower at them.

Phendaril gave Alayne a wry smirk. "She did choose the most attractive of her companions to grace her bed."

Hoping Phendaril hadn't noticed her momentary distraction or the resulting flush, Raven gave Koshika a wry smile. "He's not wrong, is he?" She looked up at Alayne. "Am I the last awake?"

"No. Jael and Ehric haven't stirred yet. I believe they were up playing cards well into the evening. And Koshika appears to be all for sleeping in." The woman shook her head at the cat and came to sit on an open edge of the bed. She gestured to the letter Raven was still holding. "What's that?"

Phendaril strode over to lean against the wall near the fireplace.

Dread tightened Raven's chest. "Marek gave it to me yesterday morning. So much happened after we came to the castle that I had forgotten about it."

"What does it say?" Alayne asked.

Phendaril said nothing, but she caught a slight lift of his eyebrows that betrayed his curiosity.

"I don't know yet." Raven opened the letter and read over it silently.

Lady Aneiris Raven Darrenton,

    I do not know what will come of this day, but I feel that I must be candid with you now as another opportunity may not arise.

I realize that I can never make up to you for my vile deeds before. I betrayed you in the worst way, and you suffered terribly for it. I admit, with no little shame, that jealousy moved me at the time. I was captivated by you. Not because of your beauty but because there is a strength in you that I find beguiling.

I am aware that my affection will not be reciprocated in kind, nor did I ever have the right to expect it to be. I do hope that, someday, I can at least earn your forgiveness and become a friend you are comfortable turning to in times of need... or any other time.

Forever, your friend and ally,
Silverblood Marek

Raven glanced up at Phendaril, then she turned her gaze to Alayne. Neither had any love for Marek. They wouldn't appreciate the rekindled sense of urgency that made her skin itch or the panic that tightened her chest. Whether they understood or not, it mattered to her what happened to the Silverblood adept. For the way he cared for her when she got sick after the night she rode back to Darrenton manor in the heavy rain. Also, for how he helped end the threat Aldrich Darrenton posed to Amberwood and guided her through it when the lives she had taken threatened to overwhelm her.

She got up from the bed and walked over to tuck the letter into her pouch. Then she went to where she had left her armor on a corner chair.

"I need to talk to the king." She had the uncomfortable sense of them exchanging a look behind her back in the momentary silence as she picked her chest piece up.

"You know you can't just wander through the castle demanding to see the king," Alayne said. "We've pushed him enough. We don't even know what he's decided yet. He could still turn you over to the Silverbloods."

Raven cast an irritable glance over one shoulder. "So I'm to wait patiently here for *him* to tell *me* what *my* fate should be?"

Phendaril's expression changed, something more introspective slipping in where the hint of disapproval had been. He stepped up beside her. "Would you like assistance with your armor?"

"Not the proper response, Phen," Alayne snapped, getting up from the bed as if she meant to bodily interfere.

Raven met his eyes, and he smirked at her. "I know Raven well enough to recognize the look in her eyes. It's time for your uncle to make up his mind or get out of the way."

Raven smiled back at him, relieved to have him on her side. "Thank you."

He helped her start buckling on the armor. As they did so, Alayne made an exasperated noise, spun on one foot, and strode from the room. Curiously, Koshika stood on the bed, stretched, and jumped to the floor, landing with shockingly little sound, then trotted after her. Raven let them go. Whatever the king had or had not decided at this point, there must be ways she could influence his decision if it appeared to be trending against her and the Krivalen elves. Or perhaps Koshika would eat him, and she wouldn't have to worry about it.

She smiled to herself as Phendaril started working on one of the buckles at her shoulder. Her gaze moved up to meet his eyes. "Will you come with me... if I go after Marek?"

His fingers stopped, and he held her gaze. "If you want me there, I'll go. Even to help that bastard." He added a tight smile to take the edge off his words.

"And if Synderis comes too?"

"Given that we'll be going after Silverbloods, I

think I would insist on that. We have to even the odds somehow." He grinned, though she caught the flash of hurt in his eyes.

"I'm sorry, Phen." She began working on another buckle, and he did the same. "Perhaps, when this is over, I should go somewhere where I can't hurt either of you anymore."

"And be alone?"

She caught her breath, looking at Synderis as he sauntered into the room through the door Alayne had left open.

His expression was guarded when he spoke again. "I would rather see you with someone who loves you than alone again."

Phendaril glanced at him briefly before turning back to finish the last buckle on that piece. "You say that with such honesty. I suspect you may be a better elf than I."

Synderis walked past them to pick up one of her bracers. He held it out to Phendaril but didn't release it right away when the other elf went to take it. Their eyes met, Synderis tilting his head just a hint to one side, searching Phendaril's dark eyes. Then he let go of the bracer. "And I have a feeling you're selling yourself short."

Neither said much after that, but they both stayed, Synderis handing them armor pieces and assisting with buckles on that side. Having them there together, tending to her needs without conflict, was pleasant in many ways. Raven focused as hard as she could on putting on the armor, determined not to say anything that could make the moment more confusing or get her sucked into any awkward vivid memories. It wasn't her own memories that posed the biggest threat. The Acridan, it seemed, had experience sharing intimacy with multiple partners at one time, and this setting called up some of those occurrences.

When they finished, she turned to see Telandora standing in the doorway, Lindyl's arms wrapped around her waist from behind. The blond elf leaned in to kiss her neck, his eyes moving up to meet Raven's as he did so. Heat rushed into Raven's cheeks as she turned her attention to double-checking a buckle that didn't need it.

"That was a great show," Telandora said in the ensuing silence, a hint of approval shining in her eyes. "What are you three doing for the next act?"

Synderis turned away, breathing a soft laugh.

Phendaril shook his head, though she caught a slightly self-conscious grin tugging at the corners of his mouth. He gave Raven a sidelong glance. "You do find interesting friends when you go out on your own."

Koshika sprinted past the two standing in the doorway like a crazed creature, bounding onto the bed as if it were elusive prey needing to be brought down, and began waging a violent assault on the covers. Liberated stuffing feathers flew into the air as the cat made good her kill. As suddenly as she arrived, she leapt back off the bed and sprinted from the room.

With feathers still floating down around them like snow, Raven glanced at Synderis. "What was that?"

He swallowed back the laugh she saw bubbling up in his expression. "She has moments. I'm not a cat. I can't explain it."

"That was like one of Smudge's rampages," Phendaril stated, the tightness of restrained laughter in his voice too, "only a lot more impressive."

Lindyl did start laughing then.

Telandora waved at Synderis to get his attention. "I'll go find the cat before she tries that on something living. You three should get out of this room before a servant arrives to change the linens."

Synderis nodded, reaching out to pluck a few feathers from Raven's hair, a casually intimate gesture. "We'll meet you back in the yard as soon as we've all gathered our things."

Raven brushed several feathers from Synderis's hair and shoulders. She caught hold of Phendaril's arm as he started to walk away. Moving around him once, she did the same for him.

"No carrying evidence out of this room," she said, offering a smile she knew was somewhat strained. This situation hadn't come up in any of the books she had read when she lived at the keep with Jaecar. She wasn't sure what to do about it. The Acridan's memories had plenty to offer, but she wasn't confident any of those options were viable for them. For now, it made sense to move forward with the things that needed more urgent attention.

The others left the room, leaving Raven to pick up the last of her belongings and clean any feathers off. They wouldn't be allowed to carry their weapons to meet with the king, so she held them in her arms, ready to deposit them wherever required. Then she made her way out to the yard.

Lindyl and Telandora were already there, standing next to Captain Reysa, and watching as Koshika sprinted around the yard. At least the lalyx respected the fence for the moment rather than tearing up the gardens outside them with her bursting energy.

"Captain Reysa," Raven greeted her.

"Lady Darrenton." Reysa inclined her head. "That creature's as destructive as the king's hounds."

"You have no idea," Lindyl muttered, grinning as he dodged Telandora's elbow jab.

Raven rolled her eyes at him before turning her attention to the captain. "You don't have to call me that. I prefer Raven."

Reysa gave her a measuring look. "In that case, Reysa is good enough for me in private conversation. I suspect we'll be working together soon enough."

Hope exploded in Raven. She tried to tamp it down before it showed, but Reysa's smirk told her she had failed.

The captain held up a staying hand. "I'm not making promises. I'm just suggesting that, maybe, King Navaran might be coming around to your side."

"He hates the Brotherhood that much, does he?" Synderis strode over to stand on Raven's right, closer to the other two Krivalen elves.

Reysa met his eyes. They were around the same height. "He hates the influence they have and their lack of respect for his authority."

Phendaril came up on Raven's left then. A few seconds later, Koshika shoved in between Raven and Synderis. Both of them set a hand on the cat's shoulders, their fingers touching. Synderis's arm tensed slightly, but when Raven didn't pull away, he relaxed, leaving his hand there. His touch calmed her, even as it ignited her desire for more.

Gathering confidence from the two elven males beside her, she met Reysa's eyes. "I would like to meet with him now, then."

A short time later, after giving up their weapons again, Reysa escorted the group and Alayne, who had managed to convince the king to grant them an earlier audience, to his throne room. Synderis and Phendaril walked to either side of her. Davon, Ehric, and Jael followed close behind or as close as Koshika would allow. Lindyl and Telandora were a few strides ahead, directly behind Alayne and the captain.

Phendaril glanced at Raven. "I never thought I would see something like this."

The amusement in his voice caught her attention. "Like what?"

"You, going to an audience with a king that you demanded."

Raven's stomach did a flip.

"He's no match for Lady Darrenton," Davon piped up behind them. "You were there, Phendaril. You saw her tame that storm drake."

All three of the Krivalen elves cast glances at her.

Synderis arched one brow. "You did what?"

Raven shrugged, afraid to speak and betray how nervous she was. Davon was right, though. She had pulled an arrow out of a storm drake while it watched her, its massive jaws hanging over her. She had faced the eliket before she knew what it really was and had kept her head about her enough to reach out to it. Why was it always people that unnerved her so?

aven bowed before the king, all too aware that her companions had fallen back behind her. It was appropriate, perhaps, given that she had demanded this audience. She only hoped her anxiety would let go of its stranglehold on her throat enough that she could speak when the time came, which was going to be any minute now.

"Lady Darrenton." The king leaned forward, resting his elbow on his knee as he regarded her through tired eyes, as though his ponderings had kept him awake well into the night. "It's my understanding that you felt our meeting today should be expedited."

Raven could hear Jaecar's voice in her head, telling her to keep her mind on her chosen target. She drew a deep breath. "I did, your majesty. The Silverblood that came here with me yesterday morning, Adept Marek, will be put to death for aiding me if I don't do something."

He leaned back, his eyes narrowing. "And the fate of this Silverblood concerns you?"

Raven was acutely aware of her companions behind her. How many of them thought Marek ought to be put to death? Did it matter? They weren't there the many times he helped her. They might disagree with her, but she hoped they would stand with her all the same.

"It does. Marek chose to help me, even though it made him a traitor to the Brotherhood. He chose to stand by me at the risk of his life, and I can't let him die for that. I will do whatever I can to help him, but I would prefer to do it while working with you rather than against you." Someone cleared their throat softly behind her, and she quickly added, "Your majesty."

The king was silent for what felt like several minutes before he stood up. He walked down to her, his grey eyes hard and unyielding. "I like you, Lady Darrenton. I think much of that comes from how passionately your companions are willing to stand up for you, my niece included. If you only heard her arguing for you yesterday, I think you might have been surprised by the glowing praise she gave you."

Raven fought the urge to glance back at Alayne. The king's words, given that stern look he gave her, were not what she expected. Nor had she expected Alayne to defend her with such fervor. She held her silence, sensing that he had more to say.

"If I am going to get people to accept a decree that women and elves can be Silverbloods and that Silverbloods created outside of the Brotherhood are not criminals that should be handed over to the Brotherhood to be put to death, then I am going to need you to be seen." He wandered to one of the alcove windows and gazed out, rubbing at his chin with his thumb and forefinger. "I would require you to travel with Captain Reysa and a unit of her choosing."

Raven caught a slight stiffening in the captain's posture, where she stood to one side of the dais. The king apparently noticed it as well. He turned to consider her. "Don't act surprised, Reysa. I know you've been itching to get away from the castle. You and the soldiers you choose will spread the word of my decree and help our elven Silverbloods move safely around the kingdom until the message takes on a life of its own."

Reysa frowned. "Your majesty, you'll make targets of them."

The king turned to look at the trio of Krivalen elves behind Raven, then his gaze settled on her again, and she inclined her head slightly. "They already are. This way, they will at least have the support of the law and the right to move openly through my kingdom."

A shiver of excitement raced through Raven. This was far more than she had dared hope for. At the same time, it did not solve her current problem. "This will undermine the power of the Brotherhood here?"

The king nodded. "It will, and they won't like it, but they will have to declare war against my kingdom or follow my laws. There are risks, but the Silverbloods don't have the numbers to take down my entire army, despite their efforts to steal all my promising recruits. Too many of them die simply attempting to become Silverblood. No offense, but the knowledge that women and elves can also be Silverblood will strip away that elite status and remove some of the appeal for many of these young men. I will send an immediate missive to King Saldin. Our alliance is stronger than the Brotherhood. Together we can put those Silverblood bastards in their place." He looked around at the four of them. "I am, of course, not including the present company in that grouping."

Captain Reysa lowered her gaze but said nothing.

"I can't speak for the others..." A hand came to rest on Raven's shoulder.

Synderis leaned close to her ear and whispered, "You can."

She glanced over her other shoulder at Lindyl and Telandora, who both offered slight nods. She swallowed hard. It was easier to offer up only herself to this madness, but she could not deny them the right to make their own decisions. In this case, the decision to make her their voice.

"Apparently, I do speak for all four of us. We are willing to travel with Captain Reysa and help change the power dynamic with the Brotherhood. Still, I must ask your help freeing Silverblood Marek first."

The king grinned and shook his head as he walked back up to his throne. He sat, taking a moment to get comfortable in a chair that looked too rigid for such. "You are an interesting woman, Lady Darrenton. No one has ever come to me for help, which I have graciously granted," he added with a look that dared her to challenge the statement, "and left me feeling like I owe them a favor."

She had no trouble meeting his eyes this time. "You did put me in your dungeon."

"Granted. Though I gave you a cell typically reserved for the most elite prisoners." He rubbed his chin again and smiled to himself. "It would be a bold way to start this campaign. To notify the Brotherhood of my decree and demand the release of Silverblood Marek."

He cocked his head to the side as he considered her. "I will, of course, recognize your claim to the Darrenton name and holdings, but as those holdings are across the border, the ultimate authority, in that case, falls to King Saldin. I will include that in my missive to him. For now, we will start with the Silverblood Brotherhood and freeing your companion. Are we in agreement?"

Raven bowed. It felt like the right thing to do. "We are, your majesty."

"Very well. Captain Reysa, gather your troop. I will have a missive and my decree prepared within the hour. I expect everyone going to the Brotherhood temple to be ready to leave by then. You may go."

Raven bowed again, guided by the bow that Reysa offered the king. Then she turned and joined her companions in filtering from the room. If any of them objected to rescuing Marek, they didn't say so. They went to gather their weapons and get ready for departure.

By the time the hour was up, all of them, even Alayne, were in the courtyard, mounted and ready to ride with Captain Reysa's troop to the Brotherhood temple.

Reysa arrived with a unit of fifteen mounted soldiers she directed to surround Raven's group, arranging them to make sure the four Silverbloods were together at the center. When she was satisfied, she turned to lead them out, and Raven began to pull up her hood.

"There's no need for that," Reysa called to her. "Not only has King Navaran declared you legal, but the four of you are also under his protection. The time for you to be seen starts now, assuming you're still willing."

The idea of going out into the busy city streets, of all the people who would be staring at the elven Silverbloods, made Raven's blood run cold. Her hands trembled as she lowered the hood back down. Phendaril's voice reached her then, an anchor amidst the threatening panic. She turned to see that he had moved his mount up beside Synderis.

"Stay close to her. She's not one for crowds."

Synderis gave a nod. "At all times."

She caught Phendaril's eye as he backed his mount up to move behind the Krivalen group and offered a shaky smile of gratitude. His subdued return smile made her wonder what it cost him to ask Synderis to be there for her when there was little doubt he would prefer to be the one in that position.

The group started to move, and Synderis eased his mount closer to her. "This time of day, there will be many people out. Focus your attention on Captain Reysa if you need to."

The comment reminded her so much of Marek's

advice when they came to the castle that it twisted a place of guilt deep inside. Had she waited too long? How fast would they judge and punish him for helping her? Fear and worry made way for anger.

"What good am I if I still can't face a crowd without feeling sick to my stomach," she snapped.

His chuckle surprised her, and she jerked away from the hand he put on her arm, which earned her another soft laugh. She caught herself before snapping at him a second time, realizing her fear was making her temperamental.

His warm smile was open and full of affection, helping to keep her mind, for the moment, off the large number of citizens parting before their sizeable party as they moved into the streets.

"Raven, you're instrumental in events that could change the future of this country, especially for our kind. But if that isn't enough to convince you of how amazing you are, I'm happy to start listing all of the things I find remarkable about you."

Raven's cheeks grew warm, and she faced forward, taking his advice to focus on Reysa's back. The woman's posture was so rigid it almost looked uncomfortable and gave Raven something to contemplate. The people in the streets did precisely what she expected, turning to stare, first at the troop riding through, then, more specifically, at the four Krivalen riding openly at the center of that group. Given that they were heading toward the temple, people might assume they were taking the elves to the Brotherhood as prisoners. However, the extensive weaponry the *prisoners* carried suggested otherwise.

Cyrleth, excited by the attention, started to prance, drawing more eyes to her. Swallowing back her rising panic, Raven used a touch of magic to calm the animal down. Then she began to try doing the same to herself. It made sense that if she could put herself to sleep with her own magic, she might also be able to calm herself. She didn't get to test the theory, however, before a sense of comfort eased into her along her connection with Synderis.

Raven cast a sidelong glance at him and caught his faint smile. A smile tugged at her lips, and she held her head a little higher.

"Look at that cat!"

The shout came from somewhere in the crowd of onlookers. Suddenly, they were no longer staring only at the Krivalen. Many were moving around, trying to get a look at Koshika, who padded along beside Synderis's horses inside the barrier of guards. The lalyx cat ignored their attention. Raven did her best to emulate the cat's confidence and lack of concern. She almost felt like she was getting the hang of it when they turned a corner, and a structure that was the twin of the Brotherhood temple in Pellanth rose before them, all dark stone and harsh angles with several spires piercing up into the sky.

Her breath caught in her throat. A cold sweat formed on her forehead, and the hair on the back of her neck rose. Memory swept in. The pain of glass cutting her skin, of the blade slicing against her breastbone. Her head throbbed from the blow Wayland had dealt her. Her death danced in his eyes as he stared down at her, gathering magic to claim her spirit.

They were crossing into the courtyard when Cyrleth balked and reared, reacting to the surge of panic in her. The move broke her from her memories. She leaned into the rear as the mounts around them startled away. When his front hooves struck the ground again, Phendaril drove his horse up into the newly cleared space beside her.

He wrapped a hand around hers on the reins and met her eyes. Comfort came from simply knowing that he had been there. He had seen her come crawling out of the Pellanth temple covered in blood. He knew what she was remembering.

He leaned in close. "You don't have to go in there," he said in a low voice. "This part can be handled without you."

Cyrleth was still now. She knew it must be one of the other three Krivalen influencing him since her own influence was undone by her panic. No matter how she tried, awareness of their audience made her skin prickle with discomfort. "I do, Phen."

She forced herself to look at the temple as if meeting the eyes of a dreaded adversary. This might look the same, but Wayland wasn't here. No wings of a stuffed wyvern were visible through the half-glass walls and ceiling of the display room to the right of the courtyard. These men were Silverbloods. They still meant her harm, but they weren't the same men, and she wasn't facing them alone. She was also stronger now than when she had fought Wayland. This time would be different.

Raven met Phendaril's eyes. "I'm all right." She turned her hand to squeeze his. "Thank you." Then she let go of him and met Captain Reysa's gaze. The woman's brow furrowed, and she wondered if Alayne had told King Navaran and his captain something of what happened to her in Pellanth. Raven nodded to her.

The captain gave a quick nod back.

The group started forward again, resuming their formation. Phendaril held his mount back, allowing Synderis to move in beside her as they advanced.

"Are you ready to face these Silverbloods?"

Raven drew a breath and let it out slowly. "I am."

It wasn't comfort or safety that swept across their connection this time. It was love and pride, and it helped her to believe that she might truly be ready.

Entering the temple of her own volition, surrounded by her companions, Captain Reysa, and five soldiers, broke down more of Raven's fear. Ten more soldiers waited with the horses out front, ready to rush in at any sign of trouble. In Pellanth, she had only ever seen this entry hall from the balcony the day her companions convinced Aldrich Darrenton to ask for her release. Today, she was merely a visitor, standing on the protected side of the king's new edict, of which Captain Reysa held one of the first copies.

The man she had met briefly at the castle, Father Markon Mallebron, came striding into the room. Five Silverblood warriors followed him in, enough to make for a total of seven in the entry hall, which evened the odds a little. Unlike Wayland, he seemed to prefer a slightly more ornate version of the Silverblood armor instead of fine clothes for his daily attire. His shorter hair, while still the same liquid silver color as Wayland's, gave him a marginally less surreal and dominating presence. Or maybe it only felt that way because she was flanking Captain Reysa, who had quite a severe presence of her own when she wanted to.

His molten gaze swept over them, taking in the Eyl'Thelandran elves, then lingering the longest on Raven. He started to turn to Reysa, but then his gaze jumped back to Telandora for several seconds before he narrowed his eyes at Raven.

"Why are *your* eyes so different?"

Reysa inelegantly cleared her throat. "We're not here to discuss Lady Darrenton's eyes, Father Mallebron."

When he looked at the captain again, a blade of open disdain cut across the distance between them. "That is awkward, given that I had been expecting a transfer of the prisoner. Your collection of elven Silverbloods is... unexpected. It appears the king has been hiding things from us."

Reysa, ignoring his accusation, held out two folded parchments, both bearing the king's seal. "The first is an edict from the king stating that Silverbloods of any race or gender, even those whose creation was not sanctioned by the Silverblood Brotherhood, are recognized as legal citizens by the crown. This copy is for you should you wish to read through the additional details. The second declares that Silverblood Marek is to be released immediately by order of the crown."

The muscles in Markon's jaw tightened as she spoke, his eyes narrowing to angry slits. It looked to Raven as if he wanted to spit on the captain, though he restrained himself. The silver in his eyes flashed, but Raven found it didn't bother her. Somehow, *he* didn't bother her, even though he did share Wayland's last name.

Markon cast a disgusted glance at the two items Reysa held out to him. His gaze flickered to Raven. "Your Silverblood is no longer here."

Reysa lowered her hand a fraction, recognizing that he was in no hurry to take the documents. "Where is he?"

Raven was suddenly somewhere else, sucked into the Acridan's memories.

A massive old forest rose around her. She leaned in the doorway of a structure, weakness dragging at her limbs.

Inside, Markon stood next to an Acridan who lay back on a partially reclined resting chair, breath coming in shallow rasps. The Acridan's skin was covered in open sores. The bone plating over parts of its body was cracked and broken, the disease turning it brittle. In places, the plating had broken off entirely, the exposed flesh raw and inflamed.

Markon—his eyes and hair only touched with silver, newly transformed by the Krivalen magic—looked up at her, a challenge in his narrowed eyes.

"Where is he?" she asked.

"Wayland rode out with a group this morning," Markon answered, dropping his gaze to the Acridan who lay dying before him, a defensive edge in his tone.

She looked at the conspicuous empty spot on a desk made of woven branches behind him, not surprised but profoundly disappointed. "He stole the book."

Markon glanced up, his lips pressed together, eyes full of disdain. Every bit the image of a pouting child. "You refused to teach us any more of your magic, so we took what you denied us. What good is the book to you once you're all dead anyhow?"

She shook her head, even that tiny motion requiring more energy than it should. "Why take a book you can't read? What do you hope to gain?"

He lifted his head now, defiant and proud, but still a child. "You underestimate our linguists. We will figure it out in time."

Raven gasped, slamming back into the present moment. Her magic was already extended, weaving around the defenses of Markon's magic like it had a mind of its own. It pushed into him the misery of the illness he and his fellows brought to the Acridan and the pain of watching everyone it cared for dying around it. It finished with the fear and desperation of being hunted when it knew it was the last of its kind. She walked forward as the magic insinuated itself deeper, stepping past Reysa. Markon's gaze locked on Raven now, his eyes widening.

"You still can't read it, can you?" Raven asked, her voice speaking words that were not hers. "Everything we taught you, you twisted to your purposes and corrupted, but you're still little more than children trying to puzzle out a complicated new toy." Something else flowed through her, riding on the wave of her magic. Angry darkness. Loathing. She fed that into him, and Markon sank to his knees, fear shining bright in his silver eyes. "It was never meant for you," she growled at him.

"Raven."

Synderis's voice was soft, barely loud enough to bridge the distance between them. The accompanying powerful surge of concern and love sweeping across their connection broke the moment. She looked at Markon, kneeling there before her. A few silver tears ran down his cheeks as he stared up at her.

"You're right," he whispered, "we can't read it, but you can teach us. Please. Teach us. Teach me."

The dark magic swelled up again, and Raven snarled down at him. "Never." For a second, she fought to remember why she was there. It wasn't this. That patient, calming flow from Synderis continued to push against the lethal hatred. Then it came back to her. "Where is Adept Marek?"

"Wayland had plans for him. I sent him north yesterday, up the inside passage."

As Raven turned away from the Brotherhood priest, Reysa stepped forward, throwing the papers on the floor at Markon's knees.

"The king will expect your cooperation."

Once Raven's back was to him, the pressure of the strange memories and magic lifted. She strode swiftly for the exit, managing, with an almost painful exercise in resolve, not to run. Synderis turned to join her as she passed, concern furrowing his brow. In a matter of seconds, the rest of the party was also following. Powerful nausea roiled in her gut, improving only marginally when they left the temple and hurried down the steps into the courtyard.

Raven reached for Cyrleth's reins.

"Stop!"

Her skin prickling with dread, Raven slowly turned.

Reysa stormed up to her, face flushed, her grey eyes blazing. "What was that?" she demanded, cutting the air with one hand to point back at the temple. "If we've traded the threat of the Brotherhood for something worse, I want to know it now."

Synderis, Phendaril, and Davon came to Raven's side immediately. They were quickly joined by Ehric, Jael, and the other two Krivalen. Alayne stood off to one side, glancing from them to Reysa and her soldiers, shifting her feet as if not quite sure which way to go. Reysa's soldiers moved closer to her, their postures becoming more aggressive.

Synderis held out a staying hand and stepped past Raven, catching Reysa's attention. "You have not. We will explain everything to King Navaran when we return, but we must go now if we want to help Marek."

Raven sent a wash of gratitude across their connection, both for his intervention and his assertion that they needed to go after Marek now. If he felt it, he gave no indication.

"You can't just leave. There are things that need to be done here if we're going to start changing people's beliefs about Silverblood elves and women, about the Brotherhood. You need to work with us. This is not the way to do that."

"Marek would come for me if our situations were reversed," Raven said, stepping up next to Synderis.

Reysa met her eyes. The muscles in her jaw jumped as she gritted her teeth. Then she signaled her soldiers to stand down. "Fine. We'll go after him. I doubt we could stop the lot of you anyhow. We'll take two of the king's galleys upriver."

"The inside passage is faster," Phendaril countered.

"The king's river galleys are at least as fast. The Silverbloods have a full day on us, and we would have to stop at some point to rest and feed the horses. If we take a full crew, we can cycle out our rowers and keep up speed through the night on the galleys."

A glimmer of hope fluttered in Raven's chest like a butterfly with fragile new wings. "Will the king let us take them?"

Reysa met her eyes. "I have the authority to do so, but when this is all done, you are going to explain to him what happened in there. To both of us." She glanced around at them, then at her soldiers. She ordered one to take a message back to the king and watched him as he rode away. A stern scowl pulled the corners of her mouth down. She cast Raven an irritable look. "You owe me."

Raven nodded. Some debts were difficult to pay, but she was willing to risk it this time.

•

Synderis watched Raven swing up on her black horse. Cyrleth started to prance and toss his head in anticipation, reacting to the same anxious energy he could feel along their bond. Then she placed a hand on the animal's shoulder, her gaze turning inward for a second, and the gelding calmed. She was getting good at that. Unnervingly so.

The Delegate's warning played back in his mind. Was this what they were supposed to be careful of? Had the power he felt coming off her in the temple been Krivalen magic she gained from the Acridan she Accepted or some of the fey magic that had corrupted that Acridan? Both perhaps. No matter the answer, getting her out of the city where he could dig into the situation a little more safely seemed the best course.

Some of the others, Phendaril included, were now keeping a subtle watch on her. All except Davon, whose affection and loyalty appeared almost worshipful. Whatever he had seen her do—involving a storm drake, apparently—had placed her high above them all in his esteem. Maybe she needed someone like that. Someone who didn't know enough of the Krivalen magic or of Raven herself to fear what they saw moments ago.

He caught Telandora's eyes. She gave the slightest shake of her head, her usual easygoing nature buried beneath an uncommon stiffness of bearing. Her jaw tightened as she, too, had to calm her mount when it responded to the anxious mood of its rider. At his side, Koshika growled low in her throat, as sensitive as the horses to the disquiet in the air. Synderis scratched behind her ears, offering comfort from a place that lacked such emotion. A sense of dread weighed heavy in his stomach as he swung up on his horse.

The next couple of hours went by without the opportunity to talk to Raven. They rode directly to the king's docks, the guards granting clearance at Reysa's orders. It took some time to get the crews and supplies together on such short notice, but once they did, loading proceeded quickly. With four Krivalen to keep the horses calm, the animals boarded easily. Telandora and Lindyl offered to ride on the second galley to keep up the management of the horses, eliminating the risk to the animals and the crew who had to work around them. Alayne, Jael, and Ehric also boarded the second galley, leaving Raven, Phendaril, Davon, and Synderis together with Captain Reysa on the first.

It was an awkward division in some ways but not an unpredictable one. Of the five who went to ride on the second galley, only the Stonebreaker, Ehric, was noticeably reluctant to part from Raven. He was even more hesitant to split from Jael, however, who followed Alayne to the second ship. Like Phendaril and Davon, Synderis was unwilling to be separated from Raven. At least Davon didn't appear to share his and Phendaril's intimate affection for her. That was another reason he thought the young guard's presence might be good for her.

The rowers who descended below decks to make good on Reysa's promise of speed were made of lean, powerful muscle. They looked well-fed, and many smiled and laughed, joking crudely with one another as they vanished below, making it apparent that they were compensated at least fairly for their labor.

Whatever they were paid, they were worth their weight in gold. Before long, the galleys were sweeping upriver. One man's entire job appeared to be blowing a horn near the captain's wheel to warn other vessels out of their path, and he took to that job with gusto. Reysa watched the horses the first few times the horn blew. When they remained calm, she grinned and gave Synderis a nod, acknowledging the positive side of her new allies' powers.

CHAPTER TWENTY NINE

For most of that afternoon, Raven stayed up the bow. Koshika curled next to her on the deck, alternating between dozing or grooming. None of them bothered her. Synderis waited, working out how to approach the subject of what happened in the temple without making it sound like he was accusing her of anything. Phendaril stayed away for reasons of his own. Davon's reluctance was more obvious. He looked as though he wanted to join her but opted instead to hang back, wandering restlessly from one side of the galley to the other, eyeing Koshika from a distance. He appeared to be waiting for the lalyx cat to depart.

As evening moved in, Phendaril approached Synderis, plucking a stubborn fall leaf from a tree branch that hung out over the galley as he came to stand beside him at the railing. Synderis offered a nod of acknowledgment that the other elf returned before turning to gaze out over the water.

"I want to talk to her," Phendaril stated in a low voice, "but as much as I hate to admit it, I don't think I'm who she needs right now. What happened in the temple... that seems more like your area of expertise. I don't think she should be left alone much longer, however."

Synderis reached out along the connection, careful not to alert her, but with enough magic to feel that her mood had quieted, her fear and confusion no longer spiraling into a hurricane of directionless anger. Phendaril was right. It was time for someone to talk to her. "It would please me to talk to her with your approval."

Phendaril smirked. "I really want to dislike you, but the more I get to know you, the harder I find it to do so."

Synderis grinned. "I'll take that as a compliment."

Phendaril crumpled the dry leaf and tossed it overboard. "Regardless, I'm not sure my approval matters in this case. I have no jurisdiction over what she wants or needs."

Synderis watched the mangled leaf floating on the water for a few seconds before one of the oars swept it under. "Nor do I, but we are the ones whose thoughts and opinions she values most. How we treat that power, and each other, does matter."

Phendaril answered with a crooked smirk. "Not to denigrate your words, because I know they're true, but I would still be much happier if I thought I was the one best suited to help her. Unfortunately, after what I saw at the temple, I feel ill-equipped for the task. You are far better prepared to understand what she's dealing with right now."

"If it helps, I know what you're feeling." Synderis turned toward him. "I've led a very... protected life. There are many things about her that you're better suited to understand. This is just the one thing I can help her with, and to be honest, even I'm a bit out of my depth in this case. I will do the best I can for her."

Phendaril glanced down at the water. "I know you will," he said softly.

Recognizing that for the approval it was, Synderis made his way to the bow of the boat. Koshika stood when he got close, unwrapping herself from around Raven's feet to make room for him. The big cat sauntered a few strides back from them and sprawled across the deck, forcing anyone else who might try to join them to have to pass by her. Synderis smiled to himself, appreciating the animal's efforts as he stopped a step away from the railing.

Raven didn't turn. She would know it was him, both because of the cat's reaction and because she would recognize his footsteps. She was remarkably attuned to such details.

"You're welcome to join me." She moved her hand off the railing enough to indicate the space beside her, then rested it back down.

"You've been up here for a long time. You must be cold," he said, stepping up next to her.

"Stand closer, then," she countered.

Synderis glanced back to see that Phendaril was no longer where he had left him. Looking around, he spotted him descending below deck. Whether or not they had an audience, he would offer Raven whatever she needed. Still, it was a relief not to have to torment the other elf in the process.

He slid one arm behind her waist, and she shifted, turning a little to lean into him, her head coming to rest against his shoulder. A soft breath escaped him, and he tightened his hold, allowing himself a moment to relish how wonderful it was to have her close to him again. He kept a grip on the railing with the other hand, supporting them both as the sweeping of the oars pushed them forward, defying the current.

He placed a kiss on her head. "Are you all right?"

"I'm not." Her voice was tight, and he suspected he might find the damp of tears on her cheeks if he touched them. "I feel like something else is trying to take control of me, of who I am."

"What happened back there?"

She pulled away, and he reluctantly let her go. When

she looked at him, he could see the faint shimmer of dampness on her cheeks in the moonlight. "I had one of those vivid memories, but it wasn't my memory. It was the Acridan's, of Markon. The memory dredged up so much anger and hatred. It was as if those emotions unleashed something darker. The power came from the Acridan, but not as it was in the time that memory occurred. As it was after the fey magic fed upon its fear and rage for all those years in isolation. What if I can't stop it next time? What if you're not there to break me out of it?"

Her voice started to rise and get faster as she spoke. Synderis cupped the side of her jaw in his hand and brushed a thumb lightly over the damp track of her tears. "I will be there. I will be there for as long as you need and want me. Until we figure out how to control this, I won't leave your side unless it's at your bidding."

The moonlight picked out the brighter flecks of silver in her dark eyes, making them look more than ever like stars in the night sky. Her mouth hung slightly open as if she meant to speak, but her gaze was searching his face now, perhaps looking for some indication that his words weren't true.

He swallowed a touch of fear, forcing his voice to be steady and confident. "Not even to go home. I will not return there without you, Raven, not unless you want me to."

"I don't want you to," she whispered.

Her eyes flickered down to his lips as she stepped closer. He met her halfway in a soft kiss. Her lips were cool from standing in the breeze at the bow for so long. After much too brief a moment, she drew back a little, still near enough for him to feel the warmth of her breath on his lips.

"Do I ask too much of you?" she asked softly.

Synderis smiled. "You do."

Then he drew her in, pulling his cloak around her, and kissed her until her lips were warm again. They would have no true privacy on the galley, but fewer people were on deck than usual, with some of the crew and passengers gone below to rest. This was the best they would get, and he intended for her to feel how much he loved and wanted her.

When they finally parted, she slid her arms around him and rested her head against his shoulder again. "I missed you. I'm glad you're here, even if it makes some things harder."

He didn't have to ask what things those were. Phendaril might have gone below deck, but his presence was still very much there. Nothing could be done to solve that now. They all had more important things to deal with first.

"I could guide you into a dreamwalk with the Delegate. She's the only one who has ever Accepted an Acridan that I know of, though even she admits that your situation is different."

Raven didn't move. "You've talked to her already?"

"I was worried."

Her soft laugh had a bitter edge. "I can't imagine why."

He took her hand and pressed it to his chest. "I told you I would help you through this."

She breathed a sigh. "If we get Marek back, then what? We follow Captain Reysa around the countryside, undermining the power of the Brotherhood and making life better for our kind? Can we do that? It seems presumptuous to think that someone like me could have that kind of influence. After spending most of my life hiding from everyone, I'm not sure I know how to be seen."

"As someone else who spent most of their life isolated from the outside world, I can honestly say this isn't the way I saw my life going either."

She drew back from him and leaned against the railing, looking at him with thoughtful little lines furrowing her brow in the dark. Her scrutiny went on long enough to make him shift his feet with a hint of unease.

"I suppose not," she finally agreed. "Do you regret it? Meeting me? Having your life thrown into all of this turmoil?"

Synderis matched the graveness of her expression. "All this change you brought into my life wasn't something I ever wanted. I was comfortable. Everyone I cared about was safe. Now I've had to kill people. I'll even have a scar forever reminding me of one of those fights. I'm out in the world trying to help change how you and other Krivalen like you are treated. I've seen more of this continent already than almost anyone from Eyl'Thelandra will ever see. I've seen its cruelty and its beauty. Through it all, I've loved and been loved by the bravest woman I've ever met." He smiled fondly. "I regret nothing, anweyn."

She gazed at him with such affection then that he no longer noticed the chill in the air. "You're too good for the world out here."

She took his hand as she sank to the deck alongside the railing, drawing him down with her. When they were settled there, sitting side by side, he wrapped his arm and cloak around her. She shifted to lean against him.

"What happened when you faced Wayland before?"

"I could show you if you're up for it." She held one hand out. "It isn't pleasant."

He had seen the scars from her fight with the Silverblood priest. They covered most of her body. It would be hard to bear witness to, but it was a memory she currently shared only with the Silverblood priest. Perhaps it would do her good to share it with another in this way.

Of course, it would mean reliving it herself, but she was no fool. She knew that when she offered.

He took her hand, twining his fingers into hers.

An uncertain amount of time later, he was still reeling from the blow to the head she had taken. Pain coursed through him from myriad cuts, mostly from the glass shards that had fallen from the ceiling. The worst was the cut down her breastbone; the blade tip pressed deep enough to touch bone. Even experiencing it with her that way, it was hard to believe the amount of injury her body had sustained, the pain she had managed to think through enough to get herself out of there.

She had taken him right up to the moment she blacked out. He saw Phendaril fighting the Silverblood, intent on trying to rescue her. He also saw Marek betray his Brotherhood to let her go. He was grateful to them both for the parts they played in saving her life that night. It was getting harder to want Phendaril out of it.

Raven trembled against him, her hand clutching his so tight that it hurt. He squeezed his arm around her, hugging her close. "Show me something else now. Show me Jaecar."

He let her draw him into her memories again, much farther back this time.

A slip of a young half-elven girl, perhaps fifteen, faced off against a bear of a man, his long hair tied at the nape of his neck, showing the first hints of grey. He wielded the wooden equivalent of a broadsword while she danced in with a blunt-edged metal short sword and dagger. It looked like a grossly imbalanced match, but no fear showed in the silver eyes of the girl, only excitement tempered by an intense focus for one so young.

She darted in suddenly, her Silverblood speed bringing her almost into striking range before he managed to block her. She leapt back and lunged in again, feinting to one side and then darting away so quickly that she succeeded in catching him with a swipe to the well-padded ribs. The man grinned and gave a shake of his head, twisting to face her again. He was fast and remarkably agile for his size, but the girl was faster and even more agile.

When she feinted to one side again, he was ready for it, feinting in response and then swinging back before fully committing to the move. He managed to block her blade this time, but his attempt to retaliate wasn't quick enough. She leapt out of his reach.

They danced like this until exhaustion added pounds to the weight of their practice blades, both of them struggling to lift the weapons. Their attacks and blocks grew sluggish and stumbling. Their breath came in heavy gasps. They circled, each looking for an opening they had enough energy left to take advantage of. Then Raven's sword dipped, and the warrior lunged. She was gone before he could strike, rolling under his attack and coming up behind him, her sword point pressing hard into the armor on his back.

The warrior held up his hands, letting his wooden sword drop. When he turned to face her, he was grinning proudly. "Well done, little Raven. I think you've finally earned a real sword."

She beamed at him, sweat tickling as it dripped over her face and ran down the middle of her back. The point of her sword sank to the ground as if she really could no longer hold it up. "And a hot cider," she countered.

The man chuckled. "You drive a hard bargain."

"I could have demanded your life," she boasted boldly.

He picked up the wooden sword and started strolling toward the door of the crumbling keep behind them, dragging the point along the dirt. As he passed her, he ruffled her hair. "Then who would warm the cider?"

"Good point," she answered, falling into step next to him, her sword point dragging like his, a tiny mirror of the exhausted warrior. A sense of weary accomplishment

rolled off her.

The memory faded. Raven was no longer trembling against him. She was quiet and calm. She freed her hand from his and reached up under the collar of her shirt. When she brought her hands back down, she held the arrowhead pendant Phendaril had made her.

"What are you doing?"

"Going for a dreamwalk. Can I anchor to you?" she asked, draping the pendant across her leg.

Synderis tensed. "I don't think it's a good idea."

"We may not get to Marek before they get him to Pellanth. Maybe, if I tell Wayland I'm already on my way, he won't feel the need to torture him."

"I still don't think it's a good idea," he repeated, "but I would rather you do it safely anchored to me than try to do it on your own, which is what I suspect will happen if I say no." He took her lack of argument as a firm confirmation.

"Thank you." She placed her hand back in his.

"Remember, the Acridan almost certainly had memories with Wayland as well. There's a risk of those surfacing and causing the same loss of control you experienced with Markon." He could feel her muscles tense at his words, and a flicker of hope rose in his chest. Maybe she would change her mind now that she realized the additional dangers.

"Hold me. Send the comfort and safety you've given me before across our connection. The... the love," she added with more hesitation than he liked. "I think that will help."

"Do you doubt that I love you?"

Raven shifted enough to look up at him. "No. I doubt whether you should."

"Let me worry about that, anweyn. You worry about getting in and out of the dream unharmed."

Raven moved to lean against him once more. With

her physically touching him, their connection was strong enough that he felt it when she anchored to him and plunged herself down into sleep. His part in this was easy. All he had to do was love her. He could think of no way to stop doing that.

aven stepped into the dream and shuddered at finding herself standing in a strange bedroom. Everything, from the canopy over the bed and the draping curtains to the cushioned chair by the fire, was done in the black and silver of the Brotherhood. Even the wood had a black stain that mostly hid the natural color. The only brightness came from a vase of yellow and violet flowers sitting on a table near one window.

At the center of that window, Wayland stood with his back to her, long liquid silver hair cascading down over his black and silver robe. Her stomach tightened at the idea of being alone in his bedchamber with him. The hair on the back of her neck lifted when he spoke without turning, somehow aware of her presence.

"My Raven. How could you leave me so alone?"

Raven stared at his back, unsure how to respond to the odd question. After a few seconds of uncomfortable silence, she said, "I was never your anything, and I never will be."

"You are meant to be one of my trophies," he countered, a sinister pleasure in his voice.

He turned then, and memory swept in, crashing over her with the force of a storm wave. Not just a single memory but a barrage of memories overlapping one another until a particular one forced its way to the front.

Wayland stood at the edge of a dense thicket, his hair shorter and much less silver. He stared down at a cowering Acridan. The scars and degenerated bone plating of the disease that had killed most of its kind were apparent over its weakened body. She watched from inside the tree line, hidden and trying to keep her panicked breathing soft enough that they wouldn't hear. Long, chalky blue fingers gripped the bark of one tree so hard it made her hand hurt. Her limbs trembled with fatigue, still not fully recovered from the sickness these men brought to the Acridan. A dark feeling deep within her compelled her to no longer entirely believe the illness they delivered to her kind was unintentional.

Four more men traveled with Wayland. Some of his new Silverbloods, as he and his companions had dubbed themselves, choosing to abandon the Acridan name for the magic in order to claim it as their own. They stood over the fallen Acridan, pitiless silver eyes glaring down at it. It put one hand in front of it as if to ward them off.

"Where's the other one?" Wayland demanded.

The Acridan trembled as it lied to them, protecting her. "I exist alone," it answered in broken Thedan.

"Kill it," Wayland growled.

Pain flared from the center of her being as if something was tearing its way out of her chest when one Silverblood swung his sword, cutting through the fallen Acridan's hand and into its neck. Her hand tightened convulsively on the tree, breaking two brittle fingernails.

Love and warmth swept through Raven, breaking her free of the memory and pulling her back into herself. Synderis. Still, the pain of the Acridan's loss lingered, feeding into her hatred of the man in front of her.

"Why are you the only one whose dreams I can enter? And why can't I enter them anymore?" He took several steps closer to her. His eyes narrowed, brows pinching together. His voice rose with every word. "You've changed. Your eyes are different. Why? You found your mother's people, didn't you? What did you learn from them?"

The barrage of questions caught her off guard, opening her to a fresh surge of memories flashing through her mind. Wayland, Markon, and another man helping the Acridan repair one of their shelters. Wayland laughing with the Acridan as they shared drinks and foods that were strange to each other. So many memories, all blackened by betrayal, tempered only by the connection that Synderis continued to flood with love and safety. Raven shook her head, trying to clear it, drowning under thoughts and emotions born from someone else's experiences.

"We never meant that knowledge for you." She bared her teeth at him in a feral snarl.

His lip lifted in an answering snarl. "I'll have Marek soon, and I will find out from him what you know."

The change of focus to Marek, someone the Acridan never knew, helped clear her head. With support from Synderis bolstering her, Raven barked a laugh. "Do you think me an idiot? Marek betrayed me once before in favor of the Brotherhood. Do you really believe I would share anything important with him after that?" It was too easy to recall the night she had fought Wayland and died for her trouble. But she didn't bear that memory alone anymore. Synderis shared it with her now, which made it less terrifying somehow. She lifted her chin, glaring a warning at him. "Let Marek go, and I may be more forthcoming when I get there."

"You're still coming here? Even though Darrenton is gone?" He arched one brow in disbelief.

"Will you ever leave my companions and me in peace if I don't?"

He eyed her warily and slowly shook his head. "Not until I have what I want."

Raven gave a nod to indicate she had expected his answer. "Then, unless you're willing to come and meet me at Darrenton's manor, I see no alternative."

Taking a few more steps closer, he leaned in to glower down at her. "I will never come to you."

Anger swelled up in her, bringing a wave of magic with it. "Sit!"

The room changed around them, becoming the massive central chamber of the crumbling keep she had grown up in, complete with threadbare carpets and rough-made furnishings. A rickety wooden chair had appeared in the center of the floor, with Wayland now sitting in it. The surprise in his eyes matched that she barely kept hidden. This was the first time she had succeeded in fully taking charge of someone else's dreamwalk. Not only that, but she had changed his dream. She had controlled it and remade it the way Synderis had done with hers a few times. The way he glanced around, his hands gripping the sides of the chair, told her she had managed to unsettle him.

Then a fire lit in his eyes, the moment of surprise giving way to fury. Knowing how strong he was, she wasn't about to allow him the opportunity to act on it.

"You will let Marek go. He's of no use to you." She took a step closer, looming over him for once as she reached for her anchor to Synderis. "I'm the one you want, and I am coming."

•

Raven jerked awake. Synderis tightened his arms around her, and she curled in against him. The strength of his love coming across their connection was nearly overwhelming now that sleep no longer separated them. She placed her hand over his heart.

"Do you really feel this much love for me?" she asked, her voice barely rising above a whisper.

"More," he answered as softly. "Did you accomplish what you went in for?" He brushed a lock of hair back from her face, concern shadowing his gaze.

"I hope so," she murmured, closing her eyes to savor his touch.

Raven stayed curled against him for a time in contented silence. When she started to drift off to normal sleep, she made herself sit up and slipped the pendant over her head. The Amberwood arrowhead rested warm in her palm. A memory of the day Phendaril had given it to her tried to take over, but she resisted, pushing it back. As lovely as that memory was, it was also bittersweet at that moment.

She wrapped her fingers around the pendant. "We should get some rest."

Synderis closed his hand over hers. "Yes, we should." He kissed her forehead, then got up, offering a hand to help her to her feet.

Raven took his hand. The help wasn't needed, and she was confident he knew that, but she liked that he always offered.

•

It was impossible to miss the two royal galleys sweeping up the river toward the Amberwood docks. Under the circumstances, though Karsima couldn't come up with any sensible reason that the king would send two of his ships to Amberwood, she was confident this meant things had gone their way in Chadhurst. Within minutes of the sighting, Karsima was riding hard toward the Amberwood dock in the company of a small group of scouts and Stonebreakers. Given the condition

Phendaril had been in the last time he returned, she also brought Synal along in case anyone needed healing.

An alternating group of townsfolk remained stationed by the docks in Karsima's old quarters. The building they had used as their healer's facility was restored to its original purpose as a warehouse for goods coming to and from the town. When Karsima's party reached the dock, the first ship had already unloaded and moved to anchor a little farther up. The second ship was tied at the pier, and they were leading the horses off.

Raven, once scared of horses, now stood in the middle of the horse line with her black gelding, scratching under the animal's forelock. The guard Raven and Marek had hired from Darrenton's band of mercenaries, Davon, whose devotion to her was mildly disconcerting, was standing next to the animal, a hand resting on its shoulder, conversing with Raven.

Not far away, Phendaril, Ehric, Jael, and Synderis were talking with the king's bastard daughter, Captain Reysa, whom Karsima hadn't seen in over a year. The large, feathered cat sat at Synderis's side, her eyes drooping half closed as she enjoyed the absentminded scratching of his fingers along the back of her head and neck. Alongside the warehouse, the other two Silverbloods, Telandora and Lindyl were standing, hands clasped, leaning close to one another and talking in low voices, the white wisps of their breath mingling in the cold air. Their attentive looks and physical nearness attested to the intimacy of their conversation.

Not seeing Alayne among them, Karsima rode toward Reysa's group, forcing a smile she hoped hid her rising concern. They were short a few other people they had left with. Another of Darrenton's mercenaries who had hired on as a personal guard, Gerrod, she thought his name was, and Marek were still unaccounted for. Their numbers had grown, however, by at least ten or more royal guards at a glance.

Jael trotted over to intercept her group. Taking hold of the reins as she stopped her mount, he glanced up at her with a knowing smile. "Alayne's on board talking to the ship's captain still."

Karsima smiled her gratitude in return, a knot of dread uncoiling in her gut. "Thank you. What of Marek and Gerrod?"

Jael's gaze shifted to Raven and lingered there for too long a moment. "It's a long story, but Gerrod's dead and Marek was taken by the Silverbloods. We came north in pursuit. Some of us will ride east to the cross-roads and see if there is still any chance of heading them off. If not, we'll come back here to Amberwood to dis-cuss our options. King Navaran's guards can't go charg-ing across the border unannounced, so we need to be mindful of those restrictions."

Karsima grimaced. The potential for things to go wrong was extremely high. But that was often the case with anything that mattered. "The king is backing Raven?"

Jael nodded. "It's a good thing the other three showed up. I think he was considering handing her over to the Brotherhood. One half-elf wasn't enough to risk an incident with the Silverbloods over. A whole group of magically transformed elves, he was willing to put his influence behind. Once we resolve this Marek situation, Raven and the Silverblood elves are to go with Captain Reysa to start making it known that elves and women can be Silverbloods and that any such are to be recog-nized as legal citizens within the kingdom of Andioch."

Karsima grinned, pride welling inside her. Alayne was right. Though it had been a risk that almost went bad, it sounded like they would get Raven her freedom, at least on one side of the border.

Something he said registered then, and she frowned. "But you're here now to save Marek, the man who dragged Raven to the Silverblood temple, where she died at the hands of that bastard Silverblood priest." She shuddered at the thought of him, and her horse shifted uneasily beneath her.

Jael shrugged. "Raven insists. Whatever happened between the two since then, she seems to feel quite strongly about trying to help him." He nodded toward the galley, the corner of his mouth ticking up in a slight smirk. "I think she can tell you more."

Karsima's heart gave a little jump in her chest when she turned and spotted Alayne striding toward them, a smile spreading across her lips. Leaving her mount in Jael's hands, Karsima hopped to the ground and strode out to intercept her. She loved that Alayne didn't hesitate to embrace her, kissing her as though they hadn't seen each other for months. Karsima fell into that kiss, forgetting everyone else as she slid her hands around Alayne's waist to pull her closer.

Alayne pulled back a little, resting her arms on Karsima's shoulders. "I knew you'd come to meet us. I'm going with the Silverbloods and Captain Reysa to the crossroads. Want to join us? Oh, and Davon. He doesn't get far from Raven if he can help it."

"No Phendaril?"

Alayne's lips pressed together for a few seconds, and her gaze flickered to where the group stood around Captain Reysa. "No. We're planning a fast ride. His leg isn't quite ready for that."

Karsima frowned. Davon wasn't the only one who preferred to stay close to Raven. Had Synderis's arrival heralded the death of whatever remained between Phendaril and Raven? It wasn't that she disliked Synderis. He came across as a good person. But she couldn't pretend that she didn't have a favorite. "Is that the only reason?"

Alayne gave her a soft, affectionate smile. "It's been a little rough for him. You could stay and head back to town with him. We'll only be gone a couple of hours."

"And if you find out the Silverbloods are close?"

Alayne grinned. "We'll let *our* Silverbloods handle it. I have a feeling the four of them can handle things. The Brotherhood had a full day on us. It's unlikely we made up enough time to catch them, and Reysa won't cross the border without going through the proper procedures. I promised I wouldn't either."

Karsima kissed her again, a lingering kiss full of desire and unspoken promises that left them both breathless and flushed.

"I liked that," Alayne breathed, her emerald eyes bright with longing. "What was that for?"

"Just making sure you remember to come right back," Karsima answered with a teasing grin.

"Mm. You can count on it." She placed one more quick kiss on Karsima's lips before extracting herself and walking toward the horses. "Let's get moving," she shouted to the others. "We haven't got all day."

CHAPTER THIRTY ONE

I t took a few hours to ride up to the town and get everything sorted with Captain Reysa's troops. Then Synal insisted on checking Phendaril's leg and hand to see if he had done any additional damage on his adventures. Karsima saw Synal off a short time later. The healer reluctantly admitted that, despite her misgivings about him going with Raven, he was healed enough to start walking without the brace some and could begin more strengthening work with his hand. After Synal left, Karsima retrieved a decanter of wine and two goblets and returned to the sitting room.

"I'm surprised you didn't go with Alayne," Phendaril commented as she handed him a goblet and filled it.

It had been hard to watch her beloved ride off again, but it would be a much shorter absence this time. Ehric and Jael had graciously taken charge of getting Captain Reysa's soldiers settled with the possibility of them being there a few days. The fact that they had volunteered for the task as quickly as they had, giving her some time alone with Phendaril, confirmed Alayne's assessment of how her friend was doing and made her glad she decided to stay behind.

"Alayne isn't my only family here, Phen. I'm glad to have you back."

"And you're worried about me." He cast her a knowing

glance as he took a sip of his wine.

Karsima shrugged and sank into one of the other chairs. "I am."

Smudge sprinted into the room and came to a bouncing halt before the fire, tail in the air and hackles up as if he'd found some worthy foe. Then he spotted Phendaril. His imaginary opponent instantly forgotten, he bounded up onto Phendaril's lap and started to knead and purr enthusiastically. Setting aside the wine, Phendaril turned his attention to meeting the little cat's demands for affection. The nubs of his tiny horns were becoming more visible through the fluff of his grey-and-black kitten fuzz, and he butted them into Phendaril's hands, insisting on all the pets and scratches he could get. It was a treat to see a smile tugging at Phendaril's lips, though he hadn't looked as upset as she thought he would be even before Smudge's intervention.

"I was reluctant to send the Silverblood elves to Chadhurst."

"You did the right thing." He flipped the kitten on its back, and it wrapped its needle-sharp claws around his hand, kicking his palm with the ferocity of a far more impressive beast. Phendaril chuckled at the antics before continuing. "I think their arrival convinced King Navaran to stand behind Raven. Things might have gotten messy otherwise. Besides, Synderis seems like someone who can give her the support she needs."

Karsima regarded him thoughtfully for a moment, taking a few slow sips of the wine. He didn't look angry or particularly upset, but she knew him well enough to recognize how skilled he was at hiding his emotions. "Why do you say that?"

"He can help her work through the issues she's having with the Silverblood magic. It's clear he wants what's best for her."

"And you don't?"

He gave her an irritable scowl, a hint of emotion finally breaking through. "Of course, I do, but I don't have the patience and understanding he does. Nor do I have the knowledge of the magic to help her with it."

Karsima scowled back at him, a deliberate challenge. "You sell yourself short, Phen. And you didn't have that magic knowledge when the two of you fell in love. What if you are what she needs?"

He gave her a stern look. "I'm not sure it matters at this point."

"She's made her choice?" She watched his expression turn inward, and her heart ached for him.

"I don't know. The night before the others arrived—"

A knock on the door interrupted him.

Karsima finished swallowing a sip of wine and called, "Come in."

Jenner appeared with Sameth on his heels. The scout stepped ahead of Jenner as they came into the room. He gave Karsima a quick nod and offered a respectful but hurried bow to Phendaril.

"I just got back from a scouting circuit when I heard you were back and that some of your party went to check the crossroads. We've been crossing up to check on the Darrenton holding every few days. I thought you should know we spotted some Silverbloods up near the manor yesterday evening."

Phendaril set Smudge on the floor and stood. "How many?"

"There were six, though one of them was bound like a prisoner."

Karsima met Phendaril's eyes, seeing the same worry she felt in them. What if they were still up there?

"Get a couple of the others and meet us at the dock. We'll take a small boat up to Darrenton's dock and go in that way."

Sameth nodded and spun, hurrying from the building.

Karsima didn't try to argue. Instead, she went to grab her sword and join him. There was a good chance the Silverbloods had moved on, but what harm was there in going up to ensure Alayne and the others weren't walking into danger?

•

Raven kept to the front of the group alongside Captain Reysa. She knew the paths through the forest well enough now that she was comfortable being in the lead. It allowed her to focus on her current goal without other distractions creeping to the fore. She kept to a controlled canter wherever she could, weaving around the trees. It amazed her how smoothly she and Cyrleth worked together now. Going from terrified of horses to riding through the forest at speed like this seemed such an unlikely thing not long ago. Perhaps, if she could do this, there was also hope for her learning to control the changed magic in her.

A dull grey sky hung overhead, holding secret its intentions. As they got further inland, spots of frost and even a few patches of snow appeared on the ground. She suspected that it wouldn't be long before snow crept into the town. Would King Navaran want them to move about throughout the winter months, spreading his edict and exposing the lies of the Brotherhood? As exciting as the idea of traveling the land as a legal citizen was, she was growing tired of being on the move. It might be nice to hole up somewhere through the winter and relax for a time.

Where, though? Where was the place she would choose to stop moving? Amberwood? Eyl'Thelandra?

Somewhere else?

She fought the urge to glance over her shoulder at Synderis. He rode a little back from her so he could drop behind in areas where the path was narrower. Their pace and the variable trail made conversation impossible. It allowed her to sit in her own mind and consider what she would do if they had missed Marek, which she suspected they had. She would not give up on him, not after all he had done for her since the day he chose to help her escape the Brotherhood temple. They were a good team, and no matter what came of her other relationships, she found she liked the idea of having the adept in her life in some way.

There was Davon, too, of course. She appreciated him. The young man's devotion made her a little uncomfortable, but she recognized the value of it all the same. If she decided to take on the role of Lady Darrenton in any real fashion, she might keep him on as captain of her guards, but what did she do with him otherwise? It seemed insensitive to send him away, but keeping a personal guard like she thought she really was some noble lady made no sense. Maybe he could be convinced to work with the mercenaries that were settling into Amberwood. It might be worth investigating.

Raven spotted a small pack of wolves moving through the trees some distance ahead. The large canines, their coats thickened in preparation for winter, glanced in the riders' direction. They looked curious but not concerned. She recognized them, with the big grey alpha stalking near the back, from her time helping scout around Amberwood.

She missed it here. Eyl'Thelandra was like a paradise, but it was an exclusive one. Her father would not have been welcome there. If not for Dellaura, she never would have found welcome there either. Amberwood was different. They were open to everyone here. They had even allowed her to stay, despite the risk she posed. Life was more demanding and dangerous, but they all worked together to benefit the community. She admired that. Jaecar would have loved such an environment.

Then again, Eyl'Thelandra could protect her better, and the Delegate might be the only one who had a chance of helping her manage the changes in her magic. There were no simple answers.

Cyrleth kicked up his heels in a small buck, responding to her growing frustration. She gave a light tug on the bit to get his attention, then tapped him with her heels to focus him on the path ahead again.

It was hard to know what to do, but the idea of having options felt good. Not only that, but she was thinking as if she might live through the trials ahead and have the freedom to make those complicated choices. That was new. Maybe the situation wasn't so bleak after all.

They slowed the horses when they finally came up near the crossroads, bringing them down to a cautious walk. Alayne moved beside Raven, riding silently next to her until they got to the actual roadway. Then Raven stopped them. She dismounted and wandered along the rough track that led to the Darrenton holding. There was no sign of riders passing this way recently. With Aldrich Darrenton dead and construction on the manor halted, there wasn't much need for anyone to go out that way.

After a few minutes more, finding nothing of interest, she mounted back up and led them to where the more established road cut across, heading north and south. This road saw more frequent use, though not as much in the colder months when the rain and snow made the route less hospitable.

The rest of the group dismounted then. Reysa, Davon, and Alayne held back, watching the Krivalen investigate the roadway. A brief search found the recent tracks of five riders heading north. One horse moved along on the flank of another, close and consistent enough in its placement that it was almost certainly being led.

"These tracks are a good six hours old," Synderis commented, standing up from where he had crouched next to some of the prints.

"And moving fast," Raven added, meeting his eyes. It was discouraging, though, truth be told, she hadn't expected to come even this close.

"You're sure it's them?" Captain Reysa asked, gazing north as if she might spot them ahead.

Raven nodded. The timing was about right. The numbers and configuration matched. They had come close to catching them with the galleys, but not close enough.

"Then they'll be in Pellanth before we get to them. I can't take my soldiers after them into King Saldin's territory without following the proper protocols. I'm already pushing the limits by coming this far."

Raven simply nodded again. She'd known they weren't likely to catch the group, but somehow, she was still disappointed. All she could do now was hope Wayland was willing to recognize that Marek wasn't worth torturing. Despite how she had ended the dreamwalk, she didn't expect the Brotherhood priest to set him free after everything that had happened. She only hoped he wouldn't waste effort tormenting Marek when there was nothing to be gained from it. Maybe, if Wayland believed her, then Marek would be in decent shape when they finally did get him free.

Synderis strode over and placed a hand on her shoulder in silent comforting.

Reysa's regard was unexpectedly sympathetic. "We can take one of the galleys north tomorrow with a few guards. As long as we register with the proper authorities and explain our business in the city, we should be able to avoid any incidents. I have a copy of King Navaran's edict that I can use if they question any of you. King Saldin will respect that you are under King Navaran's protection."

"Thank you, Captain Reysa." Raven glanced at Alayne. "I'd like to look in on the manor before I go back. It'll add some time to the return trip, so I understand if you want to turn back directly from here."

Alayne looked instantly uncomfortable. "I don't think Phen would appreciate me leaving you out here."

"We'll be with her," Synderis indicated Telandora and Lindyl with two quick nods, "if you and the others want to take the more direct route."

"As will I," Davon added.

Raven smiled to herself, entirely unsurprised at that. A little too attentive, Davon caught her smile and offered a dashing grin in response, tossing his head to get a lock of his lengthening dark hair out of his eyes. He would be better off as a lord's guard somewhere, making young ladies swoon with those dimples of his instead of following her around. Perhaps she could persuade him to move on after this.

CHAPTER THIRTY TWO

It didn't take long to reach the edge of the woods behind the manor. Along the way, Raven felt a familiar presence lurking nearby. For now, the storm drake was quiet, not bothered by their passage, but it was as aware of her as she was of it. She hadn't intended to create any kind of long-term connection between them, but it was becoming clear that she had inadvertently done so. It must have found a place to nest in the area and chosen to stay. She hoped she hadn't influenced that choice in any way that might harm the beast. The sense she got from it now was one of contentment, so she would take that as a positive sign.

Things weren't as quiet at the manor, however. As they dismounted at the edge of the paddocks, Koshika growled low in her throat at a couple of corpse eaters. The scavengers were tearing at something in the shade beyond the south edge of the manor. Over where Aldrich and his men were buried. The faint smell of rotting flesh drifted to them on a light breeze.

"We buried them better than that," Davon said. "The corpse eaters shouldn't have been drawn to the graves."

Synderis handed his reins to Telandora. "You and Lindyl take the horses up by the other barn. Davon and I will investigate."

He looked at Raven, and she could see by the way

his gaze flickered from her to the other two Krivalen that he wanted to tell her to go with them as well. Part of her was inclined to do as he wished, but a stronger part felt like this was her problem to deal with. Still, Synderis alone could handle two corpse eaters. With Koshika and Davon there, he was in virtually no danger, so her solution fell somewhere in the middle.

"I'll check on things in the house. Be careful."

A hint of relief eased the tension on his face. "Always."

Leaving Cyrleth with Lindyl, Raven walked to the back door and stepped quietly inside. It felt odd to be there without Marek. She'd come to associate the big house with his presence. It was dark within and cold. Abandoning the building untended like this wasn't good for it. Still, it wasn't her property unless King Saldin chose to recognize her claim since this land was technically on his side of the border. That meant that caring for the place could actually get her into trouble.

As she moved through the hallway leading from the back entrance up to the front, she caught a soft scuffing sound somewhere ahead. Rats, perhaps, hopefully of the smaller variety. Fell rats in the house would condemn it to much faster decay. Another shuffling sound reached her from down the side hall she had just passed, and Raven froze. She listened carefully and heard someone breathing. Then movement started up in both side hallways and behind her. Boots scuffing the floor.

She softly drew her sword and advanced into the large entry, searching the dark corners for danger. The increasing sounds of approach came from three, possibly four, different directions. Whatever or whoever they were, they were closing off the route between her and the back exit, so she set a course for the front door. It occurred to her that if the sources of the sounds in the house were sentient, they might be intentionally driving her forward. Still, she would rather face whatever they were in the open where she could have plenty of room to maneuver, so she would take the chance. If a trap lay ahead, she would simply have to deal with it.

Her nerves crackled when she reached the front door and quickly threw it open. There was a very brief instant of relief at stepping out into the open, then she saw what she had been driven to. A stump was set about twenty feet beyond the entrance. A figure knelt with their torso lying over it, their hands bound behind them, and their head lying on the ground a few feet beyond. Raven didn't have to get closer to know who it was. She recognized his build, his hair, and the massive two-handed sword he carried that lay useless beside him.

For a moment, she couldn't draw a breath. Pain and rage sucked the air from her lungs, constricting her chest so she couldn't take any air in. Her legs went weak, her knees threatening to buckle. Then she heard a blade sliding from its sheath off to her right and more footsteps from within the entrance of the house behind her.

Raven glanced toward the sound of the weapon being drawn as she moved away from the door. She drew in a breath that tasted of loathing and darkness.

A Silverblood pushed off from the front wall of the house where he'd been leaning, admiring their handiwork. "We were wondering when you'd get here."

The other four Silverbloods came out through the door as she backed away, moving off to the left to avoid Marek's body and get to the open ground closer to where the mercenary camps had been. The grey sky started to darken, and a few fat drops of icy rain hit Raven's head. One of the Silverbloods scowled up at the sky, but they continued following after her, spreading out.

"You're not going to beat us all," the one who had spoken before said.

She realized then that she recognized him. He had been one of her guards during her brief imprisonment at the Pellanth temple. His blond hair had grown out some, but he looked the same otherwise.

"Try me," she growled.

The breeze began to pick up then, and the pale light of an overcast day dimmed as though night were coming on. A soft rumble sounded above them. Another of the Silverbloods gave the sky a wary glance.

The loathing that filled her now took on a life of its own. It rippled out from her, a confusion of Krivalen and fey magic blending with the rising storm, adding to the darkness. Wisps of white mist swirled in on the fast-rising breeze. A separate mist started to rise from the ground around Raven, but this mist was dark, almost black.

"Something's not right," one of the Silverbloods commented, his steps faltering. He hefted a battleax with blood drying on the blade.

"Stop whining." The blond sneered. "Remember, Wayland may have said alive, but this one can survive a hefty beating."

The blond lunged then, and Raven leapt in to meet him, blocking his strike and managing to leave a gouge in his leather breastplate as he attempted to jump clear of her attack. The air around them started to crackle, and thunder rolled overhead. The blond bounded to his left and darted in, forcing her to turn as two others broke off in different directions, working to surround her.

The sky overhead had gone dark charcoal, and the wind whipped up, swirling together the thickening white and black mists. A crack of thunder blasted above them, shaking the ground under their feet. Underneath the sound, she thought she heard someone call her name, but it became lost in the noise. The Silverblood with the battle-axe backed a few steps toward the house. An arrow appeared in his dominant arm, and he lost his hold on the weapon with a cry.

The blond and one of the others came at Raven together. She blocked one and dodged under the other's attack, swinging in as she twisted away to catch the blond with a satisfying slice to the back of the knee. His leg buckled, and he fell hard on one knee, his face red and twisting with pain.

Pillars of lighting struck down around them. Another of the Silverbloods was leveling a crossbow at her now. The blond's companion lunged in from the front as the fifth came in on her left with a mace in hand, forcing her to turn her attention away from the crossbow. A blinding pillar of lightning struck down where the crossbowman was. She felt the bolt graze her shoulder as it went wild. Then the drake landed behind the Silverblood with the mace, lightning crackling over its scales. Massive jaws snapped closed around the Silverblood's torso, tearing into armor and flesh as he screamed. Without turning its attention from its victim, it swiped out with one foreleg and raked the injured blond across the back, claws cutting through his armor as if it were skin.

Raven lunged at the one in front of her, slicing a gash in his sword arm with her sword and bringing her dagger around into his side. Leaving the dagger where it went in, she bolted forward, following the magic through the darkness. It led her true, and she cut into the back of the man with the arrow in his arm as he left his axe and turned to run for the house. He staggered a few steps before falling to his knees, then face-planted on the ground.

The drake dropped its victim and reared up, letting out a mighty roar as lightning crackled through the air. Raven followed the magic back to the body slumped over the stump. Her sword fell to the ground. She sank to her knees next to it. Somewhere in the chaos that still raged around her, she heard more than one voice calling her name. She was aware of the storm drake coming to stand facing her over Marek's body, the lighting and wind slowly calming. The white mist began to dissipate. The black continued to swirl around her.

She hunched over, curling in on the pain. The drake lowered its head until its nose was mere inches above Marek's back. Raven reached up one hand and placed it on the cold, smooth muzzle of the beast. Tears began to stream down her cheeks, hot in the chill. The dark mist sank into the ground around her.

"Raven."

Phendaril spoke her name first, triggering a distant surprise since he hadn't come with them. She heard Synderis behind her, softly telling someone else to stay back. The drake growled a warning at them, small flickers of lighting arcing along its wings.

Part of Raven wanted to let it stay to keep them away. She didn't want anyone's company right now. She needed to feel this pain. Marek deserved her sorrow.

Then she noticed a dampening parchment tucked in the waist of his armor where it would be easy to spot. She pulled it out and read the bleeding ink.

I'm waiting.

She had convinced Wayland that Marek was of no use to him, so he'd found a way to make him useful.

Raven threw back her head and screamed. The drake did the same, letting out a roar that the sky echoed back at them, lighting flashing out from it. When she stopped, the roar and the thunder still echoing in her ears, she crushed the parchment in her fist and stood.

She placed a hand on the side of the drake's jaw, feeling the smooth scales crackling with energy. "Go," she whispered, sending a sense of gratitude into the great beast.

A rumble sounded in its chest, almost more of a purr than a growl. Then it reared up on its muscular hind legs and lunged skyward, buffeting her with a gust of wind from its wings that swept her hair back. She closed her eyes for a moment, and her face turned up into the wind the drake created. When she opened her eyes, Phendaril was standing beyond where the drake had been, with Alayne and a few others from Amberwood. She didn't need to look to know Synderis wasn't far behind her. She could feel him through their connection.

Raven turned and walked toward the house. When she was beside Synderis, she stopped, not looking at him. "I know it's a lot to ask..." Her voice cracked, and she lowered her gaze, swallowing against the tightness in her throat.

"He's human. You want him buried here?"

She nodded. "Not with the others, but I don't know..." She drew a shaky breath and tried again. "I don't know where else to bury him. This was our home, if only for a short time." A few tears slid down her cheeks.

"It's not too much to ask," he answered gently.

Raven only nodded and continued past him and the other three into the house. Koshika followed her. Inside, she shut the door behind her and leaned against it, resting her head on the hard wood. Outside, they spoke in low voices.

"After we returned to Amberwood, Sameth told us they had seen Silverbloods up here," Phendaril said. "We got here as fast as we could in case it was a trap."

"It was a trap," Synderis answered, a dark edge of anger in his voice. "One we should have been warier of. It didn't occur to us that they might have cut over somewhere north of the crossing."

"Let's take care of this and get back to Amberwood. We can talk more there," Phendaril said softly, perhaps realizing that she might be listening.

"I happen to know all too well where the shovels are," Davon stated, the weight of sorrow in his voice.

Her guard captain was right. They had seen too much death here.

Raven pushed away from the door and wandered to the sitting room where she and Marek had sat the night they took over the manor. There, she sank into one of the chairs. Koshika climbed halfway onto the chair and pressed her head against Raven's cheek. Raven sank her hands in the soft feathery coat and wept.

CHAPTER THIRTY THREE

Captain Reysa shook her head from where she stood leaning against the wall to the left of the hearth with her arms crossed over her chest. "We have no reason to go to Pellanth now. The Silverblood she wanted to free is dead."

Synderis cast a glance at the front door, wishing Raven would walk in. She'd had them dig a grave for Marek, coming out to place his sword in the grave with him before they filled it in. She stood by the grave for perhaps a half an hour in silence before consenting to head south to Amberwood. They dragged the bodies of the other Silverbloods out into the trees far away from where Marek was buried, also at her bidding.

Karsima tried to get Raven to join her and Phendaril on the boat, but she declined. Instead, she led the group back on horseback, pushing as hard a pace as the terrain would allow. By the time they reached the town, evening was setting in with a brisk cold that chilled the bones. Once she finished bedding Cyrleth down, she simply vanished, though Synderis could feel through their connection that she hadn't gone far.

At his feet, near the hearth, Koshika lay gently playing with the fierce kitten bounding around between her forelegs. Smudge butted his nub horns into her chin, and she pinned him under one paw, leaning down to groom his head as if he were her offspring. The kitten

304

squirmed, mewling his indignation. The sight brought a smile to the lips of almost everyone in the room, though Phendaril's smile looked as strained as he knew his own was.

"Raven is going to want to confront Father Wayland, especially after this," Phendaril stated, making it apparent by his tone that he meant to stand with her.

"I don't think attacking a respected figure in Pellanth will help us gain King Saldin's support," Reysa countered.

Synderis hated the idea of putting Raven within the Silverblood priest's reach, but she would never walk away from this. Not now. And, from what he knew of Wayland, the priest wouldn't let it go either. "We'll ride to Pellanth." He inclined his head to Reysa. "You and your men can stay here until we return."

"You can take Amberwood's galley," Karsima offered. The comment earned her a sharp look from Alayne, but she didn't waver. "The bastard owes us for Veylin, don't forget."

Alayne lowered her gaze and took a long drink from her wine before setting it down and giving a stern look to both Phendaril and Synderis. Alayne was notably left out of the nonverbal warning. "You're talking about taking the life of a Brotherhood priest. This is a delicate situation. If we get King Saldin's support, any Silverblood, regardless of race or gender, could become a recognized citizen under the crown in both kingdoms. Even Raven's claim to the Darrenton name and holdings might be recognized. Isn't that a better revenge than risking her life by confronting him directly?"

Karsima pushed back, the fact that she was willing to argue against the woman she loved attesting to the strength of her conviction. "Wayland killed Raven once already just for being what she is. The fact that they brought her back doesn't make that any less true. Since then, he's killed Veylin and Marek and had a whole household of servants murdered just because he wanted to get to Raven. He was even helping fund Aldrich Darrenton's plan to attack Amberwood. How much more damage might he do while we wait on politics to sort things out?" She glanced at Koshika then, her gaze turning inward and her brows rising slightly. "Besides, I saw Raven call a storm drake down on her enemies a few hours ago. I will not stand in her way if she wants to go after Wayland."

Recognizing that she was getting no support, Alayne gave a slight nod and held her silence this time.

Reysa looked around at them, her gaze lingering a few seconds longer on him before finally stopping on Phendaril. She appeared to have gleaned that there was something more to their relationships with Raven. "Please tell me one of you two is willing to talk sense into her."

Synderis caught Phendaril's eyes and offered a slight nod. Phendaril returned the gesture and faced the captain. "We'll stand behind whatever she decides."

"Find out what that is, then," Reysa snapped.

Karsima stood. "One of you go find Raven. The rest of us will head over to The Bear and Raven. Meet us there when you have a better idea of what she wants to do, and we'll figure the rest out."

The others followed Karsima, Telandora and Lindyl only after a nod from him. Phendaril waited until they had all left to stand.

"I know there's some kind of connection between the two of you," he said, a faint edge of pain in his tone. "Can you... sense how she's doing?"

Synderis ran his magic along the connection, delicately seeking her. He met up with an unfamiliar darkness. It wasn't the simple shadow of sorrow and fury over her emotions but rather a darkness that thrived on the pain and anger that ran strong beneath it. The fey magic from the Acridan. It recoiled from the tentative touch of his magic. He suspected she could control it if she asserted the Krivalen magic, but this exact moment wasn't the time for testing that.

"She's hurting, and she's somewhere close by. Do you know where she might be?"

Phendaril nodded. "On the roof of the healer's building."

Synderis could feel the cold through the link as soon as he said it. He could tell she was shivering after a moment of deeper focus. He grabbed his cloak from where he'd draped it on the back of his chair. "Take this. She'll recognize it as mine. Maybe it will help her to know we both support her."

Phendaril draped the cloak over his arm. He took a few steps toward the door before turning back. "You're sure."

Of course he wasn't sure. He wanted more than anything to be the one to go to her, but the way the fey magic reacted to his Krivalen magic suggested that Phendaril might have better luck this time. He nodded, not trusting that his voice wouldn't betray how he really felt.

The other elf gave a solemn nod, his expression saying he knew and understood what Synderis was going through. "I'll do everything I can for her."

They left the house together, parting outside the door, and Synderis made his way over to The Bear and Raven, deliberately not looking up at the roof of the healer's building.

•

Raven watched them all emerge from Alayne and Karsima's home. Most of them, even Synderis, though he lingered at

the house a little longer, went down to The Bear and
Raven. She knew he could find her. She'd felt him reach
out to her. Part of her wanted to be angry with him
for not coming after her, but she had also noticed how
the fey magic reacted to him and had done nothing to
counter the message it sent. It was Phendaril who went
off on his own, so it didn't surprise her when she heard
his footsteps on the roof, still altered by the limp but less
so than before.

He stopped behind her and wrapped a cloak over
her shoulders. As he sat next to her, she pulled the garment tight around her, realizing in that moment how
cold she actually was. In fact, she was shivering, something she'd failed to notice until then.

It didn't escape her attention that the cloak was the
grey-green one Synderis wore. That confirmed that he
and Phendaril had aligned on a plan of who would speak
to her. If Synderis had come, she might have climbed
down to head him off. This place was too significant to
the start of her relationship with Phendaril. She wanted
to keep that about it.

"You know," she said when he had settled, "I was
terrified of Veylin when I first came here."

"Veylin?" A hint of surprise lifted his tone.

"Yes. I expected the judgment I received from you
and Marek and the wariness I got from the others. I
didn't like it, but I expected it. I mean, I feared Marek
because I'd lived my whole life learning to fear Silverbloods, but Veylin... No one told me how to deal with
someone being nice to me right away the way she was.
She had so much energy, and she was so friendly. I had
no idea how to react to that."

He laughed softly, though sorrow restrained his
nostalgic smile. "I suppose she would have been terrifying for someone in your situation."

"Wayland tortured her." Her voice cracked as she

said it, and he placed a hand on her arm. "He inflicted injuries on her like those I suffered the night he and I fought. She felt all my pain, but at least I could fight back. Can you imagine how frightened she must have been?"

He cleared his throat. "I would rather not, and you shouldn't either."

"Wayland killed her to get to me, just like all those servants he had slaughtered. Now Marek is dead too, just because he chose to help me. I'm not going to let anyone else die because of me."

"It isn't your fault, you know. You didn't ask to be made what you are, and you certainly didn't create the doctrine that made your life forfeit to the Brotherhood."

She pressed her lips together, tempted to argue with him. Rationally, she recognized that it wasn't her fault Wayland so desperately wanted her dead. But if they hadn't dragged her back from the far edge of death, the others would all be alive now. That wasn't really her doing either. She wouldn't have expected anyone to work so hard to save her. That was why she had to do something now to protect those who were still here.

"I know, but I mean to end this." A violent shiver shook her, making her voice tremble.

Phendaril took her hand and stood, lifting her with him. For a second, she considered resisting. With the Krivalen magic in her, she could overpower him without too much difficulty. She was cold, though, and it was far too chilly to expect anyone else to want to sit there as long as she had.

"Let's get you warm and fed. Then we can talk about dealing with Wayland."

Raven followed him off the roof and back to the house they had shared. The warmth from a blazing fire and the smells of savory foods struck her as she walked inside. Her stomach growled noisily.

Phendaril chuckled. "I expected as much."

Two plates sat on the table near the fire, still steaming. Raven glanced around the room, looking for whoever must have just put them there.

"Jenner helped. He has a way of being there when you need him, then vanishing."

She met Phendaril's eyes, her heart pounding a little harder when he gazed back at her, his eyes full of thinly veiled affection. Would she ever stop reacting to him that way?

"What if I had refused to come?"

He smirked. "I would have eaten very well." He gestured to one of the chairs.

As she sat, she pulled the cloak tighter around her, still feeling the chill from outside. Synderis's cloak. She glanced up at Phendaril again. Having him near still made her want to be closer to him, no matter her feelings for Synderis. What a restless heart she had. It was an unrelenting source of confusion. "I'm sorry. I didn't expect both of you to end up together here. I..." She looked into the fire. "I don't really know what I expected."

He poured her a warm mead that smelled exactly like that she'd first had with Eamon what seemed a lifetime ago. She took hold of the mug, appreciating the heat that was almost painful under her icy fingers.

"I can't help you with that, Raven. I can get you fed and warm. I can tell you who I would choose." His quick wink and scoundrel grin brought a small smile to her lips. "I can help you get to Wayland," he added soberly.

She looked at him in surprise. "You what?"

"Don't think for a minute that we'll let you go alone."

"You don't mean to talk me out of it."

His gaze was calm and patient. "We were talking

about it earlier. Even Karsima supports you confronting him. Alayne tried to discourage it, but the only one strongly against it is Captain Reysa and, I imagine, King Navaran. The rest of us are behind you and will do what we can to help if that's your choice. You're stronger now, and you're not alone. Besides, you can always call in a storm drake or something if things go poorly."

"I don't think there are a lot of storm drakes in Pellanth." She smiled, surprised that a hint of genuine pleasure managed to push through the sorrow. Tears stung her eyes, but they were tears of gratitude this time. "Thank you."

They ate and chatted about simpler things, like the progress in Amberwood and how his injuries were coming along. Trying to avoid subjects that were painful or difficult. Given their history, the occasional comment subdued the mood, such as when he mentioned a few places he hoped to take her. The future remained a subject of profound uncertainty. Once she had eaten, and the warmth worked its way through her, drowsiness crept in, the stress of the day catching up with her.

At a break in the conversation, she yawned and stood. "I should go."

"You can have the room upstairs again," he offered, standing with her and helping her drape the too-big cloak over her shoulders.

She turned to face him, a little surprised by how close he was. An ill-mannered lock of hair slipped forward, and he reached out habitually to brush it back, freezing when his fingers touched her cheek. Their eyes met, a dizzying rush of wanting sweeping through her. Their lips met before she realized what she was doing, his hand sliding into her hair. She started to melt into that intimate contact for a second, then she stepped hastily away.

He grimaced and took a step back as well. "Raven,

I'm sorry."

"It wasn't your fault." She turned from him, wishing she didn't want so badly to stay. "I'll use my old room in the healer's building. Goodnight, Phen."

She felt his gaze follow her as she hurried from the house.

CHAPTER THIRTY FOUR

But Raven didn't go to the healer's building. She bunched Synderis's cloak over her arms to keep it from dragging the ground and wandered down the road in the opposite direction, toward where the Stonebreaker camp had been. She had relaxed into Phendaril's presence for a brief time, remembering what it was like to be with him. Remembering the ease of his company. It was so effortless to love each of them for different reasons. It was never going to be simple, but now all she wanted was to make sure neither of them got hurt helping her stop Wayland. There was a time when she might have been foolish enough to try to face him alone just to avoid the risk, but she needed them. Trying this alone was suicide.

She stopped alongside the river, realizing after a few seconds that it was the very spot where Marek had knocked her unconscious all those months ago to take her to Pellanth. Until that moment, she had started to entertain the possibility that Amberwood could be her home for the first time. It was strange to stand at the edge of that drop and mourn the man who had betrayed her there. She missed him. Whether it made sense to or not, she really did miss him, and the confusion between Synderis and Phendaril only made her miss him more somehow.

She had meant to protect him by telling Wayland he knew nothing. Perhaps she should have known that, by showing her concern, she would only be giving him another way to hurt her. It never occurred to her that he might believe she truly cared for Marek enough to make him a target.

"It was my fault, Marek," she whispered to the darkness. "I made you worthless to him alive. I'm so sorry. I needed you with me too. I wanted you with me." Her voice cracked then, and she sank to her knees at the edge of the drop-off. Though she would have thought her sorrow spent by now, she curled over, her arms wrapped around the ache inside her, and wept. The harder she tried to stop them, the faster the tears came.

•

The hour grew late, but Raven and Phendaril didn't join them at The Bear and Raven. At some point, Karsima took pity on Synderis and had Jenner show him and the other two Krivalen elves to a house that was currently unoccupied. A Stonebreaker smith and his family had been living there. They moved out only a few days ago to relocate to a restored home next to the smithy.

Telandora and Lindyl stayed downstairs to share some wine with him for a while, but he could see by their frequent glances that they wanted time alone together. He sent them off, insisting he didn't mind, and they retreated to one of the upstairs bedrooms. Then he sat before the fire, his feet on an empty chair, and turned to the effort of finishing the wine.

For all that he loved Raven and wanted to give her whatever she needed, it was hard not to imagine everything she and Phendaril might be doing at that moment. Through the window at the public house, he'd seen them descend from the roof of the healer's building within minutes of Phendaril going up there.

Were they in the house they shared here before? Were they still talking? Part of him wanted to reach out along the connection. He had refrained from doing so since he and Phendaril parted ways earlier. The two deserved their privacy. Besides, what they might be doing together didn't bother him as much as the knowledge that she felt compelled to choose between them. He didn't want to lose her.

Koshika sat up and rested her big head on his lap, gazing up at him with brilliant emerald eyes. A sense of sadness added weight to her bearing that he knew was a product of his mood. He scratched behind her ears, appreciating the low purr that rose in her throat. Her companionship was a comfort, even if he hadn't intended for it to become this powerful of a bond.

A storm drake.

It was hard to believe that Raven had managed to influence such a creature to the point that it would come to her aid in combat. Without the beast, the Silverbloods still wouldn't have stood much of a chance against their entire group, though he and the others would have had to get there fast enough to help Raven. As skilled as she was, taking down five Silverbloods alone would have been a lot to ask. With the storm drake fighting with her, there wasn't much contest.

In his mind, he could still see her there, facing down the Silverbloods, lightning flashing around her while an unnatural wind raged under a dark sky. The mist bothered him. The black mist that appeared to rise out of the ground around her. That wasn't the storm drake's doing. He'd never seen one in the flesh before that, but he knew enough about them. Perhaps he should have gone to Raven himself after all. Phendaril didn't have the tools needed to deal with the fey magic manifesting in her now. Though, truth be told, neither did he.

Still, it was an incredible sight, watching her fight with the storm drake, incredible and terrifying.

A nagging unease settled over him then, interrupting his thoughts. He reached across the link and met up against a stifling surge of sorrow. She wasn't in the town any longer, either.

Synderis got up and strode to the door, Koshika bolting out alongside. He wasn't sure if Raven was alone, but the fey magic was silent and the need he got from her was so intense that he didn't care. He broke into a jog outside, Koshika loping along with her tail up and her ears perked forward, excited to be moving. The sense of Raven drew him down the street and toward the river. He found her alone at the edge of an abrupt drop, curled over, shivering and crying. Though he wanted to be angry with Phendaril for leaving her on her own, he had a feeling, knowing Raven, that the other elf was unaware of her current state.

She didn't resist when he drew her up and lifted her in his arms. It had never struck him before what a delicate creature she actually was. All her strength and skill made it easy to miss that about her.

"I got your cloak dirty." She sniffled, and her voice shook with the shaking of her body.

Synderis chuckled, a flood of affection tightening his chest. "There is one thing I care about right now, and it isn't the cloak.

She slid a hand around his neck and nuzzled her cold face against his shoulder, shivering in his arms. Neither of them spoke again as he carried her back to the house, Koshika bounding around them, chasing nocturnal insects all the way to the door.

Inside, he set her down and went to stoke the fire. She had his cloak wrapped around her and bunched in her arms as though she were still trying to keep it up off the ground. She looked tired, her eyes rimmed in red from crying.

"Are Telandora and Lindyl here?" Raven whispered, glancing up at the ceiling as if she might see the other two elves upstairs.

"Don't worry. I doubt they're asleep, though they have been remarkably quiet for them."

The whisper of a smile touched her lips. She came across the floor toward him. He waited for her, wanting her close to the fire where she could get warm. She walked around the chairs and stopped in front of him, letting the bundled length of the cloak go, so it gathered on the floor around her feet. She gazed up into his eyes. The cold from outside radiated off her.

"I kissed him," she admitted, averting her eyes.

He unfastened the cloak pin and slid the chilled garment off her shoulders, letting it pool on the floor. She still wore her armor, a few spatters of blood dried on it. Cold clung to the leather, to her clothes, to her skin.

"I'm not worried about that." He took her hands in his and kissed each of her fingers, noticing how icy they were against his lips. Then he retrieved the remains of his wine and handed it to her as he began unfastening the buckles of her armor. "Can you even feel your fingers?"

"I didn't know where I should be." The tightness in her voice spoke to her pain.

He kept working to remove the armor, encouraging her with a touch on her wrist to take a drink of the wine and guiding her a few steps closer to the fire. "Where did you want to be?"

He tossed a bracer to the side where he had already dropped the matching piece and went to work on the chest armor. When she didn't answer, he looked up to see a few tears sliding down her cheeks.

He stopped and gently wiped one away. "What can

I do for you?"

"I don't want anyone else to die." Her voice cracked, and the tears came faster.

Synderis took the wine and set it aside, then pulled her into his arms. She trembled against him, though the more violent sobs he expected didn't come. Perhaps she had run those dry already. He kissed her head and hugged her close.

"We won't let anyone else die. If you want to confront him, you know we'll go with you." He avoided the priest's name, unwilling to sully this space with it.

"I know," she murmured. "That's what I'm afraid of. What if..."

He moved her to face him and placed a finger to her lips. "You know you need us. Don't try to sacrifice the one person we can't stand to lose."

"Love me," she whispered.

His pulse quickened, responding to the request behind her words, but he hesitated. "I do."

"You know what I mean."

For a second, he considered asking her if she was sure. Perhaps he should verify that this was indeed what she wanted now. That he was who she wanted, but he let the thought go and kissed her. She slid her icy hands into his hair and kissed him back, a firm, demanding kiss that he hadn't the will or the desire to refuse. He slid his hands around the curve of her waist and pulled her closer, tasting the salt of tears on her lips.

She brought her hands forward and tried to untie his shirt's laces with numb fingers. He caught her wrists and stopped her.

"Let me," he murmured.

Holding his gaze, she gave a slight nod. He removed the rest of her armor, unfastening only as much as was absolutely necessary to get it off. Then he untied the laces of his shirt and pulled it off. A faint smirk touched her lips, and she placed her hands on his chest. He sucked in a breath, his muscles drawing back reflexively from the cold. Then he made himself step closer, pressing her hands against flesh that had been quite comfortably warm moments ago, and claimed her mouth in another ardent kiss.

They remained that way for several minutes, kissing before the fire, then he led her to the downstairs bedroom and shut the door behind them. He finished undressing them and drew her into the bed, folding her close against him. It would be enough to hold her and get her warm. He could be satisfied with that.

Her feet touched his legs, and he gasped in surprise.

"Sorry," she whispered. Then she kissed his chest and murmured, "I want you closer."

She hooked one leg around his and rolled onto her back, drawing him with her. For a second, he hesitated again, wanting to be sure she was ready for him, but the demand in her eyes held his answer. He eased himself into her, finding that her body was as eager to embrace him as her eyes said she was. She wrapped her legs around him then, and he leaned down to kiss her as he started to move in her. The need and love in her eyes made it unimportant if she loved Phendaril too. She loved him, and that was what mattered. He would love her back with every bit of himself and help her, whatever it took.

CHAPTER THIRTY FIVE

I t was late when the *Syrasenne* pulled into the dock in Pellanth. Captain Narene's crew came below deck and began hauling up the cargo they'd brought to trade, giving a legitimate front to their presence there. The *Syrasenne* came to Pellanth for supplies and trade quite often, so it was unlikely to draw too much attention. Tonight, several of the crew deliberately kept the hoods of their cloaks up to "ward against the cold" if anyone asked. In truth, it provided Raven's group an opportunity to merge with them coming off the ship before slipping away. They didn't want someone tracing their activities back to the galley if things went wrong.

Synderis and the others remained hidden below deck while Davon went up first. Raven had initially told the guard to stay behind, but he had made a quick and compelling argument for coming with them. Synderis could still see the young man's smug grin when he declared that he had a friend in the city who ran a coach service. He could get them a coach that would hasten their trip from the docks to the temple while dramatically reducing their chances of being spotted. That made him too valuable an asset to leave behind.

The rest of them split off one at a time, each moving in to help with a load going ashore. Phendaril was the first to go up after Davon. Raven had made no effort to convince him to stay behind. He still had something of a limp, but Synderis had seen him fight in Raven's memory. Even though he wasn't Krivalen, he was worth having around, both because of his skills and what his support meant to Raven.

Raven gave a slight nod to Phendaril as he headed up.

Throughout the few days it had taken to reach Pellanth, she had kept a friendly distance between herself and both of them. Strangely, Telandora and Lindyl adopted that same social distance between themselves for the duration. The six of them had occupied themselves with a great deal of sparring and sharing of weapon and combat styles during the two days. Raven and Davon noticed a significant similarity in their fighting styles. It turned out to be attributable to the fact that he was trained in Pellanth by a woman who trained under her adopted father, Jaecar, before his disappearance. That discovery kept the two occupied in conversation for most of that afternoon and evening.

Synderis had found himself unexpectedly engaged in comparing combat techniques with Phendaril for much of that same day. Their styles were extremely different, which led to several demonstrations and an extended analysis of ways in which the two styles might complement each other. An entire evening was passed sharing drinks and stories, many of which ended up being from Phendaril, Davon, and Narene, as those three had traveled more than the rest.

Perhaps Raven was more clever than they gave her credit for. With her offering no special favor to either of them and keeping relations on the galley non-romantic, he and Phendaril had found common ground other than their love of her to connect them. A connection that might prove quite valuable now that they were heading to the Brotherhood temple.

Telandora went up top next, then Raven, giving the

same nod to him as she left that she had given Phendaril. He returned it, letting her set expectations for now. As he watched her head up the steps, he caught himself reaching to his side for Koshika. How strange it was to be without the big cat now. His efforts to get her to stay in Amberwood hadn't impressed her. Somehow, Raven had succeeded where he failed, convincing the lalyx cat to remain there with Karsima and Alayne. He hoped they all survived the experience, but there was little choice. An unusual companion like Koshika would be too hard to hide in the city, even just long enough to get her to the coach.

When it came Synderis's turn, he stepped in to grab a heavy sack full of some edible mushrooms that grew in Amberwood's forests. They were popular delicacies among the nobility and fetched a fine price at the city markets. Once he set the sack on the dock with the other cargo, he stopped and leaned against a stack of crates as if to catch his breath. He waited until no one was paying attention to wander away.

It was easy to follow the directions Davon had given them, each taking a slightly different route so he could move the coach a few times. Synderis's path took him down a few dirty alleys that were mostly empty at this hour. He stopped at the edge of the street where he was to meet up with them, spotting the black coach where Davon told him it would be, in front of a closed tailor's shop to his right. The young guard was driving, an arrangement that allowed them to avoid having to let a stranger know where they were going.

When he walked up to the coach, Davon glanced back, giving him a slight nod from under the hood of his heavy cloak. He tapped on the roof. The door opened, and Synderis stepped in. He sat beside Phendaril, across from Raven and Telandora, leaving the spot next to Telandora available for Lindyl.

"One more," Raven said softly.

In the darkness of the coach, with no light to reflect, her eyes appeared black. She rubbed the arrowhead pendant between her fingers and looked at nothing in particular. An air of apprehension filled the coach, or perhaps anticipation. It was hard to tell which. If things were different, he might have reached out to Raven physically for the comfort it would bring them both, but he would have to lean across Phendaril to do so.

The coach started to move. Phendaril glanced at Synderis, and he gestured subtly toward Raven. The other elf gave a slight nod, then he reached out and touched her hand. Synderis followed by sending calmness and affection along their link. Raven's gaze focused on Phendaril, then shifted to him.

"You're not alone this time," Phendaril said.

Raven smiled, glancing around at all three of them. "I know. Thank you."

The coach stopped. A few minutes later, Davon tapped on the roof, and Phendaril opened the door again. Lindyl stepped in, gravitating immediately to the spot beside Telandora. He hesitated after looking around at the current arrangement.

He grinned. "Are we doing one of those gender splits that they do in human society?"

Telandora grabbed his hand and yanked him down. "Sit."

He did as ordered, chuckling to himself. Telandora elbowed him lightly in the ribs, though the corners of her mouth curved up as she did so. The rest of them smiled as well, appreciating the normalcy of their behavior. The coach started to move again, and the smiles vanished. The next time it stopped, it would be near the Brotherhood temple.

"We need to be careful," Raven said, leaning back into the shadows. "There shouldn't be many Silverbloods there, but not drawing them all down on us at once would be preferable, regardless of how many there are. Four of us can knock them out without hurting them using magic if we can get close enough. Try not to kill anyone, but your lives come first." She gave each of them a stern look, her gaze lingering the longest on Phendaril.

They all nodded their understanding, more than one hand sinking to a weapon in absent reassurance.

They had already determined that, as the only non-Krivalen among them and an archer of extraordinary skill, Phendaril would hang back with the short bow. He also carried his sword, but his lingering limp and lack of magical enhancement would put him at a disadvantage against the Silverbloods. He would be responsible for ranged support, where he would have a broader view of the action. Also, though Raven wasn't aware of the arrangement, he was to prioritize her safety if the encounter appeared to be going in the Brotherhood's favor. The important thing was to ensure she didn't end up in Silverblood hands when this was over.

Far too soon, the coach rolled to a stop. Something about heading into danger alongside the female he loved was both invigorating and terrifying. He had to remind himself that she was at least as capable as he was, probably more so. There was always that risk, though. No matter how competent one was, something could still go wrong, and he needed to trust that she could handle it if that happened. Otherwise, worry for her could lead him to make a foolish mistake. He took an odd sense of comfort from knowing that Phendaril likely struggled with the same fears.

No one moved until a tap came on the roof to let them know the area was clear, then they opened the door and slipped out into the cold darkness. Raven glanced up at Davon, and they exchanged nods. He clucked the horses and drove away. They had arranged a different place to meet on completion of their task, and a period of time after which he had instructions to go back to the *Syrasenne* without them.

They crept up the side street along the high wrought-iron fence surrounding the Brotherhood temple grounds. When they snuck around the front, Raven hissed softly, and Phendaril cursed under his breath. The low gate from her memory had been replaced with a higher wrought-iron one tipped in points like the rest of the fence. There would be no climbing over this one.

"Anyone know how to pick a fence lock?" Telandora whispered.

Lindyl stepped forward, drew back the bolt on the gate, and gently pushed it. It swung open a few inches. "No, but I know how to tell if they bothered to lock it," he whispered with a grin.

Telandora planted a quick kiss on his lips.

Phendaril glanced at the two, his gaze flickering briefly to Raven as though he would like to do the same with her. "Let's hope all our problems are so easily solved."

"I wouldn't count on it," Raven answered in a low voice.

Without hesitation, she moved through the open gate and strode toward the Silverblood guard heading their way from his post at the temple door. He had set his hand on his sword hilt, but he had no reason yet to think he couldn't handle the five intruders. With their hoods up, he would likely assume they were nothing more than a group of drunks or adventures seekers looking to amuse themselves by sneaking around where they didn't belong.

Synderis matched Raven's quick pace, noting that, while Telandora and Lindyl did the same, Phendaril hung back a little, taking up his assigned position even before they entered the temple. It was a smart move. The guard might not notice the bow he was carrying if his attention remained on the four in the lead. It also gave him space to draw and use that bow if the need arose.

"You're not supposed to be in here after dark," the Silverblood declared, stopping several feet back from them. "You'll have to leave. You can come gape at the temple in the daylight if you must."

Raven continued, gesturing discreetly behind her back for the rest of them to stop. The guard took a few steps forward, his swagger more pronounced now that he was facing one woman. She walked up beside him and pointed at the impressive glass dome that rose out of the side of the structure.

"Can you tell me what that's for?" she asked.

The Silverblood grinned at her and faced the dome, shifting closer to her as he did so. He opened his mouth to speak. Synderis saw her hand come up to touch his wrist, and he collapsed before he could utter a word.

Another Silverblood stepped out of the deep shadows to one side of the entrance. He looked at them, standing near his fallen companion, and bolted for the door. Synderis sprinted toward him, but he wouldn't be fast enough. The Silverblood's hand was already on the handle.

An arrow whistled past his head and sank deep into the man's thigh. The man fell to one knee with a cry. Before he could make another sound, Synderis grabbed the back of his neck and put him out with the Krivalen magic for his own safety. He offered a nod of appreciation to Phendaril, who was putting away his bow as he strode up to join them.

They took a moment to move the unconscious guards into the shadows to one side of the entrance. With that done, they eased open one of the big doors just enough to slip inside. The massive entry chamber was empty. Every other sconce along the lower wall was lit, providing a few narrow pools of light that left the middle of the room shrouded in darkness. The quiet had its own presence, lingering like a predator in waiting.

They were halfway to the dais at the back when a door to their left opened. Five Silverbloods walked in, weapons in hand. Another door opened to the left of the dais in the front and two more entered. Raven cast Synderis a worried glance. This was more opposition than they had expected so soon.

Their party drew weapons. Not killing anyone just became considerably harder. Synderis still meant to avoid adding to the list of dead, but he wasn't going to do it at the expense of himself or those he cared about. He made his way closer to the back of the room, declaring with his actions that he intended to engage with the two near the dais. Telandora and Lindyl moved in between Phendaril and the five spreading out from the door they had entered through. Phendaril stepped back, his bow lowered, but drawn, evaluating his possible targets.

"We spotted your antics out front through the windows." One of the group of five Silverbloods took a half-step closer. "Who are you?"

Raven matched his step, moving toward him, and Synderis noticed that, of them all, she alone hadn't drawn a weapon yet. She pulled back her hood, and the man's eyes widened.

"You." His sword came up as he moved into a fighting stance. "You little whore," he snarled, advancing more aggressively now. "You're going to pay—"

He cut off with a pained grunt when an arrow appeared in his upper arm. Synderis would typically object to drawing first blood. In this case, he silently applauded Phendaril and moved to engage the Silverbloods now advancing on him.

Blades whispered through the air, the clash of steel against steel echoing throughout the massive room. All four of them had more Krivalen magic in them than the Silverbloods they faced, though none so much as Raven. Synderis twisted out of the way of one attack and drove the other man back with a quick flurry of strikes. He used a series of attacks and dodges to put himself where he could see Raven as she jumped clear of an attack. The Silverblood who had tried to engage her suddenly found himself facing Lindyl instead. Raven danced ahead, moving twice as fast as the Silverbloods. She dodged a sloppy strike from the Silverblood with the arrow in his arm and grabbed his neck, dropping him instantly.

Synderis had to focus on his own fight then. He ducked a high swing, a move that took him out of range of the other Silverblood's attack as well. The two came at him together, forcing him back toward the wall. The point of one's blade grazed his neck, a small wound with a powerful emotional impact. He grabbed the candelabra next to him and thrust it at the Silverblood. The man's blade became tangled in it, and he dropped back to free himself. It gave Synderis the opening he needed. He caught the other Silverblood's blade with his and thrust him backward, then twisted and lunged forward, driving his blade deep into the side of the one still struggling with the candclabra.

The Silverblood went down, blood draining from his face as he dropped his sword and threw a hand pressed to the deep wound in his side. There wasn't much chance he would survive that injury, but the blood trickling warm over Synderis's collarbone was enough to convince him he hadn't had a choice. He spun to continue his fight with the other, noticing as he did so that a third Silverblood was down and another impaired by an arrow in one leg. The most important thing, however, was that Raven was gone.

He twisted clear of another attack. "Phendaril! Find Raven."

The other male scanned the room, then bolted through the door she had been closest to. She was in his hands for now.

CHAPTER THIRTY SIX

Raven padded down the hallway and ducked up the first set of stairs she found. As she moved, she took off the arrowhead pendant and tucked it into the pouch on her belt. Hints of a black mist seeped from the walls and rose from the stone floor as she passed, wrapping around her, perhaps in response to her desire to remain hidden. She had no idea how the fey magic worked, only that she had inherited it from the Acridan and hoped it didn't change her the way it had that tormented being. For now, it appeared to be acting in her favor.

With the arrowhead pendant removed, she could feel her links to Synderis and Wayland much more intensely. The former surprised her a little. With Synderis near, the link to him already felt crisp and potent enough that she forgot the pendant interfered with it. Now the connection was so vivid it was almost as if he were beside her, holding her hand. For the moment, however, she did her best to push him aside and focus on the other.

At the top of the stairs, she halted, catching the sound of someone walking down the hall. She ducked back into the shadows of the stairwell and sucked in a breath of surprise when the fey mist folded in around her. The Silverblood stopped at the edge of the stairs and peered intently down, having clearly heard something.

Raven froze completely, not even breathing. She could fight him and probably win, but the more time she wasted on others, the more time Wayland would have to discover that something was happening and prepare himself if he wasn't already doing so.

After a few seconds, the Silverblood continued down the hall. The mist unfolded as she stepped out. A handy trick for a thief or an assassin, though she had no interest in being either under normal circumstances. Tonight was different. Quickly, she darted around and up the next flight of stairs. Her destination was on the third floor. She wanted to confront Wayland, but she wanted to set the stage for that encounter, not give him a chance to choose his own grounds on which to face her.

She crept up the stairs, listening for movement on the next level. At the top, she stopped, waiting in silence while she reached out along the connection to the Brotherhood priest. She found only a sense of darkness and quiet. He was sleeping. It was becoming increasingly apparent that the Silverbloods who confronted them in the entrance hall hadn't bothered to raise an alarm, arrogantly assuming they could handle the threat. Raven stepped out and padded down the hall, tendrils of the dark mist coiling over the walls and floor in her wake. A tug at their connection woke him. Confusion swept back to her, followed by the thrill of anticipation. He would come quickly to find her. She needed to set her stage.

Raven ducked into Wayland's study just as she heard footsteps heading down an intersecting hallway. It wasn't him yet, so she simply shut the door behind her and waited for them to pass. When they had gone by, she stepped out and grabbed a candle from a wall sconce, taking it back into the room with her. She used it to light a candle on one of the tables, then hurried to the column amidst the bookshelves and pressed the bird's wing carved into it. The doors to the Collection room swung open.

The filtered grey moonlight of a partly overcast night barely lit the room, but her Krivalen vision was enough to reach beyond the candlelight. The half-glass walls and glass ceiling had been restored. She lit the sconces inside the doors and glanced around, noting that the case she'd broken to get to the sword was replaced and the damage to the wyvern's wing from Wayland's pole-arm repaired. The polearm itself was gone. An ornate spear now hung on the wall in its place.

What Raven cared about, however, was the book. Set upon its pedestal near the base of the stuffed wyvern, the book the Acridan wrote to preserve their knowledge of Krivalen magic lay open on its stand. She walked over and started to flip through pages, her vision swapping back and forth between her present reality and the Acridan's past. The book, both new and old, sat simultaneously on the pedestal in the Collection room and on a stone table in an Acridan structure. The strange characters blended together, forming words that she could now read. Words that spoke of controlling minds, changing the seasons, and altering the natural world. Words that could be incredibly dangerous in the wrong hands.

Wayland was close now.

Raven lifted a fragile page and lowered the candle to it, letting the hungry flame taste the aged paper. It lit the corner and then hesitated as if waiting for something. With a sudden bright flare, it began to consume the page, quickly spreading to others. She laid the candle alongside the book, allowing the flame to lick at the edge of the cover, and drew her sword. Then she stepped away from the burning book and turned to face Wayland as he swept through the entrance, his liquid silver hair tied hastily back, a few strands slipping free already around his face. His shirt was only partially buttoned, and he hadn't bothered with his usual accessories. Two guards flanked him, though they stopped outside the door at a gesture from him.

He froze there, longsword in hand, his face paling as he took in the scene before him. The fire ate away at the book with great enthusiasm now. There would be no saving it, even if she was willing to let him try. He seemed to realize that fast enough, his shock turning to a twisted expression of rage.

"What have you done?" he shouted.

"I've taken your hope from you as partial repayment for everything you've taken from me."

Hatred curled his lip in a snarl. "I'm not done with you yet."

He charged her, not giving her time to speak again, and Raven twisted out of his way at the last second. Her blade nipped at his back just below his shoulder blade, leaving a small gash in the fabric and the skin beneath. He was alarmingly fast, but not as fast as she remembered him being. She danced out of his reach.

He twisted to face her and hesitated there, drawing in a deep breath to focus himself. She did the same, struggling to keep hold of who she was in his presence. The Acridan's memories grabbed at her awareness. She fought them back, clinging to the powerful sense of Synderis along their link.

"You have proven that you cannot be trusted with the knowledge you already have. It is better to lose what's in that book than to risk someone like you ever gaining access to it."

Wayland sneered at her and took a step toward the book. "You may be faster and stronger than before, but you have a long way to go to match me, my little Raven. Who are you to decide what knowledge I should have?"

Raven reached into herself, drawing on a little more

of the fey magic, pulling tendrils of creeping black mist up from the floor between him and the book. He back-pedaled, wide eyes staring at this creeping darkness.

"There's no one alive more suited to making that decision now," she growled, shifting into a fighting stance.

They moved on each other at the same time, meeting in a fast and fierce exchange of blows that left both of them nursing a few new shallow cuts. The guards at the door shifted uncomfortably, holding their ground for now rather than risk angering the priest. Wayland managed to throw her balance off with a powerful block. A dagger appeared in his hand, and he struck at her side. Raven leapt back as it nipped at her flesh, escaping with a shallow but painful reminder of the threat he posed.

The tendrils of black mist rising from the floor thickened, weaving around them. Some started to creep up at Wayland's feet, and he retreated, his attention pulled down to the strange darkness. Raven lunged in, her blade slicing a more substantial gash in his chest before he managed to knock it aside. He hissed in pain and came at her with a full-force strike that nearly disarmed her. She staggered back, and he surged after her with a second powerful attack, the weight and length of his blade driving her into an awkward block. Then he twisted and sank slightly, moving so fast she didn't have time to avoid the sweep of his leg.

Raven hit one of the display cases as she went down, taking it with her. Glass shattered, spraying across the floor around her, and cutting into her palm. Memories of their last fight swept in, making her breath catch in her throat. Panic threatened to break her focus.

"Did you even care about Marek? You must have known pleading for his life would kill him. Perhaps you just wanted me to get rid of him for you."

Sorrow and guilt crashed in on her. She felt herself slipping, the Acridan's memories forcing their way to the front. Then a surge of pride and love from Synderis flooded through her.

Wayland's thrust his blade down at her.

Raven rolled to the side, the point hitting the floor where she had been hard enough to sink into the wood. She struck out with one foot, connecting with his ankle and kicking the leg out from under him. As he struggled to catch himself, she sprang to her feet and drove her sword through above his collarbone. With an outward cut, she sliced away the muscle, her blade emerging above his shoulder. His arm dropped to his side, his weapon falling from his hand as he cried out and sank to one knee.

She knew his guards would attack any minute, though she couldn't see them past her rage. She only had a few seconds to finish this. Raven grabbed the back of his neck and lifted, rage bolstering her already enhanced strength. She hauled him to his feet, blood pouring down his arm and torso.

Hatred moved through her like poison, darkening her vision. More black mist swept out around her, wrapping Wayland in its embrace. She leaned close to his ear, dimly aware that his blood was soaking into the front of her armor.

"I did care," she hissed.

Someone moved in the doorway then, and she focused enough to see that Phendaril stood there, blood running from a cut on one arm and another near his temple.

For a few seconds, Raven met his eyes as a stranger, the hatred of the Acridan melding with the fey magic that swirled around her and Wayland.

Phendaril took a few steps into the room. "Raven," he said softly.

The worry and love in his eyes drew her back to the fore, helping her take control. She wasn't a killer, and she didn't want those she loved to fear her.

Pain burst through her leg then. She looked down to see Wayland's hand let go of the dagger he had buried in her thigh. Glancing up again, she saw Synderis rush into the doorway behind Phendaril, bright blood running from a cut on his neck. Time seemed to slow. She stared at the two elves, the black mist dissolving around her. Krivalen magic surged through her in its place, seizing the connection between her and Wayland.

Memories flooded her mind, none of them hers. Hundreds of lessons learning the Krivalen magic, the theory, the practice, and all the right and wrong ways to use it. Everything written in the book existed in those perfect Acridan memories.

Raven closed her eyes, riding a wave of furious power as it plunged across the connection into Wayland. The magic in him resisted, but the surge of power in her rolled over it, knowing how to subdue it. Acridan knowledge guided her, taking hold of Wayland's magic and ripping it away, removing it from him with almost surgical precision. Little by little, she unmade him.

A sudden blast of energy threw Raven back off her feet, dropping Wayland where he was. Her thigh screamed in agony, the blade still buried in it. When she opened her eyes, Wayland knelt on the floor, one trembling hand reaching for the mangled flesh over his collarbone. His hair was grey now instead of silver, his face deeply lined with age.

Synderis entered the room, gesturing for Phendaril to stay back. "I can heal better than you can," he said over his shoulder.

As he moved toward her, he glanced up as if expecting an attack from above. She followed his gaze, seeing that the glass ceiling and walls were spider-webbed with cracks. He looked at the burning book, almost beyond recognition now, as he passed, a hint of pain flickering across his features.

When he reached her, he lifted her in his arms and carried her from the room, not giving Wayland another glance. Raven did, peering over his shoulder at the priest once. He sagged against a display, too weak to stand, his listless dark eyes staring at her. His face was ashen, and his breathing strained. Blood ran free from the wound above his shoulder, the front of his shirt and pants glistening wet with it. He had no magic. It hadn't come into her. It had dispersed rather violently around them.

Wayland's two guards lay unconscious or dead beyond the doorway. Phendaril didn't follow them as they started across the study toward the hallway. She heard an arrow release behind them seconds before the ceiling and walls of the Collection room crashed down. She looked over Synderis's shoulder to see Phendaril lowering his bow. She couldn't be certain, but she thought the link to Wayland had gone silent before the glass had time to hit him. It didn't matter now. All that mattered was that he was no longer a threat. She relaxed into Synderis's arms when Phendaril's uneven footsteps rejoined them.

A slightly bloodied-but-alive Telandora and Lindyl waited at the main entrance. Raven smiled wearily in response to their relieved grins.

Wayland would trouble them no longer.

Raven was standing by Marek's grave when the storm drake came. Three weeks had passed since their return to Amberwood. Three weeks since Synderis departed with Captain Reysa and the other Eyl'Thelandran elves.

Wind from the drake's mighty wings buffeted her as it landed, and she smiled faintly to herself as the flowers she had placed on the grave took flight. Marek might not have even liked flowers that much anyhow.

She wasn't worried about its arrival. No dark clouds swept around them, and no lightning crackled along its wings. It was peaceful. Merely coming to visit. After it landed, she approached and reached out as it lowered its head, her hand sliding over the smooth scales of its jaw. Intelligent eyes regarded her, welcoming her into its company. The drake had bonded to her. That was unintended and unplanned, though she understood how it worked better now with the Acridan's memories, but she was pleased to see it again.

A soft rumble rose in its chest. A sound of contentment. Raven moved in closer and rested her head against its chest, feeling the powerful heartbeat. It curled one wing in as if to shield her from the outside world. After a few minutes, she walked back along its long neck and placed a hand on its jaw again.

"I can't take you with me, my friend. I don't think the kingdom is ready for a storm drake companion."

The kingdom was barely ready for Krivalen elves, not to mention Koshika, who had gone with Synderis. The three elves had struck out with Captain Reysa to spread the word of King Navaran's decree. It was also crucial for them to be seen in other locations to support Reysa's narrative that they could not have been in Pellanth at the time of the attack on the Silverblood Brotherhood temple. There were few enough living witnesses to their presence there that her word held significant weight, with King Navaran behind it.

It wasn't necessary to have all four of them on that journey, and Raven's injury to her leg was severe enough to require a period of rest and rehabilitation. However, with her enhanced healing and Synal's treatments, it was little more than a scar now.

A few nights ago, Synderis dreamwalked her to let her know they were coming back up the river if she was ready to join them. They received an invitation for an audience with King Saldin in Pellanth. He had considered King Navaran's decree and was willing to discuss complementing it with a matching one of his own in light of "recent changes" in the Silverblood Brotherhood. Wayland's demise had left the Brotherhood there in disarray. Father Markon was visiting to deal with his brother's death and figure out who would take charge of the temple.

If things went well, they might get permission to travel around King Saldin's territories the way they had Navaran's. She could also end up the heir to the Darrenton holdings, including this land, although she wasn't particularly concerned about that. Whatever happened, Synderis thought they should meet with the Delegate in Eyl'Thelandra before too much time passed to learn more about managing the Acridan spirit she had

Accepted and all that came with it.

The drake lifted its head, turning toward the manor house. Phendaril leaned in the doorway, watching them.

"I think that's my summons."

It looked back at the sound of her voice. She stroked the smooth scales one last time and moved away from the creature. As if understanding their visit was at an end, the drake reared up and launched itself skyward. When it got high enough, it circled above her once before flying off into the trees.

When it had vanished from sight, she turned and strode toward the house, admiring the lean figure of the elf smiling at her.

He pushed away from the edge of the door when she got close. "Charming beasts again?"

Raven offered a teasing grin. "I charmed you, didn't I? After that, I figured anything was possible."

Phendaril laughed.

It was a good sound. One she had heard more of lately, and she loved it. Smiling, she walked up and slid her arms around him. He leaned in and kissed her, pulling her into a welcoming embrace. Raven lingered there, tasting his lips, memorizing how it felt to have his strong arms holding her.

He drew back a little, his voice deepening with emotion. "Do you have any idea how much I'm going to miss you?"

"I have something that might help." She stepped back from him and dug into her belt pouch. She pulled out a delicate chain on which hung an arrowhead that matched the one she wore, only this one was carved in a black stone with fine fragments of sparkling green gemstone throughout. "I haven't much skill in these kinds of crafts, so I found a woman in the Stonebreaker camp who makes things like this out of gemstones and rock. I used my magic to work this and my pendant as companion talismans. They're connected, so you can wear it at night if you want me to dreamwalk you while I'm away."

Phendaril took the stone in his hand and gazed down at it. "This is beautiful."

"You don't have to wear it," she added quickly, "if you'd rather not have me constantly reminding you of us when I'm not really here."

He cocked an eyebrow. "I seemed to recall a very vivid, passionate dreamwalk we had when you were in Eyl'Thelandra." Then his brow furrowed. "Wait. When you dreamwalk Synderis—"

She placed her finger to his lips to stop the words. "Some questions shouldn't be asked." Then she moved her finger and replaced it with her lips for a quick kiss.

"Probably good advice." He fastened the chain around his neck and leaned in so his lips nearly touched hers, his breath warm upon them. "I will never take it off."

He wrapped his arms around her, kissing her with such passion that she almost forgot she still had things to do before the ship arrived.

She drew back to look up at him. "Scoundrel. You mean to make it so I'm not ready to leave when they get here."

He offered her a crooked grin that supported her accusation. When he answered, it was with playful sarcasm. "That would be tragic."

"Very funny. Let's get back." She took his hand and started walking toward the Darrenton dock.

A few hours later, she checked Cyrleth's girth once more and made sure her bow was secure on the packs, then turned back to Phendaril. She'd said her goodbyes to most of the others. Jael, Ehric, Synal, so many people she would miss when she was away. And little Smudge, of course, who wouldn't be so little when she next saw him. Davon had gone ahead to await the ship, offering her some privacy for this moment.

She took hold of the sides of his cloak in her hands, staring at the arrowhead pendant at his chest out of fear that meeting his eyes might bring tears. "You know, you could come to Eyl'Thelandra when we go. You would be welcome there, and I think you'd like it."

He touched her cheek, and she glanced up, a tear slipping free the second she met his eyes. With the softest touch, he brushed it away. "Let me know when you turn south again. Maybe I'll be ready for an adventure with my lady and her other love by then."

She met his eyes. "I never meant—"

It was his turn to place a finger on her lips. "For such a feral creature, you do love very deeply."

Raven rolled her eyes at him. "I was never that feral."

He placed his hands on her waist and smiled down at her. "You were feral and beautiful. Fierce and remarkable. So much so that I feared falling in love with you the first time I met you."

Raven grinned and stepped a little closer. She traced the line of his jaw with a light touch. "You're just lucky I didn't smell that fear when I got here."

He chuckled, knowing as well as she did that she'd been near petrified by her own fear when she first arrived in Amberwood. Rather than call her out on it, he leaned in and kissed her. She kissed him back, promising herself she would leave as soon as they parted.

When they did so, both a little breathless, she gazed into his dark eyes, realizing that she would miss him when they were apart as much as she missed Synderis now. "It's so hard to walk away."

He kissed her again, a soft, brief kiss this time. Then he regarded her thoughtfully. "Do you know how hard it will be for me to watch you leave? Not just leave, but leave to go with someone in whose arms you'll spend your nights? Tell Synderis..." He trailed off and shook his head. "Who am I kidding. You couldn't be in better hands." He smirked. "Nor could he, for that matter. Look out for each other."

"We will." She gave him one more quick kiss. "Until I return, heleath le'athana."

"Heleath le'athana," he returned, reluctantly releasing her.

Leaving would never be easy, so she hurriedly swung up on Cyrleth and urged him to a trot. She glanced back once to see Phendaril watching her, sorrow in the smile he found for her before she faced forward again.

Alayne and Karsima met her at the edge of town. They had offered to ride down with her to talk to Captain Reysa and say their goodbyes. They kicked their mounts up to a trot to keep pace, not trying to force her to slow and talk while she struggled not to cry.

Raven's heart ached, but anticipation blossomed there as well. After several weeks, she would see Synderis in the flesh again. Dreamwalking him would never be enough, though it was better than nothing.

She could feel his presence before they reached the dock. As soon as they rode into sight, she spotted him walking in their direction from where he had left Telandora and Lindyl standing next to the storage building. He smiled, and her heart soared. Cyrleth broke into a canter in response to her excitement, leaving Alayne and Karsima behind. When she reached Synderis, she swung off, leaping into his arms before the gelding had entirely stopped. Her arms wrapped around his neck, and he returned the embrace, lifting her off the ground.

Raven buried her face against his neck, breathing him in for a moment. Then he set her down and kissed her. Raven kissed him back, celebrating the feel of him, real and strong, against her. A low whistle from Alayne finally parted them, Raven's face growing hot. She gazed up at Synderis for a moment, the paler scar along his pale cheek, the beautiful silvery-white hair, as light as Phendaril's was dark.

He grinned at her. "Still satisfactory?"

Raven's cheeks warmed a little more. "You've never been merely satisfactory, my love."

He kissed her forehead. "How's Phendaril?"

Raven shook her head at him. "Of course you would ask that. He's well. He said we should take care of each other."

"Hmm. I was counting on you to take care of me." He winked at her. "It's dangerous out here in the world."

He spoke in jest, but there was a new hard edge to his gaze that hadn't been there when she was with him in Eyl'Thelandra. It made her want to take him back there. The world outside that haven wasn't kind, and she knew from his dreamwalks, from the things he didn't say as much as those he did, that he'd seen plenty of that cruelty on his travels. Perhaps they could find some of the better things now that they were together again.

"I will take care of you," she said, trailing a light finger over the scar.

"I know." He caught her hand and placed a kiss on her palm. "You gave him the talisman?"

"Yes."

"Will he come to Eyl'Thelandra with us?"

Raven narrowed her eyes in mock suspicion. "He might. Why, do you plan to life-bond him off to some Eyl'Thelandran woman?"

"Anything could happen," he answered with a wink.

Raven gave him a playful shove, then fell back into his arms when Koshika came up behind her and leaned heavily on the backs of her legs. She grinned as she straightened up, giving Koshika a scratch behind the ears.

"Come on, you can do all of this on the boat. We have places to be." Reysa stalked past them, grabbing

Cyrleth's reins.

Telandora chuckled as she and Lindyl walked over to them. "Reysa sets our schedule. Makes you wonder how we're always running behind."

"Not so fast," Karsima challenged her, dismounting next to them. "We haven't said our goodbyes."

Reysa rolled her eyes. "It isn't as if we won't be coming back through here."

Raven disregarded the captain and walked up to the two women. "I expect you to look after each other and make sure Phendaril doesn't brood too much."

Karsima smirked. "When doesn't he? But don't worry. There's still rebuilding to do. I'll keep him busy and feed him plenty of wine on those cold evenings by our fire."

"And make him take care of Smudge. Little monster needs a supervisor," Alayne added.

Raven felt moisture well in her eyes, though she managed not to cry this time. "Thank you both. Knowing you all have each other makes leaving a little easier."

"Be careful out there," Karsima said, giving Synderis a meaningful look.

He inclined his head slightly. "Of course."

The two women each gave Raven warm hugs before they turned to Reysa. It felt awkward, but she found that she liked it.

Raven took hold of Synderis's hand then. "Come. I have something to show you."

Davon, who had taken Cyrleth from Reysa, gave their hands a curious look, though she knew he would stand behind her, no matter how peculiar he found some of her behaviors. The idea of loving both elves didn't bother her much now. Primarily because the Acridan's memory held many such relationships, which they viewed as healthy and normal. It was hard to deny memories that felt like her own.

They followed Davon onto the galley. Once Cyrleth was settled with the other horses, Raven took her packs and led Synderis below deck. They sat on one of the bunks, and she took out the leather case still holding Jaecar's documents. It held something else now too. She opened it and pulled out a stack of pages, handing them to Synderis. He started flipping through them, his eyes going wide.

"This is Acridan," he breathed.

"I know. I'm rewriting the book."

He glanced at her, his mouth slightly open, speechless.

"Not all of it. Some things never should have been written down, but the Acridan's memories hold a great deal of knowledge that was meant to be shared with your people. I can make that happen now."

Synderis set the pages aside and slid his hand along her jaw, his fingers slipping into her hair. The wonder and adoration in his gaze made warmth blossom in her chest. "Our people, Raven," he said softly. "No one has ever been more worthy of Eyl'Thelandra, Amberwood, or any other place you want to call home."

Raven marveled at that for a moment. Somehow, she had gone from having no home to having several. From living in fear to a place of strength and security. Here she was, sailing on a king's galleys, not as a prisoner, but as a guest, protected by that king's decree. She and the other Krivalen were going into the world to be instruments of change for others and to undermine the power of the Silverbloods. She had no one when she left the keep in pursuit of Jaecar's killers. Now she had many friends and allies, including two remarkable elves whose love she cherished above all else. Somehow, she had accomplished everything Jaecar wanted for her and more.

It was strange, but ending Wayland's threat didn't feel like an ending at all. It felt like just the beginning. She didn't feel fear looking forward, only excitement and hope. So many things waited to be discovered and understood about the fey magic in her, but even that was less overwhelming now that she had exerted a modicum of control over it when facing Wayland. She had the strength to face whatever lay ahead, and she would not have to do so alone.

She leaned in to kiss Synderis, sinking in the warm, unbridled love that swept through their link.

"Raven."

She drew away from him and glanced at Telandora, who stood on the stairs. If anyone would be unbothered by interrupting an intimate moment, it was her.

She simply grinned at them. "Davon insists you can best me at archery. Care to support that claim."

"On the galley?" Synderis asked, arching one brow.

"It's got a long deck, and we've little else to do."

Raven grinned back. "I'll be right there."

Telandora trotted up the steps, calling to the others to set up a target. Koshika bounded up the stairs after her like a cat on the hunt, tail twitching with playful mischief. Raven tucked away the pages in Jaecar's leather case, her hand lingering for a second on its surface as his face rose vivid in her memory. A nostalgic smile curved her lips. Then she grabbed her bow and took Synderis's hand, taking him with her as she stood. There would be time for intimacy later. Now was the time to enjoy friendships she never believed she would have.

The End...

ACKNOWLEDGEMENTS

After several years spent rebuilding my life—finding a new place to call home and finishing my degree, among other things—I am happy to have found inspiration again with Raven. Her story came to me as I was pondering the effects of pandemic isolation on our social skills (which were never my strongest skills in the first place). Those thoughts led me to wonder what it would be like to grow up isolated from other people. Throw in a dash of fantasy, and Raven was born.

As such, I must give a nod of acknowledgment to everyone for surviving in these challenging times. Whatever hardships you have faced over these last few years, I hope you find something in Raven's story to inspire you.

There are a few people I could never leave off this list. That includes my dearest friends and family to my heart, Rick and Ann, my most ardent supporter and loving mom, Linda, and my patient and all-around extraordinary partner, Kai.

As always, I want to acknowledge Robert Crescenzio, my amazing cover artist; M Evan MacGregor, my wonderful editor; and Brian Short, my fantastic formatter. I value everything you do and the people you are. Thank you for being such a pleasure to work with.

To my other friends and family, know that I value your place in my life even if I don't call you out specifically here. Supposedly you aren't supposed to turn your acknowledgements into a second book, so I have to end it somewhere.

Lastly, I would like to take a quick moment to remember a few of those I have personally lost over the last few years. My beloved Huma, may you find a paradise of books waiting wherever you are now. My friend and fellow author, Jeffrey, who will be deeply missed by the many lives he touched. My dear equine companion and friend, Cody, who is now running free in a place where his body can once again keep up with his spirit.

AUTHOR BIO

Nikki started writing her first novel at the age of 12, which she still has tucked in a briefcase in her home office. She lives in the magnificent Pacific Northwest with her wondrous cat-god. She feeds her imagination by sitting on the ocean in her kayak gazing out across the never-ending water or hanging from a rope in a cave, embraced by darkness and the sound of dripping water. She finds peace through practicing iaido or shooting her longbow.

•

Thank you for taking time to read this novel. Please leave a review if you enjoyed it.

•

For more about me and my work visit me at
http://elysiumpalace.com.

OTHER NOVELS by NIKKI McCORMACK

CLOCKWORK ENTERPRISES
The Girl and the Clockwork Cat
The Girl and the Clockwork Conspiracy
The Girl and the Clockwork Crossfire

FORBIDDEN THINGS
Dissident
Exile
Apostate

ELYSIUM'S FALL
Dark Hope of the Dragons
Dark Savior of the Dragons

STANDALONE WORK
Golden Eyes
The Keeper

SILVERBLOOD RAVEN
A Path of Blood and Amber
A Path of Secrets and Dreams